BOOKS BY N. RICHARD NASH

THE LAST MAGIC

THE LAST MAGIC

N. Richard Nash

Atheneum   New York
1978

Library of Congress Cataloging in Publication Data

Nash, N. Richard.
The last magic.
I. Title.
PZ4.N254Las   [PS3527.A6365]   813'.5'4   78–55022
ISBN 0–689–10905–9

Published simultaneously in Canada
by McClelland and Stewart Ltd.
Manufactured by American Book–Stratford Press,
Saddle Brook, New Jersey
Designed by Kathleen Carey
First Edition

THE LAST
MAGIC

One

OVERNIGHT, spring came down from the seven hills and
fell on him like a curse. Every year it had been that way in Rome; in
not one of the six Aprils had it been otherwise. It was as if the
greenery were at war with the blackness of his cassock, as if the gusts
of the new season tore at his turned collar. The Ave Marias and the
Kyries and the Glorias seemed swept up in a worldly wind. The
spiritual pains of Lent were over and the earthly pleasures of Easter
were on the hillsides, and guiltily in his heart.

He should have known the morning would be that way; the night
had been full of trespass. He had had the dream again, the old
nightmare that he had hoped would never return to plague him,
which had come only once during the eleven years of his priesthood.
The animal fondling him, the dark seductive creature moving out of
the mists, kissing his mouth, sucking his tongue, pulling at his nipples
and his penis; then the awakening in wetness, and all the old shames,

3

and Hail Mary, full of grace, *Deus noster refugium et virtus,* with every verse inappropriate to the transgression.

All morning, things struck him as ill assorted. His room seemed too bright, too frivolously decorated for a man of the cloth; he was too cannily sensible of his trick: making his bare bedroom vivid with an opulence of bright books and religious paintings chosen, not for their radiance of holy spirit but for the resplendence of earthly color. It might be time, Michael thought, to go on a retreat. He needed a straw mattress, or none at all, a kneeling bench of unpolished rock, a handmade crucifix on a rough wooden wall. Bread and water, and a test of pain.

Until nearly noon he tried to work, and couldn't. He had a long digest to write for the papal foreign office; Cardinal Fellinger had sent a fifty-page report from Chicago. The Holy See's nuncio to Spain had written what he called a re-evaluation of the canonical misunderstanding in Madrid, and the Sacred Congregation for the Doctrine of the Faith had asked for the Secretariat's reaction to its set of *dubia.*

Dubia. How could he ever deliberate on the dry *dubia* for Monsignor at the Congregation when so many of his own inchoate questions shrouded his room? Smoke without flame . . . and the sucking creature still there, within the vapors, waiting, watching . . .

Just before midday, the phone rang.

"Michael," the voice said. "You've been granted an audience."

Granted audience when he had not asked for it. The poor old dying Papa had made an error.

"With His Holiness?" he asked.

Such an idiot question, and Cardinal Feradoti, his superior, the Secretary of State, was not one to let it pass. "Come, come," he said with affectionate impatience. "A touch more wit, if you can manage it."

"But I have not requested an audience," the young man said.

"You are being summoned, my friend."

If there was something disquieting, Michael thought, it might be of his own making; certainly there was nothing portentous in Feradoti's voice. Still, "What have I done?" he asked.

What fault have I perpetrated, he always meant, what frown have I brought to the papal countenance, what offense to God? Surely, the Pope was not privy to nocturnal creatures, he did not see the vanities of color in Michael's room, the pride gone awry, the corruptions by doubt.

4

Nor could he possibly have known the violences; no, of course he couldn't. They were, at any event, in the past. Even the one savagery, in the long-gone distance, back home in America, atoned for and nearly forgotten.

"When am I to go?" he asked.

"You are to attend. He will send for you."

That too seemed unusual. But there had been other unprecedented happenings lately.

"I will attend," he said.

The following morning, after saying Mass, he called the office, asked for the nuncio's Spanish report to be sent to his apartment, and it arrived at ten-thirty. He worked at home all day. Writing was easier in his own study, and faster; besides, it gave him a soothing illusion of being a student again. The only disturbance, as he sat at his desk, was the vague worry of waiting, listening for the telephone, suspending himself for the summons from the Pontiff. But there were only two calls through the day, one from the typist asking when the *dubia* could be picked up, the other from Feradoti, late in the afternoon, to inquire if the Pope had as yet given him audience.

He finished his report, rough draft and revision, the typist picked it up, the day passed and still he had not been summoned. Not actually hungry, he opened a can of Livornese sardines, tried one, didn't like the mushiness of it, finished yesterday's *formaggio dolce* and drank the dregs of Saturday's wine. All evening he had a restless sense, not so much a foreboding as an unaccustomed acceleration of the blood, as if his pulse were someone else's and he was detachedly aware of its unfailing beat, puzzled by its stubborn continuance.

Not, at best, a sound sleeper, he knew it would be a wakeful night. He put off saying Compline, hoping that the delay of the last canonical hour of worship would induce fatigue. It made him even more alert and he took it as a punishment for using prayer as a barbiturate. Yet, he thought with wry self-justification, if the layman can use Coitus as a soporific, why can't a priest use Compline? Capitalizing them both in his mind seemed, by some obverse logic, to be slyly profane, and he wished he hadn't done it. Once, when he was taking his doctoral courses in theology, Michael had made a scale of sin which he called *Peccatum et Culpa*. He was told by an old professor of dogmatics that he was the typical computer-crafter Amer-

5

ican, indulging in the accountancy of self-abuse. The professor was right. It bothered Michael that he had to tally the strokes, the pulse beats, the calibrations of sin.

He heard the wind batter his outside shutters. It would be a good night to walk in, he thought, exciting, with an April gust roiling the darkness, making a tumult at the street corners.

As he came out of the corridor and onto the steps, he pulled his topcoat tighter; the wind was more turbulent than he had expected, and colder. The street was deserted; the Romans, he mused, hate the last winds of winter; they run from them as if from betrayal. He wouldn't walk far, he imagined, only to the little piazza, once around the fountain, then return.

Perhaps he had been wrong in thinking the street was deserted. One could never be sure on the Vicolo Storto, which by its very name meant twisted; it gave no long views; all one could know of presences was the sound on cobblestones. His own sound, his own footsteps. Yet, why did he have the sense someone else was there?

Someone *was* there. He was sure of it. Not wind. Someone. Behind him, in the twisted blackness of the street, the footsteps were paced to his own, slow when his were slow and rapid when he hurried across the cobbles to the other side.

Well, why shouldn't someone be there? The Vicolo was public, the Italians had signed no concordat that the streets must be deserted on wind-racked nights. Besides, the sound had ceased; he heard no footsteps any longer, only his own.

Again. Behind him. Faster now, as if the pursuer had paused momentarily and was now catching up. Why did he say "pursuer"? Why did he allow himself to be gulled, intimidated by an old Latium superstition about the gusts of winter, *vento di malizia,* the wind of malice; there was no malice in the night.

But there had been, many nights. At first, the secular stage, as *L'Osservatore Romano* had called it: the man from the Parma auction gallery, kidnapped, then one kidnapping after another; the two newspaper editors, in Naples and Bari, both shot in the legs, crippled; the Torino automobile designer, beaten to death in the men's room of a theater. Now, the second stage, the attacks on clerics and churches: the sacristy in La Spezia vandalized; a priest stabbed to death not a hundred yards from Santa Maria of the Angels; another one, on pilgrimage, mutilated; the explosion of a bishop's Lancia and an English lorry, both blazing against the silhouette of St. Peter's, followed the next morning by the headline, *Inferno e Paradiso.*

6

Such pat ironists, the Italians, finding hell and high heaven in everything. There was no heaven in the terror. Not tonight, certainly, with the botheration growing: footsteps.

He would test the sound; it might not be footsteps after all.

He stopped walking. He waited. Behind him, silence.

He started to move again, hearing his own footfall, listening for the other.

There was no echo behind him.

Relief. He had imagined it all.

Perversely, the consolation didn't last. Whatever comfort he drew from the specific moment, there was a general misgiving. It occurred to him that he had of late been devising warnings for himself. He had been awakening nights to monitor the empty darkness. He had begun to walk with precautionary slowness. He had recently started to alert himself for bells that didn't peal, alarms that never sounded; he had been on vigil this entire day, listening for the telephone to ring catastrophe. But it hadn't.

It was total nonsense, of course. There was no threat hanging over him, he had had no premonishments from his superiors, from his confessor, from his doctor. No menace lurked in a dark *vicolo*. Yet . . . if no cold winds had actually blown his way, perhaps he was taking his easement too soon; the winter might not yet be over.

He came out of the crooked street and onto the piazza. It was not by any means a grand square, only a little one with a modest fountain. The jets made a unison spume of whiteness that didn't seem to fall but to be lifted and carried like a windswept curtain. How frosty beautiful it looked, he thought, sheer as organdy, yet motionless against the night.

Through the gauzy curtain, he saw the dancers. Three of them, quick and tentative, not choreographed to any music except the hush of falling water, a fluttering dumbshow. He couldn't tell who they were, what they were, whether they were men or women, or in what combination; only that their charade was a tremor of pleasure; except, there was a spasm in it, swift, quivering. Then, terminated.

They were gone.

Michael was still. It had happened so fleetingly, he was not altogether certain he had seen them; perhaps the dancers too, like the minatory footsteps, were not real. Yet, it was easier to disbelieve his ears than his eyes, and the three figures, unless there was bedevilment, were palpable.

But gone was gone; no sign of them. He circled the fountain, avoided the spray on the distant side, turned homeward into the *vicolo*. The wind was in blasts behind him now, ice blades piercing his spine.

He was within sight of his own apartment entrance when he saw the three figures again. They were not twenty feet from his doorstep. The dance was not a dance anymore, it was a scuffle. Two of them striking blows, the third cowering, scurrying to be free, getting caught and beaten again, grotesque, comic almost, like a macabre pantomime with slapsticks. Then the horror quickened. The nature of the blows changed and, in some indeterminately dismaying way, they were tearing at him as if stripping away his flesh. Now, for the first time, voices, animal sounds, from one, from another, low, muted, terrible. And only one word clearly:

"Aiuto!"

Over and over, the muffled plea for help, *"Aiutami!"*

Michael raced toward them. He shouted something—meaningless—lost in the darkness. Abruptly, the whole moment was over. The incident had run its course. The victim fell, the attackers fled and Michael came, running and breathless, to the man on the ground.

He was naked. He had been stripped of his clothes, every stitch had been torn away from him, and his garments lay all around him, on the pavement, on the cobbles, whipped by the wind. He moaned and he was bleeding. A middle-aged man, he was whimpering like a child.

"Aiuto," he kept repeating, *"oh, aiutami."*

He struggled to his knees, his body death-white in the moonlight. Michael reached down to help support him to his feet. At the priest's touch, the man cringed. He tried to talk but his speech was thick. He gagged with terror. But not terror alone: mortification. He was shamed by his nakedness. In the midst of his agony, he kept shielding his bare body with his arms, more pained by his vulnerable nudity than by the bruises, by the blood pouring out of his mouth. He groped for his clothes, scrounging along the pavement for a shoe, a sock, a white scrap of underwear, picking up one object, dropping another, pathetic and clownish.

"Aiuto," he sobbed, *"aiutami."*

Michael said, in English, in Italian, that he was trying to help, that the man should not worry about his clothes, but come indoors, out of the cold wind, hurry, they would call the police.

At the word *polizia*, the man's panic became frenzied. "No, no!"

He would have run if Michael had not had possession of his shirt, a

8

shoe, his briefcase. Now, forcibly almost, the young priest directed him up the steps and into the entryway.

The instant they came indoors a new humiliation assailed the wounded man. His nose and mouth were bleeding as profusely as before, his blood was gushing on the carpet, first in the hallway, then in the study. *"Bagno,"* he muttered in misery, *"stanza da bagno."*

Michael opened the door to the bathroom. The man was momentarily struck immobile, unable to budge; he began to shake again, with cold and shock. At last, he gathered his clothes with his left hand and with his right snatched at what Michael was carrying. He rushed into the white-lighted room, shutting the door behind him.

"Can I help you?" Michael called. "Can I get you anything?"

Worried over the man's bleeding, he debated about doctors and police. He should certainly be calling the *carabinieri,* but there had been the terror when he had suggested it. Michael wondered if he had any brandy, or whether to make some tea. He couldn't see how the man could put anything into that lacerated mouth, but he did need something, he had been trembling with cold. Hastening into the kitchen, Michael poured the water, turned on the gas under the kettle, pulled the tea canister down from the shelf. He speculated about the victim, who he might be: a working man going home perhaps, carrying a briefcase, a clerk or an accountant returning late to his family, waylaid by thieves.

Waylaid by thieves, what an archaic expression and, he mused with a chill of suspicion, probably untrue. There was something darker in this assault, something more dismaying than thievery.

He heard the movement in his study. Hurrying from the kitchen, Michael went to his guest. The man stood in the center of the room. He was fully dressed. He held his handkerchief to his bleeding lips and then, as he uncovered his mouth and let his hand drop to his side, Michael saw the man's collar.

A priest. His turned collar was untidy now, wet where he had tried to wash the bloodstains away. He wore an alpaca coat, badly torn, as was his vest; a white undershirt stared through the rips. His face was already beginning to swell with the bruises.

"Is there anything—can I do anything?" Michael asked.

"No, I thank you—I will go—I thank you."

But the man, hesitant, still uncertain of time and place, didn't move. He seemed suspended.

"My name is Michael Farris."

But the man did not respond to the overture, made no recognition that they were both priests; in fact, Michael had the strange sense that he wanted none made. The cleric, apparently sensing the flow of blood again, put the soiled handkerchief to his mouth. Through it he murmured something and Michael wondered whether the man had reconsidered and was offering his name. "Valerio," was the sound he thought he heard.

Probably in his fifties, Michael guessed; nondescript, like a hundred *parrocchi* he had come across, getting portly just as most of them did, hair graying, eyes fading. Drinking the wine of middle-aged contentment, gliding easily in the oiled grooves of daily living . . . how singular the terror must have been for this curate; his hands could never have shaken like this, nor his voice, so helplessly.

"I am very sorry," he started. "I do not know what—I do not know—"

"If you would like to rest . . . I could call a doctor." Michael hesitated. "I really feel you should have some attention."

Again the protestations, many of them, and he muttered something about being a nuisance. The actual word he used was *molestia.* It was blander in meaning than its correlative in English but the American chose to misapprehend it. He repeated the word as a way of finding out if the priest knew his attackers.

The man's response was instant. No, he didn't, he said; had no idea who they were, the world was full of hoodlums. Then, in the middle of his demurrers, he seemed to change his mind. Michael wondered if he was imagining the look of cunning in the priest's face. *"Le comuniste,"* the man whispered.

It was such an easy thing to say. The middle class, the businessmen in the *mercati,* in the Borsa, the clerics and parish regulars, if they wanted some impersonal scapegoat, they called upon the Communists. Rancor was not always meant; sometimes the remark was neutral, like blaming the weather, sometimes it was a comment on the generally deteriorating state of the world; often it was affectionate. The Communists. Right now, Michael felt certain, it was an evasion.

The teakettle whistled. Michael hurried into the kitchen. Putting the cups on the tray, he filled the teapot, got the spoons and sugar, and hastened back to the study.

The man was gone.

Michael set the tray down. I'm not surprised, he thought. Without rush, he went to the entryway, opened the outside door, stood on the windy landing. The street was dark. There was nobody. He went indoors again. Except for the bloodspots on the carpet and on the threshold into the bathroom, the man might not have been there.

How odd that the priest's flight had struck him as the least anomalous aspect of the whole occurrence. The macabre dance behind the curtain of water, that was far more curious; so was the beating on the street, the stripped-nakedness of the victim, the turned collar of the cleric. And even those aspects of the incident did not seem so bizarre as something else. Something minor, an almost trifling detail.

The priest was clearly Italian and not uneducated; yet in naming the Communists as his assailants, he had made a curious lapse in grammar. While the singular word *comunista* could be either masculine or feminine, no such ambiguity obtains in the plural. And the man had said *le comuniste*—feminine.

Abruptly it occurred to Michael, the priest had made no lapse in grammar. He had meant the feminine. His attackers had been women.

Two

Fainting, a psychology professor had once told Nora, was a negative societal manifestation. She agreed with him and wrote her master's degree thesis on it. She adduced to his statement whatever pertinent allegations against fainting she could find. Among them: it was misdirected energy, an inefficacious form of family protest, a counterproductive mode of attracting social advertence, and it was, as a mode of female deliverance from peril, obsolete. Also, silly.

That's why it vexed her now, when her thesis blather was six years old and she herself was twenty-eight, that she had fainted three times within the last week. Out cold. The third time, only an hour ago, was on the bus just as it made the turn off Ben Zion Boulevard onto Rothschild. She had no excuse that the vehicle was airless or crowded; it wasn't. There were very few passengers for it was Friday afternoon, the moment of hesitancy between Sabbaths—the Arabs just getting over theirs and the Jews just starting. Somebody, seeing the young woman slumped unceremoniously between the seats, had screamed. The bus had come to a halt—Tel Aviv galvanizes to celebrate emergency—and there was scurry and flurry. A little girl rubbed her wrists, a woman blew a hot breath into her mouth and nostrils, a man twisted her into contortionate postures. What particularly embarrassed Nora was that when she came to, she had lost all her sweat-earned Hebrew. Goddamn it was the only eloquence that tripped to her tongue, goddamn it, and not in translation.

The worst of it was that she knew what an ineffectual retaliation it was against the woman who had fired her from her job early this morning, and against the man in the Government Placement Bureau with whom she had moiled away the whole forenoon. Nor did she need the retaliation; certainly not against the woman—Nora had hated the job. Media research for an advertising firm in a cramped and chromed office on Dizengoff Street. Hated it enough to have had, during her tenure there, any number of other symptoms besides fainting—hives and headaches and, once, a whole week of diarrhea. But she had stuck to the position longer than to the others. With an accession of fright—and sleeplessness—she had wretchedly clung to it for eleven months, striving for the full year but unable to make it. Better than the job of writing membership brochures for Pioneer Women (three months), or teaching in the kibbutz near Capernaum (two months), or night clerking at the King David (one week). Better even than her first important position—her appointment, she had called it—with the abused children. But that was an agony apart.

She didn't know how she could tell Yoel about today's discharge. He had begged her to hang on to the position; for her own sake, he said, and she was sure he meant it. She must embed herself here in Israel, he warned her, strike root somewhere, find a place. Place had a therapeutic meaning to him, it was a medical specific against an ailment called exile, which condition he had overcome—he was no longer a refugee from Libya, from Africa, from nonexistent whereabouts, he was by God and location an Israeli citizen. Place in time, latitudes and longitudes, zones of belonging; he often went on like that, phrasemongering. She hated it; she wondered how a scientist—he was after all an intern in a hospital—could generate such gobbledegook.

Walking along Balfour Street, she slowed down and debated whether to continue onward to Yoel's apartment, or to reverse direction and go hide in her own. She kept on going, toward Yoel's, and

13

her head began to ache. The closer she got, the more insistent the pain; she knew any minute it would start that banging thing. As she walked up the back steps, it began, bang. Quicker now, one step, bang, another step, bang.

She got out her key but didn't need it; the door to his apartment was ajar—to admit the breeze. It meant not only that the place was hot and unbearable, but that Yoel was already there, waiting, and she'd have to start explaining immediately.

He was not in the living room. She saw the box of new stuff he had picked up, the contraband artifacts, a larger assortment than usual—a number of terracotta potsherds, tin coffee cans full of ancient coins, some real, some fake, with the hard gray lime sticking to them, a green bronze table leg, a small jar full of old buttons, pins, mezuzahs. She wondered where he ever laid hands on the sorry pickings, in what unsavory alleyways. He had worked his way through Gymnasia Herzliah and then through college, selling the stuff, not only to Americans but, without any seeming compunction, to Germans. She always hated the sight of the rummage and half hoped he would get caught one day, get thrown into the slammer; serve him right. She pondered the righteous notion; it irritated her.

But she was more irritated with him. He had done something else. He had again left his soiled hospital gown, slightly bloodstained, on the back of the couch. True, the hospital where he was finishing his internship was only a three-minute walk from his apartment, but how could he go promenading, even such a short distance, in a revolting, gory smock? It's only a few spots, he would say, and who's to notice? What a slob he was. Why couldn't he once, just once, change his clothes in the hospital?

She had a wayward impulse to leave, go quickly out the door, run, hectic, down the steps. She might have done it too, if she didn't need the aspirin, and at once. It bothered her that, in order to get to the medicine chest in the bathroom, she'd have to go through the bedroom where Yoel was bound to be. Well, sooner or later she'd have to tell him about the job and the man in the Placement Bureau.

Yoel lay on the bed, unclothed. The hair on his head was as black as Libya, but from the navel downward, an auburn red. She recalled that he had told her of the peculiarity even before they had seen each other naked. It was not an earth-shaking proclamation but it intrigued her and, since she had been about to go to bed with him anyway, it had quickened her there.

14

She thought, for a moment, he was asleep; his eyes were closed. Without opening them, "Get your clothes off," he said.

Briefly silent, then: "I don't feel like it."

"You will," he said quietly. "Get your clothes off."

She would have preferred an alibi less banal, more whimsical, even freakish, if necessary. But, "I've got a headache," she said.

"Oh, I'm sorry." His sympathy was genuine. She used to wonder, when she first met him, whether his kindliness was a professional deceit, the medic at the bedside, or whether it truly touched him to see people in pain. She discovered it was one of the few uncorrupted things about him, his compassion; it would probably wreck him as a doctor, he'd burrow into research somewhere, an antiseptic laboratory.

"Can I do something—rub your head?" he asked. Then, as she went into the bathroom, "Don't take the aspirin—take one of the yellows—take two of them, they won't hurt you."

She took two aspirins, washed her hands and face and tried to kill some time, loitering, letting the cool water run off her wrists.

When she came out again, he pointed at himself. "Look," he said.

He was erect and touching himself covetously. "Come on." His voice was overzealous. "It's so hard it's going to break."

"Put a splint on it."

He tried to smile and couldn't. "Want me to undress you?"

"Can't you wait until my headache goes?"

"I'll make it go faster."

It was going to be more difficult than she had expected. Do it gently, she told herself. "I'll help you if you want me to."

"I don't want you to help me! I can help myself, goddamn it! I want to make love!"

She was constantly being surprised by his vulnerability. Having made a picture of him as a tough practitioner, a nerveless hand in maneuvering the gullible, she was always taken aback to see the hand tremble. He looked fourteen right now and she could imagine him as he must have been, those days. The runaway from ignorant, possibly cruel Libyan parents, arriving in a strange new country, lacerated, lost, yet refusing to be an alien, pretending to be Jewish and making himself believe he was Jewish.

"Maybe I am," he would say to her even today. "Who knows who is Jewish in this world? Besides, everybody wanted me to be Jewish."

He meant the American Hadassah ladies who took him in. How

15

they must have pampered and cossetted him; he was their orphan of the diaspora, home safely at last, their world-violated innocent. Innocent indeed, with his hand in their purses and privates, and his eyes darting as swift as chance. But he *has* to be Jewish, one of them said to a doubting Deborah, because he's such an intellectual, such a *scholar*. Which, in fact, he was, one scholarship after another, and no longer any need for hallway larceny. Yet he clung to the practice of it—even to this day—reluctant to lose a skill he might again have to resort to in a fickle Levant that so capriciously turned natives into exiles. In the strictest sense, he wasn't an exile, neither was she; they had not been driven from their homelands, they had voluntarily fled. Still, in some deeper way, and lonelier way perhaps, they were indeed fugitives. But from what? She felt sorrier for him than for herself. She knew she was in flight; he would deny it about himself. Yes, perhaps he was indeed Jewish, always the child of refuge.

She touched him, wanted to comfort him, but he turned away. Silently she started to get undressed. She would lie down beside him, she decided, at a distance at first. Neither would speak. Then, quietly, in a peacemaking gesture, and to bring him some consolation, her hand would reach out to him—neutrally, to begin with, on the arm perhaps. If he was too deeply hurt he would turn away, lie on his left side, shut her out of the room. If the wound was superficial but still smarted, he might pat her hand, the one that touched his arm, a forgiving pat, condescending: it's all right, little girl, you're forgiven the female flaw.

She tried to take as long as possible to get her clothes off, not out of perversity—there was little spite in her—but to give the sharp clarity of the argument time to blur. Finally, she lay on the bed, at the distance prescribed by precedent, as naked as he was. But she didn't touch him, not even neutrally, although she knew he was waiting for her to do so. She was being unaccustomedly stubborn; her willfulness bothered her. Just as her hand started to move, she realized it was too late, the opportunity had been forfeited.

There was a new tension in the air. She sensed what was going to happen. She had injured him and he was going to retaliate.

"I did a tumor this afternoon," he said.

So that was the way. "I don't want to hear about it." She hated when he talked of growths and cysts and abscesses.

He went on as if he hadn't heard her. "I really should not have had to do it," he continued. "But Dr. Bar Am said I should, so I was glad of the experience. This woman had had a mild cervicitis—that is, we thought it was mild. And then—mama, mama—this tumor. Not ordinary. Not even in color. Gray. All the blood vessels—"

"Please."

"—purple. As purple as grapes. And swollen. And when it got cut away—a wetness—"

"You bastard!"

"—it just poured out the purulence."

"Pus as an aphrodisiac."

He twisted. His arm reached out and he hit her. It was an awkward blow, he was not adept at violence. Softly, trying to make as little stir as possible, she got out of bed, put on a bathrobe and stood by the window. Her anger passed presently. She felt even sorrier for him than she had before; she knew he would be punishing himself.

"Why did you make me do that?" he asked.

"I didn't make you do anything, Yoel."

"The last few weeks you've been doing this. You like to make love—I know that. I think you like it even more than I do. Why do you put me off?"

"I don't."

"Yes—in the last few weeks—why?"

". . . I don't know."

It was an admission and he let it alone for a moment. Then: "You want to get married, is that it?"

Almost a whisper. "No, I don't, Yoel. You do."

"Me?" She heard the consternation in his voice. "Me? You know how I feel about that."

"I know, but you don't."

"I don't want to marry you, Nora—get that out of your head. I don't like you, I don't even enjoy talking to you. You're too damn complicated—the only time I can figure you out is when we're fucking, and then you're great. And I'm good at it too. We've both been honest about that being the best of it. But if that's no good anymore, then nothing is."

"Yes . . . I think you're right."

He didn't expect her concurrence; she could see it bothered him. For a doubtful moment she wanted to withdraw her agreement, but she knew he had spoken the truth.

Silent, she didn't disturb anything. After a while, he said softly, "Come back to bed."

"No."

"Please."

17

Damn, she wanted to say, don't plead with me, let's not smudge the edges so that we can't see the limits of what we're looking at. Then, as he raised his hand and gently begged her to return, she hadn't the courage to be unkind.

She lied. "I've got the curse."

"You haven't."

"Yes."

"Why didn't you say so before?"

He had switched her off as if a button had been pressed.

She had no idea she would lash out. "You son of a bitch," she said. "You can talk blood and cancer and tumors and pus, you can come home wearing a gory operating gown with blood and puke all over it, but the minute I mention a Tampax, you turn to ice!"

He didn't retaliate. After a while, he was more subdued than she had expected him to be. "Good shot," he said. "You hit the doctor right in his squeamishness."

She hadn't meant to hurt him deeply, hadn't known he would make so much of it.

He asked quietly, "You're not really menstruating, are you?"

". . . No, I'm not."

He tried to smile, but there was no pleasure in it. "I feel as if you've caught me in a shameful act, like jerking off in the public library."

It was getting worse for him, and she wanted to stop it. She started to apologize but it was apparently the wrong thing. Then something happened she could hardly believe. He began to cry. She had never seen him do that before and she sensed that he too was shocked at himself, and pathetically unable to handle it. Nor could she. There was nothing she could say or do that would bring him comfort because she didn't know what it was in him that had to be comforted. Abruptly she was angry at herself; she felt barren and ineffectual. Dammit, she thought, if I need to comfort a man, is there never any course available to me than to fuck him?

So they lay in bed, giving comfort to each other, like cold dogs on a wet night, and the hell of it was she enjoyed it as he came and as she did too, each separately, then they went at it again, and both, for the first time, came together.

Now that he's had it, she speculated, it'll be easier to tell him. He'll be more relaxed, more sure of his mind and muscles, less likely to consider her decision a frontal assault on him.

She started to dress. It surprised him, the routine being broken.

Normally, the next step would have been nakedness in front of the refrigerator, debating cheese and fruit versus nuts and raisins versus wine and apple cake; then, doing the dishes together, and bed again.

"Why are you getting dressed?" he asked. "Where are you going?"

"Jerusalem, I think."

He smiled; a joke, of course. "That's a hundred kilometers, more or less. Will you walk?"

"If I have to."

He could see she was serious. "Jerusalem—what the hell for?"

"I haven't been there since I first arrived. It's well over a year. I miss it."

"I'd go with you, but I can't. I have no days coming to me until Rosh Hashanah."

"That's all right."

"Is it?" Narrowly.

"Yes."

Slowly he sat up in bed. He added her pillow to his own and leaned back against both of them. He studied her. "Are you going with somebody?"

"No, Yoel. Just me."

"For long?"

"Permanently, I think."

She could see he was puzzled. He didn't know whether to believe her; whether she was lying, teasing, testing. "You gave up your job?"

"No, I got fired."

It seemed to relieve him; he understood the reason for her threat to flee. It wasn't on his account. Failure at work again; it had nothing to do with him. "Well, you're not exactly heartbroken about losing the job, are you? You hated it—you were expecting to quit. But there are other jobs in Tel Aviv. No need to run off to Jerusalem."

"Yes, there is."

"What?"

"I hate Tel Aviv and I like Jerusalem. And if I'm going to start a new job and stay at it for any length of time, I may as well do it where I like to live."

"And me?"

The nub of it now, and she didn't know how to tell him. How to say that there would be nothing vandalous in destroying what they had together, for nothing of great beauty or value was involved?

19

Yet—scruples—it seemed to her that even one passage by night, even with a stranger, must never be treated as nothing. But perhaps that was her need to think she never abused herself.

He waited, and when she made no response to his question, he went back to where he had been before. "Is it a new job or a new man?"

"I told you."

"Do you know what sort of job?"

"No."

"Did you see the Placement man?"

"Yes."

"What happened?"

Here was another thing she didn't know how to tell; she was not too clear about it. But he pushed her. "Well, what happened?"

"He gave me a whole barrage of tests. They were old stuff—I've seen most of them before. I've even given some of them. Then I went to lunch and returned in the middle of the afternoon. He was disgusting—sort of a creep. He sat there rubbing his head and I could see the dandruff falling down onto my papers. Then he said to me, 'You're test-wise, aren't you?' And I told him I was, a little. Then he looked straight at me and said I was supremely intelligent, but that he couldn't find anything, not a single aptitude that jumped off the tests. I could do a number of things, which meant I might not be good at anything. It all boiled down to what attracted me, what I loved. So—what did I have a passion for? I said, 'Nothing'—and he said that didn't help a hell of a lot. Wasn't there any *activity* I really enjoyed? And I said, yes, fucking."

"You said that?"

"Yes."

"What did he answer?"

"Nothing, for a while. He didn't seem particularly surprised by it. He gave me a little half-nod, he wrote something down, then went poring through the papers again. At last he looked up and he was very unctuous. And he said, 'Well, that activity—I don't exactly know what you can do with that . . . professionally.' And he had that smarmy academic smile—you know, friendly with facts that can cut your heart out. And suddenly I wanted to shock the bastard, and I said, 'Professionally, that seems to indicate I should be a prostitute, don't you think?' "

"What did he say?"

20

"Nothing."

"Was he shocked?"

"No."

"The son of a bitch—how does he get off, suggesting a thing like that?"

She smiled wryly. His mind often took a back somersault. "He didn't suggest a thing like that—I did."

"But he took you seriously, and you were joking . . . Weren't you?"

"Can you imagine that I *wasn't* joking? Do you think I would seriously consider—"

He interrupted defensively. "How the hell do I know? It serves you right if people take you seriously when you say things like that. You think irony is the answer to everything."

"Isn't it?"

Irony wasn't much help to her now. She was feeling the disturbance all over again, the dizzying confusion she'd had all afternoon. She must try to conceal it. If he saw her the slightest bit unsteady, he would nail her into a rigid position. Or he would ask questions. She was smart, he would say, she was industrious—why was she always getting fired? Or quitting—why did she cut and run? Or, he would comfort her. She didn't want questions or comforts, she wanted clarity. If only a few things could remain steady; did everything have to be moving?

Things were apparently moving for Yoel as well. She hadn't expected him to be too upset by their parting. "I didn't mean to . . . shake you up," she said.

"What the hell ever made you mention whoring to that guy?"

"You want to know?"

"Yes."

"Thinking about us."

He was shocked. "Us? Whoring?"

"Yes."

"Maybe you—not me."

"Both, Yoel. And we haven't paid each other with honest money. Counterfeit."

"What's counterfeit?"

"Every time we screw, we can't really get it off without some little protestations of love and affection. But it's all fake—not legal tender. No pun intended."

21

"It's not meant to be coin of the realm. It's a social grace. It makes lovemaking more satisfying."

"No, only easier."

"That's something."

"Vaseline."

"Listen, girlie," he patronized, "every human relationship needs a little lubricant."

Since he was too vain to be hypocritical, she thought she might be imagining how pharisaic he sounded. He must be even more off-balance than she had judged him to be; he was clinging desperately to trusted platitudes. Again, the surge of sympathy for him, but she knew it would pass. He would do something, say something punitive to get back at her for having been rejected; she wouldn't get out of here unscathed.

It came. "You know, you can keep getting fired in Jerusalem just as easily as Tel Aviv."

"I know that."

"Maybe you ought to take it seriously—whoring, I mean—you might be very good at it."

Closing in on her, he pretended he wasn't going to attack her, he was simply discussing ways and means, objectively. To hide the injury, she too pretended to be objective about herself. "You're wrong," she said. "I'd be terrible at it. I still think of lovemaking as a divine accident—it's always that wonderful feeling of 'the first time'—it's never happened before, never, not to anyone. I could never sell that."

"That 'first time' crap—it's only an illusion."

"Yes, I know. But I don't have many illusions left, and I'd like to hang on to this one."

"That's because you're imaginative. But you could be just as imaginative about being a whore—you could make a *calling* of it—a new slant on a call girl."

Cheap joke; he wouldn't let up. She made allowances: he couldn't reconcile himself to her departure and was trying, by sheer friction, to incense her, to enkindle something that had gone cold. But nothing would ignite. "Well, if you change your mind, and do take up the calling, consider that I was your first customer," he said. "How much do I owe you?"

Flinching: "Whatever I was worth."

"As an amateur you were priceless. As a professional . . ."

Still naked, he walked to the bureau and picked up some Israeli banknotes. He threw them on the bed, a few pounds, less than five dollars. With effort, she smiled. Well, it was probably all the traffic could bear.

"Thank you," she said, and took it. She looked at the money for a moment, then, approaching the door, let it slip note by note out of her hand and onto the floor. And departed.

Entering the tight little foyer of the three-story apartment house where she lived, Nora started toward the bank of mailboxes, then abruptly moved away without inserting her key. The hell with it. There had been no letters in the past few weeks, not even from her parents, and tonight she couldn't bear the void. Her loneliness this evening was not measurable, and as long as its boundaries were vague, its pain was imprecise and therefore, in some way, bearable. But if it was given limits and enclosures, quarantined, reduced to the dimensions of a dark, empty little mailbox it would be the size of tears. No, thanks.

Bad enough to deal with the smallness of the apartment. And, like the mailbox, its emptiness. She had rented it unfurnished six months ago and it was still almost bare. A bed, a secondhand bureau, some kitchen implements. Six months and there were still cartons of books she had not unpacked, two lamps without lampshades, a suitcase used as a night table. Ah well, she said to Yoel, I'm rarely here. Rarely where, then, he had asked. . . . Enough of that.

She felt hollow. It didn't matter how little Yoel signified; it was a severance, her second severance in a single day, another lessening, a shrinking of her world of connection. The worst time after a breakup was, as she had recorded on other occasions, the first evening alone. The first setting of the sun, the first insidious shade of dusk, the failure of the light, the dread of the dark reasserting itself, the cry for fires, hearth fires, home, Mama in the wilderness.

Mama, yes, that would be the answer. If there were no letters to read, there would be one to write, and it would help fill space; time, at least. But what could she say? Not talk about the end of Yoel, certainly, her parents had never even been told the beginning of him; it was too difficult, trying to tell them about the men. Written home, they all sounded like hearsay, as though they were based on unfounded rumor, apocryphal.

Nor would she talk about the loss of her job; she had long ago ceased to burden them with her failures. If she wrote at all, she'd have to make a joke of it, trick it up. She smiled dryly at how the letter might begin:

Dear Mama and Dad,

Since resigning from my position, I have explored all the occupational opportunities of Israel, I have conferred with a government career counselor, I have examined my skills, achievements and aptitudes, I have taken a searching look at the long view, and have considered being a whore. There is much to be said for such a decision. Prostitution, if not man-honored, is certainly a time-honored profession and has the virtue of not being nine-to-five. While it is somewhat deficient in fringe benefits and there are no guarantees of tenure or social security . . .

Knowing her, they would have no fears that she could seriously consider becoming a prostitute; but not knowing her, they would not realize what the ironic make-believe in her letter was hiding: that she had been a failure in Tel Aviv as she had been a failure in Boston and New York, as she might be in Jerusalem; and that she was afraid she could run out of cities to fail in. Confused, her father would drift out the back door and disappear down the flight of steps that lead into the rear of his photographic equipment store. He would slip into the darkroom, lock the door and shutter the window on the excuse that any hint of light would spoil the pictures. Gazing down into the shimmering developer, he would watch the images form in the liquid, as if hoping that some illumination would come floating up to tell him what had happened to his daughter. But since he was really afraid to know, he would give up quickly, and emerge squinting from the blackness. No pictures, he would say, none of them turned out worth a damn.

Her mother, however, would run screaming to the telephone. Therapy, she would yell, therapy, go back to therapy. But I've had eight years of it, Nora might answer, and occupational fucking is all it adds up to. Then you need a new therapist, her mother would say. Mrs. Eisenstadt was a therapy collector, all varieties. She had been in analysis, of course, concurrently with her only daughter, but there were other categories as well. Orthopedic therapy when she threw her back out, nutrio-therapy when she was overweight, physical therapy to pep up her muscle tone, cellular therapy to keep her protoplasm eternally young, socio-therapy to help her find through statistics her most potent place in, as she called it, the demography. Not one of her therapies had ever been a failure, but there were always new indispositions.

Don't worry about me, Mama, Nora would say. I just wrote the letter to hear myself talking to you. I'm not going to be a whore. Nice Jewish girls don't enter any profession that does not require a diploma, everybody knows that. It was as true as Jews don't turn into drunkards or homosexuals; some even said they don't become engineers, it was a goyish profession. Teachers, yes, lay psychologists, editorial assistants . . . never secretaries anymore. And as to prostitutes . . .

She knew she would not write that sort of letter. But she had a need to talk to them, a need to write and reach, to make a large penmanship across the vast and empty space. She wrote:

Dear Mom and Dad,

You should see Israel with the spring on it. It's so beautiful—like the first time you took me to the country-side in Perryville—remember?—and the first time in my city-girl life I realized April was all energy. Green things, pushing, shouldering up out of the ground. That's what it's like in Tel Aviv. The vigor, the rapture of growth, the green courage—life sticking its neck out.

And another thing, too, that I often forget and shouldn't. How close to the sea we are here. Suddenly, in spring, the Mediterranean comes near, becomes an alluring thing, as it must always have been, the sea of wine, the sea of longing, the sea of horizonless adventure. . . .

What inanity, she told herself, but she finished it. She enclosed the letter in an envelope, addressed and stamped it, then couldn't stand the thought of sending it. She tossed it on the table and it lay there, didn't move, didn't laugh at her nor berate her nor rise up to strike her across the face. How dead it was.

As dead as the room. The outdoor light had gone from the window, the one light on the table was stingy. Besides, cold. Unseasonably cold for early spring, everyone said, which didn't take the chill out of the clammy night. And there was no way to warm the place, no fireplace here, no snowy house in winter.

Help.

There was that damn thing again, on her wrist. She thought it had

25

faded totally, out of every existence, even the past. Months at a time it wasn't there, altogether invisible, lost in the creases of the skin, as if it had never happened.

How it had happened was sometimes vague to her, sometimes as sharp as the act itself. Once in a while, thinking of the occurrence, she would diminish its importance, saying she had not been as unique as she had always considered herself, not the Nonpareil Nora; she had, in fact, been a collegiate commonplace, the student who had attempted suicide. And failed. She was not psychotic enough to have made it. Hardly even neurotic, come to think of it.

It was simply that she found herself in a state that was pervasively minus. Not dramatically minus—the distinction had to be made— only so minus as to be hardly perceptible and hardly bearable. It was minus everything, minus love, minus accomplishment, minus beauty, minus—hideous minus for its lack of humor—self-respect. And minus, most of all, the persuasion that life had any plan or poetry to it; there was no manifest scheme that was either madly beautiful or rationally comprehensible. And the insult of insults was that she deemed herself the least significant accident in the general chaos. Unable to endure living a life of deficiency, she took a perverse pleasure in imagining, without thinking the image sophomoric, that her tombstone would read: SHE DIED OF INSIGNIFICANCE.

Except that there was indeed one significance she was always aware of: her pain. It was constant and it was real. And its special cruelty was that there was nothing spectacular about it; it was not the kind of torture in which she could find a rewarding role to play; there was no nobility in it, no bravura, no ecstatic martyrdom, not a scene's worth of drama. Her pain, too, was minus.

It was the most modest kind of unhappiness, and the most inclusive, the misery of existence being less than the worth of its parts. Its one satisfaction was that, day by day, ending it seemed not only a logical thing to do, but a way to find a missing element that might bring the minus up to the minimal zero. So she tried to kill herself.

Didn't really try, she later realized. But she had tried to do *something* with that cliché razor blade. What? Certainly nothing so petty, so banal as to get a little extra attention for herself. Then what? To quantify the deficiencies in her life? Yes, perhaps. To test how much the minuses truly tormented her, to gauge whether each lack in her life, each wanting might not be filled with a little death, a compensating death, perhaps enough death to give her the courage to say: Life, I do not need you all that much.

26

Then, at the moment when death seemed to have given her more courage than life had ever done, the blade was sharpest. But not sharp enough, apparently . . . or else she had misjudged which of the two had given her more courage.

Then, with the help of a friend, she caught a glimpse of how the whole trick was set up. It was a grim antic. A practical woman, she suddenly saw life as a practical joke, aware that a practical joke was an act of hostility; so you had to be constantly on the qui vive, and you could, with a supreme effort, manage it. Her sense of irony had nearly killed her; also, it had saved her.

Tonight, however, had no wry jest in it, the going was rough. The scar, which had begun to fade, was reddening again, a vindictive weal. Would it never go away? Would it always be there to remind her of another almost in her life, another less than adequate performance?

The scar was getting more and more vivid. Time for the bracelets. She opened one drawer of the bureau, then another, and found them, a copper one she had bought in Greenwich Village, an old brass one with delicate chasing, a tarnished silver. They wouldn't go together but, as she told herself warningly, she would need a lot of coverage tonight, so she slipped all of them onto her wrist and held her hand up in the air, making a fist, making as loud a noise as the metal hoops could jangle. No scar, she said almost audibly, only bracelets, no scar.

She picked up the letter and walked down the steps again and outdoors, to the postbox. In the night, with the faint breeze coming from the sea, she perceived that everything she had said in the letter was incontestably accurate. The Mediterranean was as close and the spring as energetic as she had described them. The letter was simon-pure truth; it was only she who was the liar.

The instant the letter was dispatched she felt, somehow, better. Her headache receded to a sufferable distance. Re-entering the foyer, she paused momentarily, feeling she now had the bravery to essay the mailboxes and risk the probability that there would be no mail for her. Poking the key into the lock, she opened the brass door.

She recognized the envelope instantly, even before she had it in her hand.

Micky McLaren. She held the letter close; it was a precious gift and she would not read it until she was well upstairs and warm in bed; a good thing to sleep on. Her heart bounded with the grateful joy of it. How like Micky it was to be there when she was most needed. It had always been so, Micky appearing with a hand, with a dollar, with a

27

double date, in the precise instant of emergency—the Mick of Time, Nora had called her. She was a rowdy and a vulgarian; she made their final two years at college a tumult, a scramble of surprise, of last-minute deliverances, and happier than Nora had imagined they could be. The room they shared was a precipitation: food and hysteria, music too loud for any eardrum, nonsense, moonshine.

"You think too much and screw too little," Micky would say. She was a hooligan besides, and a soft touch and an Irish poet; mostly, she was sacrilegious. "What do I believe in? The Old and New Testicles."

"You're a goddamn sybarite, Micky. You'll die one!"

"I believe in the Sermon on the Mons!"

"What you really believe in is love, love, love. Huge butterscotch tits of love!"

"God is a sugartit!"

"Barf!"

The evening of that same pandemonium, Micky had wound down and said quietly, "I don't *know* what I believe in, Nora. My mind's not as clear as yours. And it's certainly not very nimble—it can't change quickly. My moods change—my head just hangs around. Things shift and I never catch up with them. Everything I learned in grammar school was wrong in high school. And everything in high school wasn't worth a shit in college. And I didn't catch on until I was a flunk-out. The only thing that stayed the same was love. It's what I know I know. It's my major." Then, afraid she might be caught serious: "I'm the Summa Come."

How strange, Nora thought: here I am, six years later, as different from Micky as two people can be, and I'm nearly around to her way of being. Could we have been alike even then? No, not then. Perhaps not even now, but certainly not then.

Except that they had started in the same way, social workers, both of them, both dealing with the disadvantaged—that was the current word for the poor—Micky in a New York agency and Nora in Boston. Two months after she got the job, Micky wrote to her friend:

I can't hack this. The faces are too long and the misery is gray. None of the stories have surprise endings. Besides, the poor stink. Why can't they at least stay clean, why can't they wash? But it's not only the dirt that fills the pores, it's dumb despair. And suddenly you get the terrifying sense that nothing you can do will make a difference, nothing you can say, nothing you can give—not food, not money, not for Crissake love. I can't stand it.

She didn't hear from Micky for a year. Then ran into her in Bloomingdale's. "Come up," Micky cried. "Come up now—this minute—come to my apartment!"

It was within walking distance of the store, on the East Side, a small two-room apartment, a shock of elegance. Velours, cut velvets.

"And look at this," Micky called from the bathroom. The sink and bathtub faucets were ordinary chrome but the hardware on the bidet was gold-plated. Micky shrieked with laughter. "It's my Gilded Afterthought."

"Did you do the rest of it?" Nora asked.

"Hell, no—how would I know to decorate like this? But I did pay for it."

Nora knew Micky came from a poor family, her mother an office worker, the widow of a war paraplegic. "How'd you do it, Mick?"

"I'll show you."

She was wearing a bright green suit, suede and expensive—Gucci, she said; her shoes were Gucci too. She got out of all of it, opened a closet door and pulled forth a pair of well-worn blue jeans, patched and faded. She put them on, then a pair of canvas shoes, scuffed, colorless, down at the heel; finally, into a denim shirt that might have been azure but was now achromatized like a smoggy sky. As fully dressed as she intended to be, she pulled some books off a shelf— college texts, frayed and shabby, with broken backs and damaged corners. She stood there, posing, an enormous smile across her freckled countenance, no longer the urbane Gucci Lady of the East Side Peerage, but the emblematic undergraduate, pizza and Pepsi. She tumbled her hair and wiped the rouge off her lips, and all the paints, dyes and glazes were gone; the emerald green of the suede suit had turned into the blue-gray drab of the college campus.

Starting toward the door, she remembered something. She opened a narrow chest of drawers and reached inside for a belt. It was a leather one, as shiny as patent, with a huge brass buckle, and it was bright scarlet. She wrapped it around her books, fastened the buckle; the expensive belt was now an old-fashioned bookstrap.

"Come on," she said.

"Where?"

"We're going to the Pierre Hotel. You go in first. You sit down somewhere—as close to the reception desk as possible, so you can see and hear whatever's going on."

"What will be going on?"

"Me. I'll get there in a little while. When I do, you don't know me. Just watch. Watch and listen."

The Pierre Hotel was white and gold, sumptuous and stately. Nora sat there, restive, skittishly uncertain whether to stay or flee, unnerved by whatever charade she was expected to witness. She thought she had been watching carefully for Micky's entrance. How she missed it she couldn't tell. Suddenly there was a commotion at the desk. Someone was wailing, weeping. It was that tall freckle-faced carrot-haired girl with the red-belted books. She was a wreck, poor thing, coming apart in all her limbs like an awkward doll, badly assembled.

"But he was due tonight," she kept crying. "He was supposed to check in this afternoon."

It was her father she was blubbering about. She had come down from Bennington to meet him. He was late and missing. There had to have been an illness or an accident—mishap, mugging—had any air crash been reported? What could she do, was there someone she could call, someone to see, was there no provision for emergencies like this?

The room clerk was, at first, a starched study in detached commiseration. "Why don't you just sit down and wait a little," he suggested. She made pathetic, yelping noises and he quailed. Defenseless, his starch starting to craze a little, he looked for help in a number of aimless directions, then turned back to her. "Try not to be too—uh—loud, Miss. If he said he'll be here, he's bound to be here."

"But you said no reservation," she cried.

She had somehow turned it all into his fault, almost his want of principle, and he was suddenly devitalized. With great solicitude, and a little apprehension, he directed her to one of the nearby couches. "Please sit down," he whispered. "Please."

Dutifully she sat—not too far from Nora—but she didn't give up weeping. She would subside to near silence from time to time, sniffling and trying bravely not to, then she would again be racked by lobby-shaking wails.

In a little while, during one of her quieter intermittences, a man approached her. He was a stiff, somewhat postured man—youngish, probably in his early forties—one would have to say of him that he owned things, proprietorship seemed his essence. He sat down beside her and took charge. He gave her his handkerchief and his peppermints. Nora could not hear a syllable—he spoke softly.

Whatever he was saying did not, however, seem to comfort Micky. "But my father's never done this before," she sobbed. "He's probably hurt—or dying somewhere. It's dreadful how callous New Yorkers are."

He made a grieved gesture to his heart; he had to be protesting he was not a callous New Yorker, and finally his consolations could not be gainsaid. In a little while, Micky was talking more quietly; a little while later, she was even nodding a bit, wanly. Thereupon, the man performed a miracle: the comfortless girl was comforted; she smiled. Then she offered him one of his own peppermints. He took one and he too smiled.

They rose together and walked away from the reception lobby. As they disappeared into the cocktail lounge, Micky slung the red leather belt over her shoulder and the strapful of books bounced debonairly down her back. It was the last glimpse of her Nora caught that evening.

"It's better pay if you're a college girl," Micky said later. "You work them for the train fare back to school—and school can be a sleeper jump. Sometimes you can get airfare home. Cleveland, Tulsa, Seattle—home's the ante, whatever game you're playing. Once, with a pretty good accent, it was Dublin. Also, the fucking's better—they work so hard at the seduction. And when it's all over, they're generally so sweet—solicitous—because they've not only taken you, they've taken you for *real*. But then—once in a while—they know you're a fake. And that's the most interesting—knowing how to play it. Because sometimes it even gives them *pleasure* to know you're a phony. But you've got to watch it carefully and be sure you've got the right guy: does he want to think you're real, or does he want to know you're fake? And if you spot them right—Christ, it's wonderful!"

"You mean that? You mean there are really guys who *want* to know you've duped them, that you're a fake?"

"Oh, yes. Some of them pee for joy. For whatever reasons. Sometimes their reasons are weird. There was this guy who said to me, 'I'm glad I know now, but I'm sure glad I didn't know while we were doing it. While I was fucking you, you were my college-girl-kid-sister—and she was great! But Jeez, I'm glad you're not. I don't want to go back to Minneapolis thinking I fucked my sister!'"

"He didn't think he was cheated?"

31

"But he wasn't cheated!" Micky was indignant. "I don't cheat them! I give them value for their dollar. Better goddamn value than they get at home! And that's what I want to do, Nora—give them what they paid for, what they've got a right to expect. I have no contempt for them—not for any of them—I mean it, honestly I mean it. I like them all."

She did mean it. Actually, and this was her pathetic fallacy, she didn't call herself a prostitute at all. But what did she call herself?

She was in search of a word. She was constantly exploring, reconnoitering in the dark corner of every quick-time bedroom for a term she could live with—not prostitute, certainly not whore; seeking in every man's eye a reflection she could recognize as the best picture of herself, the least ugly, questing for a title that would rub some of the tarnish off her life.

In Micky's last letter, the one before this present one, she discussed her search openly, almost as if it were a crusade; she was thinking of joining organizations and picketing men's clubs, bowling alleys, police stations. There was, in that last letter, the first sign of social outrage and imposture, and—sad, when she thought of the carrot-headed proud spirit—the pietism of guilt. Touchingly, Micky's last words in it had suggested that Nora might, in judging her, start to love her the less. Nora had answered her letter immediately.

> Don't talk to me about new words or new names for what you're doing, Mick. That's bullshit and anyway I don't think they matter between us. You haven't changed, not so far as I'm concerned. Nor, I think, have I. I love you, Micky, I always will.

Walking up the stairs to her apartment, the new letter in her hand, Nora wondered if her friend might be writing that she had at last found a felicitous word for herself, a name that would comfort her. She knew, anyway, that the pendulum would have swung by now; Micky's last letter was dispirited, which meant that this one would be cheerful and up, and most probably lewd. Even unread, it delighted her.

Having intended not to open the letter until she was snugly in bed, Nora started to undress quickly. But she couldn't wait. She tore at the envelope, pulled the single sheet out and was suddenly aware that the writing wasn't Micky's. It was Micky's mother's.

32

Dear Nora,

I'm writing this letter in Micky's apartment. For two days the police have been coming and going, and now they've left again. I don't know what to do. Micky's dead. The enclosed clipping will give you the details. I just don't know what to do.

Sincerely,

Evelyn McLaren

The newspaper had a picture of the body with a tarpaulin over it. The young woman had been killed, it said, by a person or persons as yet unknown. The victim had been, apparently, strangled. Then the face had been mutilated, smashed almost beyond recognition by a number of shattering blows. The blunt instrument had been an exceptional one but, from the fact that it was blood-covered, there was no question about how it had been used. It was a bundle of books bound tightly together by a red-leather belt.

Nora slowly, carefully put down the letter, put down the newspaper clipping. She heard her voice say the word evenly, without emphasis. "No . . . no."

The pain in her head, flashing like light. Then the onset of the old-accustomed vertigo.

No, don't faint, she said, don't. Get some air, open the window, the window.

She hurried and pulled up the sash. Her mouth agape, she sucked at the darkness. There was not enough air, there was a scarcity, not enough to go around, a terrible scarcity.

She heard her cry. "Help! Oh, help! Help me!"

It might have been minutes later, or hours, that she knew she was lying down somewhere. On the floor. By the window. A soft breeze coming in.

From the sea, she thought vaguely, somewhere from the sea.

She must go down and look at it tomorrow, gaze at the Mediterranean in the dawn, in the early sunlight.

Or go to Jerusalem. Yes, that would be where she would go. She had been there only once. She liked Jerusalem. She would buy herself a red leather belt. It would be better than bracelets.

But no . . . she didn't have to choose either alternative. There would be no leather belts in her life. No belts, no bracelets, no blades.

The three b's. They suggested "Baubles, Bangles and Beads," a song out of *Kismet* . . . Fate.

Leave it all to Fate. What a lovely romantic notion—how she wished she believed in it. Or something. So she could let *it,* whatever it might be, take care of things.

But she herself would have to take care. On her own. It was a do-it-yourself operation.

Well, so be it. She would make another start.

Tomorrow, in Jerusalem.

Three

THE OLD MAN LAY DYING, yet the odor in the room was not the stink of mortality but a fresh fragrance, purifying and clear. Incense, Michael thought at first, but there was no smoke in the aroma, no burning; rather than having come through fire it seemed to have arisen from brooks or open meadowland. The scent tantalized him and he wondered if one of the attendants was wearing it as a perfume. It was, however, a woman's essence and they were all men—the *archiatro* and his assistant doctor, the nurse, Monsignor Griti-Eschi who had been His Holiness' secretary since time forgotten (the Pope still called him his amanuensis), and Cardinal Brunaldi, the last Camerlengo and probably the next.

They were silent in the room, standing or sitting, and seemed to tune their ears to the sounds of the Holy Father asleep, to the papal breathing: the short quick pantings like a dog in summer, the stertorous angers for breath, occasionally the low soft sigh of an ailing man suddenly relieved of the hardship of respiration.

35

Observing the men, Michael thought how differently they all grieved for the failing Pontiff: the busy and workaday distress of the two doctors and attendant, the preoccupied, list-making affliction of the Camerlengo, who would soon be charged, as chamberlain, with arranging the conclave; and the desolation, the wasted ruin of Griti-Eschi, nearly as old, nearly as ill as the invalid himself. Already forsaken, the aged secretary folded and unfolded his hands, touched the blankets on the patient's bed, touched them here, touched them there, then went murmuring into the corner of the bedchamber where there was nobody to hear what he might be saying.

Someone dying; but the room, for all the heavyheartedness, had a gentle tranquillity, and Michael thought: how different from the ferocity of last night, a priest bloodied in the street . . . and how impossible for me to be here, witness to the passing of the Pope, when I am not a cardinal, a bishop, a monsignor, only an ordinary priest. You must not think he sees you through screens of protocol, Feradoti had once said, the Papa has taken you to him, has made you his young friend. But why, Michael had wondered, always why?

The old secretary's mumbling became audible. "Is it not dark in here?"

It was indeed not very light. Although it was not yet dusk, the curtains had been prematurely drawn, and the chamber was illuminated by vigil lights which guttered and flickered like burning rubies. The old man had said he wanted no electric illumination; it was a whim of his dying delirium.

Griti-Eschi, getting no reply, posed the question again. "I think it is too dark. Does nobody else think so?"

Too dark for what, Michael was on the point of asking, but the elderly retainer would have had no answer except grief. There was enough grief in the room, Michael considered, yet not enough; some special bereavement had to be expressed, and he couldn't tell what it might be. Abruptly it occurred to him, there was no woman to lament the passing of the son, the husband; there was no daughter to make an outcry. He upbraided himself for the thought: how eccentric to regret the absence of women in a moment of mortality when he never, anymore, noticed their absence in his daily living. And yet, a woman, for the sake of the dying . . .

The old man stirred in his bed. He opened his eyes and murmured. It was as if he had divined Michael's notion. "My mother was here yesterday," he whispered, in Italian. It was a different Italian than he habitually spoke. It sounded of his youth, of Calabria.

36

Nobody responded.

The dying Pope continued. "My mother . . . brought me that picture, as a present. She was here yesterday and will return tomorrow. The picture is of a field . . . a broad field, behind our house, with many distances. . . ."

His mother had been dead for thirty years. The picture was an old one, faded sepia, its scene vanished almost beyond perception. What was visible was not particularly compelling to the eye, not picturesque in any way, nor did it stir one's imaginings, only a pastureland of sorts, a view of grasses and vetches not uncommon to the mezzogiorno . . . only a field.

"How beautiful it is," the old man said. "And the wild thyme grows . . . how it spreads over everything . . . how sweet, how bitter. It is a summer thing—in the heat of August—or is it spring? I can't remember. But the scent of it is so . . ." He searched for the word. Then he found the unlikeliest. ". . . blameless."

Michael's pulse quickened. Thyme. That was the scent he had smelled on entering. Not perfume, not incense; thyme. Yet, how could it be possible? There was not a branch, not a sprig of it in the chamber, nor, likely, had there been any, ever, in the past. Suddenly he realized that, with the help of the old man's suggestion, his mind had this very moment fabricated the herb and its savory scent. He had made it up—no thyme, no hint of it—he had created a petty arcanum for himself; there was no enigma in the room, none at all, only dying.

The Pope stirred restlessly. He tried to raise his head a little, tried to distinguish something in the darkness. "Has the American come?" he asked querulously. "Has Michael Farris arrived?"

"I'm here, Your Holiness." The young man moved closer to the bedstead.

"Have you been waiting?"

"No, sono arrivato poco fa."

How odd, Michael thought, that I now speak Italian to him, and he still, even when he is ill, speaks to me in English. That same stilted, donnish Oxonian that he must have learned, as a legate to Britain, nearly a half century ago.

The old man smiled and a glint of mischief came to his eyes. With a faltering gesture, he indicated the others. "I will have a dream and they will all recede in a little while and I will not know where they have gone . . . and we will talk."

Griti-Eschi caught the hint and tried to turn up the corners of his mouth, but good cheer didn't come easily. He opened the door to the passageway, and the others departed, Griti-Eschi the last of them.

When Michael turned to look at the Pontiff, the latter had again closed his eyes. His hand reached out to the chair beside the bed, his fingers moved unsteadily over the objects. In the dimness Farris could barely make them out, then realized what they were, the long white linen alb and the undergarment, the amice, both old, both threadbare now, vestments out of the elder's past, when he was a parish priest somewhere, after Calabria perhaps, in one of the Umbrian villages. The eyelids fluttered in the haggard face, and Michael wondered what recollections he was summoning, what visions of sunlit altars on Pentecostal mornings, what Easter liturgies, what thousand Masses he had celebrated in this worn and yellowed whiteness. He was back there once more, Michael was certain, a curate in a simple place; he had forgotten the elegant throne from which he now addressed himself to heaven. Touching the frayed linen, he had lost touch with the capes of cloth-of-gold, with the triple-tiered tiara, the diadem of jewels. Of the two of us in the room, Michael thought, only I now have the remembrance of your coronation splendors, papal gendarmes in white breeches, Knights of Malta emblazoned with crimson crosses, sandaled monks and purple bishops, and the choirs chanting *"Tu es Petrus,"* then the silence, that breath of ineffable stillness, with the ostrich-plumed fans making a heavenly afflatus out of the earthly quiet. Only I in this room know that you are that man and this one, that the afflatus has not changed, inspired as the breath was then, pained as the breathing is now.

Michael reached down and lightly passed his fingers over the timeworn amice, his younger hand not far from the gnarled, arthritic one. The sick man didn't seem to notice. He had forgotten he had summoned the young priest to his bedchamber, had forgotten he was in the room.

"Your Holiness," Michael whispered.

"Ah, yes," he responded. "You would like an imprimatur, would you not?"

"Imprimatur?"

"Your book—for your book," the Holy Father said. *"L'Ultima Magia."*

Time, tricking the old man again. It had happened years ago, seven to be exact. A young curate in Philadelphia, Michael had written a book, *The Last Magic* he had called it. He had slaved on it for the first few years of his priesthood, nighttimes, early mornings before Mass, in whatever respites he could manage between Lauds and Vespers. It was a book of mysteries—of the Christus, of the sacramental wonders, of clarity in the inscrutable, of ecstasy in the mind's astonishment by the Eucharist. Mostly, it tried to restore some luster to a word that had been darkened by the Church, abjured; the word was *magic*. It was a risky title for a risky subject—any hint of magic raised hackles in the Church, but the book had been written, Michael swore by his most sacred oath, as an act of devotion.

It was not welcomed as any such thing. It nearly wrecked his life.

When the manuscript was finished, he sent it to Archbishop Lucas Cavanaugh, who was later to become a cardinal but was then the Archbishop of Philadelphia, and asked for imprimatur and blessing. Both were refused. The prelate replied:

> You have written an unorthodox document. It does not settle doubts, it raises them. There is fallacy in this book, and delusion; there may also be heresy. Schisms have been occasioned by opinions less heterodox and less sectarian, and by milder abrasions of the Christian spirit. No blessing is given, and imprimatur is expressly withheld.

For a month after the rejection, Michael was inflamed by the injustice. He had meant no heresy, he had been, almost willfully it seemed, misconstrued. A rigid mind had not allowed the possibility that there might be a way of celebrating the greatest of human mysteries not only as an old solemnity of the faith but as a new celebration of man's creative illusion; a blind, a stubborn spirit had not been able to envision a new radiance in the passion.

One evening, abruptly, like the reversal of a telescope, Michael got a variant view of his circumstance. His judgment of Cavanaugh, it occurred to him, was as pompous as the Archbishop's judgment of the book. He was guilty of pedantry; worse, he was guilty of pride. Pride—venial, if it seeks inordinately for honor; mortal, if it goes before the joy of charity. At first he was only vaguely troubled; it was enough to know his frailty and to expiate it; humility was the balm of pride, the catholicon. But he could not detect the source of the infection, and it dejected him. More and more he castigated himself; he wrapped and tied the manuscript and hid it out of sight, he said his offices in a hushed despair.

At last, in flight from himself and needing a refuge, he went on a retreat. It was a severe one, in Mexico, in lifeless, arid, desert country where there was no relief from heat and drought. He stayed longer than he had intended, in a self-imposed hardship of excessive work and insufficient food—against the counsel of his superiors—and the new worry of sleeplessness. Finally, when his anchorite afflictions were over, when his body was so thin that the weight of his clothes hung onerously on his bones, he returned.

His spirit burned clean again. He felt washed of a culpability he had never actually been able to name. He could even think of his manuscript once more, without feeling it was a bloody cross. And in this nearly hallowed state, he came to a surprising decision. Instead of giving up the book, he would go back to it. He would push his energies to whatever painful extremities might be required in order to have it published.

But he would do it outside the Church. Circumspectly. Forswearing blessings and imprimaturs. He would not trade on his authority as a priest, nor would he embarrass his brothers of the cross by letting it be known who the author of the book was.

Choosing an inconspicuous nom de plume—Edward T. Morrison—he sent the manuscript to a secular publisher in New York. A rejection, then a second one, a third. On its fourth trip, the book was accepted for publication; a contract and a $500 check arrived.

The diffident volume, when it appeared, received scant notice. One reviewer guardedly found a trace of merit in it; another called it alternately vaporous and opaque; still another respectfully classified it with other books of esoteric interest, then defaced it with the word "sententious."

The first rabid review appeared in the *Catholic Preceptor*. It excoriated the book. Calling it anti-Mother Church, the critic guessed that the theology had been devised by a renegade Catholic. Two weeks later the *Catholic World* said the treatise was deistic, that it believed in the existence of God only on the evidence of reason and that it rejected divine revelation. This was, to Michael's frustration, the precise opposite of his conviction. Why was he so misunderstood? Was he so confused a writer?

Then the word "heretical" began to appear. One review after another, heretical, and *The Last Magic* became the favorite sitting duck of the Catholic press.

And who in the world was Edward T. Morrison anyway?

As the book began to sell moderately, his publisher begged him to let his identity become known; priestly authorship would be a boon to business. But the thought of unmasking himself terrified Michael, and he lay awake wondering why Archbishop Cavanaugh had not ex-posed and vilified him. Yet he knew that exposure was bound to come.

It came on Christmas morning. Through a leak in the publisher's office, the lay author of a relatively obscure book was revealed as an ordained priest and, by Ash Wednesday, Michael was famous and infamous. Now the diatribes were no longer leveled against the book alone, but against the man. He was a hypocrite, he was an apostate. Only Iscariot could have betrayed and betrayed, and hidden behind a false name; the false name was as abominable as the kiss. It was no defense that he had used a pen name in order *not* to betray the Church, in order to carry the burden of the book on his very own back, without lightening the load by benedictions and indulgences; that he was willing to suffer the attacks without the solace of Mother Church.

Well, he was suffering them. Mostly from Mother Church herself. For a while it was excruciating. He was kept on at the parish in Philadelphia, but relieved of his duties as a curate. If he absented himself from the parish house; his fellow priests stopped noticing his absence; then, his presence. He was shunned.

Now a more terrible—and totally untoward—thing happened. Just as the clamor started to subside, his defenders arose. Ironically, their advocacy only worsened his plight. The dying embers were fanned, the flames raged again. Uncertainly, unwillingly, he became a combatant in one of the discords within the Church. The passive intellectual, the meditative theologian suddenly became an activist. A reluctant one, he dragged his feet into meetings where he heard himself described as a fighting crusader, where he received gratis subscriptions to two radical magazines, *Rivolta* and *Paraclete,* the latter of which bracketed his name with such slogans as THE BREAD IS RISING and THE VOICE OF GOD IS NOT IN THE STONES OF THE CHURCH BUT IN THE HEARTS OF THE PEOPLE.

Then, one Sunday morning in France, a defrocked priest stood outside the main entrance of Rheims Cathedral and spoke about Michael Farris as *"un martyr de notre temps."* The word martyr was echoed in Amsterdam and in Brussels. The conflict had become ecumenical.

The extremity of the word on one side brought forth an extremity on the other. Anathema. The first time he saw the word in print, Michael began to quake. His dilemma had been part of a mad momentum; there were radical inconsistencies in it that made no sense, rages that had given it an insane energy. Anathema, how can I be a danger to my people, I have no inherent evil in me, I will not be cursed by expulsion from my brothers in Christ, nor from the Kingdom of God, I will not be cut off, I will not be excommunicated, I will not be destroyed.

In the spring of that year, Michael was summoned to the Vatican. He had been there only once, years ago, as a young student going with his class to witness the coronation of the Pope, and he had felt himself to be, in a deeply ritualistic way, a part of the communal glory. And now he was returning, in solitary odium.

On the second of May, the fourth anniversary of his ordination as a priest, he walked the length of the Via della Conciliazione toward St. Peter's, turned left around the colonnade, and entered the dark passageway that led into the vestibule of the Sacred Congregation for the Doctrine of the Faith, to answer charges as yet unknown. He was shunted from one uniform to another, then told to wait in the *cortile*.

The fountain in the courtyard plashed too softly, too rhythmically, like artificial water; the arches seemed too rigid and cold; age had not warmed them. At last another uniform appeared and ushered him into a waiting room, the yellow room, he was told. It was a silken chamber, quite small, dustless, immaculate, antiseptically foreboding. Against the wall, near the door, a gray and leaden bust of a threatening cardinal stared at him without welcome.

"He's still alive," the uniform said, "and nearly a hundred years old. He lives right here." Then he added, darkly, "In the edifice—he lives somewhere in the edifice." The "somewhere" was chilling.

Again he waited. A long time. Then somebody came, a priest this one, and told him to go away, he would be called when his "matter was in readiness."

For two weeks he lived in lay clothes, in the anonymity of a small rented room. He didn't go out daytimes, he knew Rome only by darkness. He hid from everyone, he racked himself with loneliness, he tortured his soul. Longing for a retreat again, he realized that whatever refuge he could find he would have to make for himself, and he had no way of knowing how to begin. If only he knew what charges he must answer. There could be no allegations against the book—the Index had ceased to exist—the complaint must be not against his pen but against himself. And aside from the well-intentioned indiscretion of using a false name, he could not comprehend how he had sinned. *Mea culpa,* he would be willing to say, through my fault, through my

42

fault, through my most grievous fault . . . but what *was* my fault? Did I, in writing so devotedly of the mystery, love the Lord too much? What was the difference between being devoted and devout? Did I claim my love to be special and first, of all men? Did I claim my love to be a singular communion with the Holy Spirit?

On a rainy morning he was asked to return to what used to be called the Holy Office. Sopping wet and fighting the onset of a miserable cold, he was ushered through dark corridors, up one flight of stairs, then down two flights, and brought at last into a room that was dank and smelled of mildew. It was a strange room; it dulled the mind, somehow, and quickened apprehension. The walls were hung with too much drapery, blood-red damask for the most part, faded and streaked as if it had long ago been water damaged. There was no electric light in the chamber—a short circuit had darkened this wing of the building—but there was a *torchère* that gave off a quavering oil glow, and, on the oaken table, a spirit lamp.

In the nimbus created by it, Michael saw the hawklike face of Monsignor Sgarlero. He was in his early sixties, a gray unhealthy man. One side of his face was swollen; an infected jawbone, he said, was giving him pain, and he would have to talk without fully opening his mouth. His imagination engrossed, Michael conjured a rank and unhealable corruption.

"But surely," the Monsignor was saying out of the side of his mouth, "you wouldn't want me to specify."

"If I'm charged with anything, yes—I would like to know the charges."

"You are not being charged. You are simply asked to . . . concur." The actual phrase he used was *essere concomitante;* it implied something more hidden; to be in a state of attending without resistance, in resignation.

"With what am I to concur?" Michael persisted.

"You keep demanding charges, Father," the Monsignor said quietly. "You would like, perhaps, for this to come to trial, for a large occasion to be made of it—before the Signatura Apostolica, would you say?"

"No. I don't want any trial, I don't want any charges. I simply want to know what *you* want."

"It would be a benefit—to everybody—if it could be given out that the matter has come to an end. That you have simply acknowledged your . . . guilt. No more than that."

"Guilt of what?" he exploded. "What have I done? If you say you

43

have no charges, then of what am I culpable? Is this—right here—now—is this a trial of some sort? Then who persecutes me, who is my judge, who defends me? Is it confession? What do I repent?"

The Italian was utterly still. Michael's dread deepened. He had been asking questions rhetorically—no, indeed, he wasn't on trial, he thought—yet, this Holy Office had in the past functioned as a tribunal, sometimes silently, in its own way. He recalled that its name had once been the Sacred Congregation for the Universal Inquisition. Dark mists drifted back from the Middle Ages, old chains rattled, fires blazed.

Sgarlero put his hand to his jaw; it was as if Michael's questions had worsened the pain. "In your opening chapter you justify magic." He seemed coldly angry at having been pressed. "You do it in full knowledge that the Church has condemned such paganism."

"The Church has condemned only black magic, Monsignor. Witchcraft, sorcery, yes—but not so-called white magic."

Dogmatically: "Magic is condemned, as well as other forms of superstitions."

"I beg your patience." He must withdraw a bit, conciliate. "But white magic—*natural* magic—is at the heart of modern science, and the Church has long since ceased to condemn it. On the contrary, we have embraced it. And for good reason—it is a wonder of the mind—it inspires amazement at the universe. Magic is the child of mystery."

"You mean hocus pocus."

"I do not mean hocus pocus."

"That's the way you refer to penance." He held up Michael's book and pointed a bony finger at a passage underlined in red. "You say, 'By an act of supplication, by simply invoking the mystery of penance, the sinner is absolved.' "

"Is that not good doctrine? Do we not say *ex opere operato?* Doesn't that mean by the absolution of the priest—by the act alone—we are absolved?"

Sgarlero went in for the kill. "But you misuse that doctrine to make it appear that the priest is absolutely unnecessary. And, by extension, the Church as well." The man had harried Michael from trap to trap. "It is very strange, in these practical times, to see a young man pursue such emotional mysticism. It suggests—how shall I call it?—subterfuge. . . . Are you a revolutionary?"

"No, I am not."

"It is said that you are. . . . What are you?"

44

Warily: "I do not feel it necessary to put a political label on myself."

On his way back to the hotel, after this first inconclusive meeting, Michael wondered what label he would put on himself if he were forced to do so. As a political person, he didn't always know where, in the Church, he stood; somewhere in the vicinity of Pope John. Once, while still in the seminary, he was called, aspersively, an all-embracing liberal. He probably would have been called a bleeding heart if the epithet were not clerically in bad taste. If in fact his heart did bleed it was not for a single political persuasion, but for many. It worried him not to be more focused upon a cause, not to *know*.

He knew with more certainty where he stood as a theologian. Feet on the earth, yes, but barely on tiptoe, eyes upward, peering nearsightedly, with strain and striving, at the mystery. Yearning toward it. He had said in *The Last Magic:*

> I am out of my time. This is a precarious moment for a man who yearns to be a mystic. Even in the Church, a precarious moment, for God has become the project of political, teleological people. As Man becomes aware of the larger measure of the universe, he assumes the smaller measure of God; as he becomes capable of measuring the vastness, he assumes himself capable of creating it. And of using God as the Great Employee, a kind of universal manager, but old-fashioned and not yet conversant with the new methods. Mankind would have to program Him somewhat differently, for greater efficiency. There were, one supposed, punch press operators at work on this enterprise.
>
> The justifiable charge against mysticism is that it doesn't make sense. But the question is not whether reality makes better sense, but whether it has a right to rule our lives. The danger in being an exclusively rational Christian is that sooner or later the discrepancies of reality expose one another and one has a luminous view of . . . nothing. Whereas if one is a mystical Christian, there is no discrepancy—mystery is its own integrity.
>
> So, it seems to me, we must stop pursuing the unattainable reality and look to the attainable dream. It is not enough to love God with the rational and critical processes

45

of the mind; one has to love Him with the creative processes as well, with imagination, with the eagerness to be inspired by Him; not everyone His judge, but everyone His fellow artist.

Unfortunately, this is against the spirit of our analytical age. Philosophers nowadays discuss numbers instead of numen; theologians talk about causes instead of the First Cause. Even poets, so much of whose imaginative life transcends practical thought, and who lyrically affirm that the divine spirit has blessed them in their work, deny prosaically that the divine spirit exists "in real life." Thus, in the life they call real, they submerge themselves in the muck of matter-of-factness, stoppering the single precious reed through which they might breathe the rarefied air of revelation.

We are suffocating.

If we do not become inspired with God's breath, we will expire for want of it. If we demand a pragmatic answer to His mystery, we will get many of them, all contradictory, and return to chaos. And perhaps, if no practical answer exists, perhaps, perhaps—and this is the great optimism of religion—none is needed. All meaning is in Him.

For myself, I pray that this may be so. For He is the center of my being, and its depth. He is my first Father and my last, whose word I do not doubt, the measure of my life's size, the test of its truth, the vision of its beauty.

Without God, I do not know who I am; and in my bewilderment, I may not even exist.

Two days after his first meeting with Sgarlero, he was summoned to his second one. This time, one of the questions he was asked: when he was denied an imprimatur, why did he have the book published privately? Why was it so important to him—why did he take such a huge risk?

Michael answered simply: "I am a theologian—it's my life's work. This is a product of it."

Still ferreting for ulterior motive, his inquisitor asked, "Why are these fine points of mysticism so vital to you?"

As if Michael were wasting his life on metaphysical chitchat.

"Why," Sgarlero continued, "do you overburden the head of a pin? Of what use is it to you—or to the Church?"

It was the most depressing question of all. It suggested what Michael had been suspecting. The Church was irked by its theologians; they were the troublemakers of the *Magisterium*; a nuisance. Was all his work in theology, then, a waste? Was the venerable study becoming obsolete and useless now that religion was turning more to earth and less to heaven? Was theology itself to blame? Was it apologizing away its very existence, claiming to be a modern science? Was it losing its identity in dialogue with men of materiality, was it toadying to its enemies like Sgarlero, was it forswearing the offices of prayer and trying to fit into the office buildings of the Church, was it trying to communicate in a concrete technological language it could not speak and losing its ability to utter the abstract language of the logos of God? Had it abandoned its durable vellums in the realm of eternal philosophy, for the throwaway paperbacks in the trendy marketplace of psychology, sociology and political science? Was it quietly, self-effacingly, and without anybody taking especial notice, slipping away into oblivion?

And was part of Michael's life slipping away with it? Was he, as a theologian, an obsolete theoretician in an institution that no longer had any use for him, that solicited the more worldly counsel of strangers? Was the Church simply asking him to be meekly silent, and go away . . . and if he didn't, would she persecute him?

As Sgarlero was doing.

"We will have one further meeting," he said.

For "meeting" he used the word *udienza*. The ambiguity was, Michael felt sure, deliberate. Meeting, audience—the term could mean those things; it could also mean a hearing.

A hearing was, however, not held. Not with Sgarlero. On the day it was to take place, Michael had a puzzling experience. A courier arrived and informed the young priest that he was now going to be conducted to his *udienza*. The word this time was used in its strictest sense. He was escorted, by way of corridors and stairways, along loggias and antechambers, and finally, through what his attendant called *le due camere,* into the private presence of his Holiness.

Seven years ago the old man was already in his illness. As Michael knelt to kiss the revered ring, the hand even then had begun to tremble. The quivering of the fingers seemed a contradiction, like a categorical denial of the man's power to bless, as if holy water had lost its unction. As he started to rise from his genuflection, he heard the voice:

"Stay there."

47

Dutifully, albeit baffled, Michael remained on his knees.

"Stay there, you dunce," the Pontiff said. The word was not dunce exactly, but something more affectionate, *zuccone.* "What an educated simpleton you are."

"I may be a dunce, Your Holiness, but I am not what they say of me. I am not a heretic, I am not an apostate. I have no lack of devotion, nor even of piety, God help me. I am as filled with piety as I was when I lay prostrate on the floor and received my orders."

"Piety, piety," the old man said impatiently. "Hardly anyone has gone to the stake for impiety. It is a lack of reverence that apostates burn for. Reverence, my son—do you know what that is?—reverence? It is the politics of religion."

The Pope waited until the young man had collected the empiricism, then, as if he had been guilty of an oversight, permitted him to rise.

"Why did you become a priest?"

The question was unexpected. "I . . . was an orphan very young," Michael replied. "I was raised by curates and nuns. I never thought of belonging anywhere else. The world was . . ."

"Intimidating."

"Anyway, not welcoming. And the Church was."

"The Church-as-Home," the Pope said.

"Yes."

"Most priests would have answered: 'The Church-as-Sanctum.' "

"Can't it be both?"

"I think—for you—the sanctum is more important than the hearth, Father Farris. I have read your work."

He turned his back on Michael and walked to an old credenza which stood at right angles to his desk. When he turned to the priest again, he held a copy of *The Last Magic* in his hand. It was at this point that Michael's shapeless puzzlement began to take form.

"Ordinarily," the Pope said, "I could not concern myself with so specific a matter as your book. Normally, I might not even hear of it. But by an inadvertence, I did." He paused; seemed to be beset with a private trouble. "I read your book not for any pontifical reason but because it deals with something that touches me in a personal way. Let us call it a . . . vagary." He had said the word with difficulty. Now he hesitated again, studied Michael as if measuring whether he could impart a secret to the young man. "Do you . . . understand me?"

Michael didn't. What vagary, what possible caprice could involve

48

the Pontiff in such an insignificant matter—a specific matter he had called it, with a nicety—as a minor book by an unknown priest? "I'm not sure I do understand, Your Holiness."

For an instant Michael thought he was going to explain what he meant. But abruptly he saw the Pope change his mind. A shadow of regret darkened the old man's face. Then quickly, routing it, he closed the dark personal subject, and forced himself to speak brightly once more.

"What a breath-giving book it is," he said. He had begun to speak English but lapsed momentarily to use the word *respirare* to signify the pleasure of his sigh. "When you speak of things of the spirit, when you praise the Paraclete as the advocate of the Mystical Body, you are blessed with a divine intuition." He paused, then held his hands up in mock dismay. "But when you discuss the practical matters, you are as naïve as an altar boy. You do not know the simplest *mechanics* of how the church must deal with—for example— iniquity. You speak so tolerantly of wickedness! As if 'deliver us from evil' means to be liberated from nothing more corrupt than an out-of-order public convenience. Hellfire, my son, is not magical fireworks that we manufacture in the Vatican—it's not a Roman candle. Hellfire *burns*—it does not singe a little hair—it incinerates the soul. So your little parley with yourself about confession is a—*ridicolezza*. You are excellent in dealing with the ways of love, but you are too gullible in the face of evil. That's why your chapter on Penance is sheer abracadabra. I hope when we arrange an imprimatur for the book, you will permit us to delete that single chapter."

Michael thought his heart would stop. "An imprimatur, Your Holiness?"

"Not my own, of course, but I will speak to one of the bishops," he said. "And he will see that it is well rendered into Italian. I would recommend Father Alvio Perighi for the translation. He is a delicate man. You would, likely, not have heard of him. He is something of a poet, but he has unfortunately earned a small reputation in Italy only for his translations and, as he calls it, his hackwork. He is bitter about that. 'Jesus' Janitor,' he calls himself. But I am not supposed to know that."

He smiled engagingly, and Michael couldn't believe his turn of fortune. "I cannot thank you, Your Holiness, I will never be able to thank you."

"You must try." The Pontiff smiled again. "But you have not yet given permission for the excision."

"The chapter on Penance?" He had barely allowed himself to comprehend that he might have to eliminate the chapter. But the thought was now all too clear. "Must it be excised?"

"Reverence, Father—practice reverence."

"But it is my best illustration of how mystery transcends magic."

"A better illustration than the Eucharist?"

He was embarrassed and felt juvenile. It was a twinge to think the chapter might have to go; he felt he might be cutting a cranial nerve out of the brain of the book. Worse, there was something wrong in doing it, something vaguely immoral.

He started to say so and pulled himself up short. What pride, again. What pride to vaunt his ethical sense before the Father of probity. If one questions the moral philosophy of the Pope, doesn't papal infallibility become a mere ecclesiastical catchword? Certainly, he could never mean such disrespect.

He agreed to delete the chapter. "Yes, Your Holiness," he said.

Three months later, the book appeared with Bishop di Luca's imprimatur but without the section on Penance, under the title *L'Ultima Magia.* It was the title that the Pontiff himself had chosen. The word "ultimate" did not mean the same as the word "last," but when Michael called that to the attention of the Holy Father, the latter said that the English title was too finite, suggesting the limit of enchantment rather than its endlessness and its immensity.

How gently, how quietly the book presented itself, in Italian. Hardly anybody noted its arrival in the bookshops. In Milan, there was only one review, in a lay newspaper; noting the imprimatur, the critique was brief and courteous. A few other reviews were sent to Michael—summaries, for the most part, perfunctory. Only in passing, two comments related it to the hubbub over *The Last Magic;* mentioned as an oddity, a tidbit of literary gossip. Nobody referred to the absence of the chapter on Penance; nobody seemed to notice it had ever existed.

Michael heaved a sigh of relief, and fell in love with Rome. He no longer had his Philadelphia parish to return to, and was without any assignment; almost, he felt, without a call. He was certain, however, he would be sent back to America. The thought of leaving Rome made him ache.

It was the more painful because there was nobody he wanted to go back to in the States. He had been an only child. His father, a verger in a church on the West Side of Manhattan, had died when the boy was five. His mother had abandoned Michael to a Franciscan orphanage. She could be alive somewhere, or dead for many years; he might never know, was not sure he wanted to. There was nobody else.

Except Hester. And that name would be better forgotten. Some day—some night, would be more to the point—if he could ever achieve a state of most divine grace, he might indeed forget her. But such beatitude had never come to him, and he might never receive it. Better, then, to imagine her too as being dead. And perhaps she might be. If she was indeed alive, it was no thanks to him. . . .

So he dreaded going home. And made no noises in the Italian city, for fear someone might hear and notice he was still there. But at last, his conscience nettling him, he made a telephone call to the Congregation for Religious. Then another, to the Congregation of Seminaries and Universities, now called Catholic Education, and a third to the Secretariat of State. It was from the last of these that he ultimately received his appointment. In the autumn, some five months after his arrival, he became clerk-extraordinary to the Secretariat in the office of the *collegamenti,* which meant he was an agent for general liaison in the Apostolic See.

For the first year, except at public audience and in the Easter procession, he did not see the Pope again. Then, one blustery November's day, he was summoned from the Vatican Library into the presence of the Holy Father and asked by him to explain a memorandum which had been twice explained by others, and understood by nobody. Since it had been written, in the first place, by Michael himself, the Pontiff suggested that the young priest might have some inkling of its meaning.

Michael glanced at it; a whole page was missing. The old man howled with laughter; the note had gone through three bureaus without anybody noticing that, without the missing paragraphs, the communication was senseless. He wondered what meaning could be made of worship without the Word.

From that day onward Michael, to his recurring surprise, was frequently summoned to the papal apartment. The Pope, he could see, was fond of him. And Michael came to love the Bishop of Rome, which was the way the old man consistently referred to himself, as the only person he had ever met who had remained, well into old age, totally intact. Nothing in the essence of the man had ever been damaged, nothing violated. How he could be such an irresolute man—and sometimes a cunning one—and still remain so immaculate was an amazement to the American.

And what secrets of enlightenment the old man hid on his night table. He read prodigiously, not only the tomes of transaction—the summaries, the compendia, the gists and substances—but the writings of the new novelists and poets, the fantasies of the secular philosophers, the *novelle intorno al fuoco,* the stories by the fireside. Particularly, he pored over the radical fulminations of the young, and was willing to discuss them, respectfully if somewhat vexatiously, for longer sessions than his schedule allowed.

That's why the Pope's final encyclical was such a bafflement to Michael. It had been rumored that it was going to be a major manifesto, a bull or a rare autograph written by the Holy Father's own hand, indited with his passion. It was going to be an amplification of the voice of Pope John, the poet of the Church renewed; a letter written in the handwriting of the young, the progressives predicted; *Commonweal* foresaw it as the *Epistle to Tomorrow.*

It wasn't. It was a disappointment. For one thing, it was not the major message that had been awaited, it was a minor encyclical, brief, general, even equivocal. Where it did take a clear position, it went to pains to underline the validity of the status quo. It was hard to see what purpose the missive served until the last few paragraphs, and they were adumbrations of a dark future, full of warning. This final page was the most chilling part of the encyclical. Beware, the dying Pope was saying, the so-called progress in democratizing the liturgy, beware the "priest of earthly passion," beware taking dominion over the blessing of nativity, beware *aborto e abominazione.*

The papal letter should not have troubled Michael so deeply, he told himself; the Pontiff had never been known as a radical theologian, nor a radical anything for that matter; innovation had never been the mode of his ministry. His stewardship had been in the one word, stability, and if Michael had expected that the encyclical would be another *Pacem in Terris* he had only his own visionary idealism to blame. And he would never mention his distress to anyone.

He did. To the Pope himself. "All birth control is not abortion, Your Holiness."

The old man had tricked him into commenting on the publication.

"I did not say it was," the Pontiff replied measuredly. "I said abortion is abomination. I do not see a total identity between birth control and abortion."

"But your encyclical—"

"Did not address itself to the entire question of birth control."

"Might it not have been more—elucidating—if it had? There are, in fact, some kinds of control that the Church has come to accept."

"Not quite, Father. They are not, of themselves, a control of birth, but a principle of forbearance, a discipline of abstinence. And after all, to demand self-restraint is not a singularity of our Church—nor should it cause the affliction that the secular press says it does. There are more difficult self-restraints—against spite and greed and pride . . . and sentimentality, may I add."

The last designation Michael took as a slur on himself, and he was silent. The Pontiff apparently mistook his silence as meaning a total desertion.

"I thought, Michael, that I was safe in your devotions," he said quietly.

It is he who is sentimental, Michael told himself, not I. "You are, Holiness. When have you been unsafe in my devotions? You asked me what I thought, and I told you. If I tell you the truth, does that make you feel unsafe?"

The old man smiled ruefully. "The truth—on earth—is hazardous, yes. Perhaps that's why we need Heaven."

Released by the easy aphorism, they both laughed. But some damage had been done. From that day onward, Michael was summoned to the papal apartment less frequently; finally, not at all. Cardinal Feradoti, Michael's superior, suggested it might be because the elderly man had fallen critically ill and was husbanding himself. But Michael felt it wasn't so, that his meetings with the Papa had never been a strain on the invalid; to the contrary, the Pope had arranged them for his pleasure, had stopped them when they gave him pain. . . . Michael lamented that they were in the past.

Today, for the first time in months, he was again in the papal presence, and he could not bear to see how wasted the old man looked, and how the always vacillating mind had now gone to the extremities of indecision; wandering, lost.

"Will it make you happy?" the sick man said.

"Will what make me happy, Holiness?"

"Your book—L'Ultima Magia—will it make you happy if we arrange for its imprimatur?"

"You have already done so, Papa—and it did make me happy."

"Done so? When?"

"Many years ago."

"How many?"

53

"Nearly seven."

The old man smiled and winked a few times. "I was testing your memory," he said.

They both nodded to each other. Distances shortened. The Holy Father beckoned him closer to the bed. "I have called for you. I would like you to do me a favor."

"Yes, Father?"

The Pontiff started to speak but seemed to have lost his way again. Unable to get back into the drift of things, he closed his eyes a moment. When he reopened them, he appeared to have recollected. "It was you I called because you have . . ."

"Yes?"

". . . stigmata."

The word unnerved Michael. He was very still. He couldn't believe the man had deliberately chosen the term; it was a misuse. Or, perhaps his mind had wandered to another person, another time. Stigmata . . . no, not he. There were no wounds on him, no open sores, no such noble abrasions of the spirit. He had no correspondence, not of such ecstatic sort, to the sufferings of Christ. Pain, yes, but none that would bring about the charism bestowed on persons of such holiness.

Evasively, with a smile: "Pain is *lex naturalis,*" the young man said.

"No, not the law of nature—the nature of the law."

How strange that the formalist whose last letter had hewn so rigidly to the dogma would admit such a thing, Michael thought.

"Stigmata," the old man repeated. "That is why you will understand me—and why I ask this favor."

"What is it, Holiness?"

A moment. Then he said it quietly:

"Confess me."

Michael could not believe he had heard the words; then he heard them repeated, as if from a distance. He felt a moisture on his hands, cold; he felt himself trembling. The old man saw it. "Do not be so troubled, Michael," he said. "Come and sit here."

The Pope beckoned him to his bed, on the edge of which he wanted the young priest to sit. Disturbed, uncertain, Michael could not bring himself to do so. It had always awed him, the solitariness of the papal condition, overwhelmed and filled him with pity for the loneliness. The old man sitting alone at table, precluding himself by adherence to dead custom from breaking bread with any other human

54

being, eating the dry crust of sanctity; the one light burning in the papal chamber through the vigil of the night. The bed . . . which only the doctors approached as closely as he now approached it.

"Sit, Father."

The young man did as he was told.

The elderly voice had no quaver of frailty in it. Ritually, he began. "Bless me, Father, for I have sinned. . . ."

Michael's head whirled. He must steady its rotation—or was it the spinning of the earth?—something must make fast, secure itself. This is my Pope, my father of earthly fathers, come to me as penitent, come for the sacrament of God's forgiveness. How am I to administer penance: unworthy; it was the very chapter that this man had insisted I must tear out of my book.

The sick old mind was more adrift than Michael had thought it to be. The Pontiff wanted his regular confessor. "Shall I call Cardinal della Marca?" he asked.

"No . . . it is you, Michael."

"Why me?" he asked softly.

"Because you will understand me, I believe. You have been in the magic country. You know the charms, the temptations. . . . And I have been seduced by them." Then, quietly, with a note of pleading, he repeated, "Bless me, Father, for I have sinned."

Michael hesitated, as if on a threshold. It had been a long time since he had helped to shrive a conscience . . . years ago, a new curate in an old oaken booth . . . and now he was entering the confessional again. But the sliding panel between him and the penitent was closed. He could not bring himself to open it. Yet he had no choice; he had been chosen. Steadying himself, he silently made the supplication: "Help me, oh Lord, to judge gently, as in mercy thou judgest me." Then, as if opening the panel, he looked at the humbled old man.

"In what way have you sinned?"

"I have been too much in love with the mystery of our Savior. I have wanted nothing more than to be at one with His miracle. I have not been a good shepherd. I have written the words and spoken the dicta. I have been precise in the dogma and have administered the offices. But my true soul has never been with my fellow man, but only with the wonder of the Lord. And in saying that my soul has been with my flock, I have lied. I have done a falseness to the faithful, and to the Holy Name. I have sinned, I have mortally sinned. I have been bewitched by the magic of Jesus, the risen."

55

He had indeed used the word "bewitched," there was no mistaking it. Speaking in Italian, he had said *stregare;* had specifically chosen the sacrilegious word when it could have been a less culpable one— *affascinare,* for example, or *incantare.* He was heaping on his head the ashes of sorcery, the desecration of his holy office.

Michael could not believe that such a confession could come from this man. He would have reckoned him, of all others, as a practical servant of his people—practical, yes; if anything, too close to the concerns of the world, too answerable to the expedient. A man overly pragmatic, all faults considered, certainly not overly mystical. How had he come to this view of himself? And to such suffering over it?

This, then, was the answer to the years-old puzzle—the "vagary" that had prompted the Pope to take up the cause of Michael's book . . . the aching, secret trouble.

The old man was very still. His eyes were wide. There were no tears in them, yet the agony shone in his face, more terrible than his mortality, a loving man who, in his love of God had felt he had failed mankind, whose life was then a failure.

Wrong, Michael wanted to cry, you are making a wrong confession. Possibly, without knowing it, even a false one. How can a man spend a whole lifetime with himself—over eighty years of it—how can he inhabit the same body, incite the same mind, answer to the same soul, and not know who he is, to others, to himself? How can he not know what sin to repent, as if he were asking the absolution not for himself but for a stranger? Might this not knowing, this being an alien within the corporeal region one is given to inhabit, might *this* not be—more than the mere incident of death—the true tragedy of life?

Yet, why was the knowing necessary? Had it not been only in recent times that knowing had been endowed with some special grace? At what loss to mystery! . . . the death of magic. But magic had not, apparently, died in the dying man. It had lived in him all his life, and made him judge himself a liar, and his death miserable.

"Mea culpa," the old man was murmuring, "mea culpa."

Fault, then. Had Michael stumbled on the secret of the Hamlet pontiff, a spiritual man lost in a temporal world, too frightened to make any real change in it, terrified by error, taking three steps sideward and two steps backward, unable to surge forward on any crest of certainty?

"Fault, fault," he was crying. "Through my fault."

Was this, then, the infallible one, weeping of fault? Could there be an infallible one? Save Christ, had there ever been? . . . He must not allow such thoughts. He was confusing infallibility with impeccability, just as he might confuse a transgression against the Church with a sin against God.

What comfort could he give the dying man, what absolution? Life everlasting, Michael started to say, without thinking, almost by rote. And he mused wryly how often rote strikes upon comfort. The solace of forgiveness; who repents will be exculpated, the promise went.

"Go and sin no more," Michael whispered. Where, in his death, would the old man go?—again, the ritual consolation: life eternal.

"My penance, Father?" the sick one asked.

"Hail Mary, full of grace . . ." What else could there be?

As he arose from the bed, Michael heard the soft incantation. *"Ave Maria, gratia plena . . ."*

There was such solemnity in it, such a pathetic entreaty for forgiveness, that Michael wanted to be away from the dark ruby-lighted chamber as quickly as possible. As he slipped out of the bedroom, the old man was still softly murmuring his Hail Mary.

The young priest passed the others in the passageway, the vigil-makers, waiting, and walked through the long sequence of silent rooms. Loggia after loggia, one ornate gallery after another; the gilt is only on the surface, he thought, yet how impenetrable.

At the foot of the stairway he saw the apparition.

It was Cardinal van Tenbroek. Not an apparition, really; Michael had better stop thinking of him that way. Except, he wondered if the Dutch Eminence might not encourage such a daunting epithet. The Pope had once said of the Cardinal that he did not enter a room, he substantialized. Walking too softly, always, he made hardly a sound in his black clothes. He never wore chromatic vestments except when he must, on highest ecclesiastical occasions; always black, like a rebuke. His eyes were black as well, burning eyes, Savonarola *revocatus,* and he espoused Christ with clenched fist.

"Is he dead?" the Cardinal asked.

There are many dooms in this prelate's life, Michael thought, and he is always ready for one of them. His question seemed somehow reprehensible; besides, stupid. If he were dead there would be a hastening of feet, clamorings in the passageways.

"No, he is not dead."

"Has he asked for Unction?"

It was a slip of the tongue. The Cardinal had not referred to the Anointing of the Sick, the sacrament for all people who are ill, but to its old term, Extreme Unction, balm to the dying. A minor lapse. Michael should have let it pass. But he was annoyed at the morbid question. "No, he has not asked for Unction. He has reconsidered—decided not to die."

The Cardinal smiled darkly, noting the sarcasm. "He will die in due course, and we will have made no provision."

"The Camerlengo is with him," Michael said.

"I don't mean provision for the conclave. I mean provision for his successor."

"That *is* the conclave, isn't it?"

He knew he was baiting the Cardinal; the Cardinal knew it as well, but made no point of it. "We need your help, Michael."

It had been said before. "Who is we, Your Eminence?"

That too had been said before. The older man paused to give the answer weight. Then: "I have spoken to Cardinal Galestro."

Michael was still. The man would not be lying, yet how could it be possible? It was the unlikeliest partnership imaginable. This fanatic radical here, and the moderate soft-spoken man of quiet devotion. He could not conceive a fraternity of the two. Yet, he had heard Feradoti say that if the impeding hulk of prejudice in the Church was to be budged even so much as an inch, it would take both arms to do it, the left as well as the right.

Tenbroek could see Michael's irresolution. "You do not think Cardinal Galestro and I have come together?"

"Have you indeed?"

"Come with me."

The Cardinal opened the door off the staircase and beckoned Michael to follow him. The prelate led the way through loggias and passageways, his feet pattering rapidly on marble floors. Abruptly Michael was in corridors unfamiliar to him and wondered how the black figure ahead of him could walk with such swift assurance in nearly total darkness.

Van Tenbroek was now paces away, opening a door, then another passage onto a veranda, and Michael realized they were two stories up, looking across the Borgia Courtyard to the lofty windows opposite, and little else could be seen in the lowering dusk.

Nobody present, Michael thought, except us and the shadows. Then he saw the movement.

The elderly Cardinal sat on a folding chair—how had he found such a commonplace object in the Apostolic Palace?—and held a half-open breviary in his hands. He might have been saying something from it; certainly not reading it in the failing light. He finished what he was doing, whispered the last words of the office, then rose. It was typical of the man to rise to everyone as if all the world took precedence over him. His face was clouded with distress. Before they could utter a word, Cardinal Galestro raised an unsteady hand.

"I do not want this conversation," he said.

"But it is essential, Your Eminence," Tenbroek replied.

"I do not want it," he kept repeating afflictedly, "I do not want it."

It was ambiguous what he didn't want: the Pope to die or the conversation to be held.

"But there is no time to be lost," the younger Cardinal went on. "The moment he passes away, it will already be too late. The conclave will be upon us. So we must use the time. We must send Father Farris to America—find whatever adherents we can—we have no other course."

"No!" the other cried. "I will not have this electioneering—I will not take part in it."

"But it is always done, Your Eminence—why do we delude ourselves? It is inconceivable that it would not be done."

"Not by me!" Galestro retorted.

"Dear heaven, what sin can there be when men of true belief try to convince one another?" Van Tenbroek was losing patience. "Do we not do it in all other matters?"

It was a shrewd argument, Michael thought, to use the evangelical apologia with a propagandist, a man who had spent the better part of his ecclesiastical life in the Sacred Congregation for the Propagation of the Faith.

Galestro wavered, then continued with less certainty. "But— shame—to be doing it so soon—while His Holiness is still warm in his bed—have we no sensibilities? Can we not give good grace to the dying, can we not—?"

He could not finish the sentence. His perturbation held the silence.

Tenbroek moderated the urgency. "Your Eminence, there are many who love you," he said. "We want to make you our Holy Father—"

"I have told you—I do not want it."

"But how can you refuse it?"

"I do not refuse it—my unworthiness does it for me. I cannot say yes when I know I am not worthy. I do not have the shoulders for the burden. My head is not as quick as his, nor do I have his patience. I can disagree with every bull and brief the man has written—contest

59

after contest—and still he is a truer Pope than I could hope to be. I would be found wanting—and I could not bear it. I beg you—please."

"But you are the only one who can bring us together, Eminence." His voice had a fateful darkness in it. "If you do not, someone will nail a paper on the church door."

With an outcry, Galestro struck at the phantom of Luther. "No, there will be no rioting in the church—you do not frighten me—no rioting!"

"There already is, Father. In Belgium, the radicals—like myself, you would say—write theses and hang them on the altars. Two priests were stoned within fifty feet of Chartres. In Brasília the fingers of a bishop—those he raises in benediction—were chopped off and thrown into his biretta."

"That is not true. I have inquired into it. There is a legate here from Rio de Janeiro—he says it is a lie."

"What else is he to say, Your Eminence?" Tenbroek rejoined. "The newspapers do not speak of it—why should he? And we ourselves—we hush every syllable of it—as you do now. A curate is robbed, a sacristy is vandalized—and they do not even report it to their bishops."

A priest is stripped naked and he does not report it to the police. Nor had Michael himself reported it, he realized. He had seen it happen and let it pass. But then the man had not wanted it reported, he told himself. But why? And were there other secrets—of worse atrocities, as Tenbroek related—frighteningly kept? No, not possible. Everybody knew Tenbroek was a havoc-crier; dawn always brought him a day of wrath, his every judgment was the Last.

Galestro apparently had the same opinion of the man. "You see violence in everything," the older man said.

"But there *is* violence in everything—and we're too terrified to admit it. We think if we ignore it, it will go away—but it won't. If we don't face it, it will get worse."

"What is there to face?" Galestro rejoined. "There is no pattern to it. The clerics who get hurt—some are radicals, some are conservatives. But for the most part, they are ordinary churchmen who have not been known to express any political position whatever. They get beaten, their rectories are burned—and why have *they* been chosen? Why? No pattern, no pattern."

Van Tenbroek didn't answer for an instant; when he did, his voice was unwontedly controlled. "There *is* a pattern—and we've been refusing to identify it. The violence is against *all* of us—against the Church itself. To weaken us. And if we do not conciliate our differences . . ." He paused, allowing the implications of the threat to gather. "You must help us to do that, Your Eminence. If you do not . . ."

"Then someone else will do it."

"Enzo Margotto."

"He is not the worst."

"There will be further bloodshed."

"I cannot endure your jeremiads, Cardinal. You talk of Margotto as if he were Beelzebub."

"He is, Your Eminence."

Galestro was enraged. He started to retort, but, collecting himself, waited for a moment of restraint. Then he said, with slow deliberation, "I had forgotten how opprobrious you are, Cardinal van Tenbroek."

The meeting was, for him, over. Forthrightly, he walked across the veranda, but Tenbroek hurried after him. He plucked at the man's sleeve, grabbed his arm. "I beg you to forgive me. I am not as shameful as you think—but my anger is too much for me. And my apprehension. Margotto terrifies me. If he is our next Pope—and there are many who will try to see to it—it will be as if Pope John had never lived. The revisions of his Council—God knows they were temperate enough—will be disavowed. *Pacem in Terris* will be torn into confetti and thrown into the wind, over the Square. He will turn back fifty years, Father. There will be danger from heretics and danger from pagans. We will no longer be fortified here in the Vatican. The apostates will betray us and the terrorists will butcher us. It will be the time of Antichrist—and the Church will fall to fragments."

Even if the doom he was prophesying was too cataclysmic to believe, his warning about Margotto was, nonetheless, to be apprehended. The peril in the reactionary, as they all knew, was not imaginary. And Cardinal Galestro, for all his antipathy to the grim eminence that clung to his arm, realized the truth of what the man was saying.

Unhappily, his eyes shifting from place to place across the now nearly dark courtyard, he raised his shoulders as if to lighten the burden. "We cannot talk of it here, in dim doorways, like conspirators," Galestro said.

"May we come to you tonight?" the other Cardinal asked.

61

"Yes, to my house." Then, quietly, almost to himself, and as if he knew he spoke nonsense, "There is too much mortality," he said.

Van Tenbroek didn't seem to have heard him. "Could it be at nine?"

Galestro merely nodded, then hastened away, retreating into the darkness.

The instant Michael unlocked the door to his apartment he knew something had been burned.

He saw no sign of it, no blaze, no ember, no damage anywhere, yet there could be no doubt of it. It was the second time today he had thought: incense. Earlier, one illusion had turned into another, into thyme. Now, however, no illusion. There had been a burning here, and real.

He saw it in a dish on the kitchen table. And beside it, one volume of his breviary. The first twenty pages of the book had been carefully, deliberately torn out; a match had been set to them. The ashes were black and gray in the white china saucer. The breviary lay alongside the dish, its cover open, its back exposed where the pages had been ripped from the binding.

There was no sign of anybody. No window had been jimmied, no lock had been forced. Not a thing had been taken, no clothes, no bricabrac, no food, not so much as a wafer.

Why had he thought wafer, why not cracker?

Why indeed not? Because the object chosen had not been secular but a book of religious hours. One of four volumes, it was the most precious prayer book he had ever owned. He had bought many of them and had kept them all, but this was the one he used, it was part of his daily habit. Years ago he had purchased it with the small money he had earned on *The Last Magic*. Expensive, more than he could afford, it was a beautiful set of books, simple yet full of a hundred things that moved him in prayer and to it, quiet commentaries on the liturgy, canticles from the Old and New Testaments, with end papers that were rainbows of unabashed color. And it was among the last of the breviaries that still used the old names—Lauds, Matins, Vespers—for the praises of the hours; and all the comforting old Latin words; he regretted to see them disappearing. He cherished them in the four volumes, marked the pages, interlined them, revised them to his own private devotions.

62

Considering he was a priest, he was too eccentric with prayer. He had long ago given up the consolation that prayer was the remedy for all the world's ills. Sometimes he altogether forgot to pray, completely overlooked a liturgical hour, as frequently as he passed a mealtime without eating. But when it happened, as with food, he came back hungry for it, ravening for the spiritual sustenance it gave him. And the breviary, all four lovely books of it, was the key to its benediction.

Burned. Twenty pages, burned.

He could not understand it, had no way of comprehending who could do it, or why. His hands shook as he touched the ashes. The charred remnants still had a stiff and delicate form, but as he laid a gentle finger on one gray black leaf, it disintegrated. He wanted to cry.

Suddenly he was frightened.

Strange that there had been no anger. Only heartache first, then this gelid chill, this shaking fright.

Who?

And why?

And how had they gotten in here?

And what did it mean?

Quietly, he closed the damaged book, carried it back into his study, went to the bookshelf, restored it to its place beside the other three volumes, noted again how untouched they were, how undisturbed, then returned to the kitchen.

He lifted the dish. The ashes stirred a little as he carried them. For an instant he couldn't bear to let them slip into the sink. Then he let it happen, ran the water through the gray black remnants, saw them turn to muck and disappear.

The bastards.

No. Try to ask forgiveness for them—the forgiveness of Another, if not your own—try.

He couldn't. He would have to understand it first. Forgiveness—his own—would be too difficult until he could discern how it fitted into a pattern of which he was a part. But he didn't *want* to understand it, not this soon, not if it meant giving remission; he wanted to hate it for a little while.

But hate what? Hate whom? Why had it been done?

What danger did it betoken? What revenge—against what? Against all of us, Tenbroek had said, against the Church itself. Was his warning about collective catastrophe not so overwrought as Michael had considered it? Were the terrorist attacks not so haphazard as they seemed to be, but a craftily designed series of raids, here, there, everywhere?

Or was he being personally threatened? But what damage could he be considered capable of perpetrating, what blackmail, what violence?

Violence. He must not loiter in that alleyway. . . . Dread . . . Already, dread . . . How effective the bastards were.

This brooding was not good. He must get on with daily living, with preparing his dinner, with clearing away, bathing, looking to his laundry. . . .

Think of other things. Going back to America.

Improbable. It was all academic, he told himself. This peregrination on a furtive electioneering junket, against every tradition of churchly decorum; it was all in the realm of unlikely surmises; it would not happen.

Who had burned his breviary?

Besides, Feradoti, the Cardinal Secretary of State, would not allow him to go. Not a chance. His superior was not a man to suffer one of his priests in an enterprise so lacking in what he would call seemliness. Even more significant to Michael's deliverance from the mission, Feradoti needed him. Once, when asked to spare the young man for a barren editorial chore in another office, Feradoti had written a strained but tactful refusal:

> He is always, it seems to me, in the midst of some critical urgency here, and I can hardly think of sparing him. Truth is, I suppose, I have come to lean on him too heavily; he is my most certain stay and ready comfort, and I regret . . .

Michael could rely on the Cardinal; he would cling to his assistant; keep him home.

Why were the pages burnt? Why had he been warned? Against what? What cautions must he follow, what protections must he seek?

On his way home from the Palazzo, he had bought some fruit, dark bread and prosciutto. He now bit into an out-of-season apple that was too pulpy, had a few nibbles at the bread and prosciutto, and called it a meal.

Suddenly he remembered that he had promised Feradoti to stylize the Washington missive by tomorrow. It wouldn't take long but he hadn't as yet done a word of it. Glad to have something to do, a busyness to take his mind off turmoils he could not understand, he hurried out of the apartment.

The wind of the last few days had died down. There was stillness and an illimitable sweep of spring sky, stars just winking in. More than at any other time of year, Rome was a felicity to him now, before the African summer panted its hot breath upon the city. It lasted all too briefly, so he determined to enjoy this evening fully and he strolled the long way, crossing a Tiber bridge he rarely used, entering the Vatican near the Arch of the Bells, sauntering through the gardens. He stopped. On a gravel path, suddenly aware of the Tower of St. John, he realized he had walked longer than he had intended. Turning, he hurried now, arrived at the Courtyard of St. Damasus, strode quickly into the Palazzo.

A sign on the elevator said it was being used by the workmen—artists were restoring some of the chipped painting in the loggias of Raphael and Bramante; he wondered how they could match colors in artificial light. It was a nuisance having them here, shifting people out of their offices, commandeering the elevators; sometimes, in his workaday life, he forgot that the Apostolic Palace, besides being a secretariat, was a treasury of precious art.

Trudging up the staircase, he wished it were better lighted; dimness, these days, discomfited him, especially with strangers in the building. The loggia leading to the Secretary's temporary office, makeshift while the craftsmen were here, was also too dimly illuminated and he had to walk an unaccustomed passageway.

Uneasiness.

He arrived at the double doors of Feradoti's provisional offices and was about to reach for his keys when he saw he would not need them. Under the doors, the thinnest sliver of yellow light. He opened one of the doors and entered.

He saw nobody. The light on the anteroom desk was aglow, but the rest of the room, and the chambers beyond it, were in darkness. Whoever had departed last—the new young man from Udine, perhaps—had forgotten to extinguish the lights, and to lock the door. Or else the restoration people . . . but they had no need to be in this section. . . .

He heard a sound. It was nothing he could identify, a voice and yet

65

not a voice. Abruptly, another sound. Different from the first—something metallic. Incisive, shearing the stillness as if it were a sheet of tin. Silence, then.

He thought of charred pages.

The metal noise again. He could not tell where it came from or even if it was actually here in the chambers; it might be coming from somewhere else, a distant balcony, or from the courtyard.

His impulse was: turn up the lights. Something told him to desist. Momentarily immobilized, he stood there, listening. But the sound had ceased. He was listening only to a silent darkness.

The inner hallway leading to the other rooms was pitch black. He wondered if he dared go down that corridor. The stillness held. Slowly, he stepped into the hallway, took a few steps, waited. Silence.

Continuing down the hall, he took courage now. It had been a number of moments since any noise had been heard. It could easily have come from outdoors, another office, a disorder in the pipes; it might even have been imaginary, a nervous emanation.

Scratch. A metal scratch.

He didn't move.

Again, the scratching sound. Then, clearly, the voice.

An uncanny voice, yet strangely familiar.

Feradoti's.

Michael knew now what the scratching sound had been. The cassette recorder. The playback of the Cardinal's voice; an implausibly mechanical sound for these chambers. He had heard it once before at nighttime, when the Cardinal had dictated to his secretary whatever memoranda and letters he had not managed through the day.

It troubled Michael that his alarm could be aroused by such a mundane cause; his nerve endings were more exposed than he had thought.

The cassette voice continued, slowly, in a hush. Then the real voice, even more softly than the other.

He paused momentarily outside the door, debating whether to disturb His Eminence; then he knocked. Hearing the bid to enter, he presented himself at the entrance to his superior's office.

The Secretary of State barely gave him a glance and did not interrupt his dictation. Speaking into the tiny microphone, he said, "Memorandum to Father Michael Farris. Where in devil's name have you been all day?"

Michael grinned. "It hasn't been all day—and you know very well where I've been."

"How is he?"

Michael slowly shook his had. "It can't be long."

"Is he in pain?"

"He doesn't seem so. But who can tell, with him?"

Feradoti nodded. "And you were with Tenbroek and Galestro as well."

"Your spies are everywhere." Michael said the cliché good-humoredly. "You are insidious, Your Eminence."

The man was the least insidious person Michael had ever known. He had no talent for deceit. In a political commerce where diplomacy and dissembling were functions of one another, he was an unaccountable choice for the office he held. Yet, pacts had been arranged, impossible concordats had been effected and, after each one had been signed, the Cardinal would seem surprised at how blessedly they had occurred, as if he had had nothing to do with them. A true covenant, he would say elatedly, is it not, would you not call it that? With wonderment.

Wonder, like the morning, on the brow of a tired, sixty-year-old man who dealt daily with traders who had lost the gift of astonishment. Michael marveled at him. How could a statesman of such sophistication, such expertise, a man so adroit at the bargaining table, remain so innocent? When he first met Feradoti he thought his innocence was the craftiest of guiles. But he came to know the man. Feradoti lived by simple goodness. It hadn't anything to do with what the man believed, it didn't even have a total reference to religion. The Church was, to him as it was to most Italian Catholics, a thing of custom and comfort, a simple necessity of his existence; goodness, on the other hand, was how he felt, how he behaved, what gave him his essential joy.

It made it possible for him to live with his twisted back. Years ago, in his youth, he had been in a strange accident, the collapse of a bridge over a viaduct. His spine was twisted; he limped. Days upon days he lived on codeine, possibly on other narcotics more potent; hardly ever did he sleep a whole night through. But his pain—that too, like his habituation to God—was an accepted coefficient of his life, not to be questioned. Whenever it became a conscious thing, it served to measure another essential property of the man: his humility.

"Tenbroek wants you to go to America, does he?"

"Dear God, were you there—were you eavesdropping?"

"It is hardly a secret anymore, Michael. The man hawks his wares in every corridor." A flush of embarrassment. "I do not mean to refer to Galestro as 'wares.'" A moment, then: "He is our hope."

"You agree with him—with Tenbroek?" He had meant to express a mild surprise; hadn't intended to sound so shocked.

"Come, Michael. He's an insufferable man, but he's in the right. Perhaps that makes him even more insufferable. There is a saying in Siena, 'We can forgive how the hog smells, since we do not have to lie down with him.' Well, even if we must lie down with Tenbroek, we must forgive his stench of righteousness."

"Is there nobody else we can lie down with?"

"Who, then? Margotto? We will have a worse encyclical than the last one. The wedded priests will be excommunicated. Women who have aborted children will not be forgiven, even in the confessional. Do you know what I heard him say? That he doubted the modern interpretation of absolution. The power was 'assumed,' he said. Repentance comes too easily—Christ never meant all sins to be exculpated, for He never imagined what sins we were capable of. And he said it in the most forthright way—naively!"

"Naively heretical."

"Exactly. The next step, Michael—can you see what his next step might be? The clergy will make a list of discriminate sins—and we all go as sinners to the grave. Unrepentable blood."

"He's a terrifying man."

"Because he is terrified. But can that excuse him? We all are." Again, the deliberate calm. "There was another one today. In Zurich, of all places. Can you imagine it?—Zurich. A priest was stripped naked."

Michael started. The Secretary noticed it. "You know something of it?" Feradoti asked.

"No, I hadn't heard. But last night . . ."

He told of the priest in the darkness, and of the two assailants. He did not mention his suspicion that they had been women; his supposition might be too bizarre, he could have been mistaken. And just as his account of the assault was over and he was going to put a conclusion to it, he found himself compulsively continuing:

"And my breviary was burned."

"Burned?"

Listening as Michael recounted the occurrence, the Cardinal's horror was mute and, as it seemed to be becoming more and more

68

terrible to him, he showed less and less of his feeling. His face had a drawn, empty look as if his dread and pity were too much for his features to hold.

"We must not use the word 'mystery' for such things," he said. "They are all too real."

"Then—realistically—what do we do about them?"

"It is a madness that . . ." He stopped himself, seemingly unable to clear a path with the thought. Then, "There are wounds to heal," he said.

They found themselves talking in hushed tones about an invalid bleeding internally—not the Pope, but the Church itself—an ailing Mother, surrounded by squabbling children, some dissenting, others deserting.

"Wounds," the Cardinal repeated. "The demon of it is that some of the wounds are so deep—so hidden—that—how do we put a poultice on them? And who is to do it?"

They were back, then, to the dying Pope—and to the new one. "I can think of someone," Michael said.

"I think only Galestro."

"Someone else."

". . . I have asked you not to say that, Michael."

"You are twice the man he is. You would do better in the councils, you would—"

"Stop." Then, softening the severity, he smiled. "Don't skirmish, Michael."

"Why are you so . . . intractable?"

"You were going to say pig-headed."

"Something like that." They both laughed. "Why *are* you?"

"Michael, if a man whom I admire holds opinions that are exactly my opinions—"

"What opinions? Who knows what Galestro's opinions are? When has he ever expressed them?"

"He's a loyal member of the Curia, Michael—he doesn't nip at the Pope's back. But privately I've heard him on practically every issue—harmony with non-Catholics, women's rights, even marriage of the clergy." He raised his hand to stress a point. "Do you know why I feel so fervently about Galestro? Because he has one singular genius."

"What is that?"

"Persuasion. He knows how to change opinion. He knows how to smoothe abrasion. And, dear God, that's a gift we need these days!"

"I've seen no sign of such a gift."

69

"Because he hides it. As head of Propagation of the Faith he has learned to persuade discreetly. He's made an art of it." Contemplating, he was deeply absorbed for a moment. "I have one other reason for wanting Galestro. It's not entirely unemotional. I try to imagine whom Pope John would have chosen if he were alive."

"Not Galestro. You."

"Michael . . . admit something. If you didn't have this fixed idea about me as Pope, you'd be happy with Galestro, wouldn't you? Admit it."

"Well . . . yes. But—"

"No buts." Then, composedly, and without vacillation: "Understand me, my friend. I do not want to be Pope. I have not one tremor of regret about it—no blighted hope, none. So I would take it as an act of love if you would never mention it again. Not to me, not to anyone. We must not dissipate ourselves—we must not allow Margotto's friends to disperse us."

"What if Galestro finally declines?"

"He will not decline."

"He is as reluctant as you are."

"A man elected does not decline."

"It has happened, Your Eminence."

"Yes—and there was turmoil. It will not happen again. Galestro is too good, too certain that his fate is determined. He will suffer in the choice, yes—but he is an ascetic who needs to suffer. There are men of Christ who take their ecstasy from the resurrection—I am one of them. Then there are those who take it from the crucifixion— Galestro is one of those. He will not refuse the office. He will bear it—as his cross."

"You want me to do as Tenbroek says, then? You want me to go?"

"I insist on it."

"It does not offend you—this electioneering, this time-serving— pandering for votes?"

He had put the Cardinal in an uneasy dilemma, and half regretted having done it. But he saw that the old man was doing his best to face it, grappling. At last, with difficulty: "I'm sure you will believe me—I detest electioneering. I would like to pretend it is never done, or that it is done and justified. It is a choice of deceptions. We are ultimately left with what, in an emergency, is prudential. The lowest of virtues." His voice was heavy; it lightened now, slightly. "But the electioneering will stop, in due course. Once we get into conclave, the doors will be locked, inside and out. The cracks between us and the world will be sealed. Mammon will be banned. Inside, it will be all purity and *bona fides*. We will act in a cloister of righteousness. But until that time . . ."

"How close are we to winning with Galestro?"

"I don't know. You will know better than I by the time you return."

"You knew about this before today?"

"Yes," he said with a wan smile. "I had a hand in choosing you."

"Why did you choose me?"

"Must I give you a catalogue of your excellences? Mostly, it was because everybody knows how close you have been to the dying man. You must therefore be conservative. On the other hand, you wrote *The Last Magic*. So you must be a radical."

"I'm not a radical—nor is the book!" he said hotly. "And I'm certainly not a conservative."

"You have simply said negatively what I have just said positively." He was smiling at the young man's outrage. "You should probably be described as a liberal, which is to avoid saying anything. It's a position impossible to describe and nearly as impossible to hold—it's forever untenable, always off-balance. And who knows what you actually are, Michael? Point is, you have a precious talent—we all think you are one of us. I have it too—that's why I'm a diplomat." He paused. His eyes narrowed a little. "There is a more specific reason for your being chosen. You're an American. I think—we all think—the cardinals in your country will make the difference. Especially Cardinal Cavanaugh."

The name was a sharp cut, ice cold. It was incredible how, after all these years, the memory of Cavanaugh and his frigid rejection of *The Last Magic* still had a power to chill him.

"Cavanaugh? Good God, they won't send me to Cavanaugh, will they?"

"Oh, yes— the first."

"But I could never carry any weight with him. He dislikes me. He loathed my book. He would have had me censured—excommunicated, if he could."

"Nonsense. He's not a vindictive man."

I think he is, Father. I know you were close friends at one time, and I think you're still inclined to defend him. But I wish you wouldn't—he's a lost cause. Even if he weren't hostile to me, there's no center toward which anyone can persuade him. He's a rigid, and I think a cruel, conservative."

Utterly motionless, Feradoti gazed at him. There was a look on his face that Michael had never seen before, undecipherable. "You're wrong about Cavanaugh. At one time—years ago—I used to think he was going to be a . . . saint."

"Oh, Christ!"

Feradoti remained very still. "You said that as a profanity, my friend."

"Did I?—then may I be forgiven. But not for disagreeing with you. I can't imagine Cavanaugh ever had the simple kindness that would make you think of him as a saint." His antipathy against dealing with Cavanaugh was becoming an immobilizing dread. "Is there nobody else who can be effective? I could go to Chicago and speak to Cardinal Fellinger."

"Come, Michael, you know Fellinger—he's a very private man. He will always need to maintain his distance."

He thought of the old Mexican cardinal, but he suspected the reservations would be even greater. Still: "How about Cardinal Salinas?"

With a glint of mischief: "I think Pope John characterized him with great accuracy. 'Cardinal Salinas is a man whose greatest virtue is docility.' "

Then, the inspiration. Michael knew there was one man Feradoti could find no fault with: the Canadian, in Quebec.

"How about Cardinal Halevi?"

Feradoti looked at him quickly. With perfect pitch, Michael had sounded the perfect note. He was a man beloved by everybody, and had been a favorite of Pope John. The newspapers had called him the Jewish Cardinal and the name had stuck, not only because he had been an architect, in the Second Council, of the *Statement on the Jews,* but because he was in fact Jewish. Many years ago, when he was teaching in Rome, one of his most affectionate students had been Feradoti.

"You know what I'll say about Cardinal Halevi, Michael." His voice had gone gentle. "If heaven and earth were in perfect equilibrium, he would be our next Pope. But they aren't—and the greatest imbalance is mortality. Halevi is in his mid-seventies, and I'm told he's ill." Then quietly: "Come now, you must talk to all of them, of course. But you know as well as I do that it will be useless unless you can convince Canvanaugh. Every day that he spends at the United Nations, he ties another Third World cardinal closer to himself. They think of him as the Vatican spokesman. And he *is*, really, of the conservatives."

It was true. Cavanaugh was a papal legate, an adjunct of the Permanent Observer Mission to the UN. On the surface, it seemed an insignificant use of a vital cardinal, but unofficially he dealt with the political emissaries of African and South American countries that had been guilty of savage inhumanities to Catholics, and he was doing battle for Church rights. The Third World cardinals considered him their champion. He was becoming a power. "Cavanaugh, then," he agreed. "When shall I go?"

"When did Tenbroek say?"

"He didn't. He and I are to see Galestro tonight."

"Where?"

"Galestro's house."

"When?"

"Nine o'clock."

Feradoti looked at the clock on his desk. "You are in good time."

Michael took the Washington missive off the Secretary's desk and departed.

The night had suddenly grown chillier and he wanted a heavier coat; yet, he wanted too for the chill to quicken him, to stir his senses, make him understand more profoundly what was happening to him, what might happen tomorrow.

He had had very little dinner and was suddenly hungry, but he did not want to go indoors. He walked in the darkness of the colonnade and in the moonlight of St. Peter's Square. The vastness of the square was abruptly too much for him; he could not encompass its space any more than he could, this moment, encompass its meaning. It was as if the Piazza, the Vatican, the papacy all needed encapsulation for him tonight, something that was therapeutically manageable.

It was still too early to go to Galestro's villa, but it suddenly occurred to him: I *will* go early, before van Tanbroek. I must talk to the old Cardinal before I depart on this mission. I must believe in him more deeply than I do. It is not enough—this warm feeling of approval which has radiated to me from Feradoti. I need more than that: a devotion. I must feel something about him that will vitalize me, I must become impassioned: he is—or will be—our *Petrus.*

Making his way along the Borgo Santo Spirito, he crossed the bridge and walked the long distance to the house. It was an old house

73

and had once been a noble one, the ancestral home of Galestro's own family. Michael had been there once, to deliver papers and to get a seal and signature. The entrance used at that time, as he now remembered, was by way of the garden. He could see, again, that the only light was on the garden side.

The gate was open and welcoming. A graveled pathway, long and gracefully curved; his shoes made a crunching sound on it. There was a lovely scent of early spring grass, new mown, possibly for the first time of the season. He walked toward the beautiful ancient house, an amplitude of stone, worn by age, ivy- and creeper-clad. It was a dark façade tonight, with only one window alight, on the second floor. That would be the Cardinal's quarters, no doubt, where they would meet.

Although it was the back door he came to, it lacked no grandeur. Almost as wide as his arms outstretched, it was a massive intaglio of panels incised into panels, deep-carved, old and weatherbeaten. And wide open.

He entered, paused to get his bearings in the dimly lighted vestibule, then started up the stairs. It was only when he arrived on the second floor that he heard the soft music. It came from the end of the corridor through the single doorway that was open, where the dim light shone.

Soothing, gentle music, plainsong. He recalled that it was the Cardinal's avocation, his collection of *cantus firmus,* simple melodies chanted in unison. How exquisite it sounded, austere and unadorned, like early churches.

Slowly, softly, nearly on tiptoe he walked the length of the corridor.

As if a pattern of availability had been set by the open garden gate and the open rear entrance, the Cardinal's door was not closed. Slightly ajar. The plainsong was clearer here, more lyric, the voices sounded more unison, as if they all came from a single youthful throat. It was so tender he hated to spoil it by knocking on the door. He listened a moment, then forced himself to knock once, discreetly.

Too discreetly to be heard, perhaps, there was no answer. He knocked again. Waiting, hesitant, aware that he had arrived at least a quarter hour too soon, he did not know what to do. At last he knocked again. Still no response. Slowly, deferentially, he opened the door.

The room was lighted only by the lamp over the old-fashioned record player. The long-playing record was almost at an end.

In the darkness, against the farthest wall, Michael saw the Cardinal. He hung on the wall, naked, his arms outspread. The nails went through his feet and the blood still ran from them; it seemed to have congealed at the nails that ran through the palms. Nothing in the crucifixion was different from the churchly illustrations of it. Except for one addition. Into his groin, between the testicles, another spike had been driven. While his real organ hung limp and shrunken in death, the metal one extended rigidly downward from his body, a bloody penis, angry and obscene.

The plainsong played softly.

Expected at nine o'clock, Cardinal van Tenbroek was punctiliously prompt. It was he who telephoned Feradoti. When the Secretary appeared, Michael was still unable to find his voice. Without facing the horror on the wall, his hand made a vague gesture to it.

Feradoti simply stood there, gazing, his clenched hands holding his throat in an awkward self-strangling way while his lips murmured something barely intelligible, a doggerel Italian verse out of a child's catechism.

Tenbroek alone seemed in charge of himself. The expression "Dutch courage" came to Michael's mind, but he knew it meant something else, intoxication perhaps, and the Hollander was completely sober, telephoning the Governorate and asking for the security office.

They seemed a long time coming. There had been confusion: the security force, while dependent on the Central Office of Security, was civilian, and van Tenbroek had stipulated that he wanted none other than a cleric. After a while the cleric appeared—he was Monsignor de Gamez, a Spaniard with a soft, tentative voice. With him were a young monk, a boy barely out of his teens, and a doctor who was a priest. The two of them stood beside de Gamez; they all looked and crossed themselves; the young monk continued to cross himself a number of times, until the impulse wound down in a slow motion and was spent.

De Gamez was known as a sensible person; at any rate, he appeared that way. He wore antiquated rimless spectacles, the lenses of which were so tiny that it made him seem to be focusing with pinpoint precision.

"Did anybody come to the door?" he asked. "Was anybody here?"

He barely waited for Michael's reply, then sent the monk to search

75

the enormous old house. The place was empty, totally deserted; there were no other inhabitants, no staff, nobody.

"He lived completely alone—not even a servant," van Tenbroek said. "He closed up the whole house, except for the two rooms he lived in."

Feradoti nodded. "It was his austerity. Luxury would have been torture to him."

The strange part of this aftermath was: it was being handled so unstrangely. It was so logical and composed, almost ordinary—de Gamez asking sane questions about an insanity, a man crucified, red rivulets of blood running down a white wall. Yet, certain expected elements—the stereotyped television elements—were missing. Uniformed policemen did not seize the premises, reporters did not arrive, the *paparazzi* flash bulbs didn't blaze. Only questions and answers, spoken quietly; nothing sensational—decorous, in fact—like investigating a routine robbery, stolen silverware, breaking and entering.

No ambulance was summoned, no hearse. The body was going to be transported—*sub silentio*—in the custody van. Once more, the decision was arrived at sensibly, avoiding the extraordinary.

Then the matter-of-factness stopped and the macabre began: taking the body off the wall.

The two men, the monk and the doctor, started to release the cadaver, de Gamez directing them. The instant they began, the young man began to whimper. A steady whimpering, unearthly and harrowing, and nobody tried to stop him.

It was easy enough, pulling out the spikes that had been driven through the man's feet and groin. The nails had penetrated into plaster and as the doctor pulled the heels free the nails came with them, trailing plaster dust. Even the groin spike withdrew readily.

But then came the hands, and here the horror became a ludicrousness, an absurd mockery of a crucifixion: the nails would not come free. They had been driven deep, not only into plaster, but back into a wooden member of the house. They attempted to lift the body a little, then compounding clumsiness, they tugged at it, trying to make it act as a lever for pulling the hands loose. The blood had stopped but now it flowed again, from hands, from feet, from scrotum.

"Stop!" Michael cried. "Stop it!"

The doctor turned a stricken face to him. "What are we to do?"

De Gamez went down to the kitchen of the house. In a little while he returned with a hammer, a claw hammer. The young monk, the strongest of all of them, took the hammer and stood on a chair. He no

76

longer whimpered, he cried aloud, making noises that sounded of an old agony, and he tugged at the spike and yanked at it, pulling it free. Then, with the dead man swinging by one hand, barely supported, the young man pulled the other iron free.

And they took him down.

Four

NORA STAYED for nearly two weeks in a kibbutz guest
house outside Jerusalem, in the Judean hills. It was cheap and it
was friendly but there was a gymnastic vigor about everybody,
everything got done too hurriedly, a cup of coffee in the dining room
was an acrobatic field event, a whole dinner was the Olympics.

There was a young man there, Ari Linderman, a dear sweet student
of farming with a droning voice and bad breath. Every day, at break
of dawn, Ari drove her in the pickup truck to a bus that took her into
the business section of Jerusalem where she looked for a job. It wasn't
easy. An American scrounging for employment, she was patronized,
admired, suffered, insulted, advised, berated for Washington
diplomacy—and rejected. She went to a hundred places and got
nothing. Her money was diminishing, so was her courage.

We have a shortage of people in our country, Ari explained, because we have a shortage of jobs. She had difficulty seeing how it

made sense both ways at once; it was an Israeli paradox, meant to be smiled at, not understood. After a while she did understand it, however, but only as it reflected upon her own fault. Her unemployment was retribution for her failure. She had had her share of the world's jobs, far more than her share, and hadn't held on to any of them. One day she counted the number of positions; it was preposterous—twenty-eight—count 'em, twenty-eight. It seemed to her she had attempted every vocation conceivable and had either fallen short or stopped short, had either been too dumb or too smart, had expected too much or too little, had frustrated herself or her employer, and that most of her income had been severance pay.

The one thing she had always wanted to do was—whisper the awesome word—write. While still in college, she had reveries of herself as an author. She didn't, then, think of it as a workaday occupation by which one earned a livelihood; it was a supernal art. Yet, earthly as well, as basic as eating and sleeping. She had won scholarship honors in writing, plaques and scrolls and medals, with inkwells and gilded quills. Nora Eisenstadt is a talented one, they said on campus, writes prose like a poet. They were in the middle of their felicitations when she came upon a dismaying truth: her talent was glittering and empty; she made fragile ornaments, shatterable by an emotion.

The realization struck at a sickeningly bad time; just when she finished college. Mid-winter graduates, somebody told her, had to face colder facts.

A few years later, after a number of job failures—the worst one, in the social service agency—she went in quest of the Noble Vocation: Marriage. But she discovered it was less lofty a quest than the Grail, and she soon stopped rummaging. Even if she had found someone to love well enough to marry, she wouldn't dare do it. Realist though she was, the figment still emanated *some* romantic aura, and she clung to it. Her mother and father had been married nearly thirty years and, despite sulkings and bickerings, it was a successful marriage, even a happy one. And the gist of it was that they applied themselves, they worked at kindnesses as if there were at least so many of them they had to produce per diem, there were production quotas to fill. That's what scared Nora about it: marriage as a production line. Her record in such occupations not being exemplary, she decided: no marriage, not for her.

On her tenth day in Jerusalem she landed a job. The Hebrew name of the company could be translated as Research Interworld, and the

79

slogan on its brochure exulted, in a number of languages, that it could supply information on any subject anywhere. It did more than that; it supplied the precise data the client demanded, slanted to order, true or false. The head of the company was a youngish man with black thyroidal eyes; he wore pince-nez suspended from a buttonhole of his coat by a gray silken ribbon. His name was Gamel Riktor, and he was quick to say he was not an Israeli; over a period of a few days he became, successively, a Cairene, a Cypriot and a Dane. His philosophy was simple: the truth was undiscoverable; therefore, people had to process the raw data of life in some way acceptable to them; and, since this data had become bewilderingly excessive and insufferably cruel, the starving need was for the specialist who could organize facts, statistics, opinion, hearsay into any pattern that would make the customer happy. In creating such a state of bliss, Riktor boasted, he was inimitable.

His venture was only a three-person operation: Riktor, a typist-receptionist, and Nora. The latter's task was to convert her employer's disorderly English into law-abiding prose.

She didn't mind that his writing style was miserable; that was, after all, what she had been hired to improve; nor that he was as self-contented as olive oil. She was, in fact, going along fine for the first two days, keeping an even keel. On the third day, Riktor's distorted facts, his obsequious frauds on behalf of his clients capsized her. She was working on an article which set out to prove that Egyptian tobacco was not only lower in nicotine content than any other but, according to "eminent authorities" (unnamed) might even be a calmant for respiratory ailments like asthma and hay fever.

The piece was so repugnant to her that she couldn't continue to work on it, so she passed it back to him, substantially unchanged.

Riktor called her to account. "You didn't even read it, did you?"

"Yes, I did."

"But you hardly made any changes at all."

"Well . . . when something is so blatantly phony, isn't it safer to keep the bad grammer?"

His bulging eyes popped with interest; he was always in the market for useful dodges. "Safer? How so?"

"Confusion as camouflage."

"I see." He had caught the sarcasm. "Then, if you don't fix the grammar, what do I need you for?" The point was moot and, as she was studying it, he went on. "You're a very honest girl, and the hell with you."

"Well said."

Oddly, he did not fire her. As he was debating what else he might do to her, she quit.

Ten minutes out of the office, crossing Yarkon Street, she had another dizzy spell, cursed herself out of it, caught a bus back to the kibbutz, and couldn't stand how noisy the place was.

She felt in some way she couldn't relate to logic, that she had to leave the guest house in order to change her luck. Besides, the kibbutz was too far from the center of things. So she said a final goodbye to Ari, crying a little so he wouldn't feel too unimportant. (Strange, how easy it was to cry for someone else's benefit; difficult for one's own.) In the heat of the afternoon, she moved into a one-star hotel, tacky but clean, smelling of chlorine, not as cheap as the kibbutz but more private.

Private for what, she asked with self-ridicule—fainting? Who was this Nora Eisenstadt she wanted to be alone with, how did she dare go into a bedroom with her, unescorted, wasn't it risky? Better lock up the sharp instruments, particularly the brain, a jagged knife.

On a Saturday morning, in a neighborhood where hardly any business was transacted on the sabbath, she got her second job in Jerusalem. It was work she had taken her master's degree in, social service, and although she dreaded a return to it, she felt she had little alternative.

The white cube building was a home for emotionally disturbed children, publicly supported, and run by Eda Mayer, a middle-aged woman who radiated. She radiated everything—energy, suspicion, enthusiasm, jealousy, love, sentimentality, rage, generosity. Since she was considerably overweight, she radiated heat more than anything, and her faded work smock seemed held together by the mucilage of bygone perspirations.

On first meeting, Nora liked her; even on second meeting, the day Nora went to work. On third meeting, she saw Eda pinching one of the slowest children, and smiling at the fact that the *kneip,* as she called it, seemed to quicken his intelligence.

In the next few days, Nora saw other signs of Eda's resourceful use of cruelty as a brain stimulant. And she couldn't reconcile Miss Mayer's genuine kindliness with the woman's sense that only corporal punishment could take the spite out of children.

One day Eda was being self-congratulatory. "I'm tolerant," she said. "Nobody can say I'm not tolerant. I haven't one single microbe of bigotry in me—not one. I treat all my little kiddies alike. I make

81

no distinction between the Israeli children and the Arab children—no distinction at all."

"Only between the good and the bad."

It took three hours for the cut to fester. When it did, Eda radiated more feverishly than ever, hatred. Nora was fired.

She had quit one job and been discharged from another. She used to consider it less shameful to quit than to be dismissed; she was no longer convinced there was any pithy distinction.

The number of days Nora was out of employment became too depressing and she stopped counting them. It was as if the word had gone out, all over Jerusalem: don't hire the American girl, there's something wrong with her, she's over- or underqualified for everything, she has the adder's tongue, she quits or gets fired, she *wants* to get fired. She's in flight.

In flight, yes.

"It's better to run than to be killed," her mother would say. There are muggers in the streets—her mother, trembling—don't stay out past midnight, you'll get raped. Live cautiously, watch out, don't let anyone take advantage of you, beware of heartbreak, beware of clap, beware of getting pregnant. Don't take chances. Don't stand and fight—you're not a boy. Boys have to slug it out, or they're cowards. But a woman—what odds has she got against a man's muscle, his knife, his gun? So run. Girls must run. A running girl is sensible, and alive. And womanly—a running girl is womanly. So flee, vanish, quit. Always be ready to depart, take off, on your mark; live your life in sneakers. Be frightened of everything—people who ask what time it is, beggars with crusts on their faces. Children.

Children who petition your help. A little girl, bleeding.

No, she was right to have fled, that time. That was the one single, justifiable—at least, excusable—flight.

She had been placed—years ago, straight out of graduate school—in a job with a welfare agency, at what they called the Children's Desk. It had a nice sound, Children's Desk, suggesting pleasant-faced silver-haired librarians who recommended *Winnie-the-Pooh* to golden-haired little ones. Gentleness.

It had to do with cruelty. Children—babies, often—beaten by their parents, by their step-parents, battered to deformity of limb and spine, clouted to deafness, made to eat their own feces, stood up and kept awake, hour after hour, through darkness, until they dropped, haggard with the dying stupor of exhaustion.

Standard question to parents: Why did you do it?

Answers: He doesn't mind. She pees. He's not mine, I hate him. No matter what I do to make her pretty, she looks ugly. I raise him the way I want to, you bastard, I'm his mother. I got beat, she gets beat; she'll learn. It's nothin', it's only a little red mark, what's she cryin'? I can't stand him, he's sick all the time.

One day, the policeman brought a mother and a child, a four-year-old named Marella. The mother didn't know why they had summoned her. She had been good to the little girl. When the child was sick, she tended her; when she was hungry, she was fed. She bought her a rubber kitten and a plastic clown—see, here they were. "What does she want from me?" the mother asked. "Why does she cry all the time?"

"Maybe she's ill."

"The doctor says no. Nothin'. Why does she cry?"

"Is that why you beat her, because she cries?"

"Who beats her? Is that what they're sayin'—I beat her? I don' beat her."

"Her eye has been hurt, she has black and blue marks all over her, she can't use her left hand."

"She falls down. She seems like she's dumb, she don't even know how to walk right. Four years old an' she don' walk right. Whose fault? She falls down."

"Would it make your life easier if you didn't have to take care of her?"

Suddenly no longer the wary, cunning animal, the woman started to tremble. "No," she said.

"Now, think about it."

"No—my little Marella—no."

"But it might be better for both of you." The classic line, full of accommodation, straight out of the textbook pages, haven of last resort: flee from each other.

"She's mine," the woman said. "She's all I got. I love her." Her trembling worsened; she made a terrible sound, dry sobs. "I don' want she should cry—I can' stand it if she cries. Sometimes—honest to God—sometimes if I hit her she stops cryin'. She says, 'Mama, don' hit me—I won' cry no more—don' hit me, I won' cry.' And sometimes she keeps her promise. So I *can* make her not to cry. So maybe if I hit her . . . They don' tell me no better than that. What else can I do, what can I do?"

Body shaking. The person getting smaller, retreating, skulking back into the dark cave, alone, terrified.

Even more terrified when she was summoned to the Family Court.

"So it please Your Honor," Nora's supervisor said, "the child should be taken from its mother."

"No," the woman cried. "Oh, please—no. I won't hurt her—I will love her—I won't hit her no more. Never—no more—no!"

"So it please Your Honor—"

So it pleased His Honor to see both sides of everything, to see extenuations, social inequities, social expediences. There are cruelties everywhere, he said; custom habituates, he pontificated somewhat mystifyingly. Besides—the sage pronouncement—the woman clearly loves the child. . . . So Marella and her mother went home together.

But Nora kept thinking of Marella, she couldn't get the little girl out of her mind, the stricken face haunted her. Unable to close the case and forget about it, she placed the folder in the dormant file. Every three or four weeks, unbidden, without any official requirement to do so, Nora paid a surprise visit to the mother and child. The woman was not punishing the little girl any longer; the child was getting better. One day, standing on their doorstep, Nora listened and heard them laughing. She didn't go in.

Three weeks later, determining this would be her last visit, a rare case felicitously closed, Nora walked up the broken wooden steps. She started to ring the doorbell, heard the screams indoors.

She rushed in.

It wasn't the child who was screaming, it was the mother. She stood with a knife in one hand and a bit of bloody flesh in the other. The little girl was standing by the kitchen table, hanging on, her two hands clutched to the edge of it. Great gobs of blood were coming out of the child's mouth. Her mother had cut her tongue out.

Not the same day, not even the day after, but three weeks later, Nora fled from the agency.

Flight, justifiable. Or so she told herself. But the strong would not have fled. How strong need one be to survive, she asked. What a wide range of accommodation one had to make to children's blood, to failure at one's job and the inability to dissemble in a world that was all business, to insufficient talent for the realization of the dream, to the intern who steals artifacts, the kibbutznik with bad breath, to the importunate presence of men and the aching absence of them, to all the tearing ambiguities of being a woman, and to the agonizing ambiguity of herself, loving and loving and unable to love. It does not make sense, the faceless beard had said across the couch, it does

84

not make sense that you cannot accommodate yourself to *something*. . . . Does it have to make sense to get the ache out of it?

And now, the accommodation to hunger.

She was out of money. She would not be able to pay her hotel bill and, with the exception of a piece of hard Safad cheese yesterday afternoon, had not eaten in two days. If she could stand not eating for another day or so, she might have visions, she thought . . . hallucinations . . . the fata morganas that scorn the full stomach, the luminous phantasmas that come to starving ascetics in cells, in deserts, in caves. . . .

The first sign that this might be possible was a strange malaise. Her mouth became dry. No matter how much water she drank, her mouth stayed dry. She had lost her power to spit on the world.

Dizziness.

Then, when all Jerusalem was spinning, and the air itself was marked off into sections none of which was measurable or manageable, and every step she took was a tightrope exercise, she went to the bazaar and sold her silver bracelet. As she came out of the shop, an adorable Arab boy, no more than ten years old, with a face full of eyes, offered to give her a tour of the Moslem quarter, "where no tourist ever goes—all for free, for nothing." Which meant he would want a tip, the amount to be negotiated. She thought: I would do the same for free, for nothing, for a tip, and she sent the boy away.

In the restaurant, she ordered a full meal—Israeli breakfast at dinner time, to start a day at night—cheese and olives and sliced tomatoes and hard-boiled eggs chopped with onion bits. And she could eat hardly any of it. But she had had a chill, this hot day in April, and the tea was warming and good, and her saliva came back, and she felt, being able to spit once more, human again.

When the bill came she reached inside her canvas carryall for her small purse, and it was gone. The little Arab boy had had his tip.

Disbelieving, the waiter waited. And her mouth was getting dry, but her eyes weren't. Suddenly Nora, the weepless wonder, as Micky had called her, began to cry . . . for herself. Quaking, unable to move from her chair, weeping.

Another diner got up from a table. "It's all right," he said to the waiter in American English. "It's all right—just give me her check and go away."

He was fortyish and pleasant-looking, with an accent she associated with her own graduate work in Boston.

85

"Yes," he said later. "I'm a Boston Jew—did you think they all came from Manhattan?"

She didn't know whether he was as kind as he sounded, but she needed to believe he was; needed desperately to be held in the arms of kindness. He held her tenderly. She tried not to suspect that the cryptic smile didn't give all he had, that he was keeping reserves for ruthless combat, a wary businessman, mistrustful, cautiously weighing lies.

He made love that way. Suspicious of her sounds of pleasure, as if he knew for certain they were uttered out of gratitude.

Then, when she was dressing for departure from his hotel room: "How much do I owe you?" he asked.

Oh, Christ, she thought, who was playing this shitty trick on her?

"You don't owe me anything," she said.

"Come on. It was a fake, wasn't it? The stolen pocketbook, the tears."

"You can look through that canvas bag, if you want. Any money you find . . ."

"Oh, you're too smart to carry any. You *are* smart—that's the puzzling thing."

"Whores have to be stupid—prerequisite for the course?"

"Yes, I think so." He was opening his wallet. "How much? Will thirty do?"

"Yes . . . it'll do."

When she left the hotel, she was still hungry; she had eaten very little of the meal the Bostonian had paid for. During the next few days she could scarcely bring herself to touch the thirty dollars, barely even for food. Her first meal, not a meal at all, was coffee and small honey rolls, ordered at a sidewalk cafe. She drank half the coffee but after the first bite of a honey bun, she couldn't manage a second. A phrase popped out of a play—was it Strindberg or Wedekind?—"sick on strumpet's bread."

She spent another day fasting, or nearly so, eating just enough to forestall dizziness. She was in a misery of slow starvation and an inability to eat.

Then, unaccountably, it was over. There was no reason for its being over, it simply happened. She found herself gorging on a delicious lunch of roasted chicken, dressed with mouthwatering stuffing of hot plums, walnuts, and raisins; then a dessert of lemon sherbet on a bed of tangerine slices. And no unpleasant aftermath, no

86

nausea, not a belch. The food seemed to have been an intoxicant. She felt drunkenly as if she were another person, a total stranger, foot-loose and carefree, accountable to no one, certainly not to herself.

She went in search of another customer.

But it was even more difficult than she had ever imagined. Through all the hot afternoon, she trudged for miles, endless aimless miles—restaurants, the largest hotels, the lobbies of two movie theaters—and she approached nobody. Toward sundown, she walked down the steps that lead to the Bezalel Museum. Coming up the stairs, toward her, a young man: she had seen his counterpart a thousand times. He was the high school valedictorian, the captain of the debating team, the associate editor of the college paper; he was a pair of spectacles. She knew, without ever having met him, he would be stiff with academic rigor and sexual hunger.

"Well, hel-lo!" she said, a creature all surprise.

He answered hello and stopped. He was American unquestionably. I'm as familiar to him as he is to me, she thought. I too may be a pair of spectacles. He started to talk pleasantly, with that quizzical play-fulness toward a half-forgotten acquaintance, seeming to say: tease me until I recognize. She teased; wouldn't tell him where they had met.

Abruptly he knew where it had been: nowhere. She saw him realize: being sold.

Even then she might have had him. He was attracted to her, piqued at having been played with, and anxious to retaliate; for his dollar, a pound of flesh—revenge, the Spanish fly . . . But she saw in his eyes a scurry of mice, contempt.

She ran.

She ran, her damned feet giving flight before her mind told her to do so. She could have talked the man into bed, no question of it; he was already undressing on the stairs. Why, goddamn it, did she have to run?

Why couldn't she do it?

How could so many other women do it? Even the trim suburban housewives she had read about, the ones who spent their sunny mornings selling raffle tickets for the PTA, and their afternoons working a trick or two. Not for bread, which had been Nora's need, but for the turquoise earrings to go with the azure dress. She tried to imagine some particular woman making the decision—how did she go through with it? How did she rationalize it satisfactorily? Did she tell herself she was earning a dollar, her *own* dollar, in exchange for something reckoned of little worth, that her love was held cheaply; was she convinced it was the single skill her husband valued in her, hence why not value it in herself? Why not sell it elsewhere, and come away not only with the money but with the secret? The secret, privately owned. Possibly, in a family where she herself was the public possession of everyone, the secret might be her only private possession.

How did those women manage it so successfully? Manage everything—the dustless house and lintless husband, the orthodonted kids, the silk-screened wallpaper in the study, the fuchsias blooming on a sequential schedule, the punctilious ten-thousand mile checkup, the clever little wines of discovery—how did they manage all that, plus the commercial fucking? How did they, above all, manage the lacy illusion of their amateur standing?

And how could she, Nora Eisenstadt, summa cum laude, manage nothing? Not a single job. A failure in every one of them. Even as a whore.

Well, she hadn't truly applied herself to whoring.

So, that evening she tried the Ganor Plaza Hotel.

Posh, glittering with pelf and newness, the hotel was attractive to prosperous men; it had a good bar, it served robust meals, and had an excellent health club. It was Saturday night. Traffic in the lobby was brisk; there was a hubbub of tycoons and tourists—strangers to one another, an incidental advantage—and the market was promising.

She sat or she walked; her face was impassive or it smiled; she looked dangerous, she looked vulnerable; one way or another she had to seem desirable.

Nobody approached her. When, toward midnight, she actually spoke to a prospective customer—a delicate greeting, as flimsy as tissue paper—he went off and joined his teenage daughters. A second one went into the men's room and never emerged.

"Not exactly larky, is it, ducks?"

She was about Nora's age, and very thin—skinny as a wishbone, she later said of herself—and she was, largely, mouth. It was an unpretty face, without a touch of makeup, and eyes that needed cosmetic help, too small, stingy, readier for rancor than for friendliness. Her body had a splayed look, she walked that way, everything about her seemed that way; even her breasts—she wore no underwear—hung in opposite directions, sideward, the nipples too far apart, like walleyes. But her mouth was a wonderful thing, an

88

opulence, a lushness of soft mounds, and she used it suggestively, she knew it whetted appetites.

"I been watchin' you," she said, without admiration. "Gor!"

The cockney was too thick, Nora thought, too carefully faithful to English films, old ones; it couldn't be real.

A touch of panic; she was a house detective. Thinking to disarm, Nora came out with it. "You're a detective, aren't you?"

"A tecky? Me?" she screaked. Her laughter was like sticky bureau drawers. "Hell, no, I'm in it, just like you. Free enterpriser, in the same old shop. Only I got a full inventory, ducks, and you got empty shelves."

Tagged again. An amateur in a professional business.

"I'm takin' a break, love, would you like a coffee?"

They had coffee and currant cookies at a bakery lunch counter, off King George Street.

It wasn't the young woman's accent that was phony, it was everything else about her. She affected gentility and had language pretensions—dropped words too large for her brain. Even her name seemed false. She said it was Ellen Allenby, and that she was one of the originals, by which she meant her family went back to the British mandate, General Allenby being on her father's side. Ardurous times for the British, she kept saying, ardurous times, which explained why a person so patrician as Ellen was pushing her kumquat around, as she described it, for a few pounds each time.

"Well, you've got to do it for the prodigy, don't you?"

Nora had no notion what she meant; then the light: progeny. "Do you have any children?"

"Two. And wouldn't you know—both girls. Well, it's a vindictory God, innit? Always askin' a bit of His own back." She paused, measuring Nora narrowly. "That's what I want to talk to you about."

"Your children?"

"In a manner, yes. But first I want to look at *your* side of it. You're not makin' it, ducks. I watched you all evenin', and I don't think you will. There's somethin' wrong in how you're goin' at it—somethin' skewy. Now, no matter what I *tell* you, you won't learn. The only way you *will* learn—like in all human endeavors—is by doin'. Screwin' by doin', that's the trick of it. But how are you goin' to get the experience?" She paused to let Nora's dilemma chafe a little. Then: "Well, that's *your* problem—now let me tell you mine. I got two kids and I don't get to see them, it bein' night work. They're ten

89

and twelve years old, and the older one is sproutin' boobs and buildin' a big arse, and the boys are beginnin' to blow hot breath up her dress, so I'm gettin' a bit scared. . . . Now I intend to go on with my trade, but only daytimes, while the girls are in school. So, how would you like it if I made your little trysties for you—late afternoon and nighttimes, I mean—and you give me a little somethin' for my efforts?"

Queasiness. Things worsening. "That's pimping, isn't it?"

Ellen was unruffled. "Yes, that's pimpin' and this is whorin'. What's the difference?"

Nora felt her face redden. Phony as Ellen was, it was she, not Nora, who had refused to make a hypocritical differentiation.

"What would your share be?" Nora asked.

"Fifty percent."

"That's a lot, isn't it?"

"If I was *really* pimpin', I'd take it all and give you Lysol money. Besides, you'll make out fine—better than you would on your own—because I've got my regulars. I'd tout them on to you. And I got a special *kind* of trade. On account of my kids, they don't come to my place, I go to theirs. You'd be surprised the advantages in that. You don't have to live in a dump that *allows* whores, you can live in a nice place that don't know you *are* one. And no payoffs to nasty little bellboys and nightclerks, always peekin' in your keyhole and pokin' at your tits." She leaned forward and squinted her small eyes. "Well, how about it?"

It was unclear to Nora what tattered ensign she was waving, but she had to cling to it. "I don't think so," she said.

"It's all right, ducks," the other replied. "I'm in the phone directory. Ring me."

Three days went by and Nora didn't have a customer; she couldn't brace herself to try for one. She was nearly broke again and back to buying the hard Safad cheese, which lasted a long time because she disliked it so much. Then, on the evening of the third day, the doorway started to slant and she heard the loud silence, worse than before, like a discrepancy in pressures, pounding in her ears.

She called Ellen.

"You don't have to feel so cut up about the life," Ellen said. "You're only gettin' what's comin' to you. Gettin' compensated for it, instead of havin' it beaten out of you. Men are all vicious." She meant it, too. Her husband had abandoned Ellen just as her father had abandoned her mother; it was instinctive male behavior, she said, the

90

nature of the beast. "And the life's not slavery, love—not like marriage, where you have to massage their cocks *and* their egoes, and when you've been screwed, you have to lie there and scream a big orgasm you never had, just so he'll smile himself to sleep. Or take bein' a secretary, cleanin' up the toilets of a man's business. I had a girlfriend who said about her boss, 'He's stupid, so I do his work for him and say he's doin' it. Then, after hours, I fuck him. Daytime and nighttime, I front for him.' Now, that's slavery, ducks, *that is slavery.*"

How awry it was, Nora realized, to hear the truths of liberation torn out of context, turned into bromides, twisted lame, by someone not liberated; in fact, more enslaved than the women she described. Still, she mustn't ponder this too much; liberation wasn't all that easy to live with; free choice was a killer.

"How do we do it?" Nora asked.

"Well, I've got these . . . acquaintances."

Acquaintances, thereafter, became their decorous word for customers, and Ellen did indeed have many of them.

The first one was a Maronite from Beirut. He had fled Lebanon during the war, leaving his wife behind, but bringing his money with him. He had a large suite in the President Hotel, just a short walk from the center of town but on a street so quiet that it seemed suburban.

For prelude he touched Nora's hair, gently at first, then pulling it a bit too hard. When she complained that he was hurting, he started to weep. His tears were the cue he recognized. He stripped at breakneck speed, tearing at shirt buttons and tripping over trousers. Even before he had his undershirt off, he went at her, hugely endowed, still weeping, blubbering what a wretch he was, wailing for his wife and children, caterwauling and pumping away at Nora until he came.

He paid her the fifty-dollar fee in Swiss francs—it amounted to a bit more than fifty, actually—and departed in a haste of shame.

"The Lebanese are all like that," Ellen reported, cavalier with generalization. "Arab or Christian, it's a national trait. The Arabs turn their guilt on you, it's all your fault; the Christians turn it against themselves. Either way, they get their money's worth, it's a long hard fuck."

"How about the Jews?"

"Well, I don't have so many Jew acquaintances," she said. "Only at the Hilton, that's where you get your good Jewish trade. But the sabra is Lord Proudcock—won't pay a shekel—he gets it for free."

Nora's second acquaintance was a youngish man, a redhead; he reminded her of Yoel and all her muscles tightened. It made it difficult for him and it was an inconclusive thing; when she asked him whether he had come, he said yes, without arriving. She felt that she had cheated the customer and suspected he felt the same; he left his money and, when she came out of the bathroom, he was gone. In the lobby, she saw him at the cashier's window, paying for the room. She started to wave goodbye to him, but he turned away.

She thought of him for a little while, disconsolate. If she had known where to reach him, she might have refunded her share of the money. Why was she feeling so like a cheat? After all, the man did come; was she expected to supply psychic pleasures as well, small enchantments of the mind, delicate comforts to carry him through a winter of regret? Winter, my ass, he's probably forgotten it happened.

Still, there was a professional standard at stake. And it occurred to her, with a jolt of surprise, that she wanted to produce satisfactorily. And predictably—every time—that was the criterion of the professional.

Her next customer made a total amateur out of her. He was a middle-aged Polish Jew with shabby clothes and a careworn face. He was shorter than any other man she'd had and seemed distressingly unsettled, in some way disoriented in space, as if he had wandered into the wrong world. But the minute he was naked, she realized he had no uncertainties, he knew precisely where he was. He went from one place to another, he found regions never discovered by any other man, regions she herself had never known she had. Deploying himself in a hundred areas at once, kissing and sucking and being there and not being there, loving her as if he loved her, his hands and penis and mouth and all that he was, all searched her and found her a country of delight, and they came.

When it was over he was the little Polish Jew again, faltering over the broken zipper of his trousers, embarrassed, not wanting her to see him so small when only a moment ago he had been so colossal. And he departed, ignominiously, with his trousers not completely closed.

The Pole made her see a side of prostitution she had barely glimpsed: there might be pleasures in it. Remembering his skill, the thought of professionalism recurred to her. She had never failed at a job because she had not applied herself; she was a conscientious student and a willing worker. If she applied those virtues to the enterprise of fucking . . .

Ellen had, in one of her pretentious moments, referred to the "anesthetics" of the profession. Puzzled, Nora had been unable to figure out what insensibility she meant, when it occurred to her that the word Ellen had intended was "esthetics"—she was pondering prostitution as an art. Like Micky, she was trying to find some way to ennoble the occupation—and Nora now found herself doing the same. Not good at putting a pretty face on a homely truth, she still sought a romantic name for what she was doing. Courtesan, demi-monde—one day she vaguely recalled the term "hetaera." It was a lovely word, but when she looked it up she discovered, to her disappointment, that it meant a slave. She didn't know why the pandering of one's body was any more slavery than the pandering of one's brain, but what solace did *that* give?

Then Ellen phoned to give her the name of an acquaintance who wasn't any acquaintance at all. She hadn't met him, she said, except on the telephone, but he sounded charming.

"He's from Iran," she purred, "but he refuses to call it Iran. Persia, he says, because in this life you have to cling to whatever is magnificent, even if it's in the past. Don't you think that's ungratiating?"

He lived in a sumptuous apartment house on one of the hills. The living room was overly ornate but engaging, upholstered in cut velvets, studiedly aged; the chairs, especially the two porter chairs on both sides of the fireplace, seemed to have come from a baronial castle. The door to the bedroom was black oak—the wood was rescued from antiquity, he said somewhat abstrusely—and inlaid with cross-bracings of exquisitely wrought iron.

"May I watch you undress?" he said courteously, in meticulous British diction.

Nobody had ever requested such a delicate consideration, certainly not with such politesse, and Nora, undressing, tried to make a rhythmic rite of it. This was not lost on him and he commented on her flowing movements, asking if she had been a dancer. No, she hadn't, she answered, how nice of him to think so.

When they were in bed he did everything so fastidiously and so unhurriedly that she could see things were going to take a bit longer than usual. Ah, well, she mused, such old-fashioned gallantry is not to be pell-melled; but incongruously she recalled the line from *Twelfth Night*, "He does it with a special grace, but I do it more natural."

He was kissing her arms, her wrists, her fingertips. Then he started to kiss her hair. He would kiss a strand of it, look at her face, kiss another strand, look at her face again. But Nora couldn't play whatever feeling he wished to arouse in her, for the window was open, a cool breeze coming through, and she was chilly.

She sneezed into his face. He was embarrassed; she was more so.

Silently, with as much dignity as he could summon, he got up and crossed to close the casement. As he walked, the stateliness of his carriage corresponded with the stateliness of his cock, which was at perfect right angles to his body; he was a study in erectness.

There was no reason for her to giggle, but she did; there was no reason for him to think his cock was being laughed at, but he did. He pushed it down between his legs, holding it there with his hand. Closing the window, he walked back to bed, still deflecting the aim of his preposterous member.

He lay on the bed, at a distance from Nora, chagrined far more than the circumstance warranted, hiding himself with his hand.

Slowly, gently, Nora reached over, removed his hand and touched him. He had softened, he had dwindled. Without haste, caressing him, touch by touch, fingertip by handhold, she brought him back to size and stiffness. He was hot in her hand.

He turned to her at last; his eyes smiled. Going back to where he had left off, he started to kiss her hair again, then all over, and to caress her.

But something had changed. Some imponderable had tipped the scales of the lovemaking, so that nothing seemed as gracefully balanced as before. There was a heaviness in his manner, a weighted insistence on how he wanted to touch her, what he wanted to do.

His hand was on her vagina, fondling it, spreading its moisture; then one finger, inside her, then out again, then two fingers. Abruptly, feeling them, she sensed a different pressure, rougher, more demanding, hurtful. She murmured something; gentler, please be gentler. The third finger entered and as the pain worsened, she cried out. Suddenly she felt the nails, the fingernails, scrabbling at her.

"No—don't."

He didn't stop. She heard an angry sound, wordless from his throat. The fingernails were agonizing.

"Stop it—please stop it!"

She tried to twist herself free of him but he held her back, his arm across her belly. As she twisted once again, she felt the blow of his knuckles, stinging, across her face.

The nails inside her, torture now, and suddenly the pulling, the pulling, as if he were trying to turn her inside out.

"Oh, stop!"

With main strength, all she had, she wrested herself free and out of bed.

"Come back, you cunt!"

She grabbed at her clothes, her stockings, shoes, grabbed and ran. Through the baronial living room, through the foyer, out into the hallway, naked, carrying her clothes, dropping something, retrieving it, running, dropping something else, running, running.

Now, down the fire escape, one floor, then another, trying to dress as she fled, sobbing, tripping, spilling down the stairs, hurt, cut, the blood dripping down her leg, weeping, raging, weeping.

On the second floor landing she stopped, she stanched the blood as best she could, she put a handkerchief inside her, she finished dressing.

The son of a bitch.

The sadistic bastard.

All men are vicious, she heard Ellen saying; herself saying it as well.

No. She mustn't fall into that trap. More dangerous than blood. Besides, not true. She must calm down, must think of men who were gentle—she had had some of them. It was only her trade that attracted the vicious ones; and even they might be vicious only for the occasion. Taking their vengeance for hurts that had been time-inflicted, women-inflicted.

No, she cried. I will not make excuses for them anymore, will not weep for the cruel ones, the abusers of children, the tormentors of the old—yes, and the brutalizers of prostitutes. I will not let them go free.

Why didn't I fight back? Why didn't I smash his face in? Why didn't I kill him?

Why did I *run?*

Five

"IF YOUR APPOINTMENT with Cardinal Galestro was arranged for nine o'clock, why were you there at eight-thirty?" de Gamez asked.

"I said it was shortly after eight-thirty," Michael replied carefully.

"Why so early?"

"I wanted to speak with him privately, before the meeting with Cardinal van Tenbroek."

"Concerning what?"

Michael turned and looked at Feradoti. The Cardinal Secretary had sat quietly through the questioning, uttering scarcely a word, his hands covering his distraught face. Nor did he now enter the conversation, not even with a glance; he didn't caution Michael to silence; the latter independently chose it.

De Gamez repeated. "May I ask what was going to be the subject of your private meeting with Cardinal Galestro?"

Balking, Michael had an impulse to shock the investigator, tell him it was going to be a political caucus, a smoke-filled-room session on how to elect Galestro to the papacy. Instead: "I'm afraid I can't tell you that."

The inquirer unexpectedly seemed relieved that he needn't enter another labyrinth. He walked away from the priest and, at the window, looked directly into the glare of the brash mid-morning sun. He didn't squint, seemed to enjoy glaring back at it. Turning: "Are you certain that the front door was open? Not merely unlocked—actually open?"

"Yes," Michael replied. "I'm quite sure it was open."

"And the garden gate as well?"

"Yes."

"And you saw no sign of any damage to a door or to a window?"

Michael had already answered the question, and he was annoyed. The man was not a detective. Why did he resort to the gumshoe sort of question? For all the perplexities that terrorism presented, the actual murder was startlingly simple.

The crucified Cardinal was the perfect victim. He was a man of ascetic habit. Except for a cleaning woman who came in for a few hours twice a week, he lived hermetically alone. He belonged to no organization outside the Church except for the musical society, Canto Fermo; even in music, his taste was for the simple, the unadorned— plainsong. The rounds of his life were routine and predictable; an assailant could count on them. And although he was horror-stricken by the violence of the times, it would never occur to him to fear for his own safety, or to take extra precautions to fortify his lodgings; his security was in God. As Feradoti had pointed out, he was a man more responsive to Christ's torture than to his ecstasy, and his own death, even by crucifixion, might not have seemed incomprehensible to him.

So de Gamez's questions seemed unnecessarily complicated. "The fact that the doors were open—that's not really of the essence, is it? He was expecting us, not murderers—so he left the doors open." Then, Michael added, "Even if he hadn't, it would not have been difficult to break into the house."

"But you say you saw no damage to a door, or to a window?"

"No, I didn't." Chafing a little: "You certainly had enough time last night and this morning to see for yourself. Did you see any?"

De Gamez ignored the question. "You're sure you didn't change anything?"

97

"I've answered that question twice. Do you think I've lied to you?"

"Patience, Michael," Feradoti said. "We must realize that Monsignor de Gamez has been spared—" He broke off and started again. "Blessedly, in the Vatican, one has been spared experiences that . . ." His voice trailed off, then resumed once more "He must borrow his expertise."

De Gamez was grateful for the excuse. He nodded. "Yes, it's true, I am not, thanks be to God, competent in atrocity. I am instructed only in one Crucifixion, and that is mystery enough for me. Besides, my hands are still shaking—and my brain as well."

"Then, if we are not—as you say—competent, why do we not take it out of the Vatican, and put it in the hands of the secular authorities?"

Alarm in de Gamez's face; he referred instantly to Feradoti to see how he had reacted to Michael's question. If the Secretary was also alarmed, he did not show it; silent, expressionless. Just as de Gamez was about to speak, Feradoti raised his hand, stopping him. "Michael, do you seriously suggest that we take it out of the hands of the Church?"

"We have to, don't we?" he responded. "The crime was committed outside the Vatican."

"In Galestro's house, yes—which he bequeathed to the Church during the last year of Pope John."

"It's still outside the Vatican."

"With extraterritorial privileges, Michael." The Secretary's voice was steady now, his sentences unbroken. He was the diplomat again, weighing words, measuring eventualities. "It is as sacrosanct as St. John Lateran."

"But a crucifixion—my God! Once it gets into the papers—"

De Gamez interrupted. "It will not get into the papers."

Feradoti didn't seem surprised. But Michael was. "How can we possibly keep it out?"

De Gamez paused, deliberating, then evaded the question. "A copy of Cardinal Galestro's will is on file with the Prefecture of Economic Affairs. I requested to see the document this morning. In it, in the next to the last sentence, he says, 'I pray you, let me be buried in modest state.' The phrase, as you know, is quite the opposite to being buried in state. The funeral must be quick and quiet."

"But the cause of death—good heaven, it can't be given out that he died of a cold!"

98

He could see that Feradoti was ruffled by his flippancy. "The cause of his death has already been certified, Michael—by the doctor. And witnessed by Monsignor de Gamez."

"As what?"

"*Res incognita.*"

"A thing unknown? How can we say that? Those things were not unknown—they were nails—visible! And—dear God—knowable!"

"*Res* has other meanings than 'thing,' Michael. It can mean 'circumstance.' And we do not know the circumstances of Cardinal Galestro's death. Even the main circumstance—the most perplexing —who could have done such a thing?—that is certainly unknown. So the words we have chosen are not inaccurate."

Michael was perturbed in a way he could not understand. This circumlocution was, after all, a language well known to him, he used it comfortably every day. Why was it galling to him now? And why should he be so nettled that Feradoti, whom he admired partly because he was so cogent in speaking the language, was invoking his skillful talent in it for this emergency? There must be some subtle point Michael was missing.

"Why does it seem so imperative that we keep it quiet?" he asked.

"Surely, Michael, you don't need an answer to that," Feradoti said.

Yes, he did need an answer, Michael was about to say, but he was interrupted. One of the Secretary's clerks entered and handed him a note. Reading it, the older man looked perplexed. Then: "Cardinal Margotto is here," he said.

Feradoti and Margotto were not given to visiting one another; there was no devotion between them. Only extremity would have brought him here.

"Ask him to come in," Feradoti said to the clerk. Then, to Michael and de Gamez; "You will excuse me. We will talk further."

When de Gamez opened the door to leave, Cardinal Margotto was on the threshold. He barely nodded to the departing investigator. Then, as Michael paid him just enough deference to be innocent of rudeness, the entering Cardinal tapped his forefinger on the young priest's shoulder. "If the Cardinal Secretary will permit, I should like you to stay," Margotto said.

Michael turned, saw his superior nod slightly, and remained in the room.

Margotto did not simply stand, he commandeered the space he

occupied and took up a position. He was a bulwark of a man, with a combative jaw and restlessly vigilant eyes. There was no preamble, no overture of any kind. "I am told Galestro is dead—is it true?"

"Yes," Feradoti said quietly.

"There is talk that he died by violence. I am here to find out how it happened."

"He wasn't exactly a friend of yours, Your Eminence."

"Come now, that's neither here nor there." Then, taking another tack. "I have asked Father Farris to stay because it is said he was present at the time."

Michael stiffened. "I was not present 'at the time.' I arrived afterward."

"But you do know how it occurred." Peremptorily: "How did he die?"

Feradoti gave Michael no time to answer. "Are you sure you want to know?" the Secretary asked. "Those of us who share the knowledge will share a heavy burden. Are you certain you want that?"

The question was softly spoken, but there was rarely any need to raise a voice in the Vatican; contention could rage in a whisper.

Michael watched Margotto assay the challenge. He was a tough, a fearless man, but he was not reckless. He knew that Feradoti would not stoop to a meretricious trick, that he did not need to, the Secretary was adroit at alternatives. But the moment was in some way instinct with risk, and he would have to move cautiously. This was difficult for Margotto. A man without guile, his strength was in his forward motion; he bore down on his foe like an armored tank, formidable and unconcealed.

The Cardinal was still a peasant, Michael thought, with the craggy, weatherbeaten face of the farm fields he had come from; still parching in the droughts of mezzogiorno poverty, still living in the memory of stunted wheat and sour wine. How strange it was to Michael that this man of the ungrateful soil, of privation, should have turned into a reactionary, and Feradoti, of upper-class parents, educated to the last nuance, one of the *nobili*, should be a champion of the very people Margotto had sprung from. Not an unclear paradox in the secular world, he mused, but clouded in the ecclesiastical one by mists of virtue. True virtue, not false, not in either of these two men, Michael would have sworn to that; yet, so opposite, their roles reversed. And he realized that these two, who had been at great pains through the years to hide their antipathy, would soon stand openly against each other—in the conclave. For, inescapably, now that

100

Galestro was dead, they were two of the chief *papabili* for the apostolic throne. And it was as if—in this instant of confrontation—they both knew that this was so.

It was a deft strategy Feradoti had used, asking his competitor whether he chose to share the burden or to walk away from it, running the risk of seeming a fool or a coward, no other choice available. Margotto couldn't choose the part of coward, and he was shrewd enough to know he was donning the fool's cap.

"Don't challenge me with 'burdens,' " he said angrily. "How did Galestro die?"

"He was crucified."

Margotto did something Michael had never seen a cleric do. He aborted the making of the cross; started the gesture, stopped it, as if reluctant to show anyone, even God, how the news had shaken him.

Recovering: "You meant that word," he said. "You would not use such a word as a figure of speech?"

"I meant the word."

"Dear Jesus."

They talked of how it had happened and as the account proceeded, Margotto's face, which had been fleetingly vulnerable, became a stone bastion again. When Feradoti stopped speaking, the other Cardinal had only one word to say:

"Comunisti."

Feradoti looked at him levelly, not responding at once. Then: "We do not know who it was, Cardinal."

"Communists or Jews," Margotto said, with quiet virulence. "Or are they the same? I hear a new group of Venetian Jews came into the Borsa last week. They have money for everything—even for this."

The Secretary had a facial expression Michael had come to recognize. When confronted with a matter he could not endure, his eyes squinted as if he were peering at something beyond vision—a cloud, perhaps—nonexistent. "I would prefer not to hear such things in my office, Your Eminence," he said.

"It is not your office, Cardinal—it is an office of the Church. Just as the hatred of Communists is an office of the Church." Feradoti started to reply, but Margotto surged ahead. "This is a vague argument—and there is need for action. What is being done to apprehend the monster?"

"As you noticed, Monsignor de Gamez was just here. It is in the Governorate."

"That is to say it's nowhere."

"Where would you like it to be?"

"Obviously, in the hands of the civil police. And don't let us raise the question of extraterritoriality. We simply waive it."

Measuring every word, Feradoti said, "Of course, this is not a matter for my Secretariat, but it could easily become one. I have therefore—unofficially—advised de Gamez not to bring the civil police into the matter."

"Our Security Office cannot possibly handle a thing like this. It's as good as saying the murderer goes free."

"That's a possibility, yes."

It struck Margotto like a blow. "Gesù! It occurs to me you do not *want* the criminal apprehended."

The same thought had simultaneously occurred to Michael, with the same consternation. He found himself unexpectedly—inconceivably almost—on Margotto's side. He could not believe the position Feradoti was taking, and wanted him to abandon it. For the first time, he entered the conversation, as circumspectly as possible. "I'm sure we are not understanding what is in the Cardinal Secretary's mind."

Feradoti said softly, "Yes, you are."

"You do not want the criminal apprehended?" Michael asked.

". . . No, I do not."

Margotto exploded. "My God, if the Church recognizes a Just War—! What cheek are you turning, for God's sake?"

Feradoti waited for the air to stop vibrating. When he spoke, his voice was a hush. "You will say I am prompted by fear. You could possibly be right—I may be. Yet, my only other response to this can be rage—and I would ease my conscience by calling it a righteous yearning for justice. But justice would have to be retributive—and what equitable retribution can there be for a crucifixion? We have seen the answer to that, over the years, have we not?"

"So your motive in hiding it is forgiveness, is it?" Margotto asked bitingly. "You raise the absolving hand to it, do you? Well, in this case, you know it is a lie!"

A long pained moment, searching himself. "If it is," Feradoti said, "then we are back to fear."

"Of course it's fear—why do we deny it? I'm terrified! A crucifixion—is there anything worse to fear?"

"Yes . . . a continuation of terror itself. I am afraid if we give further currency to this news . . . Today—everywhere—violators emulate violators. There are fads in atrocity. There is a plague of arson—consulates, newspaper offices, airports. Then it subsides. Suddenly there is a new fad, the kidnapping of businessmen, the murder of statesmen. Then the brutalizing of old people, of children, the sacking of synagogues. Now: the crucifixion of priests."

"You mean, then, that we simply wait for it to pass, this new vogue in atrocity?"

"It's an insanity that feeds on public notice," Feradoti said uninflectedly. "The old forms of terrorism no longer command attention. A simple murder with a knife, a gun—who is shocked by that? Who even knows when it happens nowadays? But a young boy chops off his father's head with a hatchet—that is worth a front page. And the crucifixion of a man of Christ—it can play on television like a scene out of the Apocalypse." He paused an instant. "So we must take at least that gratification out of it."

"By silence!"

"Silence as a counterweapon is not new to the Church." Feradoti spoke dully, without emphasis, his voice deeply unhappy. There was an oppression in what he was saying, heavy as darkness, and Michael disconnectedly thought of long-held secrets, and people dying in medieval silences.

"Then you will do nothing about this?" Margotto's tone had the hint of ultimatum in it.

"For the moment, I can see nothing that we can do."

"I am going to telephone the civil authorities."

"Please—no."

"You mean you will simply let it pass—without a word? Can you bear to live in a world of terrorism?"

"We have lived in a world without it, Cardinal Margotto, and it was no paradise."

"Without it? What world?"

"Hitler's—Mussolini's. We had no terrorism—except theirs."

"Dear God, are you now *justifying* these atrocities?"

"No, not justifying—simply trying to understand them. What do they mean? Is the outcry for violence to be answered by a restatement of everything we have always said—unchanged? It doesn't seem to be satisfactory, does it? Does the evil of terrorism attest to the good of everything else? Will the punishment of the terrorist confirm the virtue of the punisher? Is his discontent to be considered sinful simply because murder is sinful? Can we learn nothing from him except to lock our doors and our hearts? If we

103

do not come out of this torture with a searching eye, we have come out of it as blind as we have ever been! Can we not, out of the hell of terror, violence, bloodlust, chaos, find some hint of heaven?"

Michael was not sure whether what he had just heard was an echo of empty rhetoric, or the outcry of a deep passion. Margotto, quite clearly, had no such confusion.

"You are talking cant, Cardinal Secretary," he said astringently. "I am not surprised—you are a diplomat—a professional compromiser. You see both sides of everything—and think you get a vision of the truth. What you get is double vision—a distortion. I do not. Evil is evil to me, it can never be partly good. I do not believe in a Jesus who is part God and part devil."

"Not at all man?"

"Yes—man! But a man of pure perfection destroyed by the very demons you now wish to 'understand.' We cannot make peace with demons!"

Feradoti nodded in comprehension but not in assent. "If we were so blessed as to speak only with God we would have no need to compromise. But we must speak with one another. Does it not frighten you that, in your righteous judgment, you might be seeing only one side to the struggle? You are a brave man and you would fight to the death for a principle, but does it not frighten you to fight to the death of others?"

"You see?—you talk fright. It's the language of compromisers."

"Compromise isn't cowardice, Cardinal. Peace can come of it. Sometimes amity—even love. I wonder if that might not be a surer path to purity than righteousness."

But the subject for Margotto was summarily closed. He made an awkward little bow that had no deference in it. "I will have to report it to the civilian police," he said.

He started for the door. As he reached it, his hand on the knob, Feradoti said, "Wait, please."

Margotto turned and Feradoti took a deep breath. "There is another consideration." Whatever the Secretary was considering, Michael knew it was disagreeable to him. "The extraterritoriality of Galestro's villa has always been held in question by the secular government. There has never been any occasion to test it. If we call the civilian police, they might consider this a good time to force the question."

Margotto hesitated, but only for an instant. "Galestro's villa has always been extraterritorial—always."

"By sufferance, perhaps. The property has, after all, no religious consecration to recommend it, no shrine, no sanctuary—even its chapel is a private one. This would be a strategic time for the secular government to raise questions about it. Does it not worry you that we would be giving Italy an excuse for invading Church property? Are you so anxious to jeopardize the sovereignty we have so painfully acquired? The sovereignty not only of a small villa, but of the Vatican itself?"

Margotto bristled. "This is a scare tactic, Your Eminence—I will not be intimidated by it."

"Why not?" Feradoti had carefully built an arch of logic, now he set the keystone in place. "Ordinarily, wouldn't you be the first to point out that the government is Communist?"

The final word was the final word. Dauntless as Margotto might otherwise be, Communism was the one incubus he could not rout. He tried to depart without further loss of countenance. "If you keep this secret, you will be held responsible for its consequences."

"I had already accepted that responsibility, Your Eminence."

There was a hush in the room when Margotto departed. It had been a cunning argument and Michael felt a twinge of regret that Feradoti had had to resort to it. How much more gratifying it would have been if the Secretary had won with his earlier argument, on an elevatedly moral plane, than on the lower level of expediency. Yet, scarcely any worldly ideal, Feradoti had once written, was ever achieved by impractical means; realism was not the opposite of idealism, it was the mechanics of it. Or was it the price, Michael wondered. What an apropos symbol the crucifix was—a perfect metaphor of man's dilemma; the idealist vertical member aspiring to heaven, and the practical crosswise member, parallel to earth, manbound.

"He was more reasonable than I expected him to be," Feradoti said.

"He was not reasonable—he was afraid."

"I'm not questioning what *made* him reasonable. I'm simply relieved that he *was*." Ruminatively: "If he could be *generally* reasonable, he might be a fine Pope. He is such a principled man."

"He's not!" Michael retorted hotly. "He's a bigot, he's an anti-Semite, and he's full of rage."

"Well," mollifyingly, "he comes from poverty and ignorance and injustice. If he rages against those malevolences—"

105

"No, he rages against the enemies of those malevolences!"

"You are hard on him, Michael." His manner was gentle, he was moderating a dispute, tolerant of both sides, and, as always, seeking the concordance. "If he were to become Pope you would see all the goodness in the man."

He couldn't believe Feradoti might ever entertain such a thought, even as an abstract exercise of the brain. Only yesterday the Secretary had seemed alarmed by the possibility Margotto might be a candidate. True, Galestro's death meant a need for other recourses, but . . . Margotto? Open-mindedness—it was the trait Feradoti most prided himself on—but sometimes it looked like capriciousness. It bothered him. He didn't like the drift of the conversation.

"Great offices make great men," the Secretary was saying.

"I don't believe that. I don't think this man would change. His rage is bred in the bone. His whole life has been rage."

"His life has been repentance."

They were both, Michael realized, thinking of the tragedy in Margotto's past, yet how differently they were interpreting it.

The man had come from farm people in the South. Before going into the priesthood, he had been married. His wife had died in childbirth. But the infant, a beautiful boy, had lived. When Margotto's wife was gone, the bereaved man took desperately to his son. He cared for him and loved him and farmed his fields with the child constantly at his side. One day, however, the little boy, about three years old at the time, toddled away somewhere, out of sight. He had wandered into the stable. Squeezing his way under some boards, he got into a stall. The horse was a wayward roan; they had gelded him and still he was rampant. He trampled the child to death. Margotto went insane; kneeling in the bloody straw, he tried to reassemble the broken parts of the little boy as if it were a toy that could be mended. Then, when he saw his death, he lost his senses. He was a wild Jacob viewing Joseph's bloody coat, crying for sackcloth and ashes. At last, distraught, he opened the wicket to the horse's stall. As frenzied as the animal, he beat the gelding with his bare fists, with his feet, with all his rage. He beat the horse to death. Three months later, bereft of everything he loved, he entered a monastery of bread and salt.

To Michael, the story illustrated the man's bedeviled need for vengeance, which had continued to be the driving energy of his life. To Feradoti, it was the story of a man who had faced the brutality in himself, had repented and overcome it.

"I think the man's a nightmare," the priest said.

"Michael . . . *con calma.*"

"And I resent your being his defender, Your Eminence. The more so, since you and I both know it is you who should be our next Pope."

He was angry. "I will not hear of it, Michael!"

"You've got to! I'm going to America—not in Galestro's behalf—in yours!"

"You are forbidden!" Michael had never seen the Secretary enraged, had never heard his voice raised. It was unsteadying, it had Old Testament echoes in it. "You are absolutely forbidden to go on any such errand! There will be no electioneering in my behalf!"

Michael forced himself to slow down. "Would you, for the Lord's sake, tell me why?" he pleaded. "You would have allowed me to go in somebody else's behalf when you knew my heart wasn't altogether in it. And now, when it's you—and all my heart would be in it—how can you forbid me?"

A sharp, categorical note. "I've said what I have to say." A moment, indecisive. The old man suddenly wearied. He turned from the center of the room and walked away, limping rather more than usual, seeking a vague place to pause, neither at a wall nor at a window.

Michael too turned away, and started to depart. The Secretary's voice stopped him. Not facing the young man, he said, "I'm sorry I raised my voice to you, Michael." A difficulty, then: "What's more, I regret that I disagreed with you about Cardinal Margotto. The thought of him as Pope—it *is* terrifying. But one tries not to judge—at least, not without understanding."

Michael saw a glimmer of hope. "Then, as to my going to America . . . ?"

Feradoti's tone was kind but there was no concession in it. "No, Michael, not in my behalf." He seemed troubled and drawn, touchingly vulnerable. "I'm sorry."

Michael thought: he's trying to say what an afflictive day it's been, and that he's fond of me. I would like to say the same to him, deeply, and that there will be better days.

Instead, he pointed to the older man's temporary desk, cluttered with papers. "Is there anything you'd like me to take with me?"

The question called him back. Brightening: "Yes, as a matter of fact, there is." He walked to the desk and, opening the center drawer, brought out an envelope. It was not a large one, not of business size, but a small square, and the letterpaper it contained was deckle-edged and personal.

"It's from Cardinal Cavanaugh."

The name again, and the same cold stone inside him—would he never get over it?

Feradoti started to read the letter aloud:

> " 'My dear Paolo,
>
> " 'It has been many years, and as I consider the scurrilities of the newspapers and the invectives of the so-called liberal press—not to mention the calumnies of Cardinal van Tenbroek whom you have defended—I realize how far apart you and I have separated. There is hardly any public stand you have taken in recent years—especially your indulgence of the Third World bishops —with which I can agree. And I am sure you must feel the same about me.
>
> " 'Yet, whenever I think of you personally, I think fondly. And now that I have a grave trouble—it is to you I come for help, as I did once before, with such benefaction.
>
> " 'I shall understand, however, if, for whatever reason, you cannot help me this time. The chore I ask you to perform may be a dangerous one, and it will have to be approached with the utmost discretion.' "

Feradoti began the next sentence and stopped. He looked toward the door. His face had turned gray.

Michael quickly wheeled around to see what had frightened the man. The door was exactly as it had been before, closed. There was nobody there. He hurried to the door, opened it, looked outward. Again, nobody. When he turned to the Secretary again, the man was managing a smile.

"I can't get used to this temporary office," he said.

He had said less than he meant. He was an old creature, he was implying, needing his old lair, nervous in the new one. Then: "Didn't you hear someone out there?" he asked with studied casualness.

"No," Michael said comfortingly. "But there are still some workmen . . . restorers."

"Not in this part of the building." With an effort, he shook it off. He was embarrassed by his fall through space, and smiled wanly at his foolishness. "Do we now begin to invent monsters? Shall I look for wiretaps and small electrical eavesdroppers? . . . What is to become of us?"

He lifted the letter to resume the reading of it, but again his eye went to the door; the specter was still there. He started to hand the letter to Michael, but pulled it back. One indecision bred another. At last, with candor:

"I would not feel free to discuss it here," he said. "Come to the country. We'll talk about this—and other things—somewhere, in a field. It's Friday afternoon and I long for meadows. Will you come tomorrow?"

"Yes."

Michael left the room, walked through the chambers, then out into the loggia. The corridor was long and wide and dim. He saw the man at the other end. He was not a workman. He wore the lengthy black soutane of a priest, and it swirled more than an ordinary cassock might; he was walking more swiftly than necessary.

It was a day of days; an Italian spring, with banners. Wild poppies in the fields, crowding the season; anemones and marguerites, all too early for April. And the birds, in flocks, he had never seen so many—doves and cardinals and golden orioles, and accidental finches and starlings—all in a country walk from the railway station, a bare ten minutes of strolling.

Feradoti's villetta was larger than a cottage and smaller than a villa. It was, as Ledagrazia had described it, *la misura d'un abbraccio,* the size of a hug. *Her* hug, she meant, which was the embrace of limitless bounty, of all outdoors.

She was Feradoti's older sister, a loving woman, and it was she whom Michael first saw this morning. But she didn't see him. She was in the garden in one of the white rattan armchairs, reading, deeply concentrated, as absorbed as if someone were on a precipice.

He did not immediately make his presence known. He simply stood there, gazing at her, savoring his private pleasure in the moment. She was an abundant-looking woman, rounded wherever there was any opportunity to be rounded; she had a body wreathed in smiles. Nearing seventy, she had not yet, as she said, lost her mother-fat. Yet her face was by no means a lumpish one; to the contrary, it had an Etruscan light and shade, bright with vivacity and dark with an intensity totally at variance with the languor of her body—until she laughed; then she was all one and no contradictions, an integrity of joyousness.

Almost the instant he had met her, five years ago, his heart was gone. He fell into her deep bosom; she was the mother he had never had. And on his second visit to Feradoti's house, as if by conscious design, he contracted a spectacular flu—everything—coughs, sneezes, ache of bones, blazing temperature, so that Ledagrazia had to nurse him. She did, and he luxuriated.

So did she. She missed nursing someone. Long a widow, her children had dispersed, all of them. She had given birth to six—four daughters and two sons. Three of the daughters were married, two to industrialists in Torino, one to a postal official in Bari; the youngest daughter was a nun in a papal cloister exclusively dedicated to contemplation. The elder of her two sons was in the shipping business in Livorno. She rarely heard from any of them. The one she did hear from, Bruno, she wished she wouldn't. He was her youngest child, and a Communist. More to her heartbreak, he was not the typically Italian Communist who at least paid lip service to peace with the Church. He was an embattled enemy of it, and, she said, a *ripugnanza* to God. When she talked of him she split in two, and the dark Etruscan side of her was predominant, angular, resentful, agonized.

She was not, in this balmy April morning, any of those things. She was round serenity. A composition in orange. Her blouse was a print that looked like a citrus orchard; her loose sweater, tangerine; her skirt, a burnt Roman ocher. The only contrast to the palette of oranges was the book she was reading—bright blue; no, azure, a swatch cut out of the sky. The whole picture, fresh and clear, the colors pure; and the old woman, how bright and merry she looked.

Still unable to surrender the private moment, Michael did not stir. He watched her read. The old lady's lips moved swiftly as she concentrated on the page. She had never learned any rigid rules—no reading manners, as she would say—for she was a self-educated woman despite the wealth of her parents. Why cultivate our female brains, Leda would ask wryly, since we had no use for them. Except that her brain was richly cultivated. She was always hungry for books, she raided bookshops as children do refrigerators, and she consumed what she bought in the stealth of midnight.

He took a step toward her at last. "Ledagrazia," he whispered.

She turned a startled face, then arose from her chair and flurried welcomingly toward him. *"Mico!"* she said with a rush of warmth. *"Mico mio!"*

She embraced him, she kissed him on the cheek, she held one of his hands in both her own, she wouldn't let it go. There was no reservation; she missed him, she said; he looked terrible, she said; it was time for him to get sick again, she said.

The breeze had loosened a strand of her white hair; he straightened it. He touched her cheek. "You are such a beautiful one. . . ."

"Sometimes I *am*," she giggled. "It depends on who is here." She glanced covertly toward the house and lowered her voice. "With van Tenbroek I am a crone."

"Tenbroek? Is he here?"

"Yes. So is Leone. The cardinals gather."

"So soon?"

"Exactly what my brother said this morning. 'Galestro is dead, but His Holiness is still alive. Why do they scurry?' "

"But he allowed them to come."

The words had escaped him, he hadn't known they would sound so eager. She looked at him quickly and he suspected something disapproving in her glance. "Yes, he allowed them," she said quietly.

He pointed to the house. "Shall I go in?"

"No, he said for you to wait until they go."

It was an odd instruction. Michael was already privy to what was going on. Normally, Feradoti would have wanted his presence. He was sure there were no confidences from which he had to be excluded; certainly none that the Secretary would not entrust to him. He wondered why he had been expressly asked to stay away.

"His name will appear, will it not?"

Preoccupied, he only half heard her question. "Appear? In what way?"

"You know very well in what way. He is *papabile*." She paused, reluctant to ask the question. "Will he be a candidate?"

"I don't know. He hasn't told you?" As she raised her shoulders negatively: "Would you like him to be?"

Clearly, she preferred not to have been asked. "No, not really. I do not want him to be Pope. It isn't the work, it isn't the worry. It's the loneliness. How can a man decide that for the rest of his life he will always eat alone? It is dry pasta."

III

"Would you pray that they pass him by?"

"Oh, never that. How could I do that?" It was, for her, too woeful a subject. She changed it. "Would you like something? I have some brioches—they are very French—I made them myself."

"With currant jelly, I suppose?"

She laughed. *"Tutti i preti sono ghiotti di cose dolci."*

The first time he heard the expression he thought it meant all priests are gluttonous; later, simply that they had a sweet tooth; and later still, that they yearned for love.

As she turned toward the house: "Shall I come with you?" he asked.

"Oh, no, don't waste the sunlight. Go down to the edge of the *terrazza.* Look into the pond. Carp—mother of heaven, you have never seen so many carp. It's a pool of gold."

He followed the winding path, through wild iris and jonquils, and came to the tiny lagoon. The carp were, as Leda said, a throng of darting gold. He could see all the stages of their maturation— the deep gray ones, the silver ones, spurting, scudding, almost leaping out of the water, crazed by not knowing what they had just recently become, and the oldest ones, fully arrived, swimming sedately, preening in their scales of yellow sunlight.

In a little while, Leda was back and they were drinking cappuccino and laughing and teasing one another, and Leda was feeding him brioche with currant jelly, and hazelnut dolce and dates and figs with great dollops of Bavarian cream. And whatever reason priests had for liking sweet things, he was happy to have them.

When the two visiting cardinals had departed, Feradoti invited Michael into the solarium and handed him Cavanaugh's letter. Michael resumed reading where, yesterday, the Secretary had stopped:

> . . . and it will have to be approached with the utmost discretion.
>
> It has to do with Cory.
>
> I would not ask you to do this if I were not certain that you and Ledagrazia were at one time deeply fond of my brother; and even if you have not seen him for a good many years, I feel that you must still have an affection for him.

As you probably have heard, he has become a successful artist. The boy you remember is now a man, past thirty, and has already produced a volume of painting that is remarkable. He has had two showings in America; both were reviewed with unanimous praise.

But there is something frightening in his life. He is being terrorized. And I fear he will be killed.

For six months before he left New York, he received threatening letters, with warnings of violence and murder. Once he was actually attacked and viciously beaten. Had it not been for the fortuitous arrival of a group of college students, he would have been killed.

Whatever I think is the reason for all this—whatever I have heard or conjecture—may be altogether wrong. In any event, my telling you would only confuse the request—which is a simple one:

Cory is now in Rome. He has been there for over a year. For eight months he lived in safety—his whereabouts unknown to the terrorists, I suppose. In late January, he received another threatening letter. Again, in early March. About a month ago, he was beaten and once more, providentially, escaped with his life.

Since that time I have not been able to reach him. He has never had a telephone in Rome. My recent letters have gone unanswered. I am ill with worry. He is, as you know, more a son than a brother to me, and all the family I have. I love him very deeply.

The favor I ask of you is: please find him. And if you do, beg him to come home. Whatever the dangers in this country, he will be safer here. There will be someone who will look after him. Me. And I am not without some influence. In Rome, however, there is nobody to look after him, and he will not do it for himself. He is no more cautious today than he was when you knew him. He refuses to be afraid, or to believe that he can get killed. He's wrong; he can.

So I beg you, find him, please, and entreat him to come home. And if you cannot prevail—please, my dear Paolo—do what you can to see that he is protected.

His last address was 81 Via Raca, a studio apartment. Please go to him or send someone you can trust.

Cory will not, I am afraid, be a willing ally. What he wants most is to be let alone. I would gladly leave him in solitude, if those others would. But they are horrifyingly intrusive—and as real as the world terror they have caused. Faith of itself is, unfortunately, no safeguard against them—prayer seems unavailing. But I continue, of course, to pray. For us all.

One last word: If you cannot come to my assistance, for whatever reason, I shall understand. It will be especially understandable to me, these days, in light of the rumor you may have heard with respect to the Synod. And if that weighs heavily with you, as it very well may, please do not feel that you must explain.

In any event, I have enough to be grateful to you for.

Yours, in Jesus,
Lucas

Michael refolded the letter, put it back in the envelope, crossed the solarium and handed it to Feradoti, who sat on the windowseat. Through the squarely mullioned panes of glass they could see Ledagrazia on the terrace. She was there a few moments, then gone.

"Terror again, and always patterned a little differently," Michael said.

Feradoti nodded. "But this time, thanks to heaven, we have been given a warning."

"And you want me to do something about it?"

"You do not have to, understand. It is not part of any of your responsibilities, Michael. And as Lucas says, it could be dangerous. . . . But I must tell you—that boy—the letter is accurate about how fond we were of him. He spent a summer with us many years ago, when he was still in his teens. We fell in love with him. And the way he adored Leda—!" He crossed his arms over his chest in an Italian gesture of worship. "And what a brilliant boy! He wanted to be a priest and he had special permission to enter the Santa Trinità seminary before his sixteenth birthday. Lucas was so proud of him. And then—I don't know what happened—he ran away from the seminary, gave up all thought of the priesthood . . . and nearly broke Lucas's heart. And from that time on, it was never the same . . . the boy seemed to drift away from all of us. . . . And now there's this terrible danger." He turned gravely to his assistant. "It could be equally dangerous for you, Michael, if you go in search of him. So think prudently before you say yes."

"How can I possibly say no? A man's life . . ."

"I would have done it by myself. But there might be need for a quickness." With a fret of pique he slapped his lame leg. "Please, Michael, say no if you have any qualms."

"None. But what do I do? The Via Raca—I don't know where it is, but it must certainly be outside the Vatican—how can we give him protection? And we cannot call the civilian police."

"We will have to hire people. I will personally see to the expense."

"I'll go immediately."

"Will you? There's a train in an hour. You should be back in Rome by nightfall."

Michael was ready, but couldn't assemble himself to leave. Bits and pieces, disconnected . . . and one fragment, unassociated, niggling at him.

"What did he mean, toward the end of the letter—the reference to the Synod?"

"Oh, it's nothing," Feradoti replied too offhandedly. "As he says—only a rumor."

Michael pursued it. "A rumor of what?"

"Nothing momentous. There's been some talk that Cavanaugh was going to invite the American cardinals—and a number of Third World prelates—to a meeting of some sort."

"But he says 'Synod.' "

"Well . . . a name . . ." He seemed too deliberately casual. "He could just as well have called it a council or a conference."

"But he didn't. I've never heard of a Synod of cardinals, have you?"

"That doesn't mean it can't happen. There's certainly no canonical stricture against it. A meeting's a meeting, no matter what you call it."

"But why does he want to *call* it a Synod?"

"Because it's more . . . impressive."

It was as if Michael had wrung the word out of him. "Exactly," he said. "That's the point—to impress. To influence opinion. It'll be a political convention. He might as well carry Margotto's portrait down every aisle."

Feradoti tried to smile. "Come, Michael, you're being a bit

pungent, aren't you? He'll do no such thing. The purpose of the Synod is—I would imagine—to conciliate various points of view on the liturgy—"

"—and divorce."

"Yes."

"Would it be a conciliation toward a center, do you think? Or to the right?"

"Michael, you're beginning to panic."

"Yes, I am. If Cavanaugh's organizing it, it means to the right. And it's a political caucus—and you know it."

"No, I don't. Anyway, it's tears before tragedy—it's only a rumor. Even if he's free to call it a Synod, I can't imagine he will actually announce it without first consulting the Vatican."

"But His Holiness is ill and, certainly for these purposes, you're the Vatican. You're exactly the person he would want to bypass."

"I don't believe it." The Secretary said the words quickly, but they came out of a shadow of uncertainty. And misgiving.

The telephone rang.

As often as he had been in the solarium, Michael had never become accustomed to the telephone in this room. It seemed out of place, and an anachronism.

Feradoti went to it. He didn't speak very much; he listened. At last he murmured a few words too softly for Michael to hear. When he set down the instrument he was pale. Slowly he put his hand over his mouth; his fingers were not still.

"That was van Tenbroek," he said. "He's been speaking with Monsignor Giorgi at the *Osservatore Romano.* The rumor persists. There was an item in *The New York Times* to the effect that there will be a conservative Synod. However, there has been no announcement by Cardinal Cavanaugh. He neither confirms nor denies."

"That means there will be. When?"

"Obviously, since there's been no announcement, there's no date."

"Did you say no electioneering, Your Eminence?"

Feradoti heard the irony in Michael's voice and it unsteadied him.

"May I please go to America?" Michael asked urgently. When his superior didn't reply: "May I go and plead with him—on your behalf—not to convoke this Synod? Would you allow me—please?"

Feradoti didn't respond immediately. When he did, he begged the question. "Your immediate chore is to find his brother."

"I'll do that—I'll welcome that chore. The more so because it'll put the Cardinal in our debt." The secretary looked at him sharply, a rebuke. Michael didn't apologize. "I'll take the advantage—I'll snatch for any stroke of luck that'll give us an edge."

He felt no pangs about the opportunism he heard in himself. In matters of state, one had to be on the alert for the timely, the expedient. And he even went further with it. "I'll make a deal with you, Cardinal. I'll do this chore for him—if you'll allow me to do one for you."

He had gone too far, and regretted it. Not the words; the mode. The Secretary was too finely wrought for a presentation so crass. "I'm sorry, Your Eminence," he said. "I should not have given you the responsibility for that choice. I should take the risk entirely upon myself. Which I do. I'll find the Cardinal's brother as quickly as I can. Then I'll apply for a leave of absence—and go to New York. Some way, I have to—I must convince him not to convoke this council." Then he added, wanly, "And I'm probably the worst person in the world to attempt it."

The Secretary inclined his head. It was less a mark of approval than of sympathy.

"I'll say goodbye to Leda," he murmured as he was leaving. "Is she still outdoors, do you suppose?"

He took leave of the Cardinal and went out onto the terrace. Leda was standing there, just a few feet from the door, staring at it, watching for him, as if awaiting a verdict. Without preamble: "You're going to find Cory?" she said.

"I'm going to try."

"Good. But be careful, Mico, be careful."

He assured her that he would and, as he was about to kiss her goodbye, she said, "I'll walk with you to the station."

She took his arm. Strolling with her along the country road, he had the distinct sense that she wanted to talk about Cory. Yet, for some reason unknown to him, she was avoiding the subject. Instead, she asked a dozen questions about the likelihood of her brother becoming the Pope. And he suspected she wasn't hearing any of his answers.

"When I find Cory," Michael said tentatively, "is there any message for him?"

She looked at him nervously. "No—just my love, that's all."

And she returned hastily to the papal matter. Yet, Michael could see that her mind was elsewhere; she was preoccupied, deeply troubled.

When they arrived at the station, Leda could no longer repress it. "Michael, when you find Cory, beg him not to take any chances, beg him to go home—*beg* him! If anything happens to him, it will be the end of his brother! They have so much to . . ."

"To what, Leda?"

". . . forgive each other for."

Then, quickly, as if she felt she had said too much, she tried to lighten it to insignificance. "But then, I suppose that's true of all families, isn't it?"

The train arrived. He had the clear intuition that she wanted to pursue the subject—perhaps needed to—yet was relieved that she had been rescued from it. It was, he thought, frightening to her.

According to the policeman in the railway station in Rome, the Via Raca, where Michael was going in search of Cory Cavanaugh, was one of the streets adjoining the Piazza Mastai. Michael remembered the little piazza; he had been there during his weeks of waiting when he had first arrived in Rome. Long years ago, it used to be the cigar-makers' section—in the time before the national monopoly of tobacco—a small colony of tiny shops where elderly men used to sit in their store windows, twisting tobacco leaves, smiling, beckoning. Or so the older folk told of them. But there was nothing of that sort anymore; cigars were made in factories these days; stamps were required, it was the law.

It was nighttime and the Piazza Mastai was deserted. The balm of the day had gone, the chill wind was returning.

And no sign of the Via Raca. Michael walked into one side street after another, hoping that each one would open onto a *vicolo,* a courtyard, an alleyway that would lead to Cory's apartment. But nothing.

Nor was there anyone to ask. The streets were dark, empty, soundless. The only stir of noise, his own footsteps on cobblestones, and the rising wind. He could not recall such a gusty spring as this one; it was unpleasant, worrisome, like *scirocco* in another time of year.

Something was wrong in his being here. The Via Raca should not have been so hard to find, the night should not be so black, so troublously out of season. He would try this one turning at the end of the narrow street, he told himself, then go to brighter places, the Via del Corso perhaps, where he might, if anything was open, buy a city atlas.

When he got to the street corner, he saw a faint light. It was toward the end of the *vicolo,* on the other side. Perhaps there would be someone to help him find his way. Encouraged, he hurried toward the illumination. When he got to it, the sight stopped him. Across the street, with one naked electric bulb in the center of the store—a cigar-maker's shop. In the window, the man was at work, rolling the tobacco, his hands moving swiftly, his tongue moistening and softening the brown leaves, then the fingers twisting, sealing, hastening one cigar after another. It was the one glimmer of light in a dark place. How eerie it was—the lone survivor from another period; something strangely perverse, a man making contraband cigars, unlicensed and stampless—in this neighborhood more radical than most, and readier for quarrel— willfully exposing himself in a display window, in open defiance, challenging arrest, even perhaps welcoming bloodshed.

The man did not see Michael, he paid no attention to the outer stillness. Intent on his work, head bent, his hands did not for a moment stop their swift movement, twisting, turning, smoothing. Suddenly he looked up and Michael drew a startled breath. It was not a man, but a woman. Her hair was as closely cut as a man's might be and her jaw was square and hard. She had a forbidding look, her eyes were cold, they had an unnameable malice in them. Absorbed, Michael gazed at her, puzzled at himself, at how summarily he had judged her someone to distrust.

She stopped working. As if sensing she was being watched, she leaned forward a trifle and peered into the darkness. There was no alarm in her face, only vigilance; she could not—not this woman, Michael speculated—be afraid of anything.

Slowly she arose, walked away from her workbench, stepped down and approached the door. She opened it and simply stood there. She was tall, taller than Michael, her hulk filled the doorway. She held her body with a certain muscular rigidity he had seen in fighters outside the ring, hampered by tight clothes. Holding her hand up to shield her eyes from the light, she squinted outward. Then, apparently seeing him, she raised her hand and pointed in his direction, saying nothing.

At last: "Come closer," she challenged quietly.

Dutifully, without a word, Michael started across the street.

When he was within her orbit of light, she said, almost inaudibly, "A priest." Then, without disguising her unfriendliness; "What were you staring at?"

"I'm sorry—it was rude of me. But you—I have never seen a woman making cigars."

"Have you ever seen anyone making cigars?"

"No."

"Then why did you say 'a woman'? I make as good a cigar as a man does." Gratuitously, she made her grim little joke. "For a man to smoke—and choke on."

Trying to make light of it, he laughed. She didn't. "What are you doing here?" Cold suspicion.

"I'm looking for the Via Raca."

"Are you?" The implication was that he was lying.

"Yes, I am."

"You're in the wrong place," she said. "The wrong side of the river. It's near the Piazza di Campitelli."

"Which way?"

She pointed. "Over the Ponte Garibaldi, then to the right."

He thanked her and departed. He didn't hear the door close behind him, nor did he look back—not until he reached the corner. There, when he turned, he saw the light in her shop go out.

He walked quickly, wanting to get out of the woman's neighborhood. A half mile away, still in dark deserted streets, he had an uncanny certainty he was being followed. At the foot of the bridge he turned.

She was there.

The bridge seemed dismal to him, he could not see the other side. His figure would not be visible on it; neither would hers.

He started across. He knew she was following.

Counting his footsteps, he told himself nonsensically that the higher the sum the safer he would be. The nonsense gave no comfort, he knew her count would equal his. He could sense her getting closer now, not a hundred paces behind, the number dwindling, the gap shortening.

Frightened, he had an impulse to run. But what good would that do? She would know he was afraid, she would have an advantage, and he was sure she would be faster on her feet, and run him down.

Perhaps only fifty paces now, he wasn't sure, and didn't dare look back. Then, closer still. He had a flashing memory of two women, on a windy night, savaging a priest.

He ran.

Just as he got to the other side of the bridge, his foot twisted, he started to fall, pulled himself out of it, kept running, gave all his heart to it. Across the Longotevere and into the wide safety of the Via Arenula.

Stopping to catch his breath, he turned.

She was gone.

What a quaking idiot I am, he thought, she was probably not following me at all. It was the end of her day, perhaps, she had closed her shop, she was on her way home. His direction happened to be hers, no more than that, nothing sinister in it, no shadowy menaces, no ambushes. . . . Yet, her hostility was not an imagined thing, it had been real.

Anyway, he felt easier now. Until he got to the ghetto.

Most of the Jews had long since disappeared from the impoverished section, but it was still called the ghetto, and still had the imprisoned dreariness of a pale of settlement. Now it was occupied by hard-bitten laboring families, by the unemployed, by Communists. A priest would not be a favorite here.

The main thoroughfares were not so bad but the side streets were a shambles of defeat. For ages, nothing had been done to replace or repair anything, not so much as a downspout. Metal rusting and stone moldering to dust, everything was cramped and narrow, dank with depression; the filth of timeworn poverty was ground into every decaying wall, every garbage-strewn stairwell, every rat-infested cellarway.

Here, darkness again, but of a more intense kind, palpable, like a black cowl . . . And no Via Raca.

Wearied to exhaustion, discouraged, certain there was no such street, and about to give it up, he came upon it. It was no more than an alleyway, a filthy one. There was not only wretchedness in it, there was anger. Repulsive graffiti, a postal box torn from its moorings, windows broken, vandalized—the street shrieked its vindictiveness like a profanity.

Michael came upon the house. It had been gracious once, with a façade of great stone squares and wrought-iron balcony on the second floor. But the grillwork hung awry now, tilting precariously, threatening to drop on the next pedestrian. The facing stones were pitted and flaking; the whole building had subsided, wanting to give up long ago and asking only to fall.

Michael thought, dismally: Cory Cavanaugh, a sometime painter of promise, the beloved brother of a noted churchman, a Cardinal no less, living in this squalid neighborhood, hiding.

His gloom was worse when he entered the dark vestibule. There was a stench. It came wafting down the narrow staircase, a fetor that had no name. Dead things, he thought at first, decay, animal matter gone to corruption. Yet it lacked the insistence of corruption, it was a more passive odor, willing to go unnoticed. It had probably been here for centuries, he thought, this ancient damp, the mildews that never dried, the musks of male and female long since dead, the molds of time itself.

The stairs were narrow and steep; he started to climb. There was no light, not a glimmer. On each landing, the doors were open and ajar. It didn't seem to matter whether you entered or didn't, there was nothing you would steal, better to give free access than to encourage the smashing of locks. Nor was there a sign of any tenant at all, of anybody ever having lived here. He didn't see how it could be possible for anyone to inhabit this place, certainly not Cory Cavanaugh.

He was on the fourth floor now, the last. Up here there was only one door; unlike the others, it was not ajar. He approached it. Hesitating, he knocked. Nobody answered. He knocked again.

He entered. The room, like all the others, was pitch black. Then, surprisingly, it wasn't. A glow shone, overhead. And he could see why an artist would have chosen this place. Magnificently, like open sky, the whole ceiling was skylight. Moon and stars, which had been nonexistent only minutes ago, had now come out from behind clouds and cast shining rays, lighting the floor, throwing shadows of mullions over everything, the glow so brilliant that he barely noticed the encrustment of dirt on the windowpanes.

But all the room had was moonlight, starlight. There was no furniture, not even the remembrance of any, only the scraps and leavings of a man who had moved away. In the corner of the room, a battered broom, its straw worn to the quick; beside it, an old wicker wastebasket, torn and overstuffed with bottles, papers, debris. His first impression of the room had been of clutter, but now he saw that, except for the wastebasket in the corner, the place had been left spotless, the tenant had been scrupulous.

But . . . gone.

Well, that was that, then; Michael had done his chore. Yet . . .

what if the man had not simply moved, but had fled. Fled where, from whom, and how could he know where to look for him? And what further responsibility had he to do so?

Without any conscious design, he found himself rooting through the papers in the wastebasket. But it was useless; a variety of pencil sketches, crumpled, a printed catalogue of art supplies, a few carefully folded paper bags which might have carried groceries, and at the bottom, a number of scraps of paper, tiny and scattered. Nothing that told him anything. Well, if a man was hiding out, as it seemed Cory Cavanaugh was, what had Michael expected, a forwarding address?

Abruptly, it occurred to him: all the papers in the wastebasket were simply crumpled and tossed away, none of them had been torn. But at the bottom of the basket, those scattered scraps—why had they been torn to bits?

The problem was assembling them. There had been moonlight enough to yank a crumpled drawing sheet out and identify it as such, but putting together the jigsaw puzzle of what looked like it might have been a letter . . .

He had tried the light switch on the wall by the doorway, and it had given nothing. He flicked it again; still no light. Noticing another door in the room, he hoped it might be a bathroom, with a working electrical fixture somewhere, over a sink perhaps. He was disappointed—the bathroom was probably on another floor. This was a closet. It was large; he walked into it.

Nothing was there. As he started out again, something brushed against his forehead. A cobweb, he thought, and he reached to flick it away, but it returned. He pulled it; it was a string. A light went on. Not much of a light, a small bulb in a makeshift fixture, it had been installed by the artist, he would have guessed, to illuminate the shelves. They too were makeshift and had possibly carried art materials, books, supplies.

Something had been left behind.

He saw the back of it first, the blank side of the canvas, on its stretcher, the fabric ripped. Reaching for it, he turned it around and held it closer to the stingy closet light; gazed at it.

There were two rips in the canvas, at right angles to each other, like a cross; not accidental rips but deliberately, sharply made, with a razor blade or knife. He wondered why the damage had been done, and by whom.

It was a striking painting, meticulously executed. A true portrait, he would have judged it to be—not an imaginary person—of someone real, someone singular. The face was middle-aged, a man in his fifties, possibly older, a stern face, severe to the edge of cruelty, yet strangely at variance with the soft kindliness of the mouth. But it was the eyes that reconciled the discrepancy; such beautiful eyes, such a depth of hurt and anger and remorsefulness; eyes that spoke of all manner of pain, and everyone's, like the compassionate Christ.

It *was* Christ.

Yet, it couldn't be. This was a middle-aged man, as clean-shaven as if the razor had just left the skin, with a neatly cropped haircut, sideburns perfect, parting of the hair fastidious, the comb furrows still clear, strand by strand. An American perhaps, a businessman, a college president, a member of the board. A burgher.

Yet, it occurred to him, how could he rule out any portrait of the Savior as being beyond credibility? What graphic body need the artist create, for His *anima* to live in it? However real He was, He was also the sublime illusion. Artists had apprehended him in countless, various ways, often incongruous. They had conceived of him as carpenter, teacher, rebel, priest, prophet, beggar; they had seen him as white man, black man, yellow, red, brown. Some had made him bloodless to suggest impalpable spirit, some had made him gory to quicken pity for his palpable wounds. He was, at times, a thin and wasted being, an ascetic, many essences removed from the human touch; He was, at others, a man of flesh and substance, as close as the arm's reach, as warm as comfort, a brother in the brotherhood of man. He had been revealed immaculate, to show He had come from a sanitary heaven, or soiled, to show that men had reviled Him; in dark shrouds of mystery, and in aureoles of effulgent light. He had been painted in mud and blood and earth and sky and in gold leaf so thick as to hide His lineaments.

How many hundreds of envisionings of Him had Michael gazed on, and from how many had the splendid illusion shone? Only a few. And here was a painting, possibly the least likely to summon any of His divinity, a barbered, beardless, well-fed, stern-faced businessman. And yet . . . the touch of glory.

A burgher Christ?

Yes, it was Jesus grown older, the Nazarene who had not been crucified, the practical man who had made a compact with His captors. I am not the Lord, this Jesus had said, I am not the Redeemer, I am not the Truth, the Light, the Everlasting Life, I am not the messenger of God nor certainly His Son. It is they who have said these things of me, but I am only an erstwhile carpenter from Galilee, an occasional preacher of sorts; when have I ever claimed to be other than I am? This was the compromising Intercessor, the Go-Between of heaven and hell, the Jesus who knew that one way or another he would be calumniated, and chose the calumny that went with the sparing. They had spared Him the agony.

But only the quick agony was spared; the slow one lived on and on, mirrored in these eyes of Jesus, citizen, bourgeois workman who had cut his beard and flourished to factories, and to the slow and prosperous tragedy of the man who compromises his soul.

Michael stared at the portrait, and stared. The ache in the man's eyes was unendurable; he couldn't bear to look at it, he couldn't bear to look away. Finally, he had to make himself realize it was all of his own imagining. This was a modern man he was looking at, not a Jew on an old Judean hill, this was a contemporarily turned out middle-aged businessman, the kind he could meet on Madison Avenue or in Piccadilly or in the Piazza Venezia, and that the torments he saw in this man's eyes were not there at all, they were a trick of a skillful painter.

They were in Michael himself. It was he who was the compromiser, the deal-maker. It was he, shuffling about in offices, reconciling one point of view with an opposing one, bartering in the businesses of God, who had lost touch with God Himself.

He must get away.

Get away temporarily at least; a retreat perhaps. Back to the bare rock of his faith, to the hard fact of prayer. He didn't feel well, something was wrong. His hands were clammy, his face ran with perspiration. He tried to tell himself it was the close airlessness of this tiny closet, but he knew the airlessness was in him. He was stifling.

Replacing the canvas, turning it as he had found it, facing the wall, he walked out of the closet and into the dark room. He didn't, then, know what to do with himself. There was something desperate about him, something directionless. He felt derailed, unable to get himself back on the track. He must put his mind to it, he chided himself, he must find his place again.

He looked around the room. He noted the wastebasket in the corner, the debris. Glancing upward, he saw the moon and stars through the skylight.

That's right: he was in search of a man, Cory Cavanaugh.

He could feel himself drifting back to the minutiae, the phenomena, the one chore leading to another.

The bits of paper, torn and scattered through the rubbish. Why had they been so carefully destroyed, into such tiny pieces?

He emptied the wastebasket and gathered all the scraps of paper into a single pile on the floor. Placing them onto the palm of one hand he carried them into the closet. He set the pile down on one of the closet shelves. Then, fragment by fragment, he began to reassemble them.

He had done more difficult jigsaw puzzles in his day. The words started to form immediately.

They were nothing. They were an artist's shopping list. Orange madder . . . cadmium yellow . . . turps . . . cerulean . . .

He tossed the scraps back into the basket and turned to go.

Drearily, as he walked toward the door, he saw the thing. The moonlight hit upon the whiteness of it, seemingly suspended in the dark. But it wasn't suspended, it was sticking out of the mail slot in the door. A postcard. An ordinary plain one, with Cory Cavanaugh's name and address under the Israeli stamp. And the message, written in neat penmanship:

> Sorry I missed your call last night, and especially sorry we won't be here when you arrive. Just wanted to add my welcome to Ben's. You know where the key is. If you need anything, we'll be at the Technion in Haifa until the end of summer. Just call the faculty office— they'll say where to find us. The kids send love. So do we. Naomi.

At right angles to the message, at the end of the card, the rubber-stamped letters were blurry but legible: BEN AND NAOMI ZAKKAI, 5 SHA'AR REHOV, JERUSALEM, ISRAEL.

Jerusalem.

The name of the city awakened dormant urges in him. He had never been in the Holy Land. More accurately, he had never been there *in corpore;* spiritually he was no stranger to it. He had thought at one time to do his doctoral thesis on the Stations of the Cross, and had studied the Old City until he knew every stone and halting place, but finally had given up the subject because he would have had to leave his job in Rome for a period too long. Besides, one of his professors had said, you don't have to *see* them in order to write about the Stations of the Cross; they are everywhere. So he had not gone to see them, nor had he written about them.

For a surging moment, he had a hope of Jerusalem. There was an urgent reason for going now. He thought about Cory Cavanaugh, about the attempts on the man's life. The image of the artist's painting came to him again, damaged, slashed. Like the burning of Michael's breviary, it was more than an act of vandalism, he was sure, it was a threat of some sort, a warning of terror.

But he couldn't go running off to Jerusalem. He had to take off in the opposite direction, toward America. There was a pressure of time there, a mountain to be moved, a mission crying for fulfillment.

That was his major political chore, his worldly business. But he had another need, spiritual, too disturbing and too deep to fathom. He ached with an emptiness he had never felt before. His heart, his hands grabbled for something, he hungered for a new provender, he yearned to go on a retreat where he could refresh himself and get a new sustenance for his soul.

Suddenly he knew: he had a longing for Christ and for Jerusalem as if he had been born in that city, as if he had lived there and it was home. He yearned—not to study the Stations of the Cross, but to do them, where Jesus had done them, on the same cobbles, in the same dust.

O Jerusalem, he thought, may my right hand forget its cunning, may my tongue cleave to the roof of my mouth, if I remember thee not, O Zion.

Strange, it was a Jewish vow, not a Christian one, a prayer out of the diaspora, a cry for the Holy Land, for home, the heartache of the exile.

No matter. He too felt like an exile. He would go home again, to Jerusalem, for a respite from loneliness.

Six

ONE EVENING, toward sundown, Ellen came to Nora's hotel and handed her a slip of paper with the name and address of another acquaintance.

"This one," she said, "is special. If I didn't promise Doris and Jilly I'd take them to the Planetarium, I'd do this one myself. He's been away a while—just came back. I like him, more than most. But I have to tell you, he's a bit torqued up."

Nora had never heard the expression and wondered if it was another Ellen-word, the right one put to wrong use, but she realized that torsion was exactly what was meant.

"In what way twisted?"

"Well, I'm not going to tell you that—I want you to get some fun out of it—I want you to be surprised."

She was wary of what might be going on in Ellen's shifty head. "I don't want to be surprised by another sadist, Ellen."

"Oh, nothing like that prick—nothing like," she vowed. "I give you my insurance of that. This one wouldn't harm a hair." She smiled with unusual pleasantness. "I met him last spring. It was a terrible day—rain coming down in sheets—and no business—so I went to the flicks. He was sitting beside me and I had an idea—you know how you can have a *deep* idea—that this bloke was having a bad time. Feeling sorry for him, I said, 'Lonesome?'—just that one word, 'Lonesome?' Well, it was like unlocking his door—he was as miserable as a lonely pup. So we started talking and got shushed out of the theater and checked into a hotel. . . . What a lovely man."

She thereupon gave Nora directions. It would not be an easy house to find; it was in the Old City, past the Jewish Quarter.

"You go to the end of the Street of the Chain. Then you find the sign—it says Sha'ar Rehov—you know where it is?"

"Vaguely . . . I'll find it."

Ellen wrote a few directions on a piece of paper, one right, two lefts, then a long stairway and the tiny house at the top, beige-gray stone. Then she scribbled the name of the acquaintance, Cory Cavanaugh.

He was the most beautiful man Nora had ever seen. He did not look American, although he said he was; he seemed Greek-hewn, something in marble—Praxiteles—the statue of Hermes, a copy of which she had seen somewhere, was it Boston? She remembered it now, remembered thinking at the time: I know what they meant by Hermes the messenger; more than fleetness of foot, it described a lightning of the eye, the blaze of intelligence that flashes the message by the glance. Yet, brilliant as Cavanaugh's eyes were, there was something wrong with them, and she thought, disconnectedly, about motes that had to be cast out.

He must be at least thirty, she judged, but the leap of his reflexes when he greeted her, and the way he wore his old clothes—leftover college clothes, she would have bet—made him seem only months away from the varsity crew.

He was absolutely silent. As they sat across the comfortably cluttered room, with all his painting paraphernalia spread on a huge old refectory table, he barely moved, barely breathed, in fact;

seemed to be sending wordless tidings of some unnatural world, perhaps within himself, intimations he couldn't verbalize and didn't want to imagine.

Uncomfortably, she started the conversation. "What a lovely house." She meant it; there were hundreds of books.

"It's not mine," he said. "Ben and Naomi Zakkai—they're my friends."

He said it with a possessive pride, as if to emphasize that he could indeed have friends.

She made a vague, inclusive gesture to the desk, the typewriter, the books. "Is he a writer?"

"No, *she* is—he's a professor, a scientist." He pointed to a family picture on the desk. "Those are their children—five of them— they're all my friends." She noted the repetition. "They're very . . . kind."

He said the word as if it was filled with special beneficence.

Then suddenly that was all: he had made all the talk he could manage, he was seized with shyness.

She had to fill the vacuum, and asked the obvious. "You're a painter?"

"Yes." He was grateful she had taken up the conversation. "Yes, a painter. And you?"

She thought: he's making a scruffy joke, he knows very well what I am. But his face was innocent, no sarcasm, the question was meant ingenuously. He was asking, straightforwardly, not what she was, but who. It opened up all sorts of opportunities for small talk, and she almost jumped to it. A teacher once, she was about to reply, a social worker; a writer by inclination if not by sweat and talent. Ruminations on what she had been and might still be.

She restrained herself. It was a trap, a question that seems genuinely to ask who you are. In an ordinary meeting of a man and woman, it lowered her defense against illusion—a bit of phony love philter to spread the thighs; but this was man and prostitute, the ploy unnecessary, and therefore doubly suspect.

"I'm a whore," she said.

". . . Have you been one for long?"

"No . . . not long."

Silence, which she mustn't allow. Quiet lets them think; no good, Ellen might say—it was her job, not his, to get things going.

"Is there something special you would like me to do?" she asked.

"Ellen didn't tell you?"

"No." She was right, then, there was a trick in it, Ellen's; perhaps a risky one. Her suspicion was strengthened by his changing the subject.

"How *is* Ellen?" he asked.

"She's fine. She had another . . . commitment. She didn't know you were in the city—until it was too late to do anything about it." Besides, Nora added in her mind, she wanted to avoid another meeting with you, so she palmed you off on me. . . . In what way, risky?

He didn't move from the chair, simply gazed at her, his body as still as it was before, his gray-blue eyes the only part of him in motion, too rapidly, she thought, saying too much for her to understand, yet seeming to try—desperately trying—to transmit some account of himself.

Feeling she had better help him, she started again. "Is there something you would like to . . . ?"

She couldn't finish the sentence. It hung like a broken limb.

"Would you like me to take my clothes off?" she asked.

As if he hadn't believed her: "Ellen didn't tell you anything at all?"

". . . No."

That gave him trouble. He put his hands together; one tried to comfort the other.

The silence was tighter now, as though wrung by drawstrings, pulling the walls together, giving each of them less space.

"It's very difficult to explain," he said. "If it were not so simple, it wouldn't be so difficult." He seemed to be begging her to see the humor of it, and she tried. "Ellen should have told you," he murmured.

Trying to reassure him: "You needn't worry," she said. "It's all right. . . . What do we do?"

"Not we. I."

"You, then. What?"

"I will get undressed. But you don't have to. Matter of fact, I'd prefer if you wouldn't. Then I'll sit down—over there—and talk." She had the feeling he was making it up as he went along. And he was faking. "If I—I may talk for a few minutes, maybe even for a half hour. Then it'll happen—I'm sure it'll happen." She could see he wasn't sure of anything, and was getting more and more off balance. "You'll, of course, know that it has happened because you'll

131

be watching me. I hope—while you're watching—I hope you'll be listening as well—that's very important. Then . . . when you see that it has happened, you'll take the money—I've left it on the windowsill—and go. It'll be better if I don't see you go, because then I won't be so . . . ashamed."

"Is there anything I can do . . . so that . . . you won't be ashamed?"

"No—nothing."

He seemed suddenly in deep distress; she felt sorry for him. "Are you sure?"

"No, I'm not. But shame—it may be a part of it—I may *need* to be ashamed!"

It was an unexpected outbreak, sharp with annoyance.

Uncertain how she had upset him, she mumbled an apology. He ignored it and seemed to wait for the mood to change. When it did, he started to undress. He did it carefully, without haste, as if anxious not to make some blunder. His shoes first, dilapidated loafers; he took them off and set them by the chair, neatly, side by side. Then his socks, one into each shoe. He wore a knitted T-shirt which he pulled over his head and spread out on the back of a wicker settee; then his trousers—worn and faded blue jeans—which he laid out on the same settee as meticulously as if they were satin-striped. Finally, his shorts.

Then he turned to her so that she could note the front of him, and see that already he was erect, and that he wanted the sexual ceremony to begin; in fact, his erection indicated that it had been in process from the moment he had started to undress. Slowly, with dignity, he crossed the room and sat in the chair directly facing her. He could not have chosen a chair farther away from her, she noted. He sat down and they faced each other at opposite sides of the room, she, fully clothed, and he, naked, his feet together, his knees slightly spread, his testicles resting on the canvas upholstery of the chair, his penis extended to its maximum dimension.

Suddenly she sensed a danger: she was going to laugh.

She tried to prevent it from happening. Remembering the Persian sadist and the insult he had taken from her merriment, she stifled the impulse. And resented the need to do so. Why shouldn't she laugh? It was eccentric, this disparity of nakedness and clothedness, and the distance between them was a burlesque on what was revered as the closeness of the love act.

132

But the man's distress touched her. It was worsening. He sat there, caught in anxiety, his head to one side, his jaw tight; his whole being seemed afflicted. If there were going to be any words spoken, as he had said there would, it didn't seem possible he would say them. His directions notwithstanding, she sensed that he would need her to begin.

"Shall we start?" she asked. "What do we talk about?"

His body twisted. "I said I! Not we!" His voice was full of rage. And suffering.

With a pang she realized she had bungled again. She rebuked herself with how maladroit she was, missing every sign, too quick to speak, too anxious to be helpful. She wondered how Ellen had succeeded; surely she was more obtuse than Nora, less sensitive to mood, certainly more concerned with herself than with anyone else; how had she brought gratification to this wire-drawn sensitive man? Why couldn't Nora do as well?

She would be silent now, she told herself, not whisper a word, try to keep her hands from moving, her eyelids from fluttering.

He started to talk. It was a mumble at first, barely intelligible; art talk about middle distances and far, and whether perspective should ever be given credence, since it is by definition a falsification of distance. And that perspective was not discernible to a one-eyed man, it took two eyes to make the illusion, as it frequently took two truths to make a credible lie. Then, how best to treat sensibly with the transfer between what is actually seen and what one makes of it? It was in the transfer that something shatters and the truth is gone. As with conversation. From mouth to ear, from ear to mind, with the lie between, always the lie between; as with God, the lie in the explication, the truth only in the silent mystery. Then why pursue the explication?

Paradoxically, as his words became clearer, his meaning became more abstruse, until it all sounded like mystical claptrap. But then suddenly, out of the welter of meaninglessness, something emerged that she could understand. He was no longer talking about art but about love, aspects of the same torment, he said, a yearning for deliverance from pain. Yet, comprehensible as it now was, it was incoherent, as if he didn't want to be logical, and was afraid to understand himself. Abruptly, talking about women, he cried out:

"They make me love them too much!"

Rage, ache, confusion.

133

"Hurting and being hurt—a punishment, always a punishment—!"

He stopped.

He had apparently forgotten she was in the room, and now he noticed her. He couldn't go on. He tried. His lips moved. He murmured. His voice became muffled again. In a little while the words were blurred, like the mutterings in sleep, altogether unintelligible. At last he gave up speaking.

This was not as he had told her it would be. Something had gone wrong. He should, she imagined, have had his satisfaction by now. And she wanted it to have happened, wanted it for him almost with an ache. But it hadn't happened. He sat there, flaccid, all of him, his face, his muscles, his penis, his whole spirit.

He had instructed her: when it happens, take the money and leave, it's better if I don't see you. But now, having failed, both of them having failed, she didn't know what to do.

He saw her dilemma and pointed to the windowsill. "Take it," he said, "it's all right." Her indecision made it even more difficult for him. He seemed to be commiserating with her, pleading. "Go on—take it—it wasn't your fault."

"But it must have been . . . in some way." A need, a compulsion to know why Ellen had succeeded and she had failed. "How did you and Ellen . . . ?"

He was bewildered. "Ellen?"

Flushing but unable to inhibit the question, "What did she do?"

"But it never happened with her, either. It's never happened with a . . ." He was apparently going to say "prostitute" but was disconcerted, and stopped himself. "Never," he repeated, lamely. He was mortified. Again pointing to the money, he turned away from her. "Go on—take it."

In a rush, without taking the money, she departed. Outdoors, she realized with a blighted feeling that the day was over, even the dusk was gone; dark. She started down the stone stairs. Halfway to the bottom she had the impulse: run—another failure. Things might have gone well for him if she hadn't fumbled—the first time in a way unclear to her, the second time by speaking out of turn. No matter that he had been kind enough to exonerate her of blame. No matter also that Ellen too had failed; Ellen was a slob. She, Nora, sensitive one, bright one, sympathetic to the moods of others, should have succeeded. Another fiasco—run. She tried to resist, but

134

couldn't. The stairs were steep and she turned to water, running, running, cascading into the lower darkness.

The day after Nora met Cory Cavanaugh she had a nagging suspicion.

While she had shouldered some of the blame for the failure of their meeting, she had not faced the most important aspect of it: she had wanted to fail. As, very likely, she had wanted to fail in her encounters with the other so-called acquaintances.

She had tried, subconsciously of course, to behave like an amateur, because an amateur was exactly what she wanted to be.

She had said as much to Yoel. The greatest misfortune in being a whore, she had said, was that she loses that lovely illusion of the first time. The fantasy First Time, the ever-renewable virginity, the hymen that miraculously mends itself every time a woman falls in love. The ultimate myth that this time, this kiss, this fuck, this man—*he* is the one who knows her innermost secret, knows how to detonate her and send her skyrocketing. And this ecstasy, available time and time again—new, eternally new on each occasion—if only she can hang on to the single illusion, her amateur status. With this self-deception, she can fall in love a thousand times; without it, never. Nor will anyone fall in love with her. And she will—numbing thought—cease to believe in love itself.

But the worst aspect of her revelation: today, Nora had the appalling sense that she had wanted to be an amateur, not only as a creature of love, but in all her jobs as well. She had had a need to feel like a perennial beginner, blameless and unjudgeable; needed to be forgiven her faults as a child is forgiven them; needed even to be considered charming for them. And lovable. Love me for my frailties, love me for my innocence. Innocence . . . why did she so regret its passing?

Cory Cavanaugh . . . It wasn't her fault. He had *said* it wasn't. Perhaps it could never happen to him, perhaps he was a man in revolt against his sexual hungers; or, perhaps he was in revolt against someone he loved and was trying to violate *her,* in absentia, by having concourse with a whore; or, a man too pure for fucking, aspiring to an orderly heaven and frightened of the chaos in the fornicator's bed; or . . .

His fault, dammit, his. He had not made any professional demand upon her, he had asked her merely to sit across the room—

be an audience, an assistant . . . an amateur. As men insist. And as women have been content to be. In return for which, they live secure lives, comfortably out of danger. And therefore in dire peril.

Ellen telephoned. "What happened?" she said.

"Where?"

"Cavanaugh?"

"Nothing."

Ellen sniggered. "You too, eh?"

Go to hell, you bitch.

Ellen's laughter drifted off. "He liked you."

"What?"

"He did," Ellen continued. "He says you left your money, you idiot. He liked that. I guess nobody's ever done that before."

No, Nora thought wryly, a professional wouldn't.

"He wants you back."

"He . . . ?"

"Yes, he does," Ellen said. "Toward nighttime. Say, six o'clock. He wants to try it at twilight. Can you get there?"

An instant. Then: "Yes."

In Tel Aviv the twilights had been bronze. It was as if the sun refused to set; it would remain red-brown metal until the last instant, then die a brazen death. In Jerusalem the dusk was mauve. It went through all the shades of purpleness, magenta first, and amethyst and mulberry, and finally, in the last brief moment, a remembrance of faded violets. It was a lenitive twilight, soft, almost apologetically displacing daylight, regretful. Twilight in Jersualem was sad.

It was Nora's feeling when she came to Cory's door. As she was about to ring the bell, she saw the note Scotch-taped to the other side of the oval window.

Nora,
Go right in. I'll be a few minutes late, please wait for me.

C.

She opened the door, paused irresolutely in the tiny vestibule, then entered the studio. After having walked through the noisy bazaar, the large book-filled room seemed healingly still, and she felt sure all the other rooms would be the same. She would love to live here, she thought, for a little while. The house had been renovated well, which was to say it had been renovated little. Even inside, the tufa-like stone remained exposed except where it had to be retained with plaster; in some places the old sand-colored rocks were as rough-hewn as they had always been. The thickness of the pitted walls suggested old monuments and sacred tablets brought from the desert.

Since yesterday he had unpacked some canvases, framed and frameless. The long, ancient refectory table was now covered with old-fashioned oilcloth and his paints were spread in a jumble on it, his brushes still wrapped in newspaper, rubber-banded. The only clothes she saw were in a canvas knapsack; a sweater extruded from the top, and it all leaned like a collapsed scarecrow.

The disarray was not at odds with the friendly clutter of the room. But the paintings were. They were disturbing pictures in a way she could not understand; a man in love with perspective, all his lines going back and back, straining distance as if trying to make a single jump between near and far and nonexistent. And, for all the skill of the work, there was a lopsidedness about the artist's view, especially in the portraits. Something wrong, something perversely seen.

The twilight was settling more rapidly now. She looked at her watch. She'd been here a half hour, and no Cavanaugh. It could have been a mistake, she thought; she had come on the wrong day. But there was his note on the door. Perhaps he had reconsidered and didn't want to see her again. He might be out there somewhere, hiding, watching the house, waiting for her to go. Well, there was some relief in that. She glanced at her watch once more and decided to leave. As she started toward the vestibule, she heard the sound.

The outer door had opened and closed; he must be in the entryway. In a moment, he would be in the room, and he would again be sitting naked in one chair, herself in the other, the monologue proceeding.

It wasn't Cavanaugh. The man who stood there was a priest. He was tall, young, with the tightened muscles she had observed in men of propriety. He seemed a self-certain man, yet, at the instant, doubtful; doubtful of her, most likely, of whether he had come to the right place.

"Excuse me," he said. "The note said come in and wait. But it was addressed to Nora. Are you Nora?"

"Yes."

"My name is Farris. The C in the note—I hope it stands for Cory Cavanaugh."

"Yes, it does."

He seemed relieved. "I've come a distance to meet him," he said. "Could I wait for him?"

The request suggested an intriguing picture: the three of them sitting in a triangle, two of them listening to the soliloquy of the naked one. Restraining the smile, she raised her shoulders in a noncommittal way, and he apparently took it as permission.

He stared at her; she wished he wouldn't. Abruptly seeing her discomfiture, he seemed to realize what he was doing, and looked away. He made some neutral remark about Cavanaugh the artist as he glanced at the paintings in the failing light. The abstracts held him longest. He was talking almost, it would appear, to himself.

"I can't go back as far into the distance as he seems to want me to. It's a strain."

She looked at him. She had felt somewhat the same but would not have said it so succinctly. The line was, somehow, too neat; the man was word-sure.

"He's quite an exceptional artist, isn't he?" he said.

"I don't know anything about art," she replied. "I don't even know what I like."

He smiled. Patronizingly, she thought. She detected a certain unpleasant precision about the man; the neatness of speech, the security of movement. He had to be a pietist.

"Are you a friend of Mr. Cavanaugh's?" he asked.

An erratic thing happened. She had a sudden glimpse of Micky, dead. And an equally sudden flash of anger. "None of your goddamn business," she said.

It was an instant of absolute lunacy. The picture of Micky—why had it flashed in her mind, and what had it to do with him? Abruptly she made the connection, Micky the whore, Micky the Catholic, Micky who had died out of the faith, believing in nothing, lost. Micky whom the Church should have saved, and didn't. It was the Church's fault, the fault of this turn-collared man with the more-sacred-than-thou bewilderment on his face.

She felt a surge of shame, hot at first, then icy.

If he too had seemed shocked, as she was shocked at herself, she would immediately have apologized. But even his bewilderment was over now. He simply gazed at her, totally composed. And she was glad no apology had come to her lips.

"I didn't mean to pry," he said evenly. Then, with a touch of gentleness that she took to be smug sanctity. "And I don't think you meant to be that abrupt."

"I don't like priests."

She realized what she was doing: *trying* to shock him. She was attacking first before being attacked. Call him priest, she said, before he calls you whore. How summarily she had allied herself with the disreputable.

"Have you known many priests?" he asked.

"None. It's the Church I don't like, the organized Church."

"A lot of people don't," he said, unruffled. "Would you mind telling me your reason?"

"It lives in gaudy palaces and money-sucks the poor, it hates women and forces them to breed like pigs, it keeps its hired boys celibate while they pinch ass in the vestry."

"I don't pinch ass in the vestry."

She was surprised at his using the term. She had used the vulgar to scandalize, he had used it to disarm. Pawn to queen four.

"Are you Jewish?" he asked.

"Yes, I am."

"I don't like Jews," he said. "They're aggressive, they're clannish, they're Shylocks, all of them—especially American kikes. They'll sell their mother for a buck. Did you know they use the blood of Christian babies for their Passover services? They mix it with wine. I understand the proportions are two parts wine to—"

"That's not funny."

"I think it's as funny as anything you've said about the Church."

"I was attacking the Church, not Catholics. Not the people. You were attacking the Jewish people."

"The Arabs say the same about the Israelis. We're attacking Zionism, not the Jewish people. Doesn't that bother you?" Then, quickly, before she could answer. "Anyway, I don't believe a word I was saying about the Jews. I was hoping you'd confess the same about the Church."

She thought: how shrewd he is; watch your step. "Very crafty. I'm not as well-trained as you are."

"That's a cop-out. You're as well-trained as you have to be not to have stupid prejudices."

139

"You're a professional at this. I'm not."

She heard herself saying it, and an excitement happened in her. Professionalism: here was somebody who would shed light on the subject. Hurriedly: "You *are* a professional, aren't you?"

Warily, he evaded. "What do you mean, professional? I'm a priest—it's an odd word to apply to someone in my vocation."

"Why is it so hard to answer?"

Guardedly: "Well, yes—I do profess to a certain faith—in that sense I can be called a professional."

"Can you produce predictably?"

The question made him uneasy. "What do you mean, produce?"

"Whatever it is you make. What *do* you make anyway? Faith?"

"No, of course not." He was affronted. "You can't produce faith."

"What, then?"

"What does a doctor produce? He doesn't produce people, does he? At best, he delivers them. He doesn't produce good health—at best he delivers from ill health."

"Is that what you do? 'Deliver us from evil'?"

She had at last got at him. He was openly angry now, his rage a cold dignity. "If I had said that, I would consider I had committed a sacrilege. It would hurt me deeply to think I had fallen to that. The prayer—as you know as well as I—is to Our Father in heaven. If we are to be delivered from evil, He alone can do it. As to us, the closest any priest can come to freedom from evil is penance. It is strongly advised."

"Thanks. I'll come to confession some morning."

"It'll take more than a morning."

She felt his irony was petty, but sensed that she had behaved more shabbily than he had. Still, she could not, would not bring herself to any admission of bad behavior. On the contrary, she needed now to let him know that none of this had any deep significance for her. Not finding the proper words, she found a gesture. She raised her hand and made a frivolous movement with it, a purposely silly gesture, jangling her bracelets in the air.

They made a noise. He stared at them.

She stopped the movement. An instant of alarm. He sees the scar, she thought. But he couldn't, she reassured herself, the light was too dim, it was nearly nightfall. Bringing her arm down, she made another sudden movement with her hand. As she did, one of the bracelets caught on the pocket of her dress, and snagged. Then

140

she heard the clink of it as it hit the floor. It rolled. It was the cheap copper bracelet, the one from Greenwich Village. Now, where it stopped rolling it was nearer to him than to her. As she started toward it, he bent before she did, retrieved it and handed it to her.

Something slowed her down. Some cause she couldn't comprehend prevented her from taking it from him. Neither of them knew what the slowness meant, she felt sure of that, but she was the first to respond to the embarrassment. In an instant she would have taken it from him, but it was too late. He had already put it on the paint table, alongside the tubes of color. She didn't pick it up.

Something had happened that she couldn't understand, something that didn't make sense, that had no appositeness to anything that had occurred. She was upset and didn't know why. She had to get away.

"I won't wait for Mr. Cavanaugh anymore," she said. "Would you mind telling him I was here?"

"Not at all," he said politely. "Nora, isn't it?"

"Yes." He had said her name before, but apparently wasn't certain. "Thank you."

"You're quite welcome."

As she got to the door, she felt an onslaught of self-recrimination. She yearned to tell him she was sorry for having been a boor and a fool, and a brat with a temper tantrum, beating at the unavailing air. Too much to say, and too little. Quietly, with as much self-possession as she could manage, she departed.

As she walked out into the night, through the Jewish Quarter and into the passageway of the bazaars, she realized she had forgotten to retrieve her bracelet. She started to go back, but he might still be there, she supposed, and she couldn't bring herself to face him again. So she would surrender the copper trinket; she had never really liked it anyway. She wondered why she had ever bought such a cheap-looking thing.

141

Seven

MICHAEL HAD NO FEELING that the girl had specifically departed; rather, she had evanesced, like a cloud in variable winds, a dark cloud vanishing. Darkness, that was the quality in her that was most perturbing, the sense that she was a fathomless pit of trouble nobody could ever plumb. He didn't like her. Hostility had come too easily to her, without any seeming inner turmoil, with insufficient pain; she was a vandal.

He nipped the thought; he knew it couldn't be true. He didn't need to hear the girl in the confessional to know that every attack was self-directed. Then why had he jumped to the other conclusion, that she was wanton with animosity? To exempt himself from the obligation of thinking the other thing, that she was a needful person, asking for help? Yes, that was probably it; he wanted no part of such a burden. And why should he think of her as *his* encumbrance—she belonged to a different parish and a different faith, or, like so many educated Jews, no faith at all; her

142

priest, a psychiatrist, no doubt. Let the analyst give her absolution. That's what she paid him for, to shrive her of all those sins she committed—no, not against God, heaven forbid—but against the divinity of Self. Such pride, to derive more agony from the ego-attacking sins than the God-attacking ones. Forgive them, for they know not Whom they kill.

He was well quit of her.

He saw her bracelet.

It lay there on the paint table, forgotten, copper-red, as brash as she was. What a crudely made thing it was, badly wrought; what had she seen in it? She seemed a discerning person, and her clothes were quiet; what had she admired about such a crass thing? Perhaps it was its very unrefinement. He had known a Swiss business-man, a rich boor, who had a houseful of bad paintings, all done by terrible artists, all purchased to insult his wife who was a woman of exquisite and educated taste. Whom was the girl trying to insult?

Michael had no premonition he would do what he did.

He put the bracelet in his pocket.

No deliberation; he simply did it. When the thing was there, his fingers still on it, he didn't know which was colder, the metal or his hand. Put it back, he said, get rid of it, it's not yours, it belongs to her, and nothing that belongs to her has anything to do with you, not her hostilities, her guilts, her dark abysses of trouble, her generations of Jewish anger and hunger, nothing, not any of it belongs to you. Another diocese.

But he clung to it. At last he removed his hand from his pocket, but the bracelet did not come with it; it still lay there, hidden, resting against his thigh, and he could feel it there.

The room was dark now. He didn't hear the man enter. Nor would he have known that he was there, standing in the doorway, watching him, silent, a tall figure, sapling-thin, vigilant, ready to spring.

Michael turned from the drawing table and saw him. His first thought was: he saw me take the bracelet. But he couldn't have; too dark, and Michael's back had been to the stranger.

"Who are you?" the man said.

"Michael Farris—I'm a priest. Are you Cory Cavanaugh?"

"Yes." Measuring him: "Who sent you here?"

"Cardinal Cavanaugh."

Michael heard the click of the light switch. The room was suddenly staring white. The tall, thin man was young, with a face composed of a unity, all beauty. His skin particularly was beautiful, of a transparent fineness, like the skin of invalids; he wondered if the man had been ill.

"Why did my brother send you?" he asked.

"To beg you to come home."

"You needn't have bothered." His voice had a Gaelic lilt, but he spoke against the soft music of it, strongly, with definition. "I'm not going home."

It was final. Michael had been summarily dismissed. The young man had left him nothing, not a single fraction of hope, no unfinished business, the meeting was over. If he could think of something to talk about . . .

He found it. "I have a message for you. There was a young woman here."

"Oh, yes, Nora. When did she leave?"

"Not long ago. A few minutes before you arrived."

"Damn," he said. "I got delayed and couldn't get back in time." He considered it. "Was she angry?"

Michael smiled dryly. "Not at you. She was rather annoyed at me, however."

"At you? Why?"

"I'm afraid I asked her a meddlesome question."

"What question?"

"Whether she was a friend of yours."

He studied Michael with caution. "What did she say?"

The priest wondered whether he'd be able to say goddamn. "She said it was none of my business."

Cory breathed more easily. "Which, of course, it wasn't."

"Quite right."

"And she didn't tell you?"

"No."

Michael smiled and waited. He felt certain Cavanaugh didn't want to tell him his relationship with the girl; yet, surprisingly, he might. But the instant passed, without information. He was a man of tact, Michael supposed, who was not going to compromise a lady. They were obviously having an illicit romance of some sort; she was married, perhaps, or about to be. He liked Cavanaugh for the delicacy.

The artist was now expecting him to go. He was shutting Michael out by silence, then by completely turning away from him.

The priest reached for something else. "I like your work—very much. All of this—it's very strange and beautiful. I was especially moved by your portrait of Christ."

Cory turned and looked at him. "I've never painted a portrait of Christ."

Michael felt hindered, everywhere. "In your studio in Rome—there was a portrait in the closet."

"Oh, that. It's a study of my brother." Michael flushed and Cory noted it. "You didn't recognize him?"

As if caught in a lie: "No. I've seen a number of pictures of your brother, and that didn't look like him at all."

"It wasn't supposed to *look* like him." The artist was reproving him, at a distance. Then, more closely: "You've never met my brother, have you?"

"Not in person, no."

"You said he sent you."

"Yes—indirectly—through a letter to Cardinal Feradoti." This was his last chance to engage the man; he must use it carefully. "He sends you his affection. And especially Leda—she begs you to be careful . . . and to go home."

"Thank you for their . . . regards." He was saying less than he was feeling, and Michael sensed he had at last reached him. But the artist, not letting himself be weakened by any appeal by people who loved him, changed the subject. "That portrait . . . why did you say it was Christ?"

It had piqued him in some way, Michael realized. "Because the face had two almost incompatible sides to it. One was so ethereal —almost unbearably pure. The other side was a middle-aged man gone to corruption. I called it . . ." He paused, embarrassed.

"What?"

"The Burgher Christ."

The artist was silent. Michael couldn't tell what he was thinking. Yes, no question of it, he had gotten to the young man. He must pursue the advantage. He pointed to the other canvases. "And these—all of them—the perspective pulls at the eye, it almost hurts. It's strange."

Very quietly: "Yes, it is strange," he responded. "I don't consider that a virtue."

"But it's purposive, isn't it?"

"Yes, but it's a . . . fake."

"Fake? In what way?"

"It's not the perspective I see—it's what I feel, what I *will*. It takes two-eyed vision to draw a good perspective. That's what perspective is, isn't it, almost by definition."

"Well, if you want to do that—your vision's certainly good enough."

"I'm half blind."

He couldn't believe it. The man was making a macabre joke. He didn't know whether he was meant to smile.

Cory saw his discomfort. "I am," he continued. "My right eye is false. I was stabbed in a street fight when I was a kid. I had nothing to do with the fight—I was an onlooker." He smiled grimly. "Which I have remained—halfway." Then, as an afterthought: "I always say what I've just said as early as I can because sooner or later people notice that one eye blinks naturally and the other one's been taught. I'd like it if you'd notice, once and for all—and then not have to stare."

He stood there as if challenging Michael to gape at him. Discomfited, unwilling to stare, the priest could not turn away for fear Cavanaugh would detect some aversion . . . which Michael did not feel. On the contrary, he was drawn to the young man, and felt pity for his need to confess a frailty which was apparently so taken for granted by his brother and the Feradotis that they had not even mentioned it. No doubt they accepted his semi-blindness—as Michael accepted the Secretary's lameness—with rarely a thought. In Cory's mind, however, it was a constant presence. . . . The staring was over. It was the artist, not Michael, who turned away, grimacing as if he had a muscular pain.

"May I talk to you about going home?" Michael asked.

"No."

"I've come a long distance."

"You've come too far."

"Your brother is deeply worried about you."

"He's a fretting hen."

"No, he's not. You've been attacked and you've been threatened. You'll be attacked again. If not you, then your work. That beautiful portrait—slashed."

"I hated that portrait. The slashes were mine—I did it with a palette knife."

"You yourself did it?"

"Yes." Then, dryly: "So, if you're looking for vandals . . ."

146

Irritated: "There *are* vandals. Don't tell me you feel perfectly safe."

"But I do! I was getting telephone calls in America, I admit that, and a threatening letter, once. But the threat was not carried out—I was not kidnapped. And if I *was* in danger, it was there, not here."

"And nowhere else?"

"Nowhere else."

"Not even in Rome?"

"Not a bit."

"Then why did you leave Rome?"

"I got homesick for Jerusalem."

"Has this been your home?" Remembering his own nostalgia for a place he had never seen, he realized the question was too literal.

"No, not my home but . . . I have a companion here."

Again too literally he thought first of the girl, Nora; but it wasn't an earthly companion Cory had in mind. Feradoti had recalled him as a boy who had considered becoming a priest; hence, a person of some devotion. Michael had another quick recall—the portrait in the closet again. The artist, perhaps, had lied. He had indeed painted a portrait of Christ. Christ the companion, Christ the brother. He wondered why the man had denied the painting, had even desecrated it with a palette knife.

"Are you sure it was you who damaged the painting?"

"Why would I lie about that?"

"There have been so many ravages in Rome—atrocities. You insist that you haven't been attacked there, but your brother says—"

"My brother imagines things. We're Irish—we have banshees."

"Then he's imagining himself sick."

Stung: "Do you think that's my fault?"

"Yes, if you could ease his mind."

"Don't try to make me feel guilty about him—I've had enough of that!" His anger suddenly turned to hurt, to a specific physical trouble of some sort, and Michael again had the sense the young man was unwell. In pain.

Under better control, Cory continued. "Look . . . I love my brother. He is, in fact, more than a brother. I'm nearly twenty years younger than he is and he took care of me during all of my

147

childhood. He's all I have left—I love nobody the way I love him—if anything were to happen to him, I don't think I could stand it. But I can't—please tell him—I cannot live my life in a way that eases his mind. He doesn't live his life to ease mine. He's an inflexible reactionary. This Synod he talks about—if it actually happens—do you know what it'll do? It'll destroy everything Pope John ever dreamed of. He thinks the Christ I believe in is a sentimental dreamer—I think his Christ is ice! But mine—God help us—is nearer to the true one! Tell that to my brother! Tell him to read Matthew! Tell him—look to Matthew!"

Impassioned, quaking, on the verge of tears, he didn't know what to do with himself. His face was flushed, and when it returned to its former pallor, he was still trembling. "I don't say my brother doesn't love Christ—he does," he said. "But I think he loves the Church more. And I am certain he has no love of man."

"If he loves you—"

"It's not enough. I don't want to be the single love in his life. It terrifies me. I would almost rather . . ."

The end of the sentence, Michael knew, would inevitably have been that he'd rather do without his brother's love, never see him again. But the fact he couldn't finish the sentence, that it might be too unhappy a conclusion for Cory to contemplate, gave Michael hope.

And an even greater hope suggested itself. This young man, thinking as he did, feeling so deeply, might be an ally, a vital help to Michael's mission. "Hasn't it occurred to you that if there's any hope of changing your brother—you might be the only one?"

Startled, Cory turned. "Don't saddle me with that!"

Pursuing his advantage, Michael changed his tone. "Help me," he pleaded. "I believe as you do. I'm going back to New York—to try to persuade your brother to cancel the Synod. Please—come home and help me."

"I am not going home."

Everything in the room seemed heavy to Michael, the air, his clothes, the very passage of time. He had failed. He had done all he could do with what he knew. And nothing had come of it.

Yet, he liked the man. He had never met anyone like Cory, had never seen in any lay person a spiritual quality so disembodied, had never had the experience of a person blind in one eye who could give the impression of such clairvoyant sight, who could gaze so squarely at the truth and stand to look at it. Michael was touched by the man, and wanted to touch him. About to depart, he extended his hand. Cory took it.

Michael's clasp was not a tight one, not inordinately strong. But he again saw the physical distress in the artist's face, a dart of pain. Then, inexplicably, the head rolled back, he shuddered and slumped to the floor.

"Cory!" Michael knelt beside him. "Cory, what is it?"

Cavanaugh reached to his side. The pain didn't leave his face. Michael pulled open the young man's jacket. His shirt had blood on it. Undoing the buttons, Michael pulled the cotton back. There was a bandage; the blood had dried.

"What happened?"

"In the bazaar," the young man murmured. "Somebody came behind me—a knife—I didn't see who it was. The police came. Somebody—a doctor—he put the bandage on. It's not serious—not deep. But—not used to pain—not used to it."

"Can I get you something? It doesn't seem to be bleeding anymore—can I get you something for the pain?"

"No—nothing. Your handshake—you have strong hands."

"I'm sorry—I'm terribly sorry."

Suddenly it all came clear. "You weren't telling me the truth," Michael said. "Were you?"

". . . No."

"There have been more threats, haven't there?"

"Yes."

"And the painting . . . ?"

"They did it." His voice was dismal. "Whoever they are. . . . Oh, Christ."

"Cory—please—will you come home with me?"

"No," he said, but there was no longer any conviction in his voice. "Not right away."

"But soon," Michael urged. "How soon?"

"I don't know . . . but I will."

"You'll go home?"

A moment, then: "Yes."

"I have your promise?"

"Yes."

"When?"

149

"I don't know," he repeated. "Oh, Christ."

"Tomorrow's not too soon, Cory."

"Yesterday wasn't, either." He tried to smile. "Oh, Christ."

Immediately after leaving Cory, Michael decided to telephone Feradoti. Relieved to have won the young man's promise to go home, he was eager to report it to the Cardinal.

The priest stayed, while in Jerusalem, in an Austrian Catholic hospice bordering a tiny green park full of olive trees and oleanders. The main building had been a monastery once, and hardly any of its cloistered rigors had been softened. There was no bounty of amenities, and the only telephone was in an oak-paneled common room where anyone might overhear.

He spoke guardedly to Feradoti. "I just left him. I'm sure he'll go home. He gave me his word."

"Was it difficult?"

"In a way, yes. But then . . ." He paused, warily seeking a way to express it. "There was an accident."

"I understand," Feradoti said. "Not serious?"

"No, I don't think so."

"You've done very well, Michael. You've earned a friendly introduction to Cardinal Cavanaugh." He heard the reservation in the Secretary's voice. Then, unreservedly: "Will you stay in Jerusalem for a while?"

Michael yearned to stay at least a week. But in America there was a Synod to prevent, and in the Vatican an old man lay dying. How could he go sightseeing, poking around in Christ's dead relics while His living vicarage might be arrogated? Yet, for how long had he dreamed to see the Holy Land, and when would he come this way again? Still, if His Holiness should die tomorrow . . .

"How is he?" Michael asked.

"He is about the same, Michael. We must stop counting the poor man's breaths." Then, warmly: "You could give yourself a week of Jerusalem, Michael. Have your joy of it."

An hour later, Michael was still debating: go or stay. He felt the time pressure acutely, the Synod being planned. But there was something else bothering him, even more distressful to his spirit. In Jerusalem he felt the divine presence everywhere, although he had not yet made any personal communion with it. He was reliving Christ's history, yes, but no hint of the passion. And he felt—com-

150

pulsively—that his soul must in some way become witness to it, here in Jerusalem. And if no such thing happened, it would be a terrible sign that in some way—during these practical, transactional years in the offices of the Church—he had lost his sensitivity to the human ecstasy of Jesus.

Michael rented a car. Without itinerary, with random pleasure, a tourist, he drove everywhere, to Bethlehem and to the Shepherds' Field where the angel foretold the birth of Jesus, to Bethany to see where Lazarus arose from the dead, to Jericho where the blind Bartimaeus saw impossibly far across the desert. He stood on the Mount of Olives but couldn't bring himself to enter the clutter of the modern city where they said he would find the so-called Tomb of Mary.

He went to Mount Hermon and to the desert. In the desert, where he should have thought of epiphanies, he thought instead of the man's actual existence, that He was not only a spirit but a person of actual fact.

And it was out of the commonplace of His *physical being* that the mystery was able to spring. And to endure. So many spiritual divinities had faded, so many golden gods had turned to clay, was it not a wonder that one man, born mundane, broken in body and reviled by enemies on all sides, betrayed by His own disciples, slain time and again by crusaders who slaughtered in His name, traduced and misunderstood and misused even by those who professed to love Him, was still the most moving figure in the troubled story of mankind? And the answer for Michael—at least it must be part of the answer in any moment of uncertainty—was the very banality at the heart of the wonder: *He lived.* Here, in these hills, these villages, this desert, by this river, He walked, He slept, He was hungry and He ate. He wept tears here, He dreamed, He talked till His throat was dry, He measured wood and cut it to size and knew the use of nails long before they were used on Him; here He loved God and man, and may have been angered by both; He longed for home, He wondered how it would have been to watch the world grow older. Which He didn't do. He died.

That He got to live forever was almost beside the point. The point was He was not a myth, but a man. Which made Him lovable. So lovable indeed that it was through Christ we came to know that God too was not all awesomeness; between thunderbolts, there was love in Him as well. It was good, at last, to know this about the Almighty. Perhaps He had always been that way and

151

we had never been aware of it; perhaps He became that way as He grew older, mellowing; or perhaps His loving Son helped him to become that way. Whatever, the carpenter helped us to know this about Him. To have changed our stern Father from justice and fury to mercy and love—it was perhaps Jesus' kindest gift of all.

This was what Michael's mind told him about his travels in the Holy Land. His mind alone. Respectful, wondering, but unmoved.

One afternoon he drove along the gentle Sea of Galilee, then upward to the mountain. As sunset and a misty wind took over the hilltop, he heard the beatitudes all around him, all that were blessed, the meek and the merciful, the hungry, the mourning, the peacemakers, the persecuted, the poor in heart. He thought of Feradoti and speculated: for how many of those qualities is he blessed? More than any man he knew. How right it was that he should be the Pope. And how wrong if it should be Margotto.

He must get back to the work of it, then, he must leave the Holy Land.

He came down from the eminence and drove back to Jerusalem. All the way, he was overcome with a deep melancholy. He had felt as Cory did, that this was his home, he had a companion here. But the companion had long since disappeared. He had been tracking the remembrances of Him, a chronicle.

Enough. Tomorrow would be his final day here, he determined. And he had not even seen the Stations of the Cross. At first he had thought he would leave the best for last. He had known that nothing would ever compare with his walk along the Via Dolorosa, following the path of the final passion. He wanted it to be his last journey in Jerusalem as it had been his Redeemer's. There would not be a single step of the way that would not be familiar to him, not a station where he had not ached and loved and been blessed. He only hoped he could do it without showing the excesses of his emotion, without publicly weeping.

That was his feeling at the beginning of his tour; but later, when his disappointment with the Holy Land had dejected him, he barely wanted to see the Stations at all. He dreaded it.

But one cannot, certainly a priest cannot visit Jerusalem and not walk the steps of the last pathway. So, the following day, on a radiant Jerusalem morning, he was at the Bethesda courtyard. *Now there is at Jerusalem, by the sheep market, a pool, which is called in the Hebrew tongue Bethesda, having five porches.* It was there that Michael started, then to St. Mary's under the arch of great stones, to Pilate's Judgment Hall where Jesus was sentenced, scourged, the crown of thorns, Behold the Man. Then to the Second Station where He took up the cross. Then the meeting with His mother . . .

And it was emptier than Michael had dreaded.

He was feeling nothing.

It was as if he had stripped himself naked, had laid himself bare to feeling, had exposed every raw nerve to be touched, to be hurt if necessary; as if he had asked: let me feel something of what He felt, let me be agonized. . . .

And nothing had happened.

Worse, if he had any sensibility of the place at all, it was aversion; all he experienced was the worldly thing around him. It was a commercial marketplace, a winding, dirty, twisting alleyway of haggling and peddling. It was all pagan, an idolatry of merchandise, a Babel of many-tongued money talk, mean and noisy. Everything was for sale—plastic Marys and cardboard Christs and white Jesus donkeys, mechanized and wired for sound so they could bray.

Of the fourteen Stations of the Cross, not all of them were visible; some, he was indifferently told, did not exist. One of the signs he discovered on the ground. It was the figure 6, recently painted on a stick of dry and wasted wood. He lifted the splintery thing and wondered from what wall it had fallen. Then, seeing the nailhole on a sign that advertised Arabian camel's hair jackets, he took his shoe off and nailed up the sign again.

What he hated most was the smell of food around him. There were the huge round pretzels and felafel and, everywhere it seemed, the smell of fish and the roasting of lamb. Orange crushes and lemon squashes and Coca-Cola spelled out in Hebrew and Arabic letters.

Well, what did he expect, he rebuked himself, wine and wafers? If this was a commercial marketplace now, what was it then? Did He not have to carry His cross through the crowd of buyers and sellers? Was that not one of the meanings of the cross? Did He not have to drive the moneychangers out of the temple?

That was the reality; why was it not enough for Michael? Why did it not speak deeply to him? What romantic picture of Jesus then and Jesus now did he constantly have to reconcile? Was not the *fact* of Golgotha, like the fact that he lived, enough? Why did he need the mystery?

If he had come here for pain, he was feeling it. Of a different

153

kind. The aching, gnawing sense that some way or other he was corroding his faith. And he couldn't tell how, or why.

In the Church of the Holy Sepulcher, he finished the last Station of the Cross, he knelt and, for a long time, prayed. He begged for clarity, for divine grace, for deliverance from doubt.

Retracing his footsteps, going backward along the Stations of the Cross, he felt as heavy as the crucifix itself.

Then it happened.

It was the most commonplace occurrence in the world. And it was *in* the world. As he got to one of the early Stations, he heard the voice of a woman. He turned to look at her—an ordinary woman, middle-aged, American probably, a matron, carrying an unstylish purse, wearing worn-down shoes. And she said softly, to someone at her side:

"Here He stumbled."

With sadness, yes, but not with any dramatic display of it, only simply, as an old act of an old human tragedy.

Here He stumbled.

And precipitously, for no reason he could ever explain, Michael's eyes filled and he cried. There was no logic in the tears, simply the sense of Christ the man, the frail one.

Here He stumbled.

The fact of frailty, yes, the imperfection of the man, the liability to weakness, the defect somewhere, hence His own ache, possibly, that He might be faulty, His pathetic error that He might not be all He should have been. Here was his dread of peccability, perhaps, and the mystery of His being God's son, albeit faulty, faulty.

Faulty on the way to Golgotha. And then, perfection. Water into wine, wine into blood, wafer into body. This was the mystery.

Michael couldn't stand the joy of it. Here, he thought, here, no matter what this place looked like now, no matter what it was then, here He stumbled. Here, when He carried the fearful burden, here, through these crowds, through spittle and revilement, here, when He knew there was no earthly return, when all the way was upward to agony and Golgotha, here the man's exhaustion with life itself almost brought Him down, His heart momentarily went out of Him, and here He stumbled. Here the Son of God was all human, back nearly broken, knees bleeding on the stones, here He was all weariness, yes, even afraid, and here He stumbled.

Michael wept and wasn't ashamed. Oh, God, he prayed, give me more tears to wash away the pain. Yet, he didn't want the pain to

154

stop, for he knew he was living an ecstasy, the first he had ever had, and might never have one again. But perhaps he would never have need of another. For hours the rapture glowed in him and he knew he would have it all his life.

Toward evening, however, he had a wave of misgiving. He was worried about a quality within himself that set him at odds with his time. For all his claims of being an intellectual, he was an emotional man; for all his expertise as a doer and handler, a judicious man of affairs, he was a mystic. He might be able to hide it while maneuvering for daily bread, but he was a mystic by night, in his mind of God. And his days and his nights were ceaselessly at war with one another.

At midnight, as he packed to leave Jerusalem, his mood was getting blacker. Tomorrow, on an El Al plane, he would be bound for Paris and New York, and a task for which he felt inadequate.

In the midst of packing he had a disquieting experience. He was reassembling his clothes and books in order not to have to carry too much hand luggage onto the plane, when he came across it.

The bracelet. Seeing it again, he tensed. He told himself that he had forgotten he still possessed it, but he knew it was a half-truth, unconvincing. For nearly a week it had been subliminally in his mind, waiting to leap at him.

Why had he not returned it?

Well, he had tried, was his defense. Two days after the encounter with the girl, he had gone back to Cavanaugh's house to ask the young man to return the bracelet to his woman friend. He had been resolutely prepared to take whatever embarrassment might come with Cory's inevitable question: why in the world had he taken it in the first place? He was prepared, too, to mumble over answers.

But there had been no need. When he arrived at Cory's place, it was already deserted; the door was locked, the artist was gone; through the windows Michael could see that the house was empty.

The man, true to his promise, had returned home. Michael felt a glow of accomplishment; even felt that he had earned, in small part, his week of felicity in the Holy Land.

But what would he do with the bracelet? He had indeed tried to return it. But two days later. Why two days, why not the same day, that very evening, or at least the following morning?

Why had he kept the bracelet?

Stolen it.

Come now, he scolded, no melodramatics here; there had been no theft. Some way or other he had meant to get the bracelet back to the damnable girl. He still would. If he knew where she lived, he'd stick it in an envelope and—begone!—post haste. Not knowing, he would have to find a way, but he certainly didn't want the damnable ugly thing.

Then why had he kept it? The clue was in the word "damnable," which had occurred twice in a single thought. The fascination by the damned. And the provocation. Everything about her provoked him—her smug Jewish intellectualism, her pseudo-socio-psycho-big-city-Manhattan pap, her attack on the Church. He had taken her damn bracelet for revenge.

Revenge? He didn't have that kind of pettiness; an assistant curate had once said of him that he lacked the pissy spites. Yet, he did have rages. No . . . wrong size.

Was he, for God's sake, attracted to the girl? He had seen himself on a number of occasions, tempted; to be honest about it, enticed, almost to the edge of appetite. Hester . . . but he had been a child. As an adult . . . they had been different kinds of women—a blonde leanness once, broad of cheekbone, a young Valkyrie woman, warring; but whatever field of battle she hovered over, she could never count him one of her slain. Another time, a pixie Irish girl, born of leprechauns. Without incident.

Nothing like this Nora. They were out of romantic mists; she was a total realism. He could never be attracted to a woman so packaged in palpability. And even they, come to think of it, even those fantasy creatures had never truly aroused him, not to carnality. He had to face it: he was a wet dream man. And must always be. As the rectory joke went, that was the long and short of it. The changing of night sheets . . . oilcloth on the bed.

Oilcloth was a different image; he mustn't think of that.

Packing, repacking, suddenly frustrated with everything, he picked up the bracelet and threw it against the wall.

What an asinine thing to do, he thought, and he didn't know which he meant, throwing the bracelet or keeping it.

Slowly, forlorn and unaccountably worried, he crossed the room, bent over and picked up the bracelet. The unsightly object had something else wrong with it now; dented. Damn, he had damaged the girl's unlovely bauble.

Oilcloth.

Stay back.

156

Why did he associate the two occurrences? One had nothing to do with the other; there were no similarities, none at all. Besides, it had happened when he was a child, years out of mind. No, not out of mind; it would stay with him always. As Christ stumbling would always be the holy ecstasy of remembrance, oilcloth would be its obscenity.

He must close the suitcase, snap the locks shut, get to sleep at once, and forget about it. Quickly, he washed his face, brushed his teeth, finished his breviary and went to bed.

In deep darkness, he felt the damp. At first he thought he had urinated; then thought, a dream. He awakened with an imprecation and threw the room into electrical brightness.

There was no dampness on his bed.

Oilcloth.

He would have to face her again. Hester . . . come.

He was nine years old. He had been in two orphanages, this was the third, the worst. There was never enough of anything, not food, not love, not hours to sleep, not books to read, not playthings. Nobody got physically punished, except for an ear tweak now and then, but they were tight-faced nuns with bitter tongues. They used the catechism like a cat-o'-nine tails. Their Lord was a hemophiliac, running wounds.

Michael, at that age, had just started to think, and thinking frightened him, it was an illness. Sometimes, more aggravatingly, it was a sin. Every thought focused his mind on one unhappiness or another—fright of the dark, certainty of failure, incessant hunger, guilt plus guilt, and loneliness.

Then, at the age of nine, long after he had ceased to do so as an infant, he began to urinate in his sleep. When the wet bed was discovered, he was summoned to the Mother Superior's office and, in secret, beaten. He had never heard of anybody being beaten at the orphanage, but the woman knew she was safe in doing so: Michael would be the last to tell.

She had struck his knuckles many times with a ruler and it puzzled him, even then, why she had chosen to punish his hands. Later, much later, he realized that while there could have been no question in her mind that the soil in his bed was urine, not semen, she associated the act with masturbation; hence, the punishment fit the crime. It was his first experience with guilt by association.

He wet the bed a second time; a second time he was beaten, this time, bloody.

That morning, from the trash can, he salvaged an old piece of discarded oilcloth. It had had a design on it, squares of blue and white. Most of the blue had been scrubbed away; even the white had been abraded down to the yellow canvas backing. He folded the oilcloth into a small bundle, put it inside his shirt, and buttoned the shirt over it. Carrying it upstairs to the dormitory, he hid it under the mattress of his bed.

From that moment, his bedwetting was not detected. Nighttimes, he would stay awake until the other boys were asleep, then turn his sheet down, lay out the oilcloth and sleep on the clammy surface until dawn. Before the others were awake, if he had wet the bed, he would wipe the dampness off his mattress protector, secretly stow it away again, make his bed and face the dry world.

For four or five weeks he was able to get away with it. Then, one predawn morning, he was discovered. Not by one of the boys, not by one of the sisters, but by a girl standing at the doorway, peering at him out of the hallway's shadows. Her name was Hester.

She was a newly arrived orphan, older than Michael, in her early teens. She was not beautiful but she had a certain vivacity, a quickness of mind, a mercurial sense of self-preservation, darting, unpredictable, and eyes that were a little mad. What first captured Michael's interest in her was a habit she had, a strangely naked habit with her hands: she stroked her breasts—openly, unashamedly seeming to have a compulsion to do so, as though she had not yet, and possibly never would, become accustomed to their growing; as if she could feel the growing underneath her stroking hands.

She saw him with the oilcloth, that morning, and must have smelled it. The same afternoon, in the dark corridor behind the kitchen, she said to him softly, "Piss your bed, don't you?"

He started to run and she grabbed him. "Don't worry," she said. "I won't tell anybody."

They became friends. At least that's what Hester said they were, friends, although Michael was not quite sure what the word signified to her. There was something frightening about being Hester's friend.

"Meet me down there," she would say.

Down there was a space between the boiler room and the laundry. Nobody ever used it; there wasn't even a light. It was not really a room, not even a corridor; it was simply a darkness.

"All right—go ahead," she would say.

"No, I don't want to."

158

"Go ahead—we're friends—go ahead."

He would unzip his trousers. She would reach in and hold him in her hand. He would be erect immediately, and namelessly excited, full of fright, full of wanting and wanting, and not knowing exactly what was expected of him. What was expected of him was only what she was doing, holding him, caressing him. Nothing happened to Michael; that is, he never had an emission, nothing even remotely resembling the orgasms of his later dreams; he was either too young or too terrified. But something did seem to happen to Hester, he didn't know what. Nor would she tell him; only, at those times, her eyes were even wilder than usual, more terrifying. And he would know it would soon be over when she flung her head back, her mouth open, a rivulet of drivel coursing out of it.

The experience occurred a number of times per week, for nearly a month.

Then the Deardons arrived.

They were pleasant people, both about as old as the Mother Superior, who had once said she was forty-three. One day Michael was called to the office. The Deardons sat on one side of the Mother Superior's desk and he was told to sit at the other. Then the stern nun behind the desk started to ask him questions, disorganized ones—did he have a temper, did he know his catechism, did he ever lie or steal, did he always repent at confession and afterward—ridiculous questions, to all of which she knew the answers.

When she was finished, Mrs. Deardon asked him if he remembered his mother.

"Only a little," he replied. Then, unwittingly striking on the shrewdest answer: "I don't want to remember her."

Mr. Deardon then asked him if he was strong, if he was healthy.

"Yes, sir," Michael replied.

"Any bad habits?"

The boy's heart sank. Were they trying to trap him into telling about the oilcloth? "No, sir," he said. "I don't think so, sir."

When they departed, the Mother Superior turned to Michael, seeming to debate whether to tell him. Then she uttered the first gentle words he had ever heard from her. "You did very well, Michael. And they may adopt you."

He started to stammer with happiness. He had liked them. More important, they had liked him, he had felt that they did, he had been sure of it. He wanted desperately to be adopted by them, he wanted this joy to continue.

159

"When will I know?" he asked.

"They'll come again."

They came the next week, and the meeting went even better this time. That evening, excited, filled with more felicity than he could handle alone, he told Hester about it.

"What's so good about it?" she said.

"Adopted!" It wasn't something for words; only jubilation. "It's being adopted!"

"If they don't like you, they send you back. Like sour milk."

"They don't."

"You'll see."

Two days after their second visit, a present arrived from them. It was a locomotive, part of a set of Lionel electric trains. There were no other cars, no tracks, no sidings, nothing else; only the heavy, foot-long, handsome locomotive, brilliant blue, as beautiful as anything he had ever seen. With it, a note:

> Dear Michael,
> This is a promise of other things.
>
> Mr. and Mrs. Deardon

He carried the locomotive with him every minute of the day, and the next day as well. He couldn't be parted from it. Nothing had ever been so precious to him, not even the books, not even *Through the Looking Glass.*

On the morning of the day they were to arrive on their third visit, Michael was called out of class. He knew what it was about; his anticipation flew like a bird uncaged. Carrying the locomotive, hugging it under his arm, he ran down the fire escape stairway, three steps at a time, flung himself through the street floor doorway and streaked down the corridor to the Mother Superior's office.

As he went into the entryway, he heard Hester's voice:

"He does things to me—and he wets his bed. This is his oil-cloth."

It never occurred to him that they might be willing to hear his side of it; it never occurred to him that whatever he and Hester had done, whatever sins he had committed, whatever vile wetnesses, they might all be absolved outside the confessional as generously as they had been absolved within it. All he felt was heartbreak and betrayal, and the collapse of his hope, his world.

And rage.

160

As Hester came out, he lifted the locomotive. Down on her face, down again, down, down, till the blood gushed.

The others came running.

She was in the hospital for two months. He was arraigned in juvenile court, given a three-month sentence to reform school, and released on probation after a month. When he came out, he was mercifully sent to another orphanage.

That was not the end of it.

Years later, when he was in his first year at the seminary, somebody told him Hester was in St. Francis Xavier's, a mental institution. No, he was assured, his assault upon her had had nothing to do with her emotional collapse; she had been, nearly always had been, a sick, psychotic girl.

But he couldn't get her out of his mind. She had betrayed him because she loved him, he kept telling himself, and she couldn't bear to have him taken away. She had known no other way to show her love than by betrayal. Perhaps it was equally true of Judas. Knowing that in Jesus' lifetime the agony had already begun for Him—He knew He was going to be executed—Judas shortened his misery. Not Hester's motive, certainly—but in both cases, betrayal as an act of love. How perverted we are, he thought, since the start of time.

The thought of Hester in the asylum started to plague him. The night terrors began, the fondling animal, the suctorial hideousness emerging from sickly darkness, kissing him, his mouth, his eyes, his penis, pulling at his tongue; then the wetness, the shame of dreams.

At last he brought himself to visit her. In her twenties now, she had no resemblance to the fourteen-year-old. She was, in fact, more beautiful than she had been; she had grown up to her large features; her eyes, with the old wildness, had an exotic otherworldliness about them. There was hardly any sign of the scar on her face, and she said she could not remember him, not at all.

But the way she put her hand on his arm once, and caressed it with a fierce hungriness—he thought she might be lying. When she took her hand away from his arm, she lifted her fingers to her mouth; she sucked them, then sucked her palm, kept sucking it. Yet she didn't seem in any other way deranged, except that nothing she said was absolutely clear. Until he started to go; then she seemed desolate a moment, after which she said with a weirdly

161

lewd smile: "Priestie, eh? Won't poke your peenie in the chalice, will you?" And she screamed with laughter.

No, her madness was not of his making. Then why could he not exorcise her? If he knew the exact nature of her bedevilment—and what it had to do with the exact nature of his own—perhaps he could. Perhaps, one day he would.

But not tonight. Tonight Hester was a presence, an aching, guilty presence, a bloodlust he had never fully expiated. No matter into how many confessionals Hester had accompanied him, he had never left her in the booth. Always, she came away with him, always the curse of the unatonable.

And here she was again. Brought back by what?

By a bracelet? It was inconceivable to him that there could be any relationship between the two. One was a sin already perpetrated; the other was a sin not even contemplated. There was no connection between them, nowhere, not in the world of logic, in the world of concrete phenomena, in the world of foreseeable event. It could only be a figment of his mind.

Perhaps, that was enough.

Eight

WHEN NORA WAS in high school a teacher compli-
mented her for clarity of mind; orderly thinking, she said, came
naturally to the girl. She was wrong. Orderly thinking was a pain.
Her mind jumped from A to J, then back to B; frequently she
missed C, the major point. To overcome this fault, which she knew
she had, she forced herself to write outlines that followed the
proper successions of the alphabet and the well-behaved graduations
of 1, 2, 3. She outlined everything; made lists, graphs, diagrams—
she skeletonized her adolescence, in x-ray form.

The day after her encounter with the priest, Nora decided to go
back to Cory Cavanaugh's and recover her bracelet. Whether she
liked the damn thing or not, she ought to have it, and she outlined the
reasons:

1. It was hers.
2. It had cost money; money shouldn't be wasted.

3. She mustn't start getting sloppy with forgetfulness, leaving bits and pieces of herself here, there, everywhere.

The reasons were all in order, but they were all bull; she knew it. She didn't care whether she ever saw the bracelet again, but she did care about seeing Farris again. She *wanted* to see him. (Even *with* outlining, she had left out the major C.)

Perhaps if she went back for the bracelet he might happen to be there. Or if he wasn't, Cavanaugh might drop a hint as to where she could accidentally bump into him. Or, that failing, she might barefacedly *ask* Cavanaugh to drop a hint.

She knew perfectly well why she wanted to see him. She outlined a set of reasons:

1. To tell him off. He had gotten the better of the argument, she felt, but only because she hadn't done her best, hadn't marshaled her case properly. Who the hell did he think he was with his goddamn self-righteous ironies? The blood of Christian babies, indeed. She could tell him a thing or two about the blood of babies. She could drop the names of a few concentration camps and tell him a thing or two about the blood of babies. The Catholic-comfortable son of a bitch.

2. To apologize. She had provoked the argument, not he. She had behaved like a crud and he had behaved like a decent, civilized man. No matter how tight his collar, no matter that it was turned, he had treated her as a person, she had treated him as a priest. It wasn't his fault that he was in a Christ-bitten profession, or even if it was his fault . . . comparing professions was an idiot game for her to be playing.

That reason number 1 and reason number 2 were at cross-purposes bothered her.

What bothered her most was that Farris was attractive to her. And what the hell kind of relationship could they ever have? None. Well, what was so bad about that? A none-relationship might be the ideal kind to have with him, with any man.

He was young, personable, bright, quick-spirited. What was most fascinating: he had a few illusions left. She knew without asking—felt it in her woman-bones, saw it on his brow—that his illusions had not yet dulled or corroded. He lacked the one dismal anomie that she saw in many men, the world fatigue, the exhausted morality, the excitement for living gone, bled white. She hadn't realized that the loss of illusion was something that did not affect the spirit alone; it enervated the body. It made the muscles more flaccid, the eyes less

keen, the voice less resonant. And this man had that extra vitality
. . . hence, sexuality.

No . . . not to think that way . . . a priest.

Well then, they could talk together, perhaps argue and eat together, go on walks through Jerusalem together—and have absolutely no relationship. It would be perfect. She would not have to
flatter or pamper him, she would not have to hear him maunder
about his worldly ambitions, his deals, his trickery or betrayal of
others, his shrewd handling of the materials of art or science, she
would not have to reassure his psyche or his gonads—because there
would be no sexual score hanging in the balance. They might even
have a discussion about an abstract idea. Without ruffling egos.

Balls.

Still . . .

She went back to Cory's place. When he let her in, the studio was a
disordered mess. He was packing for departure.

His face was crimson with embarrassment. "I'm sorry I missed you
last night. I was detained longer than I . . ."

She helped him. "It's all right. I don't want to bother you—I see
you're leaving."

"Yes—going back. Something suddenly came up. I hope you came
for . . ." His discomfort worsening: ". . . your money."

"No, I don't want that," she said. "My bracelet."

"Your what?"

"Bracelet. A copper one. I left it right there."

He looked at the table she was indicating. He hadn't as yet
gathered his paints together, nor his brushes; the surface was a clutter.
He pushed a few objects around, then looked at her.

"You left a bracelet?"

His puzzlement was excellent, she thought, a marvelous fake. True,
there was no bracelet on the table, but she had seen the priest put it
there, and she had indeed left it there. Did this weird man really want
the damn thing, she wondered, and what perversity would he perform
with it?

"I'm sure it was there," she said. "It fell off and . . ." She let the
sentence dangle, then tried to find a way to save his face. "Perhaps
without noticing, you put it . . ." She pointed to his still-open knapsack.

"Oh, no," he said with a smile. "I'd surely have noticed. A bracelet,
after all."

She realized her face must be showing her disbelief. He saw it. "I

165

give you my word," he said lamely. Then, the inspiration: "Here—if it wasn't too expensive, I'll be glad to . . ."

He reached into his pocket, brought out some bills.

Suddenly he stopped and she saw his expression change. In that instant she knew what had occurred to him: *she* was fabricating. She was holding him up for more money than a sex trick would have cost him.

In a rush: "No, really," she said, "it doesn't matter—it was a cheap bracelet—not worth a damn."

They sensed that neither of them was lying.

". . . Strange," he said.

"Yes."

"Unless Father Farris . . ."

"But . . . I can't imagine why," she murmured.

"No . . . me either." He paused. "Unless he thought of returning it to you."

"But he—we're strangers."

"Yes," he agreed. "Exactly."

They were silent. She felt as if they had come to the bank of a river—uncrossable—no bridge, no fording place. She jumped in: "Do you know where I can reach him?"

He laughed sheepishly. "You know—it's peculiar—I don't. We're strangers too. I never met him until yesterday. I have no idea where he's staying. I do know he's going back to the States, however—New York. He's going to see my brother."

"Who's your brother?"

"He's a cardinal—he's—"

He stopped. He had apparently forgotten, momentarily, that she was a prostitute, and had said more than he intended. He obviously regretted it.

She wanted to ease his mind. "I'm sorry I bothered you," she said.

"Possibly you made a mistake—you might *not* have left it here," he said. She knew he was wrong but didn't want to be insistent; she said nothing. Obviously realizing she was being tactful, he said, as helpfully as he could, "Maybe it'll turn up. Maybe it'll just appear one morning, in the mail."

"But he won't know where to send it—I mean, if he really has it." An idea struck her. "Will you be likely to see him again?"

"Oh, probably, yes. I could possibly . . ." He changed his mind. "No, I can't see how I can ask him if he walked off with . . ."

166

"No, of course," she said hastily.

The absurd eccentricity of it struck them both simultaneously; they laughed and quickly the laughter was over.

"Have a good trip," she said.

And she was outdoors. Down the steps again, along the cobbled street, walking through the bazaar.

He had taken it!

A freakish excitement surged in her. Something bizarre and marvelous. The priest had taken her bracelet—possibly for the same reason she had gone back for it: he had wanted to see her again. Yet, there was something about it that didn't make sense. If he'd wanted to see her, all he would have had to do was ask Cory where to find her. And he hadn't done that; if he had, Cory would have commented on it. Good thing he didn't ask, she thought. What if he had, what would Cory have told him? "That girl? What do you want with her? She's only a harlot of Jerusalem." However, no fear of that. He'd never have admitted to a priest that he was using a hooker . . . unless, in the confessional.

She was quite sure none of it had happened; they hadn't exchanged a word about her. And she was glad.

The shine of her excitement was untarnished. Something glittered in her, a brightness that hadn't happened for weeks, for months, certainly not since she had come to Israel, a dazzle she hadn't expected she would ever feel again.

A delightful fantasy occurred to her. As she was enjoying it, she realized how long it had been since she had had such a delicious vagary.

She was, in the fiction, walking right here, through the Jewish section of the bazaar. And Farris was with her. She was teasing, offering to buy him a plastic mezuzah, complete with tacks to nail it on his doorpost, and he was telling her she didn't pronounce it properly, she certainly couldn't recite the Hebrew prayers inside it as well as he could, half-baked Jew that she was; that she knew how to say Eucharist far better than she could say *tvillin*, and whose *tzitzits* was she pulling, pretending to be an idiot Antichrist?

"Do you really eat the Host?" she imagined herself asking.

"You're going to be obscene."

"Do you chew it, lick it, or swallow it?"

"You're *being* obscene."

And the fun was over and she had spoiled it. But this time, in her reverie, she had the sense to apologize, and he smiled, a nice warm hearthlike smile, and she wondered if he ever smiled in the confessional. She enjoyed the make-believe and went back to it. They were having a good time, delighting in each other, until:

"What do you do for a living?" he might ask.

She didn't like where the fantasy was going.

"You don't have to tell me what you do," he'd continue, "but it can't be that shameful."

"I'm a prostitute."

He would look at her soberly, weighing it, wondering if she was telling him the truth or trying to shock him. He'd have no alternative, of course, than not to show his shock, just in case she *was* telling the truth.

"Why are you?" he would ask.

"What the hell kind of question is that?"

"Is there any other question I should ask?"

"Dozens."

"Like what? I don't have to ask whether you enjoy it—you can't possibly."

She would have to lie, or the jig would be up. "But I do."

"I don't believe you."

"It's absolutely true." She would unreel all the junk she had put on tape a hundred times. "It's simple and it has no painful equivocation in it. I give it and get paid for it. I don't have to care a damn, it's not expected of me. There are no double or doubtful standards of accomplishment—I've either failed or I've succeeded. If I fail, better luck next time—and I don't have to live with my failure. I'm not married to him, I'll probably never see him again. I don't have to soothe his occupational frustrations or the heartaches his children give him. I don't have to sew his torn and bleeding psyche together, I just scratch him where he itches. I don't have to worry about his cholesterol, I just massage his balls. I'm giving pleasure, that's what it's all about—pleasure. And it only has to happen once, it doesn't have to last through all eternity."

"You think you're describing freedom, don't you?"

"It *is* freedom."

"It's the most abysmal kind of slavery."

"You're a vested religionist—what else would you say?"

"I'd say you're a slave—because you're a coward. You don't fight back. You take it lying down."

"That's a bad joke."

"Then why do you tell it on yourself?"

168

How smart he was to guess she was a coward, that she was afraid of fighting back. How did he ever *know* that?

He knew it because you told him, you fool, you put the words in his mouth.

And if she could be that clever, she realized, her foolishness would never be an excuse.

She had let herself become one. Why? Oh, yes, she could give herself every excuse—hunger, sickness, exitless despair—but none that eased the guilty ache. What made the guilt more wretched was that, as a trained social worker, she could supply herself with none of the standard extenuations. She was not mentally retarded, she had no monkey of sick heredity on her back, she was not one of the untrained who, for want of education, had no skills to fall back on; she had no narcotic habit, no physical impairment. She had never been seduced by her father, never raped by a stranger. She was not as certain as other liberationists were that she had been betrayed by men as a group, and she was altogether certain she had not been betrayed by any particular man. Still, somewhere in a man's society, she had let herself be cast in the role of his slave. Why?

The only answer that came to mind was not her own. Somebody had told her about a young girl, aged fourteen, who was caught in her first act of prostitution. "Why did you do it?" a truant officer had asked.

"I was far from home."

All hunger, all loneliness, all despair: far from home.

But Christ, everybody is. From the first moment that one says "I," the distancing begins, and every cerebration adds a mile. Home, whatever that might be, one's family, friends, self-love, self-respect, the sense of being equal to one's own talents and to the demand the world had a right to make on them. Far from home—sob stuff, hearts and flowers, out of tune. There were other women, far more disadvantaged than she was, who hadn't taken to whoring.

The bracelets again, and what they hid . . . Whoring was another razor blade.

That's what being a whore meant: kill me! Beat me, bring on the flagellants, beat me to death!

She had come to the end of her walk; she was on the outskirts of the Old City. The bright fantasies were gone; she dispelled the remembrance of the priest.

She thought of money and the need for it, and wondered what the day would bring, in acquaintances.

"I've only got one for you," Ellen said on the telephone. "And I don't know him. His name is Ihsan Chartier, and I don't know what *that* is, either. First name is Turkish, I think—something like that. But Chartier—that's French, isn't it?"

"It might be. When does he want to see me?"

"Five o'clock. He's in room 200, the Holyland Hotel. Ever been there?'

"No."

"Go early. Have a look—it's a pretty place."

The landscaping of the Holyland Hotel was all cypresses. They decorated the hillside swimming pool, they framed a mineral spring in a hidden garden, they adorned the scale model of the biblical Jerusalem. Nora wondered what it would be like to spend an afternoon in the garden here. She had a fleeting glimpse of Farris in this place; he'd be restless.

Inside, the corridor of the second floor was dark. She could barely distinguish the room numbers on the doors. Then, seeing 200, she knocked.

The door opened instantly. But there was nobody in the room. She entered.

When the door closed behind her, she saw that he had been behind it, Ihsan Chartier, a clean-boned dark man, with a face outlined in black, as if painted by Chagall, black hair, black eyes, black brows and lashes. And he had the pale purple lips of the Orient, and glistening teeth. He smiled a good deal.

He wore nothing but a pair of white shorts, the front of which he brushed with his left hand as if to censure the erection. To distract her from looking at it, he indicated the untidiness of the room.

"I regret so not orderly," he said.

There were suitcases open and cartons everywhere. The ropes that had tied the boxes together were all over the place. One had fallen into a basin of water; a washcloth floated in it.

"I sprain my ankle," he said, pointing to the pan in which he had been soaking his foot. He started toward her tentatively, not crowding her. He limped painfully. The sprain, together with his excessive benefaction of parts, hobbled him and he stopped walking, mortified. Both his hands went down to cover himself.

"I almost cannot wait for you," he said.

She had thought him about forty-five but now, when he smiled with such winning abashment, he seemed younger by ten years. "It's all right—I'll hurry," she said, and started to unclothe.

As she was doing it, simply to make conversation, "You know the terms and . . . everything."

"Oh, yes . . . is everything fine. Quickly, please."

At this stage of her nakedness, with some as yet unsurrendered vestige of modesty, she turned her back on him.

Before she could discard her last stitch of clothing, she felt an arm around her neck, and knuckles in her back. He ground the knuckle-bones into her vertebrae, held her tight, then turned the knuckles so that the pain was sharp, then an instant of sightless black, then pain again.

"No—please!"

He didn't let her go. The knuckles, deeper, breaking her spine, she thought, crushing her backbone.

"Please!"

He twisted her around. His face was close to hers. He spat.

"You bastard!" she cried.

He was away from her, stooping toward the basin, the rope in his hand, dripping wet, the knot at the end flailing the air.

"No!"

Down, once, across the shoulders. She started to flee, nearly naked, toward the door, but he was there first. Down across her breast, the knot like iron; white pain.

"No, please—don't—no!"

The lash. Again, the lash. The knot across the face.

"Oh, God!"

Mind's eye: Farris.

Then she did it.

She stopped fleeing. She turned. She didn't cringe under the lash; she took it. She exulted in it for a moment. Then her foot struck. Once at his groin, then once again.

He stopped. He reached for himself. His face went gray. But then he raised the whip again. As he did, her foot, once more. This time he fell.

She couldn't stop herself. She kicked him again. In the face this time. As he rolled onto his side, she kicked at his belly, at his face, then the groin, and again the groin.

She grabbed her clothes and ran.

In the dark corridor she dressed.

She didn't know when the sobbing started. Sobbing, making the whimper sounds of animals, she put her clothes on, mindless of whether anyone might see.

171

She ran to the fire exit, down the steps. Still weeping, out through the lobby, through the gardens of cypress, along the pathway to the street.

At the next street corner, breathless, gasping, not certain she would ever catch a proper breath, she paused.

In that latent instant, the thought came to her: She had fought!

She hadn't meekly yielded to the flagellation—and after her first impulse, she hadn't tried to run again—she had fought back.

Never, not once in her life, had she ever raised her hand to anybody, not once had she ever struck back. Today she had defended herself, had even retaliated after defense was no longer necessary, taking her revenge.

She wanted to scream with joy.

Something had happened, she didn't know what; she didn't know how she had managed it, didn't know what her courage was made of, where it had come from.

Yes, she did. From him. From that priest. From her conversation with him, not the one she had had with him yesterday, but the one today, walking in the bazaar.

It was he who had helped her. It was he who had fought with her—and not destroyed her—and given her the courage to fight back.

No. The conversation did *not* take place. She had made it up. He had nothing to do with it. She had done it by herself.

Then why, she asked, had she never done it before she met him?

For days after her fracas with the French-Turkish flagellator, Nora was torn between the wry pleasure of knowing she had protected herself against a brutalizer and the self-reproaching realization that, in order to do it, she had momentarily become a brutalizer herself. She knew she was in the never-ending search for an equilibrated state where she need call herself neither Nora the Perennial Pigeon nor Nora the Groin Kicker, but one thing was, to her, glorious:

She, whose mind had once run to razor blades, had discovered in herself a lively instinct for self-preservation.

On the evening of her second day after the event, Ellen called her with the name of another acquaintance and, without thinking, Nora said, "No, I don't think so."

Then the quiet inside her, the lovely unconflicted quiet.

172

The following day—Ellen again—twice. Late that evening the woman called once more, and got nasty. Nora, without any real rancor, told her to go to hell and carefully put down the receiver.

It didn't matter that she had not saved a great deal of money. She was not going to take any further acquaintances, she decided, probably not ever, certainly not until she had studied things for a while. So she moved back to the cheapest room in the hotel, she cut down on food, eliminated breakfast and had only coffee and a roll for lunch, and one day, again without thinking very much, bought a looseleaf notebook.

That night she started writing again. It would be nothing particularly brilliant, she warned herself, and certainly nothing arty. Just a commercial piece she would wring out of her strumpet experience, a racy story she might sell to one of the gamier magazines. She could see the title on the cover, superimposed over the tits of a nude:

HUSTLING IN THE HOLY LAND

She stayed up all night and finished it. Toward dawn, reading it, it seemed much better than she had hoped it would be. An hour later, in broad daylight, it was not so good. Somehow its jet humor had pinkened from comic-bathetic-bitter to serious-pathetic-pitying. And it gave her a headache.

On maddening cue, her dizziness came back. But this time she wouldn't take it lying down; she lashed herself to a mast of stubbornness. Why the hell wouldn't she be dizzy, she berated herself, she had been up all night, with six or seven cups of coffee and no food.

So she ate a roll and a mouthful of tired egg salad, and listed hopeful things:

1. She had finished the story.
2. She would soon go on to write better ones.
3. She had written well in her day, had won childhood prizes.
4. She would go on and win grownup ones.

She would.

But the mood was gone, and the money was thin. And, despite the gutsy resolution and the egg salad, the dizziness came again.

Then, mid-morning, the letter arrived. It was from her mother. Full of minor gossip, it had cheery tidbits about her mother's brother in Florida and how she had finally thrown out the old living room couch and gotten a new one. Buried somewhere in the small talk was a reference to the new assistant her mother had hired to "help out" in the photography store.

. . . not permanently, just for a week or so, until your father gets better. He hasn't been feeling well for the past month or so, and we both thought it would be a good idea if he went into the hospital for a few days. Just for observation, you know, nothing serious. Certainly nothing to worry about.

Even if she hadn't needed an excuse, Nora would have gone home. She loved her father, and he was never ill.

Buried away somewhere—always the escape hatch, at the ready—she had the return portion of her round trip plane ticket. She dug it out, called El Al and reserved a seat on the next plane to New York.

As she was packing, she noticed her bracelets, the copper one missing, and wondered if the priest had indeed taken it. . . . Probably not.

Worried and fretful, she closed her suitcase and left Israel, to go home to her father.

Nine

O N H I S A R R I V A L in New York, Michael had an immediate decision to make: whether or not to let his presence in the city be known to the office of the archdiocese. He was on holiday, technically at least, and he had no obligation to let the chancery know his whereabouts. Besides, his mission to Cardinal Cavanaugh had to be a discreet one, and the clergy has a whetted appetite for deliciously new conversational morsels. So he decided it might be prudent to stay away from bureaus and agencies.

He had barely left the airport when he changed his mind. Somehow or other, he told himself, they would find out he was here. He was, after all, an employee of the Secretariat of State; it might seem strange, and a breach of diplomatic etiquette, for him not to visit, to greet and be greeted. The Church drew comfort from such formalities, they were ceremonially affirmative and reassuring. Broken rites of custom, especially in these nervous times, caused worry and suspicion. They bred developments.

So he directed the taxi driver to the archdiocese building on First Avenue and determined his visit would be brief, as routine as possible. He would simply make his presence known, give no address—since he didn't as yet have one—and vanish.

He had a surprise.

They were waiting for him. There was a hubbub of hospitality, of welcome and good cheer, two young priests and a Franciscan brother, bobbing and burbling around him, a messenger dispatched to the ninth floor cafeteria for takeout food, an office cubicle agog with Pepsi Cola and cheese sandwiches and unnaturally red apples as gleaming as Shinola.

It was all the prelude to the introduction of an elderly priest whom they referred to as Father Lauren. He had a leather face and worn-down teeth, badly stained, and a smile too fixed. He cleared his throat a good deal; he had what he called a "phlegmous condition."

Hawking but not spitting: "We were expecting you a week ago," he said with a smile that was meant to wind round the heart.

"I didn't know I was expected at all," Michael said guardedly.

"Oh, yes—but nobody told us you were stopping in the Holy Land."

The conversation seesawed. "I didn't know anybody told you I was going there, either."

"Oh, nobody actually *told* us," Father Lauren said, and he winked.

The conspiratorial wink made Michael uneasy. "If nobody told you, how did you find out?"

An elaborate smile; his studied recourse to good nature was discomfiting. "We always know who's on the carriers. Anything that flies or floats—we get the manifest."

He was making a joke, of course, archly. But why was it necessary; what had to be hidden?

"Come now," Father Lauren said. "You're not really enjoying that sandwich, are you? Where did you get junk like that—doesn't it taste like a dry notebook? Come along, I'll show you where you're staying."

"Staying? I had planned to go to a hotel."

"What in the Good Name for? You're staying at Mindszenty House. It's on the other side of town. Ever been to the Mindszenty?"

No, Michael had never heard of Mindszenty House. He gathered it was the chancery's accommodation for visitors. The thought made him more and more disquieted. He knew the inquisitive eye of churchmen; he could see his telephone calls delivered with the

176

kindliest solicitude—no bad news, I trust; his comings and goings cautioned with the deepest concerns—it's not a safe city, you know, you won't be out late, will you? Dear old snoops . . .

And this one, this Father Lauren, coughing his curiosity through his phlegmous condition, the worst of them.

It continued in the taxi. "Miserable little cabs," the old man complained. "Tinier and tinier every year. Break your back in a coffee can. How are they in Jerusalem?"

"The taxis? Oh, I didn't ride them very much. I walked most of the time."

"See everything, did you?"

"Not really. I was there less than a week."

"Oh, yes, too short. And had to give some time to—uh—friends. Right?" An old dog sniffing at a post.

"No, I have no friends in Jerusalem."

"It's here you've got the friends, I'll bet. Come back to see any of 'em?"

"No, I haven't lived in New York in many years."

"So you're anonymous here." Another wink, a wicked one this time, with a cackling laugh to accompany. "You can put on your lay clothes and redden the town."

"I don't think I'll be likely to do that."

Quickly, getting out from under: "Well, I should hope not, I should certainly hope not." Then the grin again, the mask of comedy back on his face. "Now, come on, lad—what *are* you doing here?"

"Didn't they tell you I was on a holiday?"

"Who's they?"

"You tell me." Abruptly he decided he'd had enough of the old man's prying questions. He tried one of his own. "So you're a Church detective, are you?"

"Church detective? What in the Good Name's that?"

"Well, what are you?"

"What am I? I'm an obsolescence. They keep me on at the archdiocese—I'm their token dotard. They call me a canonist, which I'm not. What I really am is an archivist—but who's ever heard of an archivist anymore? I authenticate old documents. The documents are obsolete and so am I. But I'm still good at it. I can tell a real one from a fake. If you were a piece of paper, I could tell you whether you were true or false."

But since Michael was a person, the implication was, he couldn't make any assessment. But the presumption, the safe one, was that the

177

visitor was lying. Michael made the same presumption about Lauren. No matter what the auxiliary functions of a chancery canonist-archivist might be, he couldn't imagine greeting and glad-handing as one of them.

They arrived at Mindszenty House. It was on the far West Side of the city, in a moldering neighborhood. Typical of any number of parish houses, Michael thought, except this was a desolation. The windows of the basement and first floor were barricaded with corrugated tin, weathered and rusty. The single flight of concrete steps was rutted, fractured, and, in some places, gone to gravel. A fitful wind, gusting from the river, had blown old newspapers and debris; they cluttered the alcove under the steps and clung to the basement doorway. On the top of the steps, as the two priests ascended, a mangy gray cat, the color of the concrete, sat waiting for them, challenging their arrival.

Father Lauren kicked a foot into the air, made threatening guttural sounds, and the cat streaked off.

"Don't let the place scare you," he said good-humoredly. "It seems worse on the outside. We don't bother to keep up the exterior. If it looks nice, the vandals smash it up. What gets me—they don't seem to want to steal anything. They only . . ."

His voice disappeared in a shadow somewhere.

Michael finished his thought: They only want to threaten. . . . He shivered. The river wind was chilly, as chilly as the wind, that night, in Rome. But only a coincidence, he told himself, no wind of malice, no similarity to the macabre dumbshow the other side of the fountain and on the person of the priest. . . . These were only vandals, the old man had said, only part of the universal wantonness.

The archivist was comforting. "The inside's not so bad." He was unlocking the front door. It had originally been a parish house, he said; then, a haven for Hungarian refugees, it had been renamed Mindszenty House. It was still furnished as a visitor's hospice, but rarely in use. Except for guests like yourself, he added.

"The first floor's not too good," Father Lauren muttered, "but come upstairs."

The second floor was surprisingly pleasant. There was a spacious front living room, not badly furnished, in the antimacassar tradition; the woodwork was intricate, heavy black oak as old as the house itself. The kitchen, comfortably old-fashioned, had a huge gas oven and a marble sink; what was supposed to be white in it was whiter than whiteness. Two bedrooms huddled together in the rear, in a kind of cozy intimacy; each had a brass-and-iron bedstead with a spread of chenille, worn but immaculate. In the bathroom, the white canvas shower curtain hung from a chrome ring; the drain was part of the tile floor. There was something old world and agreeable about the place, oddly welcoming.

"For Mass," Father Lauren was saying, "you can go to St. Malachy's. It's only a few blocks away—Forty-ninth Street. . . . And the one thing you'll be wanting is a phone." Then the colluding crinkle of eyes again: "To be calling the friends you don't have here." He went to the corridor door and pointed down the steps, toward the first floor. "We had it reconnected last week when we thought you were coming. It's a pay phone, but Mindszenty has a charge number—here it is." He handed Michael the card, complete with wink, and added, "In case you want to call the Vatican—or Rome." Then, quickly: "Unfortunately, the phone's down there, in the dark hallway, under the stairs. But you don't have to see to talk, do you?"

Michael said no, and thanked him for everything.

Lauren meandered back to the kitchen. "It's all here—you can cook your own meals," he said.

He didn't seem to want to go. Michael had the uneasy sense he was staying to ask more questions. "Everything's fine," he said, trying to speak conclusively. "And I do thank you very much."

"Do you, now?"

The distrust in the old priest's voice was an odd sort of "you're welcome." It added more evidence to Michael's certainty that the man found him suspicious. Then it abruptly occurred to him that there was no specific suspicion in the elder's mind. It was more disquieting than that : a confused anxiety that had, lately, infected the Church, like an undiagnosable ailment, an apprehension of the strange and of the stranger, a foreboding that there were fewer friends than enemies, less to hope for than to fear, and a nameless evil lurking everywhere.

By reluctant degrees, the archivist made his way down the steps, and the young priest saw him to the front door, then into a taxicab.

Back in the house, Michael tried the front door key Lauren had given him. He smiled wryly at his concern that there was something wrong with the lock, that the key worked too easily, even when it was only partially inserted. The old man had made him needlessly uneasy; indoors, the lock seemed perfectly secure.

He went to the telephone, dialed Information and asked for the number of Cardinal Cavanaugh in the Office of the Permanent Observer Mission of the Holy See to the United Nations. There was no special telephone for the papal legate. He decided to call the Office itself.

The phone rang a long time. When at last someone answered, it was a boyish voice that said, "Well, actually, the Cardinal isn't *part* of the Observer Mission—he merely has his office here. But let me give you his secretary."

Michael knew the name of the secretary, Monsignor Hanrihan, but they had never met.

"Hello, Father Farris," he heard the friendly Monsignor say. "I'm sorry but the Cardinal's not here."

"When are you expecting him?"

A silence. "Matter of fact, we're not—that is, not for a while." It was a puzzlingly vague statement and Hanrihan must have realized it. "He hasn't been here, you know—not for weeks—nearly six weeks, in fact."

"Is he ill?"

Another silence, another strange reticence. "No, he isn't."

Not amplified.

"Could you give me his phone number at home?"

"Well, I'm afraid I'm not permitted to do that." Then, trying to amend what seemed a lack of cordiality. "Father, why don't you give me your number. I'll reach the Cardinal and he'll get back to you on his own."

Michael thanked him and left his number. He waited a while and the phone didn't ring.

Two hours later, when he had showered and unpacked, it occurred to him that the phone might have rung while the water was running. He decided to call again.

"Oh, yes," Hanrihan said. "I gave him your message."

"I was in the shower. If he called, I'm sorry I didn't hear the phone."

". . . There was no call."

Perhaps he imagined it: Monsignor's voice had cooled. "He didn't call?"

"No, Father. I'm quite sure he didn't."

No mistaking the drop in temperature. No mistaking, either, the note of finality; there would be no return call.

He hung up.

He couldn't believe the Cardinal was trying to avoid a meeting.

How could he do that, having learned—as his brother must surely have told him—that Michael had convinced the young man to leave a dangerous place. Even if the artist had not gone home as he had promised he would—and Michael somehow felt certain that Cory would not renege on a promise—the priest had still done the Cardinal a service. The prelate could hardly turn his back on a favor like that, one that had cost Michael time, effort, and even an exposure to his own danger. He couldn't believe that a religious man of such high estate could be guilty of such ingratitude.

He thought, for the moment, that it was *The Last Magic* working its malediction all over again. But the man had long ago vented his rancors against the book, had denied its imprimatur, had arrested its life, had given Michael years of misery. Could the Cardinal hold a grudge for so long a time, especially against a book that had subsequently received such a respectable sanction?

It had to be more serious than that. Cavanaugh had found out, had simply guessed what Michael was here for, to block the Synod. And the man was no neophyte at such politics; he had no need to enter an arena where this battle would be fought; he could win it without raising a hand. All he had to do to change Michael's dread into a reality was simply to announce the date of the Synod.

Now Michael had an added worry: his very presence here might hasten things disastrously, might prompt the Cardinal to make the announcement immediately. Michael saw himself in a hateful role—catalyst—causing a reaction; himself a chemical bystander, unchanged and inert.

Inert. Not only helpless in a cause he was meant to benefit, but a bane to it.

His hope had turned bleak; he felt dismal. Trying to discount his gloom, he told himself he was tired, the jet lag had caught up with him; and, except for the few bites of that miserable cheese sandwich, he had not eaten for hours.

And Mindszenty House, which had seemed oppressive at first, then cozily comforting, had turned oppressive again. He thought of the place as a political asylum and imagined the wraiths of the Hungarian refugees in the dark corridors of the seedy old building. They were all gone, of course, years gone, but their voices still echoed, the phantoms were still here, frightened by the rages that had exiled them, longing for warmer, more familiar bedrooms in another land. He thought of Christ's parable of the lost sheep brought home, and realized no shepherd had ever come searching for those missing ones. He wondered if they had yearned for Budapest . . . as he now yearned for Rome.

His first day home in many years, and he was homesick for a foreign land. For Jerusalem, for Rome . . . was he always to be homesick for foreign places? That's because you have not allowed the Church to be your home, his confessor might say; remember, Michael, when nobody loves you, the Church loves you.

But somebody does love me: Ledagrazia.

He longed to see her. Today was her birthday; yesterday morning, in Jerusalem, he had cabled flowers; tonight, he would go to the nearest church and ask a blessing for her.

Once, years ago on his own birthday, she had given him a beautiful and bright-colored tie; priests are taking holidays from the collar nowadays, she said. As long as he had been in the clergy nobody had ever given him a colorful article of clothing, certainly nothing so flamboyantly secular. He wondered how she knew he would love it when he himself hadn't suspected that he would.

It was that same birthday evening that she made a slip of the tongue and called him Bruno, by the name of her youngest child, the Communist son, anathematized. It had given Michael a twinge and she, seeing it, had murmured that he was what Bruno might have been, and she had embraced him and touched his cheek. She had a healing hand.

He tried to visualize her now, in her early summer garden, the pool of golden carp, her dress all citrus colors, reading in the golden light . . .

The blessing for her; he must go to church. He looked out the window. It was a coolish night for May but his turned collar would keep him warm and he would need only his jacket. He walked down the stairs and through the dingy vestibule, then out onto the street. Tenth, Ninth, Eighth Avenue, and he was in the midst of it: pornography bookshops and workover parlors, motion pictures that were not so much a lasciviousness of sex as a mockery of it.

A cadaverous man in a shiny suit walked alongside him and asked if he wanted something. "We cater to churches and synagogues," he said leeringly. "Some of our customers just come and look. 'Now I lay me down to peep.' " He laughed wetly.

Michael was glad to get inside St. Malachy's. There was a special Mass going on, something for actors, and the young priest celebrated it with a resonant theatricality, his voice making a vivid if somewhat histrionic display of the Eucharistic prayer. But the celebrant's extra decibels were wasted, his sound reverberated in a void, the church was nearly empty. There was a scattering of people near the doorway, for quick exit; the rest was only a desolation of pews.

Broadway, however, when he walked out to it, was not empty; the show was going on everywhere, in the theaters, in the restaurants, on the streets. Everything was an entertainment—the ranting of the crazy woman who wore a shopping bag for a hat, the bloody nose squabble at the entry of the massage parlor, the policeman bad-mouthing the taxi driver.

The Church could not meet the competition. This was her worst shortcoming. She was being called a variety of unflattering names. Rich and self-satisfied; bankrupt and neurotic. Too evangelically ambitious; too clannishly smug. Too rigidly holding on to old forms; too formlessly trying to be all things to all people. Too worldly to be Christian; too Christ-bitten to be of the world . . . But they were old insults, and all of them could be borne. Now, however, there was a new one.

The Church was a bore.

This insult she might not survive. When the Church was the purest theater of all, and High Mass her star performance, she was the sublime entrancement. But when she had to compete with the temporal theater and free television that made no demand of com-mitment, when her star had to compete with Superstar, she was bad box office, and the show was failing. . . . How terrible that she had become an exhibition competing with show biz and kitsch, with the blaring music of the Broadways, when she had once celebrated sub-limely with the solemn music of the Mass.

As he walked, queasy, someone stepped into his path. A woman with bad skin made a cross with two fingers, then held one of them in an upright position. A boy, hardly in his teens, came out of a door-way, hopped into step alongside him and said not a word for half a block. Then: "I got a long tongue, Father." Michael told him to go away, but the boy didn't. "I'm a Boy Scout. I got my Merit Badge—in suck. Want to see it?"

Getting sicker, Michael reminded himself that the city was no worse than some sections of Rome. Then why did he feel so qualmish, as if he were still on the airplane, going up and down the air pockets, unable to catch up with his guts, nauseated by meals he should have digested years ago?

Years ago, that was the gist of it. Could he never come back to New York without seeing every misery as a reflection of his own?

Christ, he was a man in his middle thirties now, he had made his peace with mankind, with his vocation, with God. Could he not be satisfied with that? Who, outside the clergy, could boast of such conciliations with life? But it worried him that they might be only arm's-length conciliations, as the lawyers put it, based on civility. To mankind, work, God, the same directive: you mind your manners and I'll mind mine. That way, we don't offend one another.

Safety from hurt, that was it. It was the safety of the Church. That was what the expression meant: when nobody loves you, the Church loves you—it was love as a measure of safety. Home, without peril.

Tonight, he felt out of it, and exposed. He knew that if he were to walk ten blocks, he would come upon an old orphanage building, an edifice he had not seen for possibly twenty years; he would think of a boy with an oilcloth and the ache would be unbearable, still unbearable. That was a home, too, called safe. And what of love did *that* measure, for God's sake?

Yet, he could not believe that the old place could still have such power to pain him. So tonight, on his first trip home in many years, he had to test himself.

Hurrying, almost running, he reached the turn-off, six blocks north. Then along the dark pavements, the grim, wretched, interminable blocks, through blacks and Puerto Ricans now, not Irish, and trash cans overturned, and curses in the streets, he arrived at the orphanage.

Nothing was there. Only a parking lot, with a small wooden shack where the infirmary used to be, and a pile of old junked tires where the Mother Superior used to assemble them for chapel. Gone. He didn't have to think of its existence anymore, there was no longer any monument to his pain. . . . Standing here in the darkness, why did he still ache? The limb amputated, the pain persisting; what a cheat it was.

If only he could define it. Certainly it wasn't guilt any longer. How many thousands of dark screens had he whispered into, how many little panels had slid in and out of his sinfulness, how many white absolutions had he been granted! Surely, it had been enough. Or was there more to atone for, always more?

He walked back to Mindszenty House, let himself in, climbed the dim stairs, took his clothes off and went to bed.

He couldn't sleep. He was tortured by confusion that was burrowing deeper, disarranging parts of him he had considered in balance and well-composed. Where was the Michael Farris he had come to

184

terms with, the priest who knew what he needed by way of physical, emotional and spiritual supports, where had he gone?

And what had prompted this onslaught of self-questioning? What had caused the ache in closed-up wounds, what had burst the sutures of old scars? Simply the return to New York?

What, especially, had caused him to behave in a way so uncharacteristic of himself? *Why had he taken the bracelet?*

In the darkness he sat up in bed. He groped in the night, to find the pull chain of the bed lamp. When the room was bright, he got out of bed and walked to the suitcase.

Yes, the bracelet was still there.

Who had taken it? Who was the Michael Farris that had stolen this thing? What void did the object have to fill? And why, having it, did he feel more achingly empty than ever before?

It was cold in his hands. He held it clasped between them, but still they didn't warm it.

Dropping it back into his suitcase, he returned to bed and switched the light off. It was nearing daylight when he fell asleep.

He would have slept longer if the phone hadn't rung. He raced down the steps and snatched at the receiver.

It was a Mrs. Merrill. The voice was middle-aged, with an unusual resonance, the sort of prolonged vibration one heard in the speaking voices of singers. "I am Cardinal Cavanaugh's housekeeper," she said. "His Eminence would like to see you this morning—at his home." She gave an East Side address in the Fifties. "Would ten o'clock be all right for you?"

The music in the woman's voice was false. Mrs. Merrill's unusual vocal resonance did not come from a singer's training, but from deafness. She had apparently, at some early time in her affliction, taught herself how to produce sounds that had a musical timbre; the melody in them was probably lost on her. She wore a hearing aid, the plastic of which was burnt orange, the color that her hair might once have been; the hair was badly hennaed now; only the gray seemed natural.

Michael didn't know, when she let him into the vestibule of the old beautiful brownstone, that she was hard of hearing. When he was outdoors, still on the stair landing, she could apparently read his lips. But her hearing aid was probably not in good condition and when she brought him through the vestibule into the shadowed waiting room, he found himself repeating, then shouting his no-thank-yous, he didn't wish for coffee, he'd already had his breakfast, no thank you. Listening, he was bemused by the loudness of his voice. He wasn't in the least bit angry, but sounded so, and he wondered if people who live with the deaf foment anger in their voices. And he was certain she had taken it as anger, for she darted him a surly glance, and abandoned him.

The house was a puzzle to Michael. What he had expected was the traditional cardinal's quarters, furnished to conventional prescription: the anteroom with scarlet velvet draped over the table, the Cardinal's coat of arms carefully hung below a canopy; his biretta, in an alcove, perhaps, before a crucifix, and in another alcove or in another room of gilt chairs and scarlet damask, a portrait of the Pope above the throne reserved for His Holiness if he should ever call. True, there might be such chambers elsewhere in the house, but something, he couldn't tell what, suggested to Michael that there weren't.

And it was the more puzzling since Cavanaugh was a traditionalist. No matter what modern changes had taken place in the furnishings of cardinals' houses, they would not be alterations of this man's choosing.

Not that this brownstone was in any way modern; it wasn't. Indeed, it was exquisitely antique. The walls were wainscotted with mellow oak linenfold and the bookshelves were enclosed by doors glazed in imperfect crown glass, wavy with age. Green velour, almost black, the nap worn thin, was everywhere, the furniture upholstered in it, the draperies hung from ceiling to floor. It was the hush of the room that was most effecting; he had the erratic notion that it was an ancient hush, inherited through generations, brought over from the Cardinal's old country, Ireland, some distant Gaelic quiet.

He didn't notice the painting immediately, it was done in muted colors, all receding. It was Father Damien and, were it not for the anachronism, Michael would have called it an El Greco. The greens were fumed, the yellow was chrysolite but grudging, and over the misshapen leprous face there was a muted glow that seemed not at all intrinsic to the canvas but as if it came from a religious aura in the room. It was, as Damien was reputed to have said, a precious pain. Abruptly he had the intuition that Cory had painted the portrait, for it was half joyful and half agonized, half seeing and half blind.

What particularly interested him in the anteroom was the wall of photographs. Here, there was indeed a picture of the Pope—not, as

Michael would have expected, in solitary spendor, but as one of many. It was, however, a beautiful photograph exquisitely mounted in a mat of deep red velvet, encased in aging, yellowing ivory. In fact, all the pictures—of Third World prelates, for the most part—were superbly displayed, in frames of old woods, brass or antique silver.

Two smallish photographs caught Michael's eye and, moving closer to them, he recognized Lucas Cavanaugh in both of them. In one he was the promising monsignor, possibly Michael's age at the time, the young Irish prelate newly arrived in America, standing outside the Cathedral of the Holy Name in Philadelphia. He was wearing the violet, as the expression went, probably still unaccustomed to the vividly colored cassock and mantelletta of a monsignor. Yet, there was already the intimation of the purple about the man. How quickly thereafter he became bishop, archbishop, and how quickly this very cathedral became his own, the episcopal seat of his own diocese.

The other photograph: Lucas Cardinal Cavanaugh, ermine-caped, standing before the papal altar in St. Peter's, just risen to receive from the Pope the ceremonial red hat with its golden tassels; the youngest prince of the Church . . . And in both photographs, the reds, violets and purples notwithstanding, how hueless he looked, as if his color had been etiolated by his refusal to cast vain light upon himself.

As Michael gazed, he had the uneasy sense that he too was being gazed at. He turned.

The Cardinal stood in the doorway to the inner office. He might have been standing there a long time, Michael thought, staring and motionless. He was still staring, still motionless, even now, not so much as fluttering an eyelid.

When at last he did move, it was not toward his visitor. There was no gesture of greeting, no extended hand, simply the almost imperceptible motion of his lips: "Come in."

It was the lips of the man that Michael would always remember as his most striking impression of the face. The mouth of severity is generally a thin mouth, fleshless and tightly drawn; Cavanaugh's mouth was as severe, as unsparing as any he had ever seen; yet, it was not thin but full, beautifully molded, shaped to perfection, and sensual. It was not a mouth meant for smiling, hardly for eating, one might say, only for the tasting and delectation of . . . words. Words fastidiously spoken, as if each one were an exotic morsel, the wing of a lark.

He turned from Michael and led the way back into his study. His walk was measured; he was a tall, lean man with a rhythmical grace, his gait seemingly monitored by a metronome.

The Cardinal's study was a contrast to the waiting room. It was cold gray, his worktable topped in slate; the chairs, although their seats were upholstered, were unpainted iron, elegantly wrought. He gestured to one of them and sat in a similar one with the window at his back. Still, no word of welcome. When he did finally speak, his voice had more Gaelic lilt than his brother's.

"Monsignor Hanrihan tells me you were surprised that I have not been to my office in six weeks."

"Yes, I was."

"Were you truly surprised?"

"Shouldn't I have been?"

"You've read none of the correspondence between your office and ours?"

"No, I haven't."

It was true; he hadn't been called in on the correspondence. But he did know the situation. The Pope had designated Cardinal Cavanaugh as his *legatus a latere*—one of the newspapers had said he was the old man's "side door envoy"—ostensibly to be an observer at the United Nations, but actually to deal unofficially with the violation of human rights in Central and South America, and in Africa. The violation of human rights was understood to mean, among other things, the victimization of Catholics. In Brazzaville, Congo, a cardinal had been kidnapped and murdered, in Uganda a bishop had been doused with gasoline and burned, in Rhodesia four nuns and three Jesuit priests had been shot to death, throughout Nicaragua, Honduras, El Salvador and Guatemala hundreds of priests, nuns, Catholic laymen had been murdered, deported, tortured.

Since Cavanaugh had no real ambassadorial power, he obliquely had to solicit the influence of the United Nations—and use his prestige as the Pope's personal legate—to affect the emissaries from the hostile countries. While he could not accomplish miracles, he did come to the rescue of many desperate communities. To a number of cardinals of the Third World he became a heaven-sent protector.

Like Cavanaugh, the cardinals were, in the main, conservative. But more and more frequently the priests were not. Their parishes were poor, their people hungry and bitter, and many of the clergy were inclined to be politically progressive. Theologically progressive as well; they allowed, as one of the traditional cardinals indignantly put it, "novelties of worship." Although it was no part of Cavanaugh's function to engage himself in this matter, he had expressed strong sympathies with the conservative prelates, privately at first, then in the open. At last, he had made "novelties of worship" one of the rallying issues for all the conservatives of the Third World.

It became a Vatican worry. In the Pope's illness, the Secretary of State had been brought into the conflict, and Feradoti had expressed the opinion that a man who champions the religious freedom of Catholics against hostility *outside* the Church would do well to champion religious freedom *within* the Church as well. And he further pointed out that Cavanaugh was functioning beyond the purlieus of his mission.

"You haven't heard about my difficulty with the African bishops?" Cavanaugh continued.

Michael, carefully: "Only indirectly, Your Eminence."

"Well, let me tell you—*directly*—that Bishop Mbehru is permitting fetishes in the churches. Through Cardinal Tissot I reproached him for it, and you know what he did? He *personally* telephoned me when he was in New York, and told me that it was none of my business and that Cardinal Feradoti had written him a letter saying he regretted that the Bishop and I were having a 'difference of opinion.' That was all Feradoti wrote—not one word more—not a syllable of reproof to the man. In other words, he tacitly undermined me." His voice was uninflected; he was austerely controlling his anger. "And there have been other sacrileges. All over Africa—and in a number of South American countries—sorcery, medicine men, voodoo. I have a picture in my files of a church that has a great stone phallus where the altar should be. They are worshiping a priapic Jesus." He paused. "So, since my influence is vitiated, I have thought it prudent not to go to my office. I will simply wait."

Michael couldn't believe the intractability of the man. Balked in one way, he was refusing to function in any way at all. "Wait for what, Your Eminence?"

"When His Holiness dies, there will be a new Cardinal Secretary."

So that was it. The prelate was making no pretenses: political action. A Synod to help elect a Pope who would be a conservative and would appoint a conservative Cardinal Secretary.

His hostility was granite. It was as if, at the very outset, he wanted it known that there was an unbreachable barrier between him and Michael: no negotiation.

The instant he had defined his position, he allowed no further discussion of it; he changed the subject.

"I hear bad news from Italy," the Cardinal said. "Galestro is dead."

How unceremoniously he said the man's name, Michael thought, without even the title, and how detachedly he spoke of his passing.

Michael simply nodded his head.

"What did he die of?"

The question surprised him. They had indeed kept it secret, then, even from the highest dignitaries of the Church. He wondered how long the secret could be kept, how long he himself could keep it. Not wanting to lie, he found an evasive answer. "It hasn't been given out."

"Why not?" the Cardinal asked. "What niceties are being protected?"

Michael smiled guardedly. He knew his silence was as dissembling as a spoken lie, but the facts were Church property, not his to dispense.

The Cardinal, however, wouldn't let it go. "Doesn't it strike you as odd?"

"Yes." He certainly could say that much without compromising anything.

The older man spoke flatly, without any doubt. "It had to be violence, then." He turned to look at Michael more directly. "You notice I simply state it. I do not ask you to commit to anything. No need—I will find out for myself."

There was a cold threat in the voice; Michael tried not to suggest that he was disquieted by it.

Tonelessly, without shading: "My brother has arrived," the Cardinal said.

"Good. Is he here?"

"You mean is he living here?" Michael hadn't meant that, had simply wanted to know if Cory was present, in the house. But the Cardinal was precluding risky questions. "No, he's not living here. I wish he would—we could keep better track of him. For his safety, however, I cannot tell you where he does live."

The man was edgy on the point; Michael got away from it. "I hope he's well."

"You mean the wound in his side, of course. Not serious. And he is well protected now. Someone is near him all the time."

Michael thought of the free spirit, his footsteps dogged by security men. "He must hate that."

Cavanaugh nodded. "He says, 'I feel as though I'm carrying a gun.'" He paused. "Well, he isn't carrying a gun, actually—and there's no other way." His eyes were hooded, but didn't hide his anxiety. "I hadn't meant to see you. There is nothing I can say to you except to express my gratitude, and I could do that just as well in a letter."

How ungrateful the man was, how unyielding.

Cavanaugh continued. "But it occurred to me that there was a way I could indeed thank you, and I shall try to do it."

He arose from his chair and walked to the wall cabinet. Opening a wire-meshed door, he lifted a box off one of the shelves. It was a worn wooden coffer, no larger than a cigar box, made of tiny wood panels delicately interworked. He set it on the slate-topped table and lifted the lid. Michael caught a glimpse of a miscellany of things— memorabilia, possibly—a few letters, an orange-colored fountain pen, the glitter of some golden keepsakes, a tiny leather-bound book, and the object he withdrew.

It was a bag made of faded chamois, no larger than the palm of his hand. He loosened the drawstring and withdrew an old pocket watch. It had to be solid gold for, if it had been plated, it never could have retained such a glowing shine. And the back of it sparkled with an encrustation of tiny, many-colored gems.

The Cardinal held it so it caught the light; it glistened.

"I want to give this to you," he said, "but first I must tell you its provenance."

He removed the wooden box from the table and set the beautiful timepiece in its place. As he sat down on the other side of the table, the watch was the sole object between them.

For a long time he did not speak. His hands were lightly clasped; superb hands, long-fingered, nails exquisitely manicured; Michael thought the skin on the fingertips might be as thin as the membrane of an egg.

The Cardinal spoke at last. "There used to be a man who lived in the adjoining house. He had been there many years, long before I came to my position in New York. I hardly saw him through the winter seasons, then springtime would come and he would go to his back garden and I would go to mine, and we would talk of plantings and infestations and manures, and behave like any suburban crea-tures. His name was Ira McIlhenny and we became well accustomed to each other, and were able to talk of many things.

"There was one subject, however, which we never mentioned. I knew the man had been baptized a Catholic—yet he rarely spoke a word about the Church. So I suspected that he was a tragic person—and had lost his faith. At first I used to think it was an earmark of my social grace that I never referred to it. After a while, I realized it was cowardice. Too late, I'm afraid.

"He became ill and, from time to time, I visited him. Then one night he showed me this watch and said he was bequeathing it to me, as a token of his deep affection. I was touched, and thanked him.

"Two days later he was dying. I went to see him. He was in terrible pain, in agony—I ached for him. Just before the end, when I could no longer stand his torment, I said, "Ira—please—let me give you the Last Rites.

"It was catastrophic. He cursed me. He used the little breath he had left—he shrieked at me. Not only did he revile *me*, he profaned the Church, he blasphemed the name of God.

"That night he died. A few weeks later, his lawyer delivered the watch together with a brief excerpt from the man's will."

The Cardinal took up the timepiece and looked at it. "It is an exquisite thing," he said, "and the lawyer tells me it is a museum article, worth considerable money. But I cannot keep it. I cannot, in good conscience, cling to a gift from an apostate. Nor can I, for the same reason, offer it to the Church."

He reached over and set the watch on the other side of the table, close to Michael. "So I give it to you," he said. "For I am inclined to think you will have no such scruple in accepting it."

Michael felt his face go purple. He could not believe such an outrageous affront. His impulse was to strike, or to run. But he tensed himself against any action; he took deep breaths and waited. Then, with as much self-possession as he could manage, he said, "I think you do not know me well enough, Eminence, to speak about my scruples."

"By their fruits shall ye know them."

"You do *not* know me."

"Your work."

"One book. A single book nearly a decade ago—and you can't possibly remember it that well."

"I remember it very well. And I am not referring to the book alone. The book was honest. I hated it, I loathed the heresy in it, I loathed the twisting of doctrine, the extenuation of sin, the maudlin tears you shed for Antichrist. But it was not the book that told me who you are. It was what you did afterward." He paused, then: "You are a corrupt man, Father Farris."

"Corrupt? In the name of God—what did I ever do that lets you call me that?"

"I suspect—from the fact that your book has Bishop di Luca's imprimatur—that there was some small assistance by the Pope. I don't know how you managed that, but it was quite a maneuver." Before Michael could defend himself against the pejorative "maneuver," the Cardinal hurried on. "I read the book twice, Father Farris. Once in English and once in Italian—the last time under the title *L'Ultima Magia*. The minor matter is the Italian title. 'Ultima' does not mean 'last,' it suggests the decisive conclusion of all process—so the word is a pretension—there are more things in heaven and earth than are dreamed of in your 'ultima.' But let that pass. What gave me a sickness was your excision of the chapter on Penance." With bitter irony: "That was not a printer's omission, was it, my friend?"

Michael's mouth was dry; he could not answer.

"Was it?" the Cardinal persisted.

"No, it was not."

"The chapter on Penance was indeed central to your book, was it not?"

". . . In a way, yes."

"In fact, it might have been one of the main reasons you wrote the book, mightn't it?"

". . . Yes."

"You are, then, a contaminated man."

Michael felt hobbled, so lame that if he had been asked to run, he might fall. "I did what His Holiness asked me to do."

"That was *his* conviction. Was it yours?"

Unsteadily, he found what argument he could. "I believe in the infallibility of the Pope."

"Was that your true reason for toadying to him?"

"I did not toady!"

He knew he should have left it there, and gone. But he felt overborne and had to get out from under the weight of the defeat. "As a priest, I'm obliged to live as peaceably as I can under the authority of the Pope. If I can't, I shouldn't be a priest. But I can. His approvals and imprimaturs and sanctions—I can live by them."

Almost a whisper: "I do not live by them alone."

"You are fortunate, Your Eminence, if you have a direct word from Christ."

"Get out."

Michael walked quickly to the door. As he was about to enter the waiting room, he heard: "Just one moment."

His impulse was to keep going, to ignore the command to stop. But he turned.

"Father Farris, I know why you are here. Our Pope is on his deathbed. There will be a conclave by and by—and we cardinals will vote. I have already determined what my vote will be. I am a conservative. I do not believe in the new forms, only the old ones. The new liturgy is alien to me, even its language. English is my worldly tongue, it has the grime of earthly life on it—I cannot utter it to God, so I speak to Him in Latin. I do not believe in murder—of any kind—not even of preborn infants. If a woman were to be made a priest, I could not confess to her, for Christ was a man. There are other things, of course, and there are many who believe with me. Some of them, Mother Church has almost lost—the Traditionalists, for example. We must bring them back, we must bring them together— all who believe in the old traditions of the Church. I have spoken to Cardinal Margotto on these points, and we are in such agreement that I will vote for him in the conclave, and pray for him always. And on his behalf—and for the Church that I love devotedly—I will soon announce the date of the American Synod."

"Before you do, may I speak to you on behalf of Cardinal Feradoti?"

"You may not."

"Despite your differences, he is your friend."

"That is one good reason why you may not."

"As a favor to him."

His jaw set. "However you may be, Father, I am not corruptible . . . not even by affection."

Michael lost his temper. "My God, you wrote to him—you pleaded for a favor! And through me, he did you that favor. Now, through me, he asks you to do him one. Simply listen to him."

"No."

"Please, Your Eminence, we're talking of Mother Church—is there no human thing in her?"

"In me, you mean."

"Of course."

"We are human according to our lights, Father Farris. And I will not discuss my lights with you."

His severe mouth closed conclusively. The meeting was over.

As Michael went through the waiting room and entered the hallway, a door on the side of the entryway opened and Mrs. Merrill appeared, to show him out. How the deaf woman knew the session was over he couldn't imagine. More puzzling, he thought he heard music coming from somewhere, possibly from her quarters. They were lovely voices, a chorus of them, beautifully modulated and sweet. And quite soft. How could she hear them?

Walking down the steps, the turmoil of the meeting still roiled in him and he paid little attention to the music. As his heartbeat steadied, however, as he became more collected, the music became clearer in his mind. It was familiar.

He thought of an old Italian villa, and a man nailed to a wall. The music, then and now, was plainsong.

Ten

NORA GOT OFF the train with her two bags and her
shoulder purse, crossed the station platform to the taxi, stowed her
luggage in the back seat, got in and said, "Siders Inlet."

Siders Inlet, the town where Nora's parents lived and had their
shop, was on the South Shore of Long Island, a half mile inland from
the Bay. She had just finished her second year of high school when
they had moved there from Manhattan, moved, as her mother put it,
to seek a better life for the family. Her mother denied she was trying
to get away from "the ethnic thing"—she was a democratic woman,
she said, but she did feel one had to make a virtue of a demographic
necessity, and she would have stayed on in the city, except for the
rising cost of private schools. Glossing over the inconsistency, she said
you had to choose between paying the tuition and paying the psychiatrist; you couldn't have both luxuries. So they opted for the psychiatrist and moved to Siders where Nora's education was a public charge.

Nora neither liked nor disliked Siders. It was, simply, not a place to be. So she wasn't there. *It* wasn't there, either. When they arrived, the little shopping center—as distinguished from the great wide wonderful mall which was not yet dreamed of—was still not ready for business although Nora's father was ready to open his photography shop in it. On the day he unlocked his door to the customers, they were installing the quaint white colonial windows in the quaint phony-antique brick façades that faced onto the quaint arcade where shoppers were already promenading in unquaint sneakers.

It seemed unreal to Nora to be living in an apartment over a store instead of riding up seven stories in a graffiti-walled elevator. In her first six months in the new town, she became friendly with nobody. Midway through her first semester she was failing three courses.

"You were the smartest girl in Manhattan—don't tell me you're the dumbest in Siders," her mother said.

To her father's more reserved question, she gave a truer answer. "My skin's breaking out."

Nobody saw any correlation between breaking out and flunking out, but they sent her to a dermatologist. Two years later she still had lesions on her face but she had mastered an important skill: she now knew how to get high grades without anybody knowing she was there. Graduation day, as she accepted a scholastic award, somebody said, "So that's Nora Eisenstadt."

She had never thought she'd be able to get through that last year. Things started going out of whack. One night, not knowing where she was, she got out of bed and started to walk to Manhattan. A mile or so later, she didn't want to go there, so she turned around and walked toward Montauk. Just before dawn she had the first of her dizzy spells. When they found her, she didn't want to go home. They led her through the arcade to the outdoor stairway that went up to the kitchen, but she didn't want to walk the stairs. When she got into her bedroom, she didn't want to leave. She didn't have a friend, she had never had a date, she didn't know why she was at school, and all she could touch was bookshelves.

Things will get better, her mother said, you wait and see, things will get better. When you go to college next year, you'll have a chance to make a new start. They won't know you. You can create a whole new personality—new clothes, new attitudes—yes, even new skin—and you'll see, you'll have a new world.

In her new world, she flunked two courses, her first roommate moved out on her, and her skin turned purple. The only thing she liked about herself was her now carefully trained, outlining mind. She

197

knew how to go unerringly from point to point; and, starting with what she considered her ugliness, thence through all the ABC's of her unhappiness, she arrived at the inevitable conclusion of razor blades.

She had, of course, read that suicide was a function of derangement. Ridiculous. She didn't feel at all deranged; on the contrary, the razor blade was, in itself, a sane and rational object. It did its work neatly and painlessly; it transcended its primary function. Even the blood wasn't messy. Nothing violated the outline.

There was only one tangential factor she hadn't taken into consideration: Micky. The girl wasn't even her roommate at the time, she certainly couldn't have given a damn. But she came running, carrying a bathrobe cord for a tourniquet, promising doctors and secrecy. Illogical redhead girl, making the preposterous noises of living. I'll keep your secret, she kept saying, sit up, you dumb thing, I'll keep your secret, only tell me what it is.

What secret, idiot? Can the dry ache, the absence of choice, the sense that all life is less, growing lesser, than it should be, the void within the void, the this-way, that-way, no-way of despair be encapsulated as a secret?

Micky kept the secret that didn't exist. Especially from Nora's parents. They never noticed the scar. Bracelets, yes; not the scar. Don't clank, her mother said.

But there was the one time, during a Christmas holiday when Nora sat on the living room couch, watching television with her father. It was a film out of his boyhood. Bing Crosby and Bob Hope on the road to somewhere. Her father, laughing, running his hand through his iron-gray hair and taking his glasses off to wipe the tears, and laughing, holding her hand, laughing. Then, when the film was over and the Christmas carols played, she felt him stroking her wrist, watching and listening to the music, the gentle Jew moved by the Jesus songs, and touching her cicatrice, touching it softly, tenderly, as if it still hurt and he might be making it better.

Now he was ill. Under observation, the letter said. Somebody was watching him, that meant, spying on him, prying into *his* secret . . . trespassing upon the privacy he had never shared with anybody, certainly not with his daughter, for all she knew of him was what he might or might not know of her, the caressing of a scar . . .

As the taxi got closer, Nora wondered what she and her mother could pretend to talk about, this trip. There would be her father's ailment, of course, but how about the other times? She couldn't recall ever having had a lengthy conversation with Lily. Squabbles, yes, and, on occasion, a welkin-smashing riot of temper and vituperation. Nor did they ever do anything together—until the big mall opened.

It happened during the summer after Nora's last year in college. Stupendously, there it was, the Happy Vista Mall, its vista only the acreage of parked cars, the emporium of emporiums—Sears and Macy's and Woolworth's and numberless shops made of true plastic and false everything else. Stores within stores, escalators within escalators, and food everywhere. It was a lucite Beulah Land, with organ music soughing the soft sell through the weekend specials, and hard rock jackhammering the hard sell through prefaded jeans and see-through lingerie and sewing machines and cut-rate happiness, do-it-yourself.

Lily initiated her daughter into the rite of the mall-crawl. Nearly every Friday night they went without dinner and spent a few hours in the dollar-fat paradise of goods and wares. Unconsciously they fell into the rhythms of the various musics; they became mesmerized by hubbub.

They bought things. Little things they didn't need and forgot they had. An occasional big thing that was usually a mistake, the wrong size or it didn't match. Sometimes, clothes they would never wear—Nora bought a brassiere that felt like labial skin but who was to touch it? Lily bought a pair of jodhpurs; she had never ridden a horse.

Mostly, they ate. They never, not once, sat down to a meal; they ate at counters or while walking. They consumed countless hot dogs and hot doughnuts, they compared numberless pecan pies with French apple, they chomped and licked and lapped at ice cream sundaes with pecans and walnuts and almonds and bananas and raspberries. They indulged in the small lusts as though they were grand, libidinous sins, and were secretly regretful that they weren't. Erratically, Nora never felt guilty about the cheap transgressions. If it was a bit shoddy middle class, she didn't mind it. If it was gluttony and the smug accommodation of the overfed belly to the underfed soul, the surrender of the right of choice to the hawkers and corrupters, she said the hell with it, and licked the ice cream clean.

And so, the Friday evening would be over and—opiated—they would trudge homeward. Nora's father would be waiting for them. If he asked them anything, they would be too numb to answer, zombied.

"After the mall-crawl, the mall-pall," he would say. He said it often.

In none of those Friday evenings did Nora and her mother ever talk. Except for the do-you-like-that and isn't-that-cheap and isn't-this-delicious, they had little they could say to one another.

Once in a while, those times, a word or two almost got said between Nora and her father. Almost. Once or twice they were touchingly on the edge. Then one or the other shied away, as if caught naked.

But she had not yet given up on her father. She couldn't, she loved him too much. Some day she would ask him a direct question, and he would tell her something of himself. Some day he would ask her something. Some day he would again touch the scar and say, "Tell me."

"This is Mr. Kellman," her mother said. "Harry, say hello to my beautiful daughter."

"Let me take your bags," he said.

"No, no—it's quite all right."

"Mr. Kellman is an old friend of your father's—they used to work together at Willoughby's," Lily Eisenstadt explained. "He came to give us a hand in the store. It's only temporary, of course—until Dad's better."

"How is he?" Nora said. "What's wrong?"

The customer stood between her and her mother, and Kellman thoughtfully beckoned the lens-preoccupied young man to his section of the counter.

"I'm sure it's not serious." Her mother lowered her voice. "They thought at first it might be an intestinal obstruction, and they'd have to operate, but thank God it's not that. Then they said colitis and . . . well, maybe it's colitis."

"Has he been sick for long?"

"Who can tell? You know your father—he's not exactly Mr. Bigmouth."

She was worried, Nora could see, but it might not be more serious than the fact of his being in a hospital. "Is he in pain?" she asked.

Evasively: "He's a terrible man, your father—terrible. Not a word. He didn't complain a word. I wouldn't have known if he hadn't put a cot down where the darkroom used to be. 'What's this for?' I asked. 'Sometimes,' he said, 'when it's slow, I like to lie down and read.' That's what he said—can you imagine? Your father, reading in the middle of the day—have you ever heard such a story? I knew it was

200

fishy, so I called to make an appointment for him with Dr. Eckert. Well, he had already seen Eckert four times. And Eckert is such a nothing—! So, the next day, another doctor—and—into the hospital."

"What do they actually say it is?"

"Well, you know, tests and examinations and more tests. Now, don't get worried, honey. When you see him, you'll realize—it's not serious. He looks thin but it's that miserable diet—they give him a spoonful of this and a mouthful of that. Hospitals are terrible."

"Can I go see him now—can I use the car?"

"I'll go with you, hon. Just go upstairs—get settled—I'll be right up."

Her mother turned to a customer, and Mr. Kellman again made a move to help Nora with her bags. "No, please," she said. "I can manage, really."

He was a pleasant-looking man, a bit too plump, just turning forty, she'd have said. He wore thick glasses and he smiled a lot. The customer liked him, so did Nora; but his skin was too white and he was too shiveringly eager to please, like tapioca. She could see her mother's irritation with him; he was not the quietly skilled man her David was, not spare of word, nor the private man you went in search of.

As Nora gathered her bags, she had another glance at her mother and realized she was still beautiful and still romantic—a woman who, when her real house plants languished, watered the plastic ones. And she had quickness. She was too hurried for Nora, too swift to come to a conclusion before Nora was sure of the question. And always so enviably free to rely on her instincts. They used to bicker about that. Once, when in high school, Nora had taken an examination composed of a hundred questions. She had answered seventy-two of them correctly, and had not done any of the others.

"Why didn't you at least try them?" her mother had asked.

"I knew I didn't know the answers."

"Why didn't you guess? It was true and false—you had a fifty-fifty chance."

Nora found herself replying—and embarrassed by the pretension of the reply—that to guess at what she knew she didn't know would be a denial of what she did know, a betrayal of her mind.

"Mind, for God's sake? Your mind is only part of you."

Spoken impulsively with hardly a thought. But Nora had a hundred thoughts about her mother's statement. It was true, she had indeed denied everything within herself except her brain; subverted her appetites and desires, the needs of her muscles; dulled every nerve ending, even her will to exist. She felt like a creep.

Sometimes, she thought, as she walked up the back steps to the kitchen, she still felt like a creep. Or was it coming home that made her feel that way again?

The door to the kitchen was unlocked. Nobody lives here, Nora thought, it's too clean, no living person can survive in such immaculateness. Sanitary as Nora was—the ablutionary type, Micky had once called her—her mother's dream was asepsis. She bathed in nearly boiling water and took strong laxatives—purgation, inside and out.

Cleanliness, neatness, everything in its place, and nothing must be changed. The new couch, Nora noticed, was exactly like the old one. Whenever her mother went out to replace a lampshade, she took the worn one with her. Even when she and Nora's father went on a vacation, no matter how brief, she carried parts of her house with her, her bedroom alarm clock, the small coffee maker, the spider plant. Unlike Nora, the instant she arrived somewhere, she settled in, it became her own. If she had seen her daughter's apartment in Tel Aviv—a packing box for a night table—she would have gone back to Librium.

Nora's bedroom was as unchanged as everything. The fresh paint was exactly the color of the paint it had covered; the curtains had shortened a little, with laundering, but they hadn't been replaced.

And there, on her dressing table, a Milky Way. Near it, the scribbled note in her mother's hand, "Welcome home, honey."

Nora felt a pang of grief.

The Milky Way was not associated with her mother. It would always be a reminder of Micky.

She picked up the Milky Way and couldn't bear to remove the wrapper.

"Why do you walk like a klutz?" Micky had asked, six months after they had started to room together.

". . . I don't know."

"Come on—why *do* you?"

"Who's looking?"

"Bullturd. Why do you walk like a klutz?"

"I have bad skin."

"So don't walk on it." Then, almost as an afterthought: "Who the hell said you've got bad skin?"

"I've always had bad skin. I haven't had a Milky Way in ten years."

"Eat a Milky Way, for Chrissake, your skin is great."

Nora couldn't believe it. She looked in the mirror and still couldn't believe it. How was it possible to peer into the looking glass, day after day, toothbrush morning after toothbrush night, to look and not see that the acne was over, the pimples were gone, the miserable childhood had passed and the skin was clear? What had happened to the suppurations of growing up?

Micky got her her first date. He sent her Milky Ways. They ate Milky Ways in the movies, they ate them in the park, they ate them in his dormitory bedroom. He was as virginal as she was; they both knew more about Milky Ways than they did about genitalia; pleasure from the former was predictable; from the latter, chancy.

Now, nearly ten years later, she could remember very little of the boy, except that his first name was Clifford and he had—an overly apt coincidence—bad skin.

Here, now, in memory of Micky McLaren, she put the Milky Way aside, to save it for . . . later. Later was the time parents told you to save things for, a time when you would, presumably, have a greater appreciation or a deeper need . . . older.

Unpacking as little as possible, she got out her tar soap—she still used tar soap—and washed her face and hands. Back in the kitchen, she opened the refrigerator, studied it to catch up with old times, and ate nothing. In a few minutes, her mother appeared, ready to depart, and they hurried down the stairs to the parking alley, and got into the Plymouth.

Her mother was a good driver. As they approached Babylon, she said, "It's not a very nice hospital—what's a nice hospital?—but he's got a big room. I thought since the insurance pays for most of it, we'd splurge and go private." Then, brightly: "Besides, it'll only be a short while and he'll be home."

Nora had been worrying whether she was being sheltered from bad news: a critical illness. But the practical consideration of a high-priced private room did indeed mean a short term, and it was heartening.

"If he doesn't say he's in pain, then what is it—what does he complain of?"

"Nothing. He was just sickly, that's all. I knew he was sick—but he'd say no, he wasn't. And he *was*. Your father's a bright man,

Norie, but as a patient he's a dunce. Why didn't he complain? If he only kvetched a little, even if he made a pest of himself—!" She stopped, then said unhappily, "And he owes it to himself—he owes it to both of us. I'm making a mess of the store."

"You don't seem to be, Mama," she reassured. "You were doing very well—I noticed you."

Peevishly: "No, I don't even know where things are. My God, if you don't know where things are—"

It described for her the onset of chaos. Nora continued to comfort. "You certainly seemed to know more than—what's his name—Kellman."

"That's not much of a compliment. He's such a lump, that man. Nothing stays in his hand, it slips out. That's all we need in a camera shop—a fumbler. Every time he picks up an expensive lens or a light meter, I go for the smelling salts. Lifts things and drops them, lifts and drops. He's like a fetus that never developed fingers."

Her mother could annihilate a weak man in a paragraph, a strong one in a page. Nora wondered, where her father was concerned, how many chapters . . . What a militant feminist her mother would have made, and what a puzzle that she had thrown in her lot with the men-kept women, wedded not only to her husband but to marriage itself. Men are something marvelous—she heard her mother proclaim it a hundred times, not meaning men, meaning marriage as a bastion. Men are wonders, men are the lovers of the world, she would say; she was a one-woman relief party for a beleaguered institution. Liberated women, Lily had said, were so tight-assed about being professional —which they could never be—that they could no longer waltz gracefully, as amateurs. They had tried to make a profession of everything and failed at everything. Even marriage. Men never thought of marriage as a profession; they certainly didn't worry their busy heads about failure in it; only about failure in business. Women worried.

Not Lily. She clung to her amateur status as, before marriage, she had clung to her virginity. She was not a professional in anything. She was a good cook, she might say, but would never call herself a chef—that was a man's job; she knew nothing of her husband's business, it was too much for her, she said, too technical; she rarely expressed a political opinion because she felt she was too emotional; and Nora felt certain that in bed she was altogether passive, modestly deferring to her husband's professional masculinity while she maintained her amateur womanhood.

Liberation, Lily had said, was a menace, a male conspiracy. "They want to take away our right to be weak."

It was nearly five o'clock when they arrived at the hospital. Her father was sitting up and looking very much as her mother had described him; not really well, but only provisionally ill, as if his condition depended less on what *he* felt than on what others felt about him. Even his embrace was tentative.

"Hello, sweetie, is it you?"

She kissed him a few times, forehead, hands. "Are you sick or are you bluffing?" she said.

"It's nothing, hon," he replied. "I bought myself a cot for the old darkroom, and your mother got hysterical."

His wife made an elaborate threat to smack him and he made an elaborate gesture of fending her off.

"Stop jouncing around," Nora said, "and let me look at you."

He didn't look ill, only tired. And handsomer than she remembered. He had the head of a Roman senator, someone had said of him, square and strong, with enormous furrows across his forehead and down his jaws; a lean face always, it was leaner now, but it had kept its kindliness; there never could be meanness, not even stern judgment in it. Wearing the hospital nightgown, loose and open at the throat, the look of the ancient forum was vivified; he wore his toga fittingly. All the strong components, Nora thought; yet, when assembled, never the intrepid warrior.

When she was little, she thought him a profound thinker. Then, one spring vacation—forlorn insight—she caught his trick. He wasn't a thinker, he was a codifier. He classified other people's thoughts. This is a technological consideration, he would say, or this is an ecological one, or philosophical, or artistic. By shoving each "consideration" into its proper pigeonhole, he had no further need to consider it. He did, however, need to consider himself a man of thought; it excused him from having to consider himself a man of action.

She recalled him during the kitchen years, the years of argument while the chicken was heating up, the raised voices, sometimes the imprecations, then the back door, opening and closing quietly, and the man padding softly down the back steps, into his darkroom, to develop pictures. She wondered what quaking picture of life came shimmering up to him out of the hypo.

And he had done the slipping down the back stairs, not only to avoid his wife but his daughter as well.

She had once, uncharacteristically, cheated in trigonometry. It was a measly fraud, and senseless; she'd have gotten a high enough grade without peering at someone's paper. Thanks partly to the petty pilfering, she got the highest mark in the class. And didn't want it. For days it nagged at her. She went, at last, to her father.

"I've got a problem in math," she said.

She still recalled the smile of easy benevolence. "You'll work it out, sweetheart."

"Maybe not this one, Dad."

He kissed her, and in the tight embrace he squashed the trouble flat. "You know I don't know anything about math, honey. And you know what a worry wart you are. You fuss and you fidget and you come home with an A. So I have big confidence in you, Norie—you're the greatest!"

It was his most expedient expression: you're the greatest. He used it even when she felt like the littlest, meanest, mingiest gnat. He was a professional fortifier.

She never told him about cheating at math.

"Well, how do you like it there?" he was asking. "Still love Israel, do you?"

Could she tell him, this time, the complex truth of it? It might not be too late; she mustn't sell him short. But she settled for the easier, simpler thing. "Israel?—oh, I love it."

"What sort of job these days?"

Whoring, she might say. And he might say he didn't know anything about that, honey, he knew she could always solve these problems, he had great confidence, she was the greatest. He might . . . or he might actually listen.

"I've started in a job for the government," she said. "I'm afraid it's confidential."

"An alien doing work for the government?" But he didn't seem to think it suspicious; on the contrary, they had recognized her special talents. "Big secrets, huh?"

"Oh, not that big." She forced cheeriness.

"Always modest," he said, grinning. "I'll do all right in English Comp—and wins the Pearson Award."

"I'll do all right," she said.

I'm doing *this* part all right, anyway, Nora thought; they're sharing a pleasure, I'm making them proud. I think I'll stay a while, a few weeks, maybe, until he's well and out of the hospital. I can do a good job here, I can be his therapeutic . . . if the lies hold out.

"Do you like the Israelis?" he was asking.

"I didn't at first. Everything you hear about them—their arrogance —how overbearing they are—it's all true. And yet . . ."

"You do like them." Her mother wanted her to like them.

Then I'll like them, Nora decided. "Well, if you look at arrogance another way, it's kind of wonderful—their independence. Even when they pray, it's as if they're saying, 'Dear God—don't help and don't hinder.' "

Her parents laughed. Even she enjoyed herself. Why hadn't she thought to say something like that, back there in Israel? If she had laughed more . . .

Her father had been enjoying himself only a moment ago, easily; now he was diligent at it. As he lay back with a fixed smile, his breathing seemed an enterprise.

"Tired, Dad?"

"Oh, no—not at all."

"We'll go," she said.

"No." Surprisingly, he meant it. Then, as if her mother were not in the room: "I want to talk to you, Norie."

Lily said, "Not now—you're tired. Norie will be here—she's not going anywhere for quite a while. Are you, hon?"

"No, I'm not." She gave him a pretendedly rough pat. "See you tomorrow."

"Stay a little." Entreaty.

Nora realized then, as her mother must have realized before, that he wanted to speak to her alone. Lily muttered something baleful and indefinite and left the room.

"Your mother is a marvelous woman," he said.

It was one of those conventional catchalls, the vague compliment that is the preface to specific condemnation.

Nora smiled. "What's wrong with her that we haven't already done a thesis on?"

His eyes appreciated her. "Have we covered it all?"

"I think so."

"She's got a new one, Nor."

"She has? What is it?"

"She won't listen to the truth."

Nora held still. Then: "What is the truth, Dad?"

"I have cancer."

No, Dad, let me tell you about cheating in math. Israel's great, only I'm not great *in* it, or anywhere. About the bracelets . . .

He was wearing a white toga—would it look good in a casket? Mama, come back, I can't handle this alone.

"Please, Dad."

"It's true, Norie."

"But she says—"

"Don't listen to what she says. It's been months. Tests, everything."

"I don't believe it. How can the two of you—if she says you haven't got it—"

Softly: "Stop it, honey. There's no sense to any of it, and you can't *make* sense of it. The only thing we've got is the fact. There's nothing else to hang on to, understand? Nothing—only the fact. And if we try to grab hold of anything else, it's all . . . shifty. It is to me, anyway. So I've got to live by the fact that I'm dying."

"But what if it's not a fact—what if they're mistaken—"

For a fraction of an instant she saw him almost snatch at the brass ring, and she felt miserable for having tossed it to him. But: "They're not mistaken, Nor," he said quietly. "It's so bad they won't even open me up."

"Oh, murder."

She was about to cry, but saw his face toughen. It was the strongest she had ever seen him. "Cry on your own time, will you, honey?" he said.

By stopping her breath, she warded off the tears, but kept saying oh murder, oh murder.

"Do something for me, will you?" He was totally calm. "Tell her: no more of this charade. Will you tell her that? I can't make the gestures anymore. It's too tough, and it's taking . . . time. Maybe— if we quit playing it—we'll find something to say to each other."

She nodded and promised she would speak to her mother. He tried to smile, then decided not to invest too much in it. He lay back and this time let himself be tired.

"I love you, Norie," he said.

He had never stinted in saying that he loved her; he had said it often, and effortlessly. It had always been less of a strain than talking, or listening. It filled a lot of spaces, covered many sins of omission, bridged great chasms of loneliness. For her, it never sufficed; she always saw its uses. Yet, easily as the words had come to him always, they came with difficulty now, as if all his life he had not known what the three words meant, and had suddenly, this moment, come upon their meaning: pain. She had never thought them bad words, mean words; but suddenly they were no good, they were cruel. Don't say them to me, she wanted to cry, I don't want you to love me, if you'll die.

Slowly, gently, she put her hand to her father's forehead, to his hair. It was speckled black and white, steel curls of it. How strong it felt, how springy to the touch, how healthy. They won't even open him up, she thought; yet, his hair, how healthy.

He was breathing evenly. His eyes were closed. She had a random thought: he's in the darkroom, developing pictures. As in the old days, she wondered what images were shimmering up to him out of the water.

"Why didn't you tell me?"

"I don't want to talk about it," her mother said.

Lily held the steering wheel tighter and turned the windshield wipers on. The rain had just begun, a spring rain in summer heat, frenzied and intemperate.

Nora pursued it. "Why didn't you tell me the truth?"

"Let it wait. I can't even see through the damn windshield—let it wait."

"Let it wait for what?"

"Don't badger me!"

"He's got cancer."

"Don't scare me with a word—that word doesn't scare me."

"Then why don't you say it?"

"I'm the one who *has* been saying it. I've been saying it to *him*—I've been saying we can fight it!"

"Mama, the doctors say—"

"I don't care what they say!"

"—they won't even operate."

"Who's talking about operations? Is that all we've got?—knives? Those doctors are monsters! They don't know anything—they don't want to know anything! I hate them—I hate all of them!"

"Mama, if they've given him up—"

"*I* haven't given him up—*I* haven't! And if he didn't give himself up, we could save him. I told him months ago—I begged him—go into therapy. But he listened to them, not to me. I said chemotherapy, I said orgone treatment, I said muscle therapy."

There she was again: her therapies. She had studied up on it, she said, she had read everything, she had questioned everyone. And there was no mystery in it for her. She knew all about the rioting cells, the

209

vicious little bastards. And they could be dealt with. It took ingenuity, it took slavish work, it took the lust for vengeance, but the sons of bitches could be dealt with, they could be annihilated. There were remedies! And she listed all the nostrums and quackeries, all the linctures and tinctures, the potions and panaceas, the cures by grapes and apricots and vitamins and diets and cobwebs—yes, cobwebs—and, for God's sake, a cure by music. A person didn't have to rely on the goddamn AMA, a person could fight the fucking little terrorists, fight them, goddamn it, fight them!

"But not your father!" she raged. "Not your father! He won't do anything about it—he won't lift a finger! You want to know why? Because he's a dier!"

"Don't say that!"

"That's what he is—he's a dier! And it's a curse—it's in the blood—it runs in the family. You've got it—you got it from him. Both of you—you're diers—you're born diers—born diers!"

She was wild-eyed, distraught.

The car skidded and she jammed it to a stop. Then she couldn't stand driving it anymore, so she shoved the door open and, shouting born diers, born diers, threw herself out into the rain.

"Mama, come back!"

Nora ran after her.

"Mama—Mama! Come back!"

She caught up with her at last and grabbed her. She shook her mother. "I'm not a dier, I'm not! Don't say that, Mama—I'm not!"

She must restrain herself, she realized; she must not get caught in her mother's hysteria. The older woman started to flail at Nora, and at the rain. At last she ripped herself away, and ran again.

Nora watched her disappear into the blue downpour. Then she returned to the car and sat quietly in it, waiting for her mother to return.

Born diers, both of you. So her mother had known; had seen the scar and known; the bracelets had hidden nothing from her. Which meant, possibly, that her father too had known. Then why had they not mentioned it, why had they let her handle it alone, why had they sent her to still another psychiatrist, still another therapy, another cure that wouldn't be a cure, away from home?

Born diers. Was it truly in the blood? How stupid, how ignorant to think the allure of self-destruction was inherent. And yet, maybe that's what Micky had once meant when, a renegade Catholic, she had scoffed at the Church's notion of original sin. Maybe Micky knew better, that original sin was the love of death.

After a while, her mother returned. She was soaked to the skin, yet unaccustomedly calm. In utter quiet, they drove home.

That night, with the rain pounding at her bedroom window, Nora awoke and discovered that the lesions had returned. Not, however on her face, but on the lips of her vagina. In the darkness she felt an itching and a soreness. Turning on the light, inflicting the indignity, she held a mirror to her genitals and saw the tiny skin eruptions, barely visible but an unmistakable presence.

Somewhere in the Old Book, or was it in the Apocrypha, she had read that harlots had come out of a dark country and, for their wickedness, had been cursed with whelks and blebs. She was not quite certain what whelks and blebs were, but they had just the right preposterous sound to belittle the symptoms, the minor boils and pimples, the smaller maledictions from Sinai.

She turned the light out and stood in the dark bedroom of her adolescence and was loathsome to herself, even more now than she had been in those days. The final mockery, the final degradation—how would a jeremiad have put it?—for her whoredom and wickedness.

When it stopped being absurd, it was frightening. Chancres go with syphilis.

In the middle of the night, not knowing what purpose would be served, she started to dress. But with her first article of underwear still in her hand, she couldn't proceed, couldn't bear to contaminate her clothes with the disease of her person. She started to imagine the infection spreading, encroaching upon her body, enveloping her thighs, legs, arms, breasts, the skin of her neck, her mouth. She began to imagine the run of its discharges and the smell of them, the stench effusing from all her pores, and herself a rankness in the room.

Rain or no rain, she opened the window, wide, and stood naked in front of it, hoping the chill and the wet would freeze and cleanse her. But she didn't feel sanitized.

She got into the bathtub, lathered herself with tar soap, ran the water until it was scalding hot, and, still perspiring, went back to stand in front of the window again. Shaking from the chill of the cold rain, she forced herself to dress.

It was getting to be daylight. She wrote an imprecise note to her mother, then silently slipped down the back steps and walked the long distance to the railway station. She waited for half an hour for the first local of the morning.

Before ten o'clock she was at the registration desk of the Polyclinic Hospital, giving a false name.

The young man who examined her hastened to let her know he was not an intern but a house doctor, and he had thought of specializing in "gyne" but had decided to "stick with the female illusion."

"Looks like the big syph, but it's not. Scares hell out of a lot of women," he said with studied indifference.

"What is it?"

"Vaginitis."

It was a common complaint, she'd heard the word, but abruptly realized she had no understanding of it. "What does it mean?"

"It can mean a number of things. But this isn't the gonorrheal kind, I'm sure. I'll give you something. It'll respond."

He was already through with her, scribbling on a pad. But she couldn't let it get away from her, couldn't simply take the little paper slip and let it pass.

"What . . . does it come from?"

She thought: he's looking at me as if I ought to know. With a casualness that was too offhand, he said, "It comes from bad hygiene, in many cases."

"Not in my case," she said. "I'm more fastidious than that."

"I'm sure you are," he said tactfully, "but others aren't."

Others. He wasn't actually calling names; he probably saw a hundred women a year who were more promiscuous than Nora, and very few of them hookers. And even if he was being snide, she had no right to be angry. Not at him.

By the time she got back to Siders Inlet, and in the privacy of her bedroom, she had turned the wrath where it inevitably had to go, inward. She wondered if Micky, in the course of her services to men, had ever been bodily contaminated, and if so, how she had managed it. She must have found *some* way of concealing from the world, from herself, that she had been stupid and had been caught and had been tainted. What swagger and clank, what bracelets did she wear to hide the scar?

Why had the priest taken her copper bracelet?

She tried to push the incident out of her mind; it was unrelated: a mental impertinence; nothing in it was germane to what she was thinking. Or, it was too pedantically germane: from sinful pestilence to purifying priest. No, what a maggot in her brain; she wasn't Micky, a Catholic, she had no tropism toward any cleansing holy waters. It was simply the fact of the goddamn bracelet. Its disappearance was obsessing her.

And she had no notion, not the vaguest, where she might find the man. Well, yes, he was going to be visiting Cory Cavanaugh's brother, a cardinal; it was hardly a set of directions. She knew nothing about Catholic institutions, certainly no addresses. If someone had asked her to name a Catholic building, she would have said St. Pat's, Fifth Avenue, and that would have been the total extent of her information. . . . But maybe that was enough.

She telephoned the Cathedral, heard two men's voices consulting, then was told to write to the Cardinal at an address on East Seventy-second Street, the office of the Permanent Observer.

Nora started to write a letter and was immediately embarrassed by another lack of information: she didn't even know how to address him. Should it be Father Farris or Reverend Farris, or should she cop out and call him Sir?

> Dear Reverend Farris,
> When we met in Mr. Cavanaugh's place in Jerusalem, I inadvertently left my bracelet on his worktable. I returned the following day, but neither he nor I could find it. Unlikely as it seemed, it occurred to both of us that by some error or absentmindedness, you might have wandered off with it. If that is so, I would be glad to come and pick it up at any time convenient to you. My telephone number is 317-4422, area code 516. If this letter ultimately reaches you at some distance, please call me collect.
> Sincerely,
> Nora Eisenstadt

She wrote his name on the envelope, care of Cardinal Cavanaugh, and addressed it to the Office of the Permanent Observer of the Holy See. She ran with it, literally ran most of the distance to the Siders Inlet post office.

When she came out of the post office, she noticed that it was mid-afternoon and the day was clear. The rain had washed the town, a cool breeze blew through the inlet where the boats bobbed at their moorings, and the sails made a flapping cheeriness in the wind.

Again, as once before in thinking of him, she felt exhilarated. She was happy she had written the letter. Not for one instant, after she had gotten the idea to do it, had she had any disinclination to send it. It was a rare experience to her, making a decision in which there was not the slightest misgiving. She was pleased with herself, deliciously surprised. She felt she had performed an act of high adventure, had engaged herself in a hazardous enterprise, and she was equal to it. In a momentary surcease from her stunting sense of reality, she felt exuberant and romantic. It was like a drunkenness . . . cheers. Hallelujah!

Standing at the bayshore, a wonderful thing suddenly came to her, a golden gift, a fantasy: She was on the beach of a fabulous seacoast, in a brisk wind, scanning a vast distance. She was lighthearted; the illimitable reach of water was not frightening, it was friendly to her. A letter had been sent forth upon it, her letter—an argosy, full sail, full of hope, voyaging venturously toward an uncharted horizon. Spirit high, she was buoyantly confident it would come home again . . . but a little uncertain with what cargo.

Eleven

FOR TWO DAYS after his meeting with Cardinal Cavanaugh, Michael debated whether to admit that his mission had miscarried and return to the Vatican, or to remain in New York and . . . do what?

He might as well clothe himself in humility, as the Epistle would have it, and recognize that the task exceeded the man. The diplomatic rule of thumb to send only the mighty against the mighty had been broken; he felt utterly ineffectual.

Defeated, he wandered aimlessly around Manhattan, a tourist in the city where he had been born. He yearned for anachronisms. A tiny courtyard he had loved, cobblestoned when he was a child, was now a gunmetal tower of windows and doorways. A corner bakery that had sold sweet buns and hot bread was gone now, no scent of it remaining; the little Jewish stationery store, the secondhand bookshop, the junkyard treasure trove . . . in place of memory there was glass. Sixth Avenue, all glass, buildings mirroring each other, mocking their own images.

The city made him anxious. Everywhere—even more than in Rome—he had the sense of vigilance; quadruple locks on apartments, peepholes within peepholes, women with German shepherds trained to savagery, tarantulas doing the nightwatch in jewelry shop windows, mace and dagger canes, and leather gloves knuckled with gritstone to lacerate the skin. And the surveillance seemed a terror in itself.

He slept fitfully, he didn't eat, he said Mass in a distracted state. He wanted badly to go home to Italy, but something made him stay. He had to conquer some imponderable, he wasn't quite sure what.

Was he indeed, as Cavanaugh had indicted him, a corrupted man? Was that, then, why he stayed? To prove to himself—to Cavanaugh —that he was not guilty of any such moral perversion? What would his staying have to do with that? Non sequitur.

Besides, his conscience was clear. He needn't apologize for having acquiesced to the Holy Father's suggestion. After all, a chapter in a book—stet or cut—what was its dimension compared to the size of his respect and reverence for His Holiness? Michael's faith—need he vociferate it?—was in Jesus Christ; his probity, in the Church. He had made vows and attestations to that effect; his ordination as a priest was rooted in it. Finally—quintessentially—he had been an orphan; he had had no other parents than Mother Church and Holy Father. Those were, and had been as long as he could recall, his only parental authorities. And he followed their precepts not only because they had family jurisdiction over him, not only because he revered them, but because he loved them. And he should never be required to do penance for love. Damn anybody who made him feel he must.

Damn His Eminence.

And if his remaining in New York had anything to do with his justifying himself to that hard-bitten, stone-faced man, it would make good sense to return to Rome. He would telephone the Vatican, admit that he had failed, and tell the Secretary he was coming home.

Home meant Feradoti, it meant Ledagrazia, the house in the country, an afternoon in the garden. He missed them. Especially her. He felt a suffusion of warmth at the thought of seeing them again.

He put the telephone call in and was told there would be a delay at the Vatican. Abruptly he changed his mind. "Cancel it," he said.

He couldn't give up so soon. He knew that Feradoti had been right, that the key to all the electioneering in the Americas and the Third

World countries was indeed Cavanaugh—specifically, he had to kill the Synod, and, momentarily at least, he was balked. But was there nothing else he could do?

Cardinal Halevi, the Jewish Cardinal. If Cavanaugh was a power for the conservatives, Halevi was a progressive one. If only he could convince the Canadian prelate to set some countervailing force in motion—say, an opposing council. If he could only touch off a fight that he had a chance of winning.

He decided to telephone Halevi in Quebec. Excited, as he stood in the hallway waiting for the call to go through, the murk began to lift from his mind. A luminous and refreshing memory took its place.

He was at the papal villa at Castel Gandolfo—summer, five years ago. Feradoti's work with the Holy Father had been completed; the Secretary and Michael were about to leave when the new visitor arrived—Natan Halevi, the Cardinal from Quebec. The latter had been Feradoti's teacher—they embraced warmly—and the Canadian reminded Feradoti that the student still owed the professor one more paper in Old Testament exegesis. The cardinals bickered over it like schoolboys. As they were laughingly coming to a compromise, the Pope joined them and a picture was taken of the three prelates, with an unidentified assistant in the background. Michael was the assistant; he still had a print of the photograph.

He was smitten by Halevi, swept into the exhilarating breeze of the Jewish Cardinal's ebullience over everything. He was all ardor. Feradoti had said that Halevi could win anybody; Pope John, who had loved him, was going to deputize him to woo the devil.

Next to his pectoral cross, the Jewish Cardinal wore his Star of David. He would say, with a wicked twinkle, "Like Jesus, I have never ceased being a Jew," and he would mischievously watch people scratching at what he called the pruritis of prejudice.

His pleasure in discomposing biases became a passion during the Second Vatican Council when he gave his fervent Cross of Judah homily in a small church not far from Rome. It had been reprinted in a score of languages, posted on the walls of the ghettos, handbilled in every piazza in Italy, and argued in every loggia, on every stairway, in every crypt and courtyard of the Vatican. It helped, some said it helped the most, to bring about the Council's *Statement on the Jews,* which condemned all forms of anti-Semitism. His power had been the more efficacious because everybody knew that his defense of the Jews had not been special pleading, he had fought for all beleaguered people. When the Nixonian "even-handed" had gained currency, he wryly characterized himself: "I try to be even-handed—dear Lord, how I try. But while one of my hands is making the cross, the other is making the fist."

Remembering the man, Michael couldn't help smiling; it had been a smiling day, then, the kind of Italian afternoon that gives friendliness and sunlight, and asks nothing in return.

"*Oui!*"

The French voice at the Quebec end of the telephone was young and brusque. It was certainly not the Cardinal. "*Père Laqueux,*" the priest said to the operator, identifying himself as Cardinal Halevi's secretary. He was sorry but the Cardinal was not available, he was ill, and did the New York party wish to speak to the secretary?

"Yes."

Hearing the one syllable in English, the Canadian priest switched languages. "Who is it?"

Michael gave his name and said he was an assistant to the Secretary of State. His credentials stopped the conversation briefly, then: "I'm sorry, but the Cardinal isn't taking any calls. He's just come out of the hospital—he's had an operation."

"I hope it's nothing serious."

"No, it was minor," Laqueux replied. "But, after all, he's seventy-five. . . . Could you leave a number and we'll call back in a few days?"

Michael dictated his number, asked to be remembered to the Cardinal and left his wishes for a quick recovery.

He hung up, and wasted the rest of the day. The following morning, impatient, he decided to do some electioneering on his own. He made a number of calls to other cardinals. All were polite, some even cordial, to a man who had come from such an important office in the Vatican. But nobody would commit to anything, and the general sentiment was that it was unwise or premature for Michael to visit. Cardinals McCaffery and Salinas, of Detroit and Mexico City respectively, said they had not had word—officially—about the Synod, and couldn't comment until they did. Marquardt in Los Angeles said he was indeed a liberal but wasn't it a bit indelicate to be discussing this? Fellinger, in Chicago, a punctilious man, regretted that he could not "ventilate" the subject with anyone of lower rank than a cardinal.

He needed to attract a leader. His only hope: Halevi. The return phone call from Quebec was not due but Michael couldn't wait. He called again.

"Oh, I'm really embarrassed," Laqueux said. "But His Eminence has run away."

"Run away?"

The Canadian laughed. "He wasn't able to rest here. The callers, you know, and the telephone. So he rushed off to his cottage in the mountains where he can have a little quiet . . . without any telephone."

"There's no telephone?"

"No, just the couple who run the house for him . . . and the silence."

The hints were thick. Michael had the irksome feeling he was getting the same sort of telephone runaround he had first had from Cavanaugh. But this surely was different; this Cardinal had been personally friendly to him; it was only an overprotective secretary.

"Would you again give my best wishes to the Cardinal, and—again—my number?"

He gave up telephoning.

Full circle, he was back to the nucleus again: Cavanaugh. And no way to approach the man.

Except Cory.

Some way or other, Cory might be an access, an emotional access to the Cardinal. No matter what differences the young man might be having with his brother, he would have more personal influence than Michael had. And the most encouraging thing: the young artist was on the priest's side. If there was anybody who could talk the prelate into giving up the Synod, Cory would be the one.

But Michael had no idea where to find him. What's more, the Cardinal had made it clear he didn't want his brother's whereabouts uncovered. Well, he had to ignore such prohibitions; there was no embarrassment of choices. The Cardinal's injunctions notwithstanding, Cory had to be ferreted out of his hiding place.

Where to begin? The two brothers were devoted; one was all the family the other had. From time to time, Michael reasoned, they must meet. There would be a meal, sooner or later, a cup of coffee, an evening of talk or television. Occasionally, even if they did have disagreements, Cory might attend his brother's early-morning Mass.

The Cardinal's brownstone had to be the first focus, not necessarily because it was the best converging point, but because it was the only one Michael knew. But it meant casting himself in the role of amateur sleuth, one-eyed behind a newspaper, dogging footsteps, sniffing trails, shuffling in and out of taxicabs. No matter how ludicrous, he'd have to do it; put aside his black vest and turned collar, and his dignity.

He didn't like wearing laymen's clothes. When more and more priests were wearing them more and more of the time, he rarely did. Not because his clerics gave him civil privilege, not even because they were preferred form in the Vatican, but simply because he felt at home in them. They relieved him of the trying task of identifying himself by a costume of choice; yet, they gave him the identity he most needed: membership in a family. He hated to get out of them, and hadn't even brought any lay clothes with him. Reluctantly, the following morning, he walked down Broadway and bought himself a cheap shirt and a nondescript tie; then, in a rummage shop, a second-hand coat and trousers that didn't match.

Nighttime, in the shadow of an alcove diagonally across the street from the Cardinal's brownstone, he waited. He waited for hours and grew restless and didn't know where to sit when he was tired or where to relieve his bladder, and felt quirky and preposterous, and nothing happened, and Cory didn't appear.

On the second night he found a better vantage place. A few doors down from the alcove he had hidden in the night before, a storefront building was being renovated. Most of the frontage had been torn away, exposing the stairway. There was a metal rigging up to the third floor, a pile of broken plaster on the street, a stack of bricks with a red lantern on top. Michael went through the rigging, approached the stairway and ascended into the darkness. On the second floor, he stepped out onto the building platform. In shadow here, and above the sight line, he was concealed; yet, he had a clear view of the brownstone opposite and the whole street. He stood there and waited.

Nothing happened. Through the entire second evening of his vigil, nobody entered or left the house.

On the third night the oyster man appeared.

The priest called him by that name because the fellow reminded him of a shucker of shellfood Michael used to watch, as a child, through the window of McGrory's Oyster Bar, in the Forties somewhere. He recalled a burly man with a beet-red face, a purple-veined nose and a tongue that worked itself out of a slobbery mouth as the knife poked into the mollusk. Besides wearing the same kind of face, this one even wore clothes that suggested the oyster shell; stone-gray and as shining under the streetlamp as if they were damp.

220

The oyster man was as cannily watching the Cardinal's brownstone as Michael, two floors above the ground, was watching him. At first sight, not having seen any sign of Cory, Michael thought it was the Cardinal the man was waiting for, and that he might be an assailant. Then he noticed that the sentry was making no effort to conceal himself; on the contrary, he seemed consciously conspicuous as if to warn hostility away by his very presence. Beware the bodyguard. Cory, therefore, might be indoors with his brother; could have come visiting before Michael's arrival.

Watching, waiting. It seemed forever, and nobody else appeared. Passersby, an elderly couple going into a limestone building across the street, three women and two children entering a brick-fronted apartment house; lights going on here and there; lights going out.

Meanwhile, the oyster man stayed and smoked. One thin brown cigar after another, half sitting on a fireplug, lounging against a parked car, a lamppost, and in the alcove Michael had used two nights ago.

Just as the moon came out of clouds, brightening the whole thoroughfare, the gray-suited man looked at his watch. Michael looked at his own: exactly eleven o'clock. The oyster man pitched the stub of his cigar into the gutter, buttoned his suit coat, took one glance at the Cardinal's house and started away, walking eastward.

Clearly, the man's tour of evening duty was at an end, the surveillance over his charge was finished; Cory, if he was there at all, might be spending the night in his brother's house.

Immediately after the thought occurred to Michael, the one light in the Cardinal's building, on the parlor floor, went out, and the priest realized that if he had had any chance to speak to Cory this evening, the chance was now gone. He had been very close, perhaps, and had missed an opportunity. And he had no expertise to help him take advantage of a future one.

On impulse, annoyed at his ineptitude, he rushed down the steps and past the metal rigging. He must follow the oyster man. By doing so he might find out where Cory was living; no matter that the artist probably wasn't there this evening; or, at least, learn the address of the bodyguard. Even that might be of some use; it could start to triangulate the terrain, going step by step from points known to points mysterious.

The oyster man was walking fast. At First Avenue he turned until he got to Fifty-fourth Street, then suddenly disappeared. He was not visible northward on First Avenue, and would not have crossed the street, Michael speculated, for that would have meant going back in the direction from which he had come. Risking it, Michael turned eastward, toward the river.

When he got to Sutton Place South, it should have been easy to spot the man; the streets were practically deserted, and the thoroughfare was well illuminated. The sumptuous apartment houses threw golden shafts of light on all the pavements; carriage lamps glittered in front of the old townhouses. It was a subdued, expensive neighborhood, hiding its occupants behind a soft curtain of light.

Hiding the oyster man as well. He had totally vanished.

Telum imbelle, a lecturer in Church history had once said of someone; feebly warlike, with undertones of imbecility. That's me, Michael said. Gloomily he turned and walked in the opposite direction.

And saw him. He was in the tiny park, a children's playground, where Fifty-fourth Street jutted, between two apartment buildings, toward the river. He had a scenic dropcloth behind him, a view of the river, as pleasing as if painted, picturesque. The moon on the black shine of water, and the winking lights of Roosevelt Island in the distance, made the night glitter, onyx, silver, gold. Mid-channel, a solitary tug was plying slowly downstream; from it, by radio or television—an unlikelihood—floated the strains of orchestral music, familiarly romantic, a symphony, possibly the César Franck. A light wind lifted the melody and stirred the air with a delicate coolness, fresh and suggesting a not too distant sea.

The man was there, inside the park, a character against a cyclorama. Waiting.

Why had he indeed *not* vanished? Michael felt sure, by now, that the bodyguard knew he was being followed. Why was he waiting?

Not obviously lying in wait, nothing like that. In fact, preoccupied with something else. He was just inside the park, standing at a piece of bronze sculpture, a zodiacal world with astrological figures circling it. He gazed at the graduations, gently fingered the arrow that went through the earth. Moonlight, whether he could see the signs or not, seemed more suitable than sunlight to consider his starry fate.

A man absorbed in the zodiac at night—the priest knew it was too rococo for belief; his absorption had to be with Michael. His eyes on the bronze world, but all his other antennae reaching and questing, quivering in the cleric's direction.

All right, then, he thought, this is what the moment means: I must move toward him. It's openness now, his waiting, and I must treat it so. Apologize for following him, say honestly that I'm in search of

Cory, I'm his friend, and where can he be found? How foolish not to have done so in the first place.

He started to move toward the bodyguard.

With his first few steps, a message said beware, don't go.

But it was a false message, he told himself, better not listen to it. Besides, the alternative was to surrender the instant and surrender everything.

The oyster man still did not move. But Michael did, slowly, continuing toward the park.

If only I could believe that he's as frightened of me as I am of him. Not to be hoped for; the man would be a seasoned creature in a dangerous element; also, inescapably, some way armed.

Michael walked closer.

The man did something. He struck a match, cupped it in his hand a moment to give the flame a chance, then held the flickering light to the zodiac, the better to see the markings.

What does astrology say, Michael wondered wryly, on that matchlit thing?

Closer, every sense quickening.

The street lights were behind him now. The square's too dark, he thought; matchlight counts for nothing.

Closer, and into the park. His feet felt the difference; not concrete anymore, paving softer underfoot. Tread warily on it. A few more feet. He was deeper in the park. The place was only two people now; the space was committed to them alone.

Ten feet from the oyster man.

I'm here now, Michael might as well have said, see me now, I'm here.

The match went out. The man got rid of it.

He looked up from the dial, stared at Michael, frankly stared across the darkness.

Michael had his words all ready: My name is . . . I'm looking for . . . perhaps you can . . .

But almost at once he knew he would say nothing, and the other would do the same. It wouldn't happen that way. An action would occur, was about to, a movement was going to be made, a hurtful one.

He must prevent the inevitable, must speak, must force himself to speak.

Just as his lips began to move, another incredulity: release. The man turned away. Left the zodiac, left Michael, departed slowly, a man sauntering on an evening stroll, along a pathway in a park, along an edge of it, then out. Just as he reached the pavement, he half turned. He may speak a greeting, the priest thought, say it's a lovely evening, and farewell.

Michael didn't hear any footstep behind him, only a breath of sound, no louder than a sigh.

He felt whatever it was, felt it around his neck, an indescribable thing it seemed at first, then it was a hand, then fingers, as clearly, as severally as if he were meant to count them. Felt them tightening.

He couldn't utter anything, breath gone. He saw his arm raise as if it were not his own, reach out, gesture to the oyster man, gesture don't go, stay, please stay, do something for me.

The hand tightened.

The oyster man, still partly turned, partly watching, partly somewhere else, was poised in temporariness like a man trying to remember a thing forgotten, wondering whether to go back for it, or forward without it.

Michael's arm, still reaching.

The tightening hand did something else. Not a blow, but something. Then the pain became two, a greater and a lesser. The first was understandable, simply pain. The second was unearthly, hardly pain at all; utterly incongruous, like a seizure of color, a cruelty of color, as if lavender had punishment in it, an abuse, a hurt of lavender.

Then, no color, not a tint, and no pain either. Only darkness.

It wasn't the color that came back, it was a beam of light. Then other beams, little ones at first, then great ones, crossing one another, like a gala premiere. Then they broke into tiny sparkles, a million rhinestones, twisting, glistening, dancing in a streak; then, a myriad of tiny flies, no larger than drosophilae, with glimmering, flickering wings, hanging in gleams, not going anywhere, fluttering to stay afloat, making a shine so brilliant that it hurt his eyes and he was reluctant to open them. After a bit, he heard the insects start to hum, a low murmur in unison, with a steady rise and fall, like chanting.

Finally, the humming was a hushed weeping, and the weeper was a man.

Cory Cavanaugh, standing by a window, in a beam of early morning light, crying softly.

He doesn't know I see him, Michael thought, and I'm not sure I do.

224

But if I do see him, I'm awake, and he doesn't know I'm awake, and I won't tell him, I'll just watch. It was a childish pastime, hide and seek. . . . I wonder where the lavender went, and the rhinestones, and the tiny flies, the wings fluttering, chanting.

No lavender here. The room, my own bedroom in Mindszenty House, with the same floral coverlet and the same ivory crucifix on the dark wooden paneling . . . and I have no recollection of arriving at this place.

If I'm going to ask a question, he mused, I will have to lick my lips. It was difficult. "How did I get here?" Michael said.

Startled by the voice, Cory twisted to it, turned to the window to hide his face, the signs of weeping. "I brought you here."

The rhinestones glittering again, then gone. "How did you know to do that?"

Still not facing Michael: "Larrick called me . . . I was at my brother's."

"Who's Larrick?"

"You followed him. He's the bodyguard Lucas hired to look after me." A reluctant instant. "He saw it happen."

If my head didn't hurt, Michael thought, I could be angrier. "I know damn well he saw it happen. Why didn't he help me?"

"There were three of them. One of them had a knife. God knows what the others had."

"Your man—surely he was armed."

"No. I've been insisting that he not be. And tonight—when I got angry at him for not helping you, he said he couldn't be much good without a gun, and I said the hell with that. And I fired him . . . Lucas and his damn bodyguards."

He felt a slippage, back to darkness; stay awake, he told himself. Start moving; try to sit up. "Three, you say?"

"Yes."

"Who? Who were they?"

For an instant, sitting up and uncertain he could remain that way, he had a hope Cory would say they were people who did not signify, except as the generality of sickness signifies; muggers, that was all. He was there, simply there, an unspecified man in lay clothes; the little square was dark; they had taken him for his wallet, perhaps, or his watch. But somehow it didn't fit properly . . . there was the oyster man, watching . . . and he knew without feeling at his pocket or his wrist that nothing was taken; it was something more than that. He

225

knew it particularly by Cory's evasion of the question. So he repeated it.

"Who were they?"

"Who knows?" Cory replied. "Larrick says the older man was middle-aged. The other two were in their twenties."

"He didn't know who they were?"

". . . No."

Michael wasn't sure he believed him; or, perhaps Cory didn't believe the oyster man. "Or what they wanted?"

"No." Then the artist continued quickly, "I know what they didn't want. You. Whoever was sent to do the job didn't know us. It was me they were after."

Michael tried to see some reason, any reason. "Or me," he said.

"No." But he was thinking about it. "Why you?"

"To warn me."

"Of what?"

"Not to . . . meddle."

The thought seemed to hit Cory harder than was warranted. "Maybe it's a warning you shouldn't ignore." The young man was taken unaware by his own feeling; his eyes filled up again. "Christ, don't *you* get hurt in this!"

Clearly, he hated his show of emotion; the muscles tightened in his face. How frail the man was, Michael thought, and how unfortified against these summary outrages. He seemed even more troubled here than he had been in Jerusalem, certainly more frightened. How odd, and yet how typical of the artist's essential innocence, that he had been less alarmed when he himself had been in danger. He needed distance to judge its magnitude, and now, seeing mayhem perpetrated upon another person, it loomed too large for courage.

"Why the hell have you been watching for me?" Cory asked.

"I need your help."

"Stay out of it!" Sorry for his outburst, he pleaded: "Can't you see they're trying to kill me? You want to get caught in it?"

"If they're trying to kill you, why don't they get it over with?—it should be easy enough." Michael persisted: "And who are they?"

"Stay out!"

"Help me!"

"Listen. We all better stop 'helping.' We can do more harm than good. My brother thinks he helps by putting guards on my back. But it only makes these people more vicious, more vengeful."

"What people? For what reason?"

"Please—do me a favor—do yourself one. Go back to Rome. Get out of this." Cory too wanted to get out of it; he was starting toward the door. "I'll call to see how you are." He pulled a pencil and miniature sketchpad out of his pocket. "What's your number?"

As Michael muttered the phone number, he felt the clutch of desperation. "Wait," he said. Lifting himself, getting out of bed, he was managing quite well, he thought, the return of the tiny flies notwithstanding, the golden glister, the flapping of minuscule wings. Not well, however, when he straightened to his full height. He was about to fall.

The artist was back, holding him. "Lie down," the young man said.

"No—if I do, you'll go."

"Lie down, you idiot."

"I need your help. Please." He pulled himself away from Cory. He mustn't give in to any weakness, not now. "Talk to your brother. Or beg him to let me talk to him. If he goes on with this Synod of his . . . What's happening now—the ravages, the havoc—we all have some responsibility—all of us—you and I—*he*, possibly more than anybody. We're not evil men. Feradoti thinks your brother is a saint. Your brother thinks you should have been a priest. Not evil— none of us. Then why does evil come to us—and possibly *from* us!"

The last few words seemed to unsteady Cory. Hesitant, he delayed his departure. Michael rushed ahead. "Cory—please—we have to talk—all of us."

"My brother won't listen."

"He'll listen to you—he loves you."

"And I love him!" It was a lash of anger. "But if he were to die tomorrow, I wouldn't shed a tear over him! I think—God help me—I could love him better if he were dead! . . . You don't believe that, do you?"

"No, I don't."

"You don't believe I can love him and kill him? You don't believe I can kill him and be willing to die for him? You don't believe this miserable family lovesickness, do you? You don't believe we can love each other as brothers, and murder each other as enemies?"

"If you love each other—"

"Then we can't be enemies!" With long-suffering contempt: "You priests are all the same. You don't know the first goddamn thing

227

about love and hatred. You think they're opposites—well, Father, they're the same. But you have to keep love inviolate—all safely wrapped up in your saintly devotion. Especially the good priests, and you're one of them, aren't you? The good ones are the worst. Love without hatred—as if Christ never got angry. Purity and passion, immaculately conceived. Stay the celibate all your life, an innocent child, at home with Papa and Mama. Stay, for Christ's sake, *pure!* Well, I'm not pure—but my brother likes to think that he is. So, between the profane and the holy— no dialogue."

He paused an instant. Then he said, with even more scathing antagonism, "And between you and me, Father Farris, there is still less."

"There can't be less than none, Cory," Michael said assuagingly. "We're on the same side."

"Not a bit. I'm a radical. You're—whatever you have to be at the moment. You may, in fact, be a more dangerous enemy than my brother. You make the Church work—and in its present form, it shouldn't. It should explode, and start all over again. You make it sound honest and diligent and kindly—and even sacred. It's not. It's corrupt and lazy and cruel—and a mockery of Christ. You tell the lie—you do it, Father Farris—you do it more viciously than my brother does. Nobody can see what a destroyer you are, because you liberals—you sugarcoat the poison pill!"

Michael's strength came back, in a fury. "I'm sick of those easy phrases that cause bloodshed! 'A liberal is only a pimp for a conservative.' 'A radical who's not a revolutionary is a reactionary.' What in God's name do they mean? They mean you're out of patience with slow-moving, slow-thinking men like myself. You want it to happen quickly, in a burst of flame. You want an epiphany—with blood, if necessary. Well, I don't want you mangled somewhere in a back alley, I don't want a priest mutilated or a bishop kidnapped, I don't want my breviary burned or an altar pissed on . . . and I don't want to be strangled in a public park. What's more, I'm wondering if, after all, *you* really want that. Do you?"

Michael could see the young man's doubt. The artist was, plainly, not in any way a combatant; violence was abhorrent to him, and terrifying. But there was something else that was swaying Cavanaugh: Michael felt that Cory liked him. It was an anomaly. He had heard the man speak to him with hostility, even with contempt. Yet, he sensed that the artist, for reasons of his own, might be grateful to

228

him; or, perhaps the attack on the priest had made him feel responsible for his safety. Whatever the complexity, Michael was convinced there was affection in it.

"Cory—tell me something—have you left the Church?"

"No."

"You say you're a radical, but honestly—do you want the Church to fall apart?"

". . . No."

"Then, for God's sake, don't you realize that if your brother goes on with the Synod—if Margotto is elected Pope—the Church *will* fall apart? Help me to talk to him. He loves you—maybe the two of us together—"

"Stop it!" Pained, he made a grotesque movement. He put his hand to his eye, the useful one, and covered it with his palm, as if to shut out a hurting view. His false eye, remaining open, was able to stare. After a moment, he removed his hand and addressed himself to Michael's plea.

"I would be no good to you, Father. I've lost all the influence I ever had with my brother." Then, ponderously: "I'm a Galatian."

When Michael had first heard of the Galatians, they were part of the Charismatic renewal in the Church—not particularly radical, certainly not revolutionary. It was a congregation of joy that believed its members had been baptized—personally, not necessarily through the Church—by the Holy Spirit. Charisma had been given to them, the gifts of grace: the healing of the sick, the power of exorcism, the uttering of prophecies; and, probably most controversial, the speaking in tongues, a mystical experience by which the Spirit was believed to speak through the faithful in a language altogether foreign to the person blessed.

The Charismatics were a life-giving force in religion—burgeoning particularly in America—and the Vatican was not unfriendly to them. But small splinters of revolt had torn away from the Charismatic movement; a few groups had turned revolutionary. One of them refused to admit the infallibility of the Pope; another had demanded the right to ordain women as priests. The Galatians were a group of that kind, but Michael did not know how far toward heresy they had gone.

"Have you gone underground?" he asked.

"I suppose you could say we have, yes."

"Are you . . ."

229

Cory forestalled him quickly. "No, we are not violent."

"I wasn't going to ask that. The biblical Galatians, as I recall, were about to become . . . hysterical."

"Yes— until they took their lesson from Paul. Which is what we have done as well." He quoted the words of the Epistle. " 'And to prove that we are sons, God sent forth the Spirit of His own Son into our hearts, and the Holy Spirit cried, Abba, Father. Wherefore we are no more slaves, but sons; and God's heir, through Christ.' "

It sounded like all the biblical translations, and like none of them. Perhaps the man was paraphrasing, or perhaps it was the slanted translation acceptable to his group. "You construe that to mean that authority comes directly—and solely—through the Holy Spirit?"

"Yes, but we would not use the word 'authority.' Revelation would be better."

Michael felt he had made an unfortunate slip. "The devil can cite scripture. . . ."

"It is not the devil."

The priest quoted from another part of the same Epistle. " 'O foolish Galatians, who hath bewitched you?' "

"We are not bewitched. Come and see for yourself—we are not." Michael heard it first as a gesture of evangelism: come and be saved. But it was more than that. Again, as before, he had the sense of the man reaching out to him, in a spirit of amity; it was an offer of religion-as-companionship. The artist was looking tightly at Michael, waiting for a decision, urgently wanting his invitation to be accepted. When the priest hesitated, Cory prodded him. There was nothing cursory about the bidding. "Please come."

While Michael was weighing it, the young artist moved quickly to the table upon which lay the priest's breviary, a notepad and a glass full of pencils. He lifted a pencil, wrote the address on the notepad and continued scribbling directions. "You get off the bus at Canal Street. It's a short walk from there. Come at nine tonight." Then he repeated the petition. "Please come."

When Cory left, Michael looked at the address and directions, hardly seeing them. His head still ached.

Underground . . .

Underground—he had never attended such a meeting. These times, especially on this mission, he was quite sure it would not be circumspect to go, but he was already on his way.

Getting off the bus, he started to walk, following Cory's penciled notes, in a southeasterly direction. This was Eastern Europe here, no country, many countries, neither Polish nor Russian nor Ukrainian, yet all of these, and the Slavic mark wherever he looked. It was a late closing time; the streets were weary. In a butcher shop, the lights were going out as rolls of stuffed intestine were being pulled down from window hooks, then coiled into wooden boxes. The fishmonger was disassembling his outdoor stand, letting the bung out of the tin basin, the icy water sloshing down the pavement, gutterward; white cod into black metal bins, the squish of dirty squid into huge cheese-cloth bags. The men seemed somberly reconciled—no day could end any better than any other day; the women were going off to their housework, perhaps, their broad pale faces nearly hidden in scarves and kerchiefs, their eyes half closed against invasion. All their expressions were elsewhere, it seemed to Michael, in ancient, alien hinterlands, almost beyond memory, soon gone. Not friendly.

The alleyway, according to Cory's directions, was called Kosciuszko, but he couldn't find it. Back and forth, one street and another, the Ukrainian Church, the Russian nightclub, both dark, then St. Mark's Place, and he knew he had come too far. Lost again in his search for Cory, he was reminded of the first time, in the dark streets of Rome, looking for the Via Raca, and he wondered whether there was some portent in his repeated search for the man, not only the quest for a man undiscovered but undiscoverable.

He found Kosciuszko and realized why he had missed it. Not an alleyway at all, but a kind of courtyard, what had once been a tiny mews perhaps, nearly sealed off from the street, unfrequented and barely lighted. It was still cobblestoned, it had never been done over, had never stopped being old. How forgotten the place was. None of the buildings were apparently in use; maybe none were usable. Dark-fronted, all of them might once have been warehouses or small factories; one had been a bookbindery, a barely legible sign said so; another, brass turnings.

The number he was looking for, 329, did not exist; in fact, there were no numbers, nor anyone to query. There was nothing here, only a dismal forgotten pocket in the city night, unwanted, and available for outrage.

He had come on a fool's errand, he realized, he had traveled uselessly and far, in a place beyond vespers. And to what end? Everything he was doing was turning into something amorphous, without name.

231

He saw the figure move.

It was in an entry across the street. He felt sure there was someone there, hiding in the vestibule of the warehouse building, the other side of the glass door. It stirred again, then was motionless.

I wonder if it sees me, Michael thought. He stepped back into the darkness, out of the streetlamp's range. It was only then, as he made the motion of retreat, that he became actively frightened. And what frightened him most was the realization that there might be nothing dangerous about the figure in the doorway; it was his own fear that was a peril. He had caught it, the poisonous infection, terror, in the park last night. The strangling had done it; and it occurred to him that it was meant to do precisely this.

He mustn't run, he told himself, he mustn't surrender even if the threats became aggressions. Go forward, he said, walk to the vestibule, speak to the man, look the terror in the face.

The glass door opened. The figure came out of the hallway.

Michael started toward him.

He was a tall man, not clearly visible . . . looking to the entrance of the courtyard. Quickly now, the figure moved. Directly into the circle of light.

Startled, Michael also moved.

The man heard the stir and, alarmed, twisted toward it.

Michael's breath stopped. "Cory!"

"Father Farris—that you?"

"Yes."

"My God, you scared hell out of me. Where've you been—I've been worried."

"I got lost."

"Hurry," Cory said, "we've almost started."

Michael rushed across the courtyard. Cory opened the door. "It's dark—I'll go first." As the priest stumbled: "Be careful—the steps are uneven."

They started upward. "Where are we?" Michael said. "What is this place?"

"It used to be a tannery. Animal hides to leather. Belts, pocketbooks, stuff like that. It still smells of it—we'll never get rid of the stink."

It was an acrid odor, deep and sharp, like vinegar; it went straight to the throat. The stairs were steep, and this was the third flight. In darkness, black.

232

They heard the voices before they saw the light. Not loud; distant murmurs; many people. Then, another landing and the dim light was above them, in the passageway.

"Here we are," Cavanaugh said. He looked at the priest. His manner was friendly as he pointed to the priestly collar. "I see you've worn your starch."

"Shouldn't I have?"

"Oh, it's fine—I'm glad you did. I wondered if you would."

He opened the door. There were fewer people than Michael had imagined, and the room was huge. Its side walls were brick, rough and unpainted, powdery with an old efflorescence. All the plumbing pipes were exposed; those too were unpainted; the galvanized ones were dirty gray, the brass and copper ones were green.

Michael thought, at first, that he had been tricked, that the young artist had brought him to an art show. There were a number of paintings displayed on a makeshift wooden partition, and many drawings hanging by wires from a suspended batten. Bits and pieces of abstractly sculpted figures were mounted on plinths made of cement blocks and cardboard boxes.

The viewers—they seemed like viewers at an exhibition—ambled leisurely from canvas to figure to drawing; they talked quietly, they laughed quietly, they seemed to be fond of one another. Some carried wineglasses; the wine was uniformly red. There were not as many men as women, possibly ten of one and fifteen of the other. The youngest was in his teens, with a long growth of ginger-colored hair gathered together by rubber bands to make a pigtail nearly to his waist; the oldest was a round woman with a sweet and winning face, and Michael thought of Ledagrazia. She was the only one who, apparently, had dressed with any design. Her clothes seemed to say: I am an elderly woman of comfortable means, with a comfortably rotund body, dressed in comfortably pleasant taste.

The others wore just anything. A woman in a long, wide skirt, all lace and eyelets, wearing a man's shirt; a fattish man trussed into a tight leather coat, too warm for May; a couple, man and wife perhaps, who had seemingly thrown all their clothes in a heap, then dressed randomly, blindfolded.

Michael pointed to the display of canvases. "Is it an art show?"

Cory smiled ingenuously. "No, not any kind of show." Then: "It's a Mass—or will be. The canvases—well—we feel that the Holy Spirit is part of everything we do—how we work, what songs we sing

233

and pictures we paint, how we make love, how we live with others. So we bring our lives here—to our church—whatever it is we do. Last week it was food. Along that wall, we all set out our specialties. More desserts than anything else." He laughed. "Of course, everybody found a symbol in that."

One of the art objects was particularly beautiful. It was a picture called *Desert Anchoress* and the woman depicted was as much made of sand as the desert itself, arid and desolate. The most exotic aspect of the picture was that it was macramé, composed of cordage and twine, twisted and braided in the subtlest variations of buff, beige, ocher.

Cory saw Michael's interest in the object and pointed away from it. The macramé artist sat quietly to one side, all by herself. She was even then working concentratedly at a sennit rope, plaiting it out of strands of hempen yarn, braiding and knotting and tying. Her mind was on nobody, on nothing other than the task. She was a woman of indeterminate age, could have been thirty or fifty, with a faded Irish face, somber and work-worn, skeletally thin, her eyes on some inaccessible distance, a futility.

"Her name is Cassie—she won't tell us her last name," Cory said. "She's painfully diffident—rarely says a word. They call her Cassie Macramé."

Cory excused himself and hurried across the room. Two elderly people embraced him; he kissed them both, the man and the woman, then hugged them once more, one in each arm.

The greetings, everywhere, were like a homecoming, as if all of them had been in foreign lands, as Cory had been, and all were being joyfully delivered of a dread that they would never see one another again. It was touchingly happy. But Michael pondered whether it was spontaneous, this bounty of affection, or had become a ritual. If it was genuinely impulsive, how different it was from the rite practiced in the more orthodox church, the ceremony of dignity and decorum. And aloofness. God afar, and man keeping His distance. Surely, at one time, in the days of Jesus perhaps, these demonstrative endearments must have been the more likely way that they celebrated their love for one another. On second thought, he could not envision Jesus as a promiscuous embracer; loaves and fishes seemed discrepant, somehow, with hugs and kisses. Mass was not a New Year's Eve party, Auld Lang Syne and smooches to strangers.

Yet, ritual or not, he saw no falsity here. There was something genuine and generous in the voices. Even tenderness.

234

"Wine, Padre?"

Michael turned. A middle-aged man stood close with a small tray on which there were a decanter of wine and a few glasses. His face was medievally ugly. Gaunt as everything about him was gaunt, the man's features were as grotesque as a gargoyle. His eyes were pulled out of shape with too much eyeball exposed, his mouth twisted and not altogether closeable; the look of his skin was too smooth and shiny pink, as though it had been synthesized. But most of all it was the expression of loathing, a smiling, simpering hatred.

"Want some wine, Padre?" he repeated.

The word "Padre" came out as an unclean insolence.

"No, thank you," Michael said.

"Visitors shouldn't insult us," he said, his leer more offensive.

Before any issue was joined, Michael was rescued. The mediator edged gently between them. "It's all right, Mr. Heskins," he said to the gargoyle. "I'll see to Father Farris."

Heskins nodded a little, frustratedly, and sidled away.

Michael's rescuer had a friendly smile. "I'm glad you've come, Father Farris. I'm Lewis Warrum." His hand was firm and warm.

He was a priest, older than Michael by five years or more. His costume was as fortuitous as all the others. With his clerical collar and black vest, he wore a pale-blue caftan, striped in yellowish beige, long, flowing down to his ankles. Michael wondered if, under it, he wore no trousers; none showed. All that was visible below the billowing skirt were his brown bedroom slippers, terry cloth.

Michael tried not to betray his surprise at his apparel but the priest detected it and with endearing frankness revealed his own discomfiture. "It's a silly get-up, isn't it?" He smiled charmingly. "It's very difficult these days—the role gets confused—so does the costume." With undisguised envy he seemed to be reviewing Michael's ministerial dress. It was so uncomplicatedly black and white, so unmistakably an integer of priestliness. Farris suspected he saw a stir of nostalgia in the man, for simpler times, perhaps, remembering and envying a lost clarity.

"Cory told me you were coming," he said to Michael, with friendliness. "I want you to know how welcome you are."

"Thank you."

"I'm sorry you were greeted first by Mr. Heskins. He's an unfortunate man. He was in a boiler room explosion and his face and hands—all reconstructed . . . It's not so easy to reconstruct his spirit."

235

Michael murmured a word of sympathy and Warrum quickly shifted to a happier subject. "You've come on a special occasion," he said. "Sacramental. We're having a wedding."

Cory approached them. "Bill and Elbie have a plane to catch, Father. You better get them married."

"Yes, instantly." He hurried away, pulling up his caftan so he could walk faster. No, he wore no trousers, and his calves were bare.

"Dearly beloved," he called out happily, as if he were a Protestant. He got a giggling response and a smattering of applause. "Shall we get the show on the road?" he called. "I'll need a server—anybody available?"

"I am." It was the pigtailed boy. A flash of ginger hair, and he was standing beside Father Warrum.

Mr. Heskins turned the main lights off, someone else flipped a switch at the front of the room. The loft was all shadows now, except for the forward wall. On it, the crucifix. Michael hadn't been aware of it before. It was the single liturgical object in the entire place. Black against the only white wall, it was the strangest cross Michael had ever seen. Christ's body, as long and thin and wasted as El Greco would have done it, but not nailed to any members of wood; the arms alone were pinioned against the body of a snake. The serpent was coiled around the limbs of the Christus. It was ugly.

Cory, close beside him: "It's dreadful, isn't it?"

Revolted, Michael nodded his head.

"The sculptor thinks it joins the violation of Eden with the violation of Golgotha."

"The violations are certainly there, aren't they?"

Wryly: "Yes." He pointed to the doorway. "There she is."

"Who?"

"The sculptor."

She stood at the doorway, not entering immediately, gauging the room. She was the most awesomely magnificent woman Michael had ever seen. Taller than average, she stood taller still, as if challenging her own stature. She was foreign-looking, a darkly fervent face, with cheekbones much too wide, and blazing eyes much too far apart. Blaze, yes—that was the prepossessing quality of the woman, as if she were about to be consumed by some self-enkindled fire. And, seemingly, to neutralize this burning vividness, her clothes were almost colorless, a hesitating softness, like doeskin, except for the accident at her throat, a scarf of orange and scarlet, an escape of flame. She didn't

236

smile and, Michael thought, she never smiles, as if smiling were a reserve power she wouldn't dissipate. Power, that was it, yet altogether feminine; and throat-catching beauty.

"She's the sculptress?"

"Yes, but for God's sake don't call her that," Cory whispered. "She insists on 'sculptor.' "

"Of course."

Misconstruing Michael's meaning, he said quickly, "No 'of course' about it—she's not a lesbian—far from it. She loves men—she's always in a riot with one of them. . . . Christ, she's beautiful, isn't she?"

". . . Yes."

She moved from the doorway. Her body was exquisite, anomalously lean and lush; there was something formidable in the animal litheness of her walk, almost threatening. He wondered why he had that sense of her—did he feel her as a personal danger? No, it was something in the woman herself—more than his feeling of her power—a prescience of her recklessness. Possibly beyond recklessness, to the edge of . . . what?

He had forgotten the Christus she had sculpted. Cory was now indicating it again. "Can you imagine such a lovely creature creating a hideous thing like that?"

"No."

"Yet, if you knew her, you'd see it all fits."

"What's her name?"

"Nobody really knows—we think it's fake. She calls herself Dr. Falga Cristobal—says it was originally Cristobão—Brazilian. We have no idea what she's a doctor of, but whatever it is, she's given it up to become a sculptor. I'd say it was a mistake, wouldn't you?"

Michael suspected that the resentment was even stronger than the sarcasm suggested; yet, it was clear Cory was hypnotized by the woman.

"Let's get started," Warrum was saying for the third or fourth time. His manner was leisurely and amiable. He wasn't trying to make an august event of anything, he seemed to say, nothing full of heavenly splendor, like a Mass; only a friendly game of cribbage, say, or the rehearsal of an amateur play, come if you've got nothing better to do.

Some came quickly, some didn't. Those that didn't, lingered over the paintings a bit longer; those that did, drew folding chairs to the front of the room, or sat on the threadbare davenport along the wall.

237

When the chairs ran out, the davenport people gave up their loose pillows which were carried just anywhere. A few stood on the periphery with wineglasses in their hands; an elderly woman sat on an elderly man's lap, put a few raisins in her mouth and popped some into his.

"We have something of an evening tonight," Father Warrum said. "A sacrament or two—getting Bill and Elbie off to a happy life—and when they're gone, we can talk about another letter I've received. It's from the chancery and it takes us to task again."

Somebody tittered, but the others were silent, worried. A stillness had taken the Galatians; the merriment was gone. Warrum sensed the gloom and regretted it. "I'm sorry I put a damper on a happy occasion. I could have waited to mention the letter. Very foolish. Sufficient unto the day is the evil thereof, and the night too. Let's forget it if we can. And make a joyful noise."

A woman who had applauded before, applauded again.

Warrum lowered his head almost imperceptibly, then raised it heavenward. "In the name of the Father, and of the Son, and of the Holy Spirit."

Under his breath Michael said the amen, but nobody else did. To what the priest had spoken, they were making a response he had never heard, repeating the words:

"Holy Spirit."

It was a whisper, it was the faintest stirring of the lips, as reverent, as full of piety as any response he could imagine. And as the service continued, he heard it again and again . . . Holy Spirit . . . The words had tenderness, they had devotion. In them, he heard the essence of the worship, the direct converse with the divine truth—no intermediaries, no pomp and panoply, no complex liturgy to darken or conceal, no golden altar raised too high for reaching, no heaven unattainable: God was here. God, they said, was friendly, had accepted the invitation, and had come. He had come bringing charisma, the gift of His presence, the hearing of His voice, the seeing of His face, the speaking to Him in tongues, the understanding of His mind, His will, and the returning to His love. Not only were they intimately in touch with the Holy Spirit, they were part of it; they were God's counterpart.

Each time Michael heard the words Holy Spirit in his ears, he heard the Latin words in his mind, Spiritus Sanctus, and said amen. How strange that the amen remained the same, language to language, still the same yes, the same restorative affirmation of truth, the same promise that we are all one, orthodox and heterodox, Catholics all, upon this stone.

Yet, caution. This was not what these people were saying. Not an affirmation of our sameness, but of our differences.

He must not let this Mass become too moving to him. Yet, a Mass was a Mass, he had never attended one that did not touch him in some way—and already he felt too close to this one. The old expression, watch and pray, came into his mind, and he resisted half of it. He was here to watch, he warned himself, only to watch. He must pray in other places.

Then the cry: *"Kyrie Eleison."*

It is not fair, he wanted to shout. If you say the Latin words in English, say the Greek as well. Take the painful ones—Kyrie Eleison—and cry Lord have mercy in the most familiar agonies, in English; don't anesthetize them in a foreign tongue.

Abruptly—no prelude, no warning—someone rose.

"I have been given an extraordinary grace," the young man said.

Nobody asked the nature of his blessing. Someone whispered alleluia.

A woman rose. Her face was flushed, crimson. "Last Friday, as my little boy went off to school, I had a sudden fear. Then a great hope drove it away, and I felt raised up by the Spirit."

Alleluia.

"I spoke in tongues," an old man said. "I sang, oh how I sang—in tongues."

Alleluia.

It was sheer revivalist. It was store-window religion, drums and tambourines and ecstatic fainting spells. Surely, these people must know that this was a drama they were enacting, not a devotion—theater, not church—and their feelings were histrionic, not real . . . Then why was he feeling it?

"I drove the devil out of my father's sickness."

Alleluia. No, no alleluia, he almost said aloud, the woman is mistaken. She may think she's telling the truth, but she is deceived . . . By what, he asked, by whom?

"I had a vision of our Lord."

No.

"I had a gift of prophecy. For one moment—praise God!—I had a gift of prophecy!"

No, he said again, but they said gloria.

Gloria, gloria. Glory to God in the highest.

Prayer, then the Epistle, the Responsory and Gospel.

"There he is," Cory said softly. He pointed.

"Who is he?"

"Bill—the groom."

The man was dressed nondescriptly. He was older than Michael had expected him to be; he had thought a young wedding, and this groom was in his late thirties, forty perhaps. He came walking forward from the back of the room, simply walking, not making any ceremonious slow march of it, until he came close to Father Warrum. As the latter smiled, Bill did the same and added a little nod of his head, in much the same way as one would say hi, in a hallway somewhere.

"There's Elbie," Cory said, turning his head to a little room on the left through the doorway of which the bride was coming. Michael turned to look at her.

The bride was a young man. He was in his mid-twenties, Michael supposed, and wore a newish-looking dark suit. Thin-faced and studious-looking, he wore glasses, with nothing to distinguish him from the commonplace except for a halting uncertainty of movement, as if he had forgotten his house number.

They were going to be married.

Everything in Michael tightened. "Is he really going to marry them?"

"Yes," Cory said.

"He can't—it's unnatural."

"It's beautiful."

"It's a sacrilege!"

"No!"

Michael felt stricken. "I must leave," he said.

Cory turned a beseeching face. "No, please."

"I can't—!"

"They're two decent people, Father. They've lived together for four years. They truly love each other. It's not a sacrilege—it's a sacrament of love."

Michael couldn't answer. He wanted to cry out that there was no sacrament of love, but of marriage. And that marriage meant the procreation of the race, and the regeneration of it, and the hope of man's future in it, and that *that* was the love that mattered, the love of God. But all he could say was, "I can't."

"If you leave, you'll do them a great unkindness," Cory said. "You needn't take part. You needn't even pray with us."

Just watch, the young man was begging him. It was no different from his own warning to himself. Watch without praying. He needn't become a participant. Nor need he perpetrate an unkindness by a conspicuous departure.

Anyway, it was too late now. The Eucharistic Liturgy had begun. The service of the solemnity had started, of the Body and Blood of Christ, of the sacramental renewal of his sacrifice on Calvary. The Eucharistic prayer, then, for this is my Body, this is the chalice of my Blood, world without end, let us pray; may the Blood of our Lord Jesus Christ keep my soul until life everlasting. Then the consuming of the precious Blood.

Now, he said, now comes the communion of the Faithful—and those two, the two he thought he daren't watch, would be the first. How could he bear to observe them, in the presence of the wine and the Host? They had to be unclean and unconfessed; how could he dare to be present, willfully joining himself to their sin? And why was he not revolted by them? Why did he feel no aversion at all, but only a yearning to . . . pray for them.

May Almighty God have mercy on you, forgive you your sins, and bring you life everlasting.

Amen.

Something was changing in the room. The communicants were rising. They were clapping their hands, rhythmically clapping; some were singing. Then they started to reach for one another. A man took the hand of a girl who took the hand of a boy who took the hand of an old woman. It was a circle now, and they chanted.

The Lord be with you.

And with thy spirit.

The Lord make His love to shine upon you.

May Almighty God bless you.

The Father, and the Son, and the Holy Spirit.

Praise the Lord!

World without end.

Amen.

He hadn't known it was going to occur. He hadn't seen anyone reach for him. It was Cory's left hand that held his right; he didn't know the man on the other side of him. But he was in a circle, saying the words as the others were saying them.

God go with you.

And when the circle broke apart and they were all embracing one another, he felt that his hands were moist, and was certain that his skin had gone paper white. He knew he should leave quickly, but he couldn't; he wanted to embrace someone as others were embracing, but he couldn't.

"When we say yes in hypocrisy there is an honest no that screams to be free."

It was not exactly a homily that Father Warrum was delivering; it was certainly not in the order of things; more specifically, it was not a moment when sermons are ordinarily spoken. But it had come up naturally, almost inevitably, in the course of what the Galatians called their conversance.

"And if we celebrate our brotherhood not only in Christ the God but in Christ the man, then our brotherhood is with all men, Catholic and otherwise, poor as well as rich. Perhaps our brotherhood is even closer to those who have not than to those who have, for Christ's ministry was not to the rich but to the poor.

"But the ministry to the poor over the rich is a dangerous ministry, as dangerous as Calvary. So be it. Christ's mission was not *sub*mission, it was revolt. As ours must be. Revolt against the suffocating incenses of the Church and the silken hypocrisies and the golden chains; revolt against the dusty reasons and the tithing corruptions and the Sunday bingo-madness and the factory-made fetishes and flippancies which kill the faith.

"We must cry no to these things. Yet, there are those who say that no is a destroying word. Do not—I beg you—do not believe it. It is the word we have from the mouth of the rebel Jesus."

It was trashy rhetoric, it was passion deeply felt; it was radical fervor, it was cant. Whatever, it was the agony of a man who had left home.

"The thought must grow," he continued, "the mind must change. The doctrine that doesn't change becomes dogma, and we have suffered much from it. The man who is taken as infallible is an idol, and becomes an instrument of man's tyranny over man. When this happens, dogma and idol must be questioned to the root, and we must deny infallibility and deny the dogma. And out of this God-affirming no, we renew our minds and our almighty hopes. Even the soul renews itself, from grace to grace. Thus faith may endure, and God may remain forever new, forever radiant. And thus we pray."

He lowered his head; the others did the same. But not Michael. His

242

eyes roved the room. There was one other person whose head was not lowered. Falga Cristobal. She was looking at Michael, her eyes fixed, frankly staring, without equivocation. . . . A shiver went through him.

He heard Father Warrum's voice. The priest held a letter in his hand. "It came from the chancery this morning," he was saying. "By messenger. I had to sign for it. This one's not from Bishop Weiler, but from the Archbishop. We've been promoted."

He was trying to lighten the seriousness, but for once nobody laughed. He raised the letter high in the air and riffled the pages. "As you can see, it's a long epistle—longer than the two Corinthians. So I won't try to read it to you. What it says, in effect, is that if we do not step back out of the no-man's land of heterodoxy, we shall no longer be considered a harmless cult inside the Church but a baneful sect outside it. He says, 'You may already have wandered into the dark reach of heresy.' I am tempted to answer that a man's reach should exceed his grasp, or what's a heaven for? But I do think that would be frivolous, don't you?"

He was unnerved and needed them to laugh, and this time they did, a little. He was encouraged to go on. "He lists four general charges against us, and any number of specific ones. Among the general, he says, first, that we believe the Second Coming of Christ is imminent."

"And it is!" someone called out.

"Second, that we have an insolent certainty of salvation."

"Is faith an insolence?" a woman asked.

"Third, that we claim the Holy Spirit speaks only to the heart, and the mind is a betrayer."

"The mind is Judas!"

"And last, he says there are too many among us who have denied that His Holiness, the Pope, is the sole and sanctified Vicar of Christ, and therefore infallible. And from these four heretical beliefs come pagan practices. And he lists them. I think he enumerates twenty-one."

"Blackjack!"

This time everybody laughed, and this time Warrum was disturbed to hear it; he had not meant for the Archbishop's letter to be taken quite *that* frivolously. He went on, more soberly. "Among the specific charges are a number we have heard before, in earlier letters, We are heretical—I think he says schismatic—on matters of divorce, the control of conception, abortion, homosexuality, the marriage of priests, the ordination of women—need I continue?"

He paused. His eyes became steadier, more grave. "But it is his final statement that is most forbidding." He turned the pages of the letter and read the concluding paragraph.

" 'You must therefore, in your considered wisdom, recognize that Mother Church is one, not several, and you cannot in good faith conduct your life outside the canons of universal Catholicism, you cannot build a church outside the Church. In such sunderance there is heartbreak. How can you so excommunicate yourself? I ask you, therefore, my dear Father Warrum, to disband your congregation, to discontinue your meetings for whatever well-intentioned purposes they have been held, and return to Mother Church where you have always found love and forgiveness, and will always continue so to do. Yours, in Jesus Christ, I remain . . .' "

The silence was a density, almost tangible. Warrum slowly folded the letter and slipped it into the voluminous pocket of his caftan. As he did so, he again became aware of his hodgepodge costume. His smile was mirthless.

"We have answered three letters of the chancery. None of our responses has been easy to write. But to answer this one—the warning is specific—it is the first time the word has appeared: excommunicate. Disband or be disowned. There are those who can meet this terrifying threat with considerable fortitude. But I must admit, I have had no other country than the Church, and it is a forsaken thing to be exiled from it."

He faltered, didn't know how to use the next moment, where to look, what to do with his hands. He reached into his caftan pocket and again brought forth the letter; he stared at the pages, perhaps not seeing them.

"I . . . do not know which way to turn. It is a comfort to me that we are learning how to do these things together. For I confess that I need your help now, possibly more than you need mine." Once more, he held up the letter. "What do I do with this?"

"Burn it!"

There was a gasp from somebody. Then a murmur, almost inaudible. Everybody looked to the left margin of the room. It was

Falga Cristobal who had spoken. She stood up, incendiary. He thought again: a recklessness. But seeing her rise so strongly, so passionately in defiance, he realized that the difference between recklessness and courage could be measured by the discrepancy between the size of the risk and the size of the cause. And with a fierce woman like Cristobal there might be no discrepancy. A life for a cause; perfect equity.

"Burn it!" she said again.

Heskins took up the cry. "Burn it!" Then someone else: "Burn it!"

The muttering was general—eruptions everywhere. Only a few voices were on the sculptor's side, but their tones were the sharpest. As to the other Galatians, they were muddled, irresolute, uncertain what to say or where to attach themselves.

"Burn it!" Falga's voice had a rich resonance and its vibrations were contagious. The words were being taken up by more than her own group now; there was a rhythm starting, burn it, burn it.

Warrum raised his hand. He tried to still the mounting noise; he waved an arm in the air. Starting to speak, he desisted, then started again. In everything he did now, there was misgiving. He was immobilized.

But Cristobal wasn't. "Now—burn it now!"

"No!"

It was Cory. He had risen to his feet. A second time he shouted no, in a louder voice than Michael thought was in the man.

"No! We don't burn a letter any more than we would burn a book. If we're Galatians—if we talk friendship and forgiveness—how does a notion of violence occur to *us?*"

"It occurs to them," Falga raged. "Excommunication—what's that? Not violence? It's burning at the stake!"

"Let them be violent—not us!" Cory shouted. "We're not destroyers!"

"We're revolutionaries!"

"No, we're not, Falga! We're peaceful partisans of the Holy Spirit."

"We're radicals—I've heard you use that word!"

"Yes, but only in the sense of the original meaning—the root, the origin. The source of our sustenance—God in the Holy Spirit, God in ourselves!"

"And what are we to do—deny that? Go back to the dark before

245

yesterday? Look backward, and be attacked when our heads are turned? No! We don't look back. Anybody who does is guilty—he's guilty in the bone, guilty in the blood!"

She was pointing directly at Cory, and Michael imagined her as a priest, ordained not in Christ's mercy but in Jehovah's justice, a finger-pointing fanatic, aflame; no peace, all passion. She fulminated at him. "As guilty as all the other compromisers!"

"I am not guilty—my hands are clean!"

"Bloody with compromise!"

Somebody reached for her, not roughly, simply to restrain her. Defensively, her arm struck out, and a man grabbed her. From no-where, it seemed, someone came to defend her: Heskins. He smashed a fist into the man's face. How the two others got into it was unclear. Blows were struck, a woman started to grapple crazily with a man. Warrum hurried to the melee. So did Cory, to put an end to it. An elderly man got between him and the sculptor. Warrum shouted, begged for them all to separate; he lurched at a berserk boy to push him out of the fray; someone struck wildly at anyone, and it was Warrum who was hurt by it. Cory reached, struggled with two men; they punched at one another. A woman screamed in another section of the room, she screamed and screamed and kept on screaming and, at last, attention shifted to the outcry. Suddenly the fight was over, the woman was being ministered to and comforted, and all that was left of the turmoil was her soft sobbing, and shame.

Michael turned from her and saw Cory coming toward him. The artist looked miserable; he was mortified. "I'm sorry, Father—I can't tell you how sorry I am. Nothing like this has ever happened before."

He was asking for comfort, but what could Michael say? It's all right, it's not important, not serious? But it wasn't all right, it was important, it was serious. "I think I'd better go," he said.

". . . Yes."

Humiliated, Cory was the first to turn away. Michael started for the door. As he got to the threshold something held him there. He didn't go toward the stairs but looked once more into the large room . . . to have one more glance at Cristobal.

There was a slow and muffled movement in the place. Heavy, hushed. If she were still there, she'd be the first one he would see. But she was gone.

He departed too, slowly, down the steps.

What a fascinating woman she was, beautiful and terrible, like nobody he had ever known. He thought of the sonorous voice made strident by an ugly rage; of the exquisite being who had fashioned a most hideous Christ; of the cruelty she suggested, and the splendor. He could not make sense of the contradictions; she was remote from his experience, alien in too many ways. But why did he need to find an affinity to the woman, why did it bother him that he did not understand her?

An hour later, as he mounted the steps of Mindszenty House, he heard the phone ringing. He hurried the key, opened the door and got to the telephone under the stairway.

"Father Farris?"

The voice was unfamiliar for a sentence, then he recognized it: Lewis Warrum. The man sounded shattered.

"I can't tell you," he kept saying, "I can't tell you how grieved I am that you had to see us that way. It doesn't happen—it's never happened before."

"Yes—Cory told me that."

"It's true. And I wanted—you being a priest—I wanted so desperately to make a good impression on you. And such an ugly scuffle!"

"It wasn't your fault." Except in a larger sense, he thought.

"Will you come again?"

"Well . . . no, I don't think so."

"Please—won't you give us a chance to show you we're not that way?"

Michael wavered; but no, he mustn't lead the man on. "Really—I can't."

In the silence, he could feel what Warrum must be feeling, the rejection. Wanting to end the man's distress, he was about to say goodbye and hang up. But the other said, "Then—please—let me come to you. Father Farris, I am in desperate need of a friend." As if afraid Michael might say no again, he hastily continued. "I know what you must be thinking—I should have many friends among the Galatians. But it isn't so. I'm a priest—what do they know of a priest? Especially a . . . troubled one."

"I'm sorry." He meant sorry that the man was troubled, but apparently Warrum mistook the word as a second rejection, a total one.

Michael heard the click. Slowly replacing the receiver, he was unnerved by the man's torment. He couldn't reconcile the gifted leader, the talented public speaker, a man of power in persuasion,

247

with the pathetic voice he had just heard, forlorn and friendless. He deeply regretted not having gone to his aid in some way. Lonely . . . the voice sounded so lonely.

He must stop commiserating; nearly all priests are lonely. He could attest to that. Loneliness was the white space in the breviary. . . .

But then loneliness was not unique to the priesthood. Cory, too, by inviting him to the Galatians' meeting, had made a bid for his friendship.

His mind felt like a field of brambles. He was exhausted and went to bed.

Was that the real reason Cory had invited him to the prayer meeting?—friendship? Or was it to demonstrate how disparately he and his brother viewed salvation? What would that have proved? And what about Cristobal? If Cory was telling the truth that the Galatians were a peaceful little cult, what was she doing there? How could they tolerate a member so candidly belligerent?

I must put an end to this self-mystification, he told himself. I'm imagining difficult answers to easy puzzles. Cory had invited him to the Galatians for the most basic religious motive in the world: evangelism. Warrum had made that clear; had begged Michael to return. As to Cristobal, it was the old story: dissidence is the besetting trouble of dissidents. The Galatians had splintered away from the Charismatics; now Cristobal's group would splinter away from the Galatians . . . divisiveness, the very disease Michael was fighting.

Mystification again: how had Warrum gotten his number? It was an absurd question: he got it from Cory; there was no riddle in it.

In the darkness, Michael saw Warrum's stricken face again. And he heard the forlorn voice: "I have had no other country than the Church, and it is a forsaken thing to be exiled from it."

Exile echoed everywhere. It reverberated in this old Mindszenty House, an empty haven where refugees had ached for the friendly footing of well-known cobblestones, for rooms familiar enough to walk through in darkness. He could hear their voices as clearly as Father Warrum's, resounding mournfully in the hollow brownstone, calling to one another, trading memories of a dish that could be cooked only with homeland ingredients, of a jest that was humorous only in that one cafe, of a certain beautifying radiance in the air, back home, where there was a more becoming sunlight.

He thought of his own distances. He was nostalgic for his happy childhood, as if he had had it; for loving parents, as if they were real;

for a bygone love affair, as if it had ever happened.

Abruptly, in darkness, he thought of the real thing: a bracelet; and he recalled a real woman, with a doubting smile, with quick eyes in a troubled face.

He had no idea when he fell asleep.

The ringing sounded like cathedral bells, a carillon somewhere, an angelus pealing everything at once, morning, noon, evening.

It was the telephone.

How gray it was in this hellish hallway, how cold the wooden steps underfoot; how clammy a house was when unoccupied.

"Hello."

It was Mrs. Merrill's voice. "I'm sorry—did I awaken you? It's nearly nine o'clock—I thought you mightn't be asleep—and it just arrived by hand."

He wasn't understanding her. "What just arrived by hand, Mrs. Merrill?"

"This letter. It's addressed to you, but it was sent to the Permanent Observer's office, care of the Cardinal. . . ."

He was still half asleep. "A letter for me?"

"Yes. The Cardinal would like you to pick it up." Then there was a directive in her voice. "He said at eleven o'clock."

"Yes, I'll be there," he said.

Perhaps he was still not fully awake, or perhaps it was the voice of authority that brooked no question. At any event, he hadn't asked why it couldn't be forwarded again, why it had to be picked up at eleven in the morning . . . or, even, who might have sent the letter. Mrs. Merrill could easily have looked at the return address.

No need. He knew who had sent it. He knew as certainly as if he had torn open the envelope and seen the signature. It would be that girl, about her bracelet. It was preposterous for him to be so sure. There was nothing, not one shred of evidence that she knew he had it, that she knew he was in America, that she knew how to reach him. The supposition was to be dismissed. Yet, he knew.

Amazement: he was right.

He waited for Mrs. Merrill to leave the waiting room. The instant she was gone, he ripped at the flap, pulled out the single sheet and read the message:

Dear Reverend Farris,

When we met in Mr. Cavanaugh's place . . . wandered off with it . . . pick it up . . . convenient to you. . . . My telephone . . . Nora Eisenstadt.

He had an impulse to snatch at the phone on the anteroom table. But he couldn't talk here. An impulse, then, to hurry off, run to the nearest phone booth, hello, it's me, the bracelet-stealer, how are you, anyway?

"Is it good news, Father Farris?"

The Cardinal, as once before, stood on the threshold of his study. Michael felt the flush of festivity, yet awkwardness; someone caught in a pantry.

"Yes, it is, sort of."

With sheepish pleasure, he made sounds of gratitude for the letter and stuffed it into his pocket.

"Come in," the Cardinal said, "I want to talk to you."

Michael's spirits lifted even higher. He couldn't believe it would be that easy. All good fortunes coming at once. Days of asinine snooping and tracking, concocting outlandish schemes for storming the Cardinal's fortress, and here they were, as casual as tea, come in, I want to talk to you. Stepping over the threshold was stepping onto a new level of hope.

"Sit down," the Cardinal said. "I have an apology to offer."

Better and better. He said nothing; needn't improve upon excellence.

"Actually, it's not an apology to you, but to my friend, Feradoti."

Dear heaven, was it going to be as easy as this?

"You started to plead his case. And at the very outset you reminded me that he had done me a service—through you—in getting my brother to come home."

"I was not suggesting a quid pro quo."

"Well, your point was that I could at least be civil in hearing the case of someone who had been generous to me."

"Yes . . . I did feel that."

"And I was—shall we say—obstinate."

"Yes, Your Eminence, you were."

"And an ingrate."

Michael didn't realize that the man could, without softening a single lineament of his face, be so charming. A cultivated skill.

"Yes, I think you were a little ungrateful, sir."

250

"I have brought you here to tell you: you have no idea."

"No idea of what, Cardinal?"

"The enormity of my ingratitude."

The affected charm was gone. His face was severely set, and Michael had the sense that the man was, in some anomalous way, making a strenuous effort to hide a distress.

"I want you to know how deeply indebted I am to Paolo Feradoti."

"It's not necessary, Your Eminence. I should not have mentioned indebtedness."

"I still want you to know." There was compulsion in it. "I've known Paolo Feradoti for twenty years. Known him more intimately than anybody in my youth." He hesitated. "I'm going to tell you all of it—and then I'm going to do you a very special favor."

He started arranging things. He arranged the Austrian curtains so that the morning sun would not shine into Michael's eyes. He arranged his chair at a meticulously measured distance between writing table and bookcase, so he could swivel and lean. He arranged a calendar and a clock, a millimeter here, a millimeter there. It was the setting of scene and pause for effect, Michael considered at first; but, on second thought, it was pure procrastination; he was delaying the start of a troubling revelation.

"I was born on Kilklare Island." It was as if he had prepared himself by the diligent study of a script. "It's a tiny reef, out in the Atlantic, off Connemara. A mean place, miserable. Whatever you can say about poverty, whatever you can say about ignorance and rancor, the petty spites of man to man—you can say them all about Kilklare. Nobody has a kind word for the place, least of all the people who live there. And it's an unhealthy island. The cold comes out of the sea—and the bitter wind—it seems to go back a hundred generations, that cruel wind—it numbs your very soul. People get ill of it—they say Kilklare is the birthplace of pulmonary consumption.

"My childhood was miserable there. I've heard it told that very young children do not know, they cannot be aware when they are miserable, they cannot put a conscious label on their unhappiness. I could. I knew it very well. From the instant I was born, I knew, every brain cell told me, every cursed day.

"When my parents died and left me in charge of my five-year-old brother, I was determined that somehow or other we had to be liberated from Kilklare. The Church was my means of doing it. Deliberately—with a purpose—I made the choice of going into the priesthood. And my purpose was *escape*. It was not an act of faith, not at all. Faith came later—much later—after long study and deep contemplation, and no end of pain.

"So I went to the seminary and, with a little cadging here and there, I got my brother a free scholarship to an excellent Catholic boarding school in Dublin.

"I wanted to succeed—oh, I wanted badly to succeed. And if one wishes to go far in the Church, there are specific ways. One does not look for poor parishes or unknown cloisters or brotherhoods of charity—one goes to Rome. So, directly after I was ordained, I started my apprenticeship in the Vatican.

"It was outrageously easy. I am extremely bright, my mind is agonistic, it excels in contest. I went ahead quickly, I was respected, it looked as if nothing could interfere with my rise in a great theocracy. Then, one day, things changed.

"I cannot exactly say *what* changed. I was afflicted with an indefinable malady which I can describe with only one word. Clumsiness. Now, you cannot call that a malady, can you? But it was. I had always considered myself a man of extraordinary dexterity—I was adroit everywhere, my muscles, my mind. And suddenly I was a lummox. I lumbered up to a decision and hulked away from it. If I took a delicate thought into my head, I dropped it and shattered it into a hundred inanities. I began to disintegrate.

"Then came my understanding of it. Guilt. It was bitter medicine—the cure more painful than the ailment—and it didn't *cure.* I realized that my faith had only been poverty-deep—never more—and that I had gone into the Church as men enter banking or industry, to traffic with Mammon. And the price I would pay for affluence would not be, ironically enough, the loss of heaven—which I had not truly sought—but the decay of what I held most precious: my mind. And I could feel it happening, like a slow softening, like rot. . . .

"So I determined to leave the Church.

"It was then that I met Paolo Feradoti. He was a youngish man who had just been made a bishop, and been transferred to a secondary position in the Secretariat. He was my superior and he was kind to me. One day, when he saw me quaking at my desk, he called me to his office. He kept me there a long time, he made me talk; then he said I was too relentless with myself. He asked me: 'Why do you try to live only with the worst aspects of yourself? Why can't you find some Lucas Cavanaugh who will be at least a part-time friend? Why don't you give yourself a merciful chance?'

" 'A chance to do what?' I asked.

252

" 'Find whatever courage you have—whatever selflessness. Whatever love of God.' He was silent for an instant. Then he added, 'Why don't you try your soul?'

"Try my soul . . . What affliction could I perpetrate upon myself to test the measure of my love of God, and my love of Lucas Cavanaugh? After tormenting myself with the question, I faced it: I would go back to Kilklare—as a curate in the hell of my childhood.

"Cory was just entering his teens at the time. I arranged for him to go to a preparatory school in Florence—and I went back to Kilklare.

"It was even worse than I expected. The church had burned down, with grief to no one. Nobody missed it, nobody wanted it again. I started a parish house in an abandoned fish cannery. Not a person put in an appearance. And there was nothing to come to, no shrine, no sanctuary, and certainly not the comfort of a loving priest.

"One night there was a terrible storm. I went out where the cliffs met the shore and picked driftwood out of an angry sea, and in the morning I used it to build an altar.

"Nobody noticed. Anger was the mode of everything, anger at the tempests, anger at poverty and, of course, anger at the sea.

"I started to work with my neighbors; I went out in their boats with them, I helped to mend their nets, I set up a barter market.

"With the approach of my second winter there, when things looked most wretched for them, I gave them a stretch of marshland, a terrible vile-smelling bog that belonged to the Church, and told them to cut the peat, and sell it. It took them through four months that would have been starvation.

"That winter was so cold—I cannot tell you how mercilessly cold. It was frozen vengeance. And I was becoming ill. The winter had barely begun—there were three months of it before me—it would be spring before my lungs would clear and I would breathe again. . . . Except, I knew they wouldn't clear.

"I had tuberculosis.

"This, then, was the trial. Should I let it be known in the offices of the Vatican, and be recalled to a warm place? Or should I test my body to the soul? For the first time in my life something was more needful to me than myself. It became my obsession—I would like to say my passion—that the people of the island should have food through this winter and the next. It was more vital to me than rising in the hierarchy of the Church—more important than that my sputum was now always red.

"The winter never seemed to end, and I was worsening. One

morning I began to smell my own person, and it was the odor of dying. As a seminarian, I had attended many mortally ill people, and none of them had ever seemed repugnant to me, but now my own stench disgusted me. I wanted death, but I was not prepared for it. I knew that I lacked grace. At last, however, I reconciled myself to a meaningless mortality, and asked for Anointment. It was Feradoti who gave it to me. He arrived on Christmas morning. On the last day of the year, he bundled me in bedclothes and cotton wool, and carried me back to Italy.

"At first, I knew hardly anything of what he was doing for me. I hadn't even a sense of time—daylight and darkness were the same. Then one morning, one Palm Sunday morning full of glory, I awakened to Italian sunlight. Oh, how genial it was, how loving! Everything, it seemed everything, was loving then. Paolo—who understands every delicacy of devotion—to God, to man, to the more helpless creatures, to food, to the blessings of beauty, to the changes of the season. And Ledagrazia—do you know Ledagrazia?"

"Yes. She nursed me through a weekend chill."

"She nursed me for ten months." He stopped. His face went into shadow as if a cloud had darkened the sunlit Italian scene he had been describing. Then, quickly, the eclipse was over, and he continued. "In June, that year, they sent for Cory and he came down from Florence and spent the summer with us. The boy gave me the happiest news of my life. I had been hoping—praying, in fact—that he'd enter the priesthood. And his news was: he had applied and been accepted at the seminary of the Santa Trinità in Florence. What a wonderful summer it was! We talked and listened to music and were all in love with one another. Cory was painting a good deal—he had won a prize or two at school—and Leda encouraged him to continue at it. Once a week she took him into Rome where he had lessons at an art studio. He loved her very much and she was very . . . important in his life." He paused. The cloud again. "As to Paolo, he was the most lovable human being I have ever known. And whatever true and certain faith I have within myself was started by Paolo Feradoti."

He turned away. He had touched some tender feeling in himself and he was not at home with it. It was, apparently, a sensitivity he distrusted. When he had recovered his flintiness, he said, "Yes, he led me to my faith—but faith is not a once-acquired thing. It must be rewon every day we live. It's a never-ending war against the times, against cynicism and freethinking and against one's doubting self. Every day, a man of true belief has a battle to fight. You challenged me to a terrible one. You dared me to make a choice between my love of Feradoti and my love of the old order of the Church."

"Need it be a battle? Can you not make peace with both sides?"

"There is no peace. Whatever affection I have for the man, I abhor his persuasion."

"His persuasion is decent, Your Eminence, it is healing. He searches for a way of life between the old Vatican and the Church in a young world."

"Between the Vatican and the Galatians."

How curious, he thought, for Cavanaugh to mention such a minor group as the Galatians in this context. "Those are not the only choices. And even if they were . . ."

He caught himself. The sentence had begun almost on its own, as a figure of debate. He couldn't conceive of the Galatians as any part of his choice; the words had damaged him.

Cavanaugh pounced. "There—you idiot! You spend one night with those people—one handclapping, footstomping night—and imbecilities spring into your mouth. Well, let me warn you of something. The Church is watching the Galatians—we even know who attends their meetings. And I tell you, beware of those heretics—and especially beware of that man Warrum."

"Warrum? He doesn't seem dangerous to me."

"He's dangerous to all of us. He's wrecking my brother's life. And he will do the same to you. He will make himself an object of pity. He will lick your hand, like a naked spring lamb. He will be forlorn, he will weep. He will come to you and beg for your help in time of trouble. And you—because you are a sentimental candleholder like my brother—you will be moved to Christian charity, and you will do him a service. And suddenly you will be one of *them,* smashing the sacraments, and picking your nose in the presence of the Holy Ghost."

He had let himself get loud with anger. Now he became grimly quiet. "I used to think Lewis Warrum was a minor imp. I have come to think he is the devil."

"We are told not to dismiss the arguments of the devil."

"We are also told not to believe them."

"How can we believe or disbelieve if we do not tolerate him to speak?"

"It's easy to be tolerant on a matter to which you are indifferent, my friend. I am not indifferent to the tenets of faith. They are a passion to me. Faith may even be a function of *in*tolerance. It never

255

shows two sides of itself. It will not allow investigation, it will not suffer questions. It is a forthright, uncompromising act of the will— *to believe.*"

"To believe in what? God alone?"

Cavanaugh seemed shocked. "Is there anyone else to believe in?"

"Don't you believe in man—not at all, Your Eminence?"

"I cannot serve two masters. Can you?"

"I think I must."

"A servant of two masters—isn't that the classic description of a hypocrite?"

Michael felt the rage in his eyes, blinding him. The last time, called corrupt; this time, a hypocrite. The man was deliberately trying to provoke him; he must not give him the pleasure of knowing how distressingly he had succeeded. "Seeing both sides is the better part of diplomacy, which happens to be my business—as it is yours!"

He regretted having said business. For the second time Cavanaugh used his worn words against him. "It is not my 'business,' Father Farris. I have been sent here as an envoy of the Pope, but diplomacy is not my 'business.' I have only one calling in my life, and that is God—and God is not an article of trade. You should be aware, my friend: there is a danger that you and I and all of us in the Church may become part of a large, new, loathsome enterprise. Religion and Company, Inc. Catering to the customer's demands—something for everybody—in all sizes—Christ on a money-back guarantee. A ten-day free sample of the Eucharist. I cannot endure that thought. It shrivels me. . . . Are you not at all belittled by it?"

"You describe the worst of it, but the best of it is not belittling. It is human."

"Humanism, eh? That's what you called Pope John in your book, isn't it?—the Divine Humanist. What nonsense. As if there could be an equal partnership between humanity and God." He paused a moment, gathering forces. Then he asked the question: "Whose humanism are we talking about, Father Farris?"

There was some sort of trap in the question, and Michael paused, unsure of his footing. Abruptly he realized it was a rhetorical question—Cavanaugh was not going to allow him to answer it. What the prelate wanted was to perorate. Once more Michael had the intimation of an austere man with a self-indulgence, the pleasures of mouth; words, specifically, his single sensuality.

"Which humanism?" he repeated. "Which will give any dignity,

256

let alone exaltation, to our lives? The humanism that was dashed when Copernicus revealed that man was not the center of the universe? The humanism of Freud who demoted man's mind to his subconscious muck? The humanism of Darwin who let the baboon out of the bag? The humanism of Hiroshima, or the concentration camps or napalm? Which humanism? Ah, perhaps the glorious star-spangled humanism of democracy. That's really what you're talking about, isn't it? Would you prefer that one? Would you really enjoy a democratic Church? Is that what you're working for, in your present role as ward-heeler? The ballot in the polling booth—a vote for Christ on the democratic ticket? Does it comfort you to think there will be party whips and blacklegs and political bosses in the Vatican? That we will have pictures of our papal candidates on the billboards of highways across the world? That we will make them simpering candidates in the ecclesiastical beauty contest? That we will ask them what we ask any candidate for political office: what is your platform, what will you offer, what promises will you make? Oh, yes, they *will* make promises. To the ruttish cleric they will offer a wedding certificate which will entitle him to a thousand free sportations in a connubial bed. To the incontinent woman will be given a lifetime supply of vaginal jelly and a sharp instrument. Every freethinking idiot will receive a pad and pencil with which he can compose his own vulgar Gloria, his illiterate Gospel, his banal petition to the son of God. He will be given a roadmap to heaven and will light his way there with an obscene candle. And the profane will at last have inherited not only the earth but the dome of heaven."

Abruptly he seemed tired, and uncharacteristically penitent. "Forgive me. It is unworthy of either of us. I should simply have said—without bitterness—that the Church cannot be made many things to many people. The Church is our only Absolute. If we make it Relative, we will never again be able to distinguish between Cain and Abel. We will be defenseless in a world of horrors. What may be worse—tragically worse—we will lose the one timeless beauty ever created—the only true mystery—the last magic."

Michael was stunned. That phrase. He looked quickly at the prelate to see whether he had deliberately used the three words, the title of his book, the very book the man had anathematized. He couldn't tell whether it had been accidental or purposive. The priest felt disordered: an impulse to lay claim to the expression, to crow over the Cardinal's use of it; an annoyance at being plagiarized, an

257

enormous satisfaction at being quoted. Consciously or unconsciously, Cavanaugh had betrayed a lenity of spirit, and Michael could not lay a name on it.

Better not. Better let the moment pass, not continue the argument, get on to something else. "You said something about a favor. . . ."

"Yes, I haven't forgotten," the Cardinal replied. Rearranging himself, he spoke evenly. "You are, I am sure, a talented young man. And you are obviously very ambitious—you should go far in the Secretariat of State. Since you are apparently Cardinal Feradoti's protégé, I do not want to hinder you. Therefore, I have made a decision. The Synod will take place roughly five weeks from now, mid-June, two weeks after Corpus Christi."

What a conscious ruthlessness he had perpetrated. He had left the cruelty for the very last, so Michael could depart while still feeling the blow. But he was wrong, he saw in a moment; the man did have a special favor in mind.

"This date has not yet been given to the press," Cavanaugh continued. "I had intended making the announcement this afternoon. If I do so while you are here, it will be a black mark against you. Everybody knows why you've been sent here—it's no longer a secret—it's been bruited about in the diplomatic offices, and possibly in every cubbyhole of the chancery. The announcement—while you are here—would be an insult to you, it would underscore your failure. There would be some who might even say you were partly responsible for crystallizing the decision against your very own purposes. . . . I will save you those charges. I will not make the announcement until well after you have departed . . . if you leave within the next three days."

The favor was a vinegar sop. "So you're after all a deal-maker, like the rest of us," Michael said with quiet anger.

Cavanaugh was incensed. "This is not a deal. It's a dispensation."

"It's not a dispensation, it's not even an honest ultimatum—it's a deal! You're having difficulty squaring this Synod with your conscience. I won't help you do that, Your Eminence. I'm going to stay."

He didn't pay the Cardinal the courtesy of waiting for the nod of dismissal; he merely turned and departed.

He walked out of the study and into the waiting room. Nobody was there to let him out, there was no sign of Mrs. Merrill, so he proceeded into the hallway. He was just crossing to the inner door of the vestibule when the same sound he had heard on his first visit to the house came faintly through the corridor.

Plainsong.

Disturbed now as he had been then, he stopped to listen to it. It faded and was gone.

Could he indeed, as he had imagined it a few days ago, have heard it only in his memory of the atrocity?

He opened the inner door of the vestibule, went out into the entryway and was about to open the front door when he heard the music once more. No doubt in his mind. Quite clear.

Whether to go back and inquire about it. It was the old question of meddling: erratically, he remembered an old curate who said that not to meddle might not be the virtue of respecting privacy, but the vice of indifference. None of this had anything to do with his overpowering need to investigate. It was a compulsion now, rational or irrational, that offered no alternative. He had to know.

As if coerced, he turned, reopened the inner door of the vestibule and entered the hallway again. The music seemed to swell.

He thought of calling Mrs. Merrill, but realized she might not answer; she was hard of hearing. It occurred to him to go back to the Cardinal's study and make some comment about the music, asking frankly where it came from. But it seemed such an inapt anticlimax to his meeting—unless he could tell the Cardinal what prompted his curiosity. But that would mean telling about the crucifixion. Yet, perhaps the prelate already knew how Galestro had been killed. In Michael's first meeting with Cavanaugh, the Cardinal had indeed suspected violence, and had halfway threatened to find out what form it had taken. Perhaps, by now, he knew it had been a crucifixion. But what if he didn't? Michael might betray the confidence.

Standing in the dim hallway, vacillating, hearing the music clearly in this place, he was disturbed and didn't know why he should be. Plainsong had nothing to do with anything except his own hideous associations, he chided himself. Many people, especially church people, loved the ancient chant melodies. He himself had gone through a stage—with Leda—of collecting records which they used to play, summer evenings, with the music coming softly onto the *terrazza*. There were societies that embraced it as a special and beloved art—the Canto Fermo, for example, to which Galestro had belonged—there were learned studies in it, on its place in liturgical music. There was a whole Gregorian library on descant and *cantus*

259

firmus, there were chantries to keep it alive. The only disturbing thing about hearing it in this house was his own disturbance.

But he was haunted, he couldn't leave. He had to know more about it, where it came from and who was listening to it.

He decided to ask Mrs. Merrill.

Assuming that her living quarters were downstairs, he walked to the end of the hallway and the head of the stairs. The steps to the basement were not lighted. He looked for a switch and couldn't find one. Step by wary step, he descended into the darkness.

He couldn't tell whether the music was louder or fainter as he went down. But he still heard it.

There was another hallway, a narrow one, below stairs. He went to the end of it, still in blackness, toward the front of the house. There was a door and he knocked. Nobody answered.

He didn't want his voice to be heard upstairs, so he whispered her name. It was useless to whisper to a hard of hearing woman, he realized. He would either have to call loudly, or simply open the door.

He knocked again. Still no answer. He tried the door; it was locked. She was apparently not there; having locked the door, she might have left the house.

He listened for the music. Down here, away from the staircase, in the basement hallway, not a single strain of the plainsong was audible. It could have stopped, of course, but when he went to the stairway again, he heard it as clearly as before. The music was not down here, nor on the main floor where the Cardinal's study was, but upward somewhere.

Quickly, stealthily he ascended the stairs again. At the first floor newel post, not ten feet from the entrance to the prelate's waiting room, he paused.

The sound was growing almost imperceptibly, a faint crescendo of lovely voices. There was no question of it—the music came from upstairs.

These steps were brighter, somewhat; the chandelier was a display of crystals, glittering slightly in the muted glow. And there was deep carpeting to tread on; not a footfall could be heard.

Up, swiftly upward, and he arrived. The second floor landing and here—unquestionably he had found it—this room was where the music came from, loudest at this threshold.

It was a beautiful door. Not oaken, like the others he had seen in

260

the house, this was a darker, richer brown, a large door made of tiny panels of hard-rubbed, glowing mahogany.

Slowly, his heart speeding, he reached for the doorknob.

"What are you doing here?"

In a panic, he turned.

She stood at the end of the hallway, in the dimmest part, Mrs. Merrill, hardly more than the whites of her eyes visible, angry, cold angry.

"What are you doing?" she repeated.

"I heard the music—plainsong, isn't it?—I was curious." He heard his own silliness, the maundering.

"Don't you dare go in there."

"I'm sorry, I—"

"Get out." Icy fury.

Smarting with mortification, he retreated, started for the stairs.

Don't you dare go in there, she had said, as if the room might be filled with demoniacal terrors.

All it had was plainsong.

Or was that all?

He had only gone down a few steps when he heard her voice: "Father Farris."

He turned. She stood above him with a ring of keys in her hand. "Come up," she said.

She moved away, into the darkness, and he quickly ascended, following her. At the mahogany door, she stopped. Slowly, unhurriedly she selected a key and unlocked the door. She beckoned for him to enter.

He did as he was told and she followed him into the room. She stood there, on the threshold, unmoving, watching him vigilantly, as a guard in a museum might watch a suspect tourist.

How had he not foreseen what would be locked behind the mahogany door? Knowing the Cardinal was an archconservative, how could he not have described this tiny suite of rooms even before entering? No matter what liberties other churchmen might take with old traditions, Cavanaugh would have had to hew rigidly to the obsolete prescription for a cardinal's quarters. He would have had to have an anteroom just like this one, with a small table draped in scarlet velvet; above it, there would be a canopy from which would hang his coat of arms. There would be the tiny biretta room . . . the scarlet tasseled cap on the taboret below the crucifix. Beyond, more private than all the rest, the throne room. It was exactly as it should have been—gilt chairs covered in scarlet damask, the Pope's portrait beneath his own canopy, and the throne on which His Holiness would sit if ever he should call upon the Cardinal, in residence. So that no other person might ever sit on it, the throne was properly turned toward the wall. Everything precisely *in propria forma*. And next to the throne room, in a tiny chapel alcove, the most exquisitely carved altar Michael had ever seen. *Propria, privata e sacra.*

Mrs. Merrill had denied him access to the rooms not because they were secret but because they were sacred.

No evidence of plainsong, no record player, no cassette machine, no music-making instrument of any kind. As he passed her to go back into the hallway, her voice stopped him.

"The plainsong is the Cardinal's," she said. The subject was, for her, finished; she was dismissing him.

As he was descending the stairs, he still could not tell where the music had been coming from; at any rate, he noted that the *cantus firmus* had entirely ceased.

He walked as quickly as possible, without actually running, away from the house. He couldn't get the music out of his mind, nor his disappointment at having come upon nothing. Was that all, then, was there no secret in the brownstone, had the mahogany door told all the enigma that there was?

But what the devil did he expect? That he would come upon something that would link Cardinal Cavanaugh with a crucifixion? Was Michael losing his senses; what, in fact, did he hope to find?

Some secret about the man himself.

Some weakness.

The prelate was inviolable. That was the maddening obstacle. There was nothing that Michael knew about him that made him in any way vulnerable to Michael's persuasion. He was a man *senza macula*. And he would go on with his ruinous Synod—unassailable— and Michael's mission would fail.

If only somebody could help him find some frailty in the man, some Achilles' heel that he could pierce. But nobody could or would, not Cory, not Feradoti. . . .

Ledagrazia.

He recalled that twice during the Cardinal's account of his convalescence, in the midst of the happiest part of his recollection, something had disturbed the man. The first time the circumstance he was describing was general, the mood seemed unclear; but there was no disclarity about the second reference: it had occurred when he was relating that Leda was important in Cory's life. In what way important? Surely, not because she had encouraged the boy to paint—why would the Cardinal object to that? Then, could it have been in connection with the priesthood? Was she, in any way, responsible for Cory's decision not to become a priest? Yet, Michael couldn't believe she would discourage the boy's religious inclination. Then what?

"They have so much to forgive each other for," she had said.

Somewhere, among the three of them, there was an injury, a betrayal; in some manner, by some accident or design, Leda or Cory—or both—had wounded Lucas Cavanaugh. Leda knew; Leda would be the one to tell in what way the Cardinal was vulnerable.

Running now, racing for a taxi, he couldn't wait to get back to Mindszenty House. Even before he had his coat off, he was at the telephone. He prayed there wouldn't be a telephone delay, he had to get to her instantly.

There was no delay. He heard the buzzings and cracklings, the connections going through Rome, then Fiumicino, then inland to the village, he heard the *pronto*s, a woman, then a man, and at last—Ledagrazia.

"*Pronto*," she said.

"*Leda—mia carissima!*"

"*Mico—è Mico?*"

"Yes—it's me, darling—are you well?"

"*Oh, felice giorno—sì, grazie,* I am well—and you, and you?" Before he could answer, she rushed ahead. "I never thanked you for your beautiful birthday flowers. I didn't get your address from Paolo until today." Then, flurrying back to how he was: "*Come stai, come stai?*"

He said that he was well, and she must have suspected that he wasn't. "What is it, Mico—what is the matter?"

"I need you for something, Leda—it's very important."

"*Dimmi.*" Tell me, she was saying, only say it to me and it's done.

"It's something—delicate—perhaps difficult."

"*Dimmi, dimmi.*"

"You know about Cardinal Cavanaugh's Synod?"

"Yes—how are you getting on with him?"

"Not well, Leda—trouble. He's an inflexible man—I don't know how to get at him. There's no access, none at all. He seems absolutely invulnerable. And I was hoping—he told me about the summer—

263

years ago—when he was ill—Cory was with you at the time—and in some way—something must have happened."

He stopped. He was saying it badly, not knowing what to ask for, what information he was seeking . . . too formless.

"I don't know what you're asking, Mico."

Abruptly he knew, by the tightness of her voice, that she *did* know, that there was indeed something to ask for, if only he knew the question.

"I—Leda—I don't know how to say it. Was there an injury—a betrayal—"

The instant he said the word he realized how tactless the telephone call was. If she had indeed betrayed the Cardinal, if anybody had betrayed anybody, he was asking her to break a confidence and repeat the betrayal. Not only tactless but an unjust request, and he wanted to withdraw it. But it was too late.

"I cannot tell you anything about that, Mico."

If only he hadn't called. "No, of course you can't. I'm sorry, Ledagrazia."

"*Dimenticalo.*" Forget it. Her voice sounded fragile, ready to break. "I don't want to fail you, Mico."

"No . . . it's all right."

He had a need to pursue it, to try once more, but stopped himself. Then, distressfully, they had nothing to say to one another. Even the affection of their goodbyes was strained.

Interminably, after he hung up, he stood there, by the phone. He felt a hurt, placeless but everywhere.

Chilled, he ran a hand over his arm, and realized that his topcoat was wet; it had been raining and he hadn't noticed. He took off the damp thing and hung it in the hallway closet, not far from the phone table.

He must not think of Ledagrazia, not right now.

Think of the letter, Nora's letter. Call her.

He reached into the inside breast pocket of his jacket. The letter wasn't there. The other pockets, then the trouser pockets as well. Not there.

With alarm, he thought: I've lost it—her phone number. If I can't call her, she'll think . . . whatever she'll think, this will be the end of it. Before there was any beginning. It gave him the jitters.

The topcoat. He opened the closet, reached into the coat . . . and found it.

Suddenly, everything was better. He had a flush of anticipation that

264

warmed him against the chill that Leda had caused him. He looked at the letter and dialed the number Nora had written. He could barely wait. The phone kept ringing and his impatience made him sweat.

"Eisenstadt's Camera," the man's voice said.

"Is Miss Eisenstadt there?"

"Did you say Miss or Missus?"

"Miss."

"No, she isn't. Who shall I say?"

"Never mind," he said, "thank you." And he hung up without leaving his name.

Restless, uncertain, he stood in the hallway and thought of all the irresolutions: Nora, Leda, Cavanaugh . . . Halevi.

He hadn't heard a word from the Jewish Cardinal. He debated whether to telephone Quebec again. He decided, instead, to send a letter. He scribbled off a hurried, urgent note, marked it *Personal, Air Mail, Special Delivery,* affixed more stamps than necessary, and rushed it down to the mailbox.

Back again, he hastened to the phone once more and made a second call to Nora.

No, she had not returned, the man's voice said again.

This time, he left his name. He was about to leave his number but it luckily occurred to him: she might call back and not find him, and then not try once more. "I'll call again," he said. For he knew *he* would be sure to try.

He didn't immediately leave the phone. Something new, of only trifling interest, had just struck his mind.

Years ago, right after being ordained, Michael had read, in a clerical magazine, an article entitled "Vainglorious Humility." One of the lesser instances of this fault was the ostentatious modesty of priests who referred to themselves as Mister—notably when they left telephone messages. A priest, said the piece, should always say it was *Father* So-and-So who had called; it was more honest, not falsely humble, and prevented misunderstandings. Michael had thought it vacuous advice, yet had adopted the arbitrary wisdom and from that moment onward always left his name as Father Farris.

Just now, for the first time in eleven years, he had said Michael Farris. He wondered about it. And it bothered him a little.

Twelve

HER FATHER BREATHED DEEPLY, in a steady, unbroken rhythm, and she supposed he was asleep. Sometimes, mornings, which were his best periods, he would be able to doze off if Nora was beside him. She would have to be there alone, without the nurse or her mother, and very quiet, silent, then he might simply drift away, occasionally in the middle of a sentence. Did I doze off, he would ask in a little while; only for a few minutes, she would answer. Always the same.

It was her imagination, she assured herself, that he looked so much worse than he had appeared yesterday, or the day before, or a week ago. He couldn't have gone so far downhill in such a short time. It was not the disease itself that made him appear so ill, it was the name of it. From the moment she had heard the word, his face had begun to whiten and emaciate. It was, in a way, her fault for having accepted the label; maybe her mother was right in having denied its murderousness.

Today his breathing was more profound than usual, somehow healthier, and she thought he might sleep longer. Perhaps she could get up from the chair and sneak away, and he'd not know she had gone.

Just as she was about to do it, he slowly reached out. And he did that thing again, that holding of her hand that he had done only once before, that stroking of her wrist. Quietly, tenderly, almost as if it were part of his slumber, holding her hand, his fingers working under the two bracelets, touching the wrist, seeming to gentle it, to soothe the healed wound, to kiss it with his fingertips.

Why don't you talk about it, she yearned to say, why don't you tell me you've suspected what the scar came from, why don't you ask me when and why, and whether I have ever come upon any comfort that could keep me from doing it again? Perhaps it'll make you feel better, Father, if you know; perhaps it'll make me feel better too. Perhaps it won't, but why not take the chance? Why can't we take a chance with each other, Dad; is our love so frail?

That was it; it was. Don't overburden it.

But she deeply wanted him to know. She longed to go back to those years, to tell him what happened, as if she knew what had happened, and how she had managed the toughest times; and to make him understand that those days were over, his very knowing of them would help them to *be* over. There would be new agonies, but the old ones would never happen again. If only she could tell him without hurting too much, him or herself. If only . . .

She had such a need for him to know. Stroking her wrist, stroking; one phrase would have done it: what's this, Nora . . . tell me about this mark. . . .

He murmured something and she could feel her pulse quicken.

"What did you say, Dad?"

"So many bracelets."

"Only two," she said. . . . Go on, Dad.

"It seems like more."

She waited. Seemed to be waiting in stages; she could count them: one . . . two . . . three.

Go on. Ask me. Go *on.*

He didn't proceed with a further question. On the contrary, he turned his head a little, away from her.

"You don't have to stay, honey," he said. "I think I'd like to sleep."

She took his hand away from her wrist and touched it to her lips.

267

Straightening the bedclothes a little, she moved noiselessly to the door.

Down the long white corridor, into the car, along the back road, the shortcut, as if she were in a hurry to get somewhere, then the highway, so many bracelets.

Not that many, Father, why didn't you ask me? Why didn't you make me tell you about the cut, the razor blade . . . the bracelets?

There used to be one more, she thought, a copper one, lost, strayed, stolen. And no one to return it, to claim the reward, whatever reward she could give.

The letter hadn't been answered. Three days; that meant it wouldn't be answered at all. Perhaps he hadn't gotten her message, or didn't know what to make of it, hadn't taken the damn bauble in the first place, had scarcely noticed its presence. Ah, well, she had fabricated the man, he didn't exist. She must stick to the commonplace, she reminded herself; she had never been able to write her way through a credible fantasy.

She drove into Siders, parked outside the store, and entered to return the car keys to her mother.

"You got a telephone call," Lily said.

"I did? From whom?"

"Ask Kellman. He took the message."

She turned to the sluggish man. He was putting things in a paper bag, making change, mumbling counter talk. (Her father was always embarrassed to take people's money; he used to chatter through the sound of the cash register.) When the customer was gone, "You got a call," Kellman said. "He called you twice."

"Who?"

"His name is—I wrote it down—Michael Farris."

They were looking at her as if her manner were extraordinary; trying not to seem that way, she did feel extraordinary. "Did he leave a number?" she asked.

"No, I asked him for one, but he was cagey—both times he was cagey. He said he would call again."

"When was this?"

"Oh, an hour," Kellman said. "Maybe more."

"Why didn't you call me at the hospital?"

She had asked one question too many, had made it sound too important. Her mother noticed. "Is it something special, Nora?"

"No," with studied casualness. "Just a friend of a friend."

She left it there, went out the back way and started up the stairs. In

268

the kitchen, she opened the refrigerator door, closed it, opened it, closed it. She wished she could get out of the damn habit of going straight to the icebox; there was no need of Milky Ways anymore. Still, she wished she had one.

Oddly, she drifted to the liquor cabinet in the dining room. She drank very rarely, and never in the daytime, and didn't know what she was doing there.

He wouldn't call again. She could make a list of very logical reasons why he would, since he had already done it twice, but she knew he wouldn't call again. She was certain of it even when she heard the telephone.

"It's all right, Harry," she said to Kellman, who had picked up the store extension. "I've got it."

She waited to hear the downstairs phone cut off. "Yes," she said. "This is Nora Eisenstadt."

"I have your letter," the voice said. "And I have your bracelet."

He sounded as she remembered him, but not so sure of himself. Possibly he was uncertain because he couldn't remember her exactly, was trying to visualize what she looked like.

"I wondered if you might have it," she said.

"I do. May I return it to you?"

"Yes, if you will—I'd appreciate it."

"I'll mail it. Would you give me your address?"

It was all going to fall apart. She had purposely refrained from writing her address, so that he would have to telephone. Now she would give it to him, he would put the bracelet in an envelope, with a brief note perhaps, altogether void of content, words that made the paper blank, and that would be the end of it.

Slowly she dictated her address. When she was through spelling everything out, there was a lengthy nothing, as if the phone had gone dead.

"Did you get the whole address?" she asked, filling in.

". . . No." The silence was even longer now. "I didn't write it down."

She had no idea what he meant. Each stillness, lengthening. At last he said, "You mentioned coming into town."

"Yes, I'm there often," she said. It was a lie. She had been to the city only once since her arrival.

"Then why don't I give you *my* address?" he suggested. "When are you coming in again?"

This instant, I'll leave this very minute, she wanted to say. "I have an errand or two this afternoon."

"Can you make it an errand or three?"

"Yes, certainly. Where are you staying?"

He gave her the address, then: "I'll give you the number too—in case something comes up."

She took the phone number but knew it was unnecessary; nothing would come up.

The door was enormous, almost as wide as the spread of her arms. It was black oak, weathered to gray in places. Four strap hinges, each a yard long, heavy and scroll-carved, battened the boards together. Between the middle two, the cross. Since the wood was mottled with age, much of the shiny finish having peeled away, and, since the intaglio that made the cross was not deep, she hadn't noticed it at first. It was the severest of cruciform designs, the Latin cross, one vertical member and one horizontal, nothing more, no ornaments, no serifs. She felt a queasiness; she almost didn't ring the bell.

When she did, she heard it a long way off, a chime, then a series of tones like a carillon. Quiet followed; only a distant fog horn from the river. And no one came.

It was the right address. Mindszenty House, he had said, and the old bronze tablet on the stone façade called it by that name. But the place looked tenantless, and drearily deserted.

To the right and left of the doorframe there were long vertical panels of glass. She peered through the left one and saw the figure. It was a shadow at the top of the stairs. It didn't move for an instant, seemed irresolutely poised between going and coming, then quickly descended.

The door opened and he stood there. He was tentative; didn't seem to know a proper greeting. "Come in." He smiled, as if surprised he had found the words.

"I'll lead the way," he said. "Be careful, there's very little light."

It wasn't the darkness she minded. It was the odor. She knew the scent was not here and now; she had to be remembering. It came out of some distant moment in her childhood. The mystery of the corner church, the doors open on a summer's afternoon, pouring the dark coolness out on the glaring hot pavement; then the curiosity, like an itching garment she had to shed. Nine years old that doesn't know what organ music's made of, that doesn't know what lurks in Catholic darkness; nine years old that has dismay to deal with, delicious and terrifying. Up the shallow steps, in through the wide, wide doorway, then into frightening penumbra, the rays of stained glass light with colored motes dancing, the genuflections, the soft secret murmurings, the scent she doesn't know as incense, and the candles, the candles, the odor of sanctity, the thick, sickly strange alien odor of terrifying sanctity . . . Run.

As now, climbing the stairs behind him: run.

But upward, slowly, grown women do not run; upward, into the antimacassar room, oh God, do they still use antimacassars here, is there a stringent rule about them, have they an unknown meaning?

"It's rather a tacky room," he said. "But—come in."

His smile was unsure. He looked unprotected, as if he were about to apologize for not being bigger or brighter, or someone else. He kept looking around the room, searching for the sophisticated key to things, an object he might have mislaid.

She tried to put him at ease. "I didn't know people used antimacassars anymore—they're charming." What they lacked most was charm. They were stiff, unyielding. She wished she hadn't lied.

He nodded, seeming to understand she had only meant part of it. "I wish the room were somewhat more . . . giving."

It was precisely the word, she thought. Ungenerous.

Then he added quickly so as not to seem to be derogating a friend, "But the very fact they allow me to use it—that's the most giving part. And I'm grateful."

Good for you, she thought, a noble Christian sentiment. She didn't like herself, patronizing him, even if only in her mind. He might be inexperienced as a worldly man, she thought, perhaps even credulous. But there it would stop; he was brighter than she was. She must not mistake sensitivity for naïveté.

"Can I get you something?" he asked reservedly. "I could make some tea. Or—I have a little wine."

She wanted the tea, or wine, or anything they could both sit down to and make a moment with, but some childhood bashfulness prevented her from accepting food in a stranger's house, and this house—no matter how many Christian homes she had ever visited—was a primal alien place.

"No—don't trouble—thank you," she said.

"Are you sure?"

"Yes. I'm sorry—I haven't the time."

Damn. She had all day, she had tomorrow and next week.

He seemed crestfallen by her need to go so quickly and she,

271

delighted by his disappointment, almost changed her mind. But it was a breath too late. He was already leaving the room, mumbling something about the return of her property. "I'll go and get it," he said.

He came back with the bracelet in his hand. Here it was, the physical object, the trifle of little worth, misshapen, not beguiling to look at, something meant to be lost.

He didn't hand it to her at once. Looking at it in confusion, he said lamely, "I don't know why I ever took it."

Quickly: "An error—absentmindedness."

"I'm not absentminded."

He said it quietly but with absolute definition. He was taking the total blame for a consciously perpetrated act. And he was disturbed.

She felt sorry for him. She wanted to open a back door through which he could retreat from his embarrassment. "People woolgather. I do—lots of times—and I find myself doing strange things."

"No," he said softly. "I stole it."

She tried to laugh. "Did you? How nice. I used to steal things all the time. From the five-and-ten."

It almost did the trick. It was the first release he partially accepted. "How old were you?" he asked.

"Oh, eight—nine."

"I'm thirty-six."

"Good," she said, not knowing exactly what she was approving.

"What did you used to steal?"

"Anything. Once I snitched a pair of glasses."

"Did you need them?"

"For my eyes? No."

He heard the differentiation and smiled. "What did you need them for?" When she didn't answer, he continued. "What did you do with them?"

"I left them in my bedroom. Nobody noticed they were there."

He lowered his head a bit, sympathizing, humoring. "Ruined everything, didn't it?"

"Everything . . . That's what the analyst said."

"What, exactly?"

"Stealing attention." She gazed at him steadily and wondered if he'd be more honest than she had been. "Is that why you took my bracelet?"

". . . Yes, I think."

If he was going to stay honest, he might be more difficult; she might not be able to reciprocate. "Well . . . I'm attending."

He flushed. "I . . . don't know exactly what it is I want you to attend to."

"Try to think of something."

"Yes," he said, almost dutifully, like a child. "I'll try to think of something." She could see him actually doing it, actually setting his mind to it. "Somebody—yesterday—another priest—called me on the phone and said, 'I want you to be my friend.' When a full-grown person says that to another full-grown person—says it in need—I can't tell you how that distressed me."

"You've thought of something."

"Yes." He smiled ruefully. "I wish I had thought of it myself. I can't even claim it to be original."

"I'm not very original, either."

"Would you, then?"

"Be your friend?"

"Yes."

"I'm not sure I know how to do that . . . with a man." She had been on the verge of saying "a priest."

"And I'm quite sure I don't know how to be anything else, with a woman. In fact . . ." He stopped and reddened.

"Yes, I know the fact."

". . . Yes."

Something had languished. Everything had had a bloom about it, and suddenly the room was full of faded flowers, and regret. And she felt that she had spoiled it. She looked at him, a might-have-been man who could never actually be anything in her life, and questioned why she had so avidly hoped to hear from him; questioned, especially, why she had damaged it, why she had caused nothing to come of something. Wouldn't a friendship have been enough? Would it not have been better than the nothing she had now? Might it not be possible for this man to fill the emptiness Micky had bequeathed to her? Why had she ruined it?

She took the bracelet from him, said something that had gratitude in it, and turned to go. She felt miserable.

At the doorway, she turned. "I owe you something," she said.

She mustn't do this sloppily, mustn't tell him too much. Choosing word by word: "Back in Jerusalem—when I returned for the bracelet and it wasn't there, and it occurred to Mr. Cavanaugh and me that you might have taken it—I thought it was one of those weird accidents. Then, when I got the notion you had done it on purpose . . . I was glad. And something happened—I had a nasty situation with

273

a man—I won't go into that—except—I handled myself with more guts than usual and I was . . . quite proud." Then, quickly: "Now, understand—it had nothing to do with you, but I *thought* it did. And something . . . worked."

She had cued him to ask, and hoped he would. "What worked?"

"I've always wanted to be a writer. I'm probably not very talented, but what's that got to do with anything? So . . . guts in one thing gave me guts in another—and I started writing again. It's always impossible for me to finish anything. I start to write, I hate it, I tear it up. But this time—I did one page and a second and a third, and before I knew it, I had a whole piece. *Finished.*" She paused. "It's not important whether you actually helped me, or I imagined you did, is it?"

"No."

"I'm surprised you agree with me. Isn't that a little like saying it doesn't matter if there is a God, just so you believe in Him?"

He gave her an oblique smile. "I think there's a difference."

She felt too good to stir up the difference. "Anyway, I can say you helped me, and I do. If you didn't, I want to imagine it."

The obliqueness was gone. His smile was straight and full. "I've got the better of it—I don't have to imagine you're thanking me."

"No, you don't."

"Could I read it, do you think?"

The title came to her mind, "Hustling in the Holy Land," and she grinned.

"Is it a funny piece?" he asked.

"Somewhat."

More than somewhat, she thought: a priest reading her raffish story—written for the dollar—on the subject of whoring in Christ country; thanking him for inspiring her to write the scrubby thing, practically dedicating to him what he might consider outright pornography.

But if it was funny, the joke was not on him, she realized, but on herself, on the no-bullshit, totally debunked Nora Eisenstadt. She wanted him to read it, not to violate the priest but to get him to tell her she had not totally violated herself. Because something inside her, an insidious hope, as treacherous as it was uplifting, needed to be told that the story was not so bad after all, was indeed better than she thought. Under its grimy surface was a clean truth, the clean truth about her; she was as decent as the story was—only seemingly— indecent. Suddenly this tremulous hope steadied itself, became a wonderfully still thing in the air around her. She would show him the autobiographical article and thereby tell him about herself. She would reveal to this man that she had been a whore, that she had shamed and sickened herself. She had diseased her life not only with petty lesions on her private parts—those were healed now—but with wounds upon her deepmost being. She'd say psyche, he'd say soul—it didn't matter, tell him . . . and he would understand.

"I'd like you to read it, if you would."

"Could you bring it to me?"

"When?"

"Today? Tomorrow? As soon as you can."

"Tomorrow then. What time?"

Some reserve seemed to halt him momentarily. "Could you break bread with me?"

She smiled at the archaic, or was it religious? "It sounds very hallowed. I have to warn you, I don't believe in sacraments."

"Bread doesn't necessarily mean the Host, you know. It can be rye, if you like."

They both laughed. She thought: wouldn't it be comforting—and weird—if we could simply enjoy each other, like this. How quickly he thinks, how kind he is. We could be friends.

"We could go out for dinner, if you like," he said, the following evening. "Or we could have it here. I've put some things in the refrigerator."

She could see his preference was to stay. "Let's have it here."

"You'd better not agree too soon. Come and see what's to eat."

It had been raining, off and on, for the last few days, and Nora was wearing a lightweight raincoat. He didn't offer to take it from her; clearly he didn't want to commit her to stay here for dinner, not until she approved of the provender.

She followed him into the kitchen. Everything was old-fashioned, the obsolete porcelain drainboard, the brass faucets in the sink, the pullcord light in the center of the room. The refrigerator, however, was a white scream of newness. He opened the door. "Look," he said.

She looked and giggled. "Oh, no."

"I got both kinds—with and without caraway seeds. I didn't know which kind you preferred. And bagels, of course."

"Murder, how much lox did you *buy?*"

"Too much lox is a contradiction. It's Nova Scotia, to be precise."

275

"It's something to be precise about."

"Oh, the difference—it separates New Yorkers from all the others."

He had not said the Jews from the Christians. She wondered whether he considered it a more up-to-date distinction or a more tactful one.

They set the table in the kitchen alcove. The silverware didn't match, the china plates were crazed, her tumbler was glass and his was plastic. He straightened the tines of her fork with a butter knife and invited her to sit. She did, so did he; but neither of them began to eat.

It occurred to her; he wants to say a benediction. Thinking of yesterday, she reassured him. "I didn't mean to sound crass about the sacraments. You can say one, if you like."

A mistake. The words were hardly out of her mouth than she knew they were wrong. You don't *say* a sacrament, she felt sure of that; but she had no idea what one did with it. *Celebrate* came to mind; she wished she had said it. He would correct her; she could see by his hesitation that he would.

He did, but as deferentially as if not at all. "Nothing as lofty as a sacrament. Only a small blessing."

"Well, go ahead. I'll look out the window."

"I've already done it."

"Have you? I didn't hear you."

"I wasn't praying to you."

She put her hand over her eyes in an elaborate gesture of embarrassment.

"Are you blushing?" he asked.

"I hope so."

They ate lox, cream cheese, herring in sour cream, bagels and rye bread of both kinds, without prejudice. He apologized for the absence of garlic pickles but bragged that the onion was Bermuda, so they had huge slices of it, then cups and cups of coffee and sloppy mounds of French apple pie. Daintily they ate like pigs, and talked penitently of diets.

She was enjoying herself but had a restless sense that the evening was off center. They had made their engagement ostensibly for him to receive her story. But she hadn't given it to him, nor had he asked for it. By not mentioning the story, they were tacitly acknowledging that it had only been an excuse for them to see each other again. How strange it would be, she thought, if they went through the entire

276

evening and neither of them alluded to the typed manuscript in her purse; how strange if they never mentioned it again.

"Did you bring your story?"

"Yes. I have it in my bag."

"Is it long—could I read it now?"

"Now—while I'm here?" She felt a flutter.

"I read quickly. No prepositions."

"I could do the dishes while you skip the prepositions."

"Skip the dishes."

"No—really—I want to do them."

"All right. Where is it?"

She hurried from the kitchen, found her purse, pulled out the pages. "Hustling in the Holy Land"—the title was like a shriek on an Eighth Avenue marquee. She couldn't bear to give it to him. She thought of sneaking away.

Entering the kitchen, she held the manuscript behind her back.

"Before you read it . . ." She waited.

"Author's disclaimer."

"Yes. I have to explain what I wrote it for."

"Well?"

"Money."

"Pis aller."

"It *was* a last resort. I was broke and I thought—all those magazines—you know, the ones that pretend to be literate and are really dirty—I thought I could make the rent. . . . So that's what I wrote it for."

He was genial, and amused. "I'm not an expert on those magazines. I hope you don't expect me to be critically helpful."

"No . . . I only want to know what you think."

"Why?"

She evaded. "Well, you were partly responsible for my writing it."

"Is that the real reason?"

She was about to tell him the real reason, that the story was personal, it was true, it had happened, and she needed to talk about it. But she resisted the impulse. "And you did ask to read it."

He didn't pursue it and she was glad she had avoided telling him. He would view the thing as a literary exercise, no more than that. No digging around in personal histories, guilts, no sharing of aches and pains. As to her yearning to confide in someone, this man was a stranger. And it had been whimsical to think she could unburden

277

herself to a man so remote from her experience, so uncontaminated by the temptations of body and bone. Better to hear him on the subject matter before hearing him on the subject. Time enough for that later . . . if ever.

She gave him the story, and cleared the table.

As he sat there reading, she tried not to clatter too much. She had the erratic feeling that if she did the dishes quietly, without sharp noises, not only would he be able to think more clearly, but she might be able to hear him think. She would be able to eavesdrop on all his yeses and ahas and how-right-you-ares, and she would hear his noes as well.

She heard nothing. And the dishes were finished now. She slipped furtively away from the sink and out of the kitchen.

In the living room, she was annoyed by the precise placement of the antimacassars. She pulled one down too far and another up too far; then, when they were more annoying in their askew positions, she straightened them again.

Sitting in the most upright chair, by the open window, she watched the last ray of twilight disappear. She thought about turning a light on, but couldn't make a decision about it.

She heard him but could barely see him in the dark doorway. "Don't you want a light?" he asked.

"Yes, I suppose."

There was a small lamp on a marble-topped table. Alight, it made a rosy glow. She thought: the light illuminates the silence, and makes it seem longer than it is. It became longer still.

"If you don't want to talk about it, you needn't," she said.

"As I told you, I'm not an expert on . . ."

He couldn't finish the sentence; now he was the disclaiming one, and uncomfortable.

"It's all right," she said, trying to ease things for him. She saw the manuscript in his hand. "You think it's terrible, don't you?"

Long, long. ". . . Since you press me."

There were many kinds of terrible, and she wondered which he meant, but didn't want to trouble him any further.

"I finished it quite a while ago," he said. "I just sat there, trying to find nice things to say. Like 'You write very well,' which you do. You say things with a charming crookedness—wry—what a lopsided world—and it's a pleasure straightening out what you mean. You're quite a clown—you mimic things in a funny way. That makes every-

278

thing worse—to think of your using all that talent to write all that swill."

I daren't say anything more, she thought. I can't ask why he thinks so, or he'll tell me. I've got to pick up my coat and go. Instead:

"Why do you say it's swill? Because it deals with a whore?"

"No. Because it doesn't deal with a whore. It says it does, and doesn't."

"What does it deal with, then?"

"With . . . how to titillate the reader. With how to tease—sexually tease . . . so that someone who buys a cheap magazine can get a cheap thrill." He carefully put the manuscript on the marble-topped table. "I think you'll sell it very easily."

"I *said* I wrote it for money!"

"I'm sorry—so you did. I'm the wrong person—you shouldn't have let me read it."

"You shouldn't have offered."

"Yes, I know. But I thought . . ." He was troubled, and trying to accept his share of the blame. "Look, what are you doing, writing this kind of stuff? What do you know about prostitutes, anyway? Why don't you write about something you know?"

Christ, was he going to pull a dead-headed bromide like that? Fool, look into your heart and write. Easy, isn't it?—quick, where's the pencil?

"What *do* you do for a living?" he asked.

I do *that* for a living, she was going to say, or have done it. How does that jibe with your appraisal of character, Father Righteousness? . . . But she didn't say it. It would have been a petty revenge, at a price she didn't want to pay.

"What do *you* know about prostitutes?" she said.

"Not a great deal, I admit." His difficulty was worsening. "But I've heard them in confessions, a number of them. It's a merciless life. Drearier than you've written it, much drearier. There's not that kind of hyped up excitement. And it certainly doesn't have the . . . glitter. The terrible thing is—none of them could ever be like that girl. They can't be that rational—or articulate. They're—it's the most hopeless thing—they're submerged—they're way below any kind of thinking that could pull them up. If they're depressed, they have no idea what depresses them. If they get mean and vengeful, it's general, it's against the whole world, and they don't know what to get angriest at. When they come into the confessional to repent, they don't know what they're repenting for. It's a low level infection of the spirit. It's full of the kind of despair that doesn't know it's despairing . . . and almost beyond help . . . even God's."

She couldn't stand the sanctimony; felt she was slipping around in holy oil, sliding, falling, making a fool of herself, being made an idiot by someone holier- and craftier-than-thou.

And he wasn't letting up. "You've made a small sensation of it," he continued. "You've cheapened a serious thing. Are you cheap?"

She saw herself hitting him: lashing out, striking him across the face, once, then again, scourging him with something, a whip, a thong, a leather belt; she saw him grabbing her, throwing both his arms around her body, clutching her to himself, closely, in a grapple or an embrace, hurting or kissing her, she couldn't tell which, or which she wanted.

"Let go!" she cried. "Let go!"

The words were, of course, all he heard of her reverie, and he seemed unnerved by the frenzy of them. "I'm sorry," he said at last. "I'm terribly sorry. I didn't mean to be so cruel."

She got her coat, her bag, her manuscript, and ran away.

All night, Nora didn't sleep. She lay in bed tossing from one side (she had failed), to the other side (the failure was his). Toward morning, she came to the conclusion: the botch was totally Michael Farris's. She had come to him, all willingness, accessible, with none of the hostility she had shown at their first meeting, offering amity. She had opened a private door into an intimate chamber of herself, and what had he done? Walked in and befouled it.

Morning, she got out of bed, bathed, dressed, and tore up the manuscript. Not that she had changed her mind about his being wrong; he *was* wrong, in all respects except one. His judgment of the story itself. Maybe that was the real reason she had brought it to him. She wanted to be told precisely what he had told her, the story was no good, so that she need no longer burden herself with the hope of being a writer. Talentless. She could give it up now. Free.

She borrowed her mother's car, drove into the city and registered with three employment agencies: the first, as a teacher; the second, as a secretary; the third, as an editorial assistant. She would, she decided, take the first job that came along, anything, and go back to being a hewer of wood and a drawer of water.

She was in the middle of an interview when her head flew off.

He had asked her to be his friend; she had wanted to be his. Why couldn't she take his criticism, rough as it was, and not shatter to pieces? If it had been Micky criticizing, she'd have listened, fought back, and listened some more. Why not with him? Maybe it was all crap, that business about friendship with him, maybe she had simply gone there to get laid. To get laid by a priest. If she was cheap enough to have written that story, based on true and tawdry experience, she was certainly cheap enough to have gone in search of a shabby thrill.

"Is there something wrong?" the interviewer asked.

You bet your ass there's something wrong. I'm a creep, that's what's wrong—and telling myself I'm not is tough work, short pay. None of the self-deluders worked, they never did—not bourbon, not hops and hemps, not Zen, none of the promiscuities with idols and images—nothing ever helped her avoid the truth about herself.

And in this case, the truth was she wanted to go to bed with him. He was the classic temptation, the man beyond reach; the craving perversity, to profane the sacred. And what he had most was charisma —wasn't that a divine blessing of some sort?—anyway, a vibrant energy of belief, and battling it would have given her that ultimate goatish excitement. Even while she was beating him, in her fantasy, she saw him hurting her, kissing her.

You fucking creep.

"No, you're quite right," she said to the interviewer, "I don't see myself in that position."

In what position, creep?

After leaving the last employment agency of the afternoon, as she descended in the elevator of the municipal parking garage, a ruggedly handsome man in a suede leisure suit with a bit of foulard at his neck studied her minutely. His eyes started at her hair, investigating all of it as if he were combing every strand, then went down to unbutton her blouse, remove her brassiere, unzip her skirt, pull off her underpants, stockings and shoes, nudge her backward into the corner of the elevator.

I could charge you for looking, she thought bitterly; I'm in the business, or have been.

Suddenly she had a catch of fright: what if this tendency of mood and mind was now rooted inside her, and unchangeable? What if she never again saw men as other than contemptible customers, creatures despised? What if *this* was the hideous social disease—not syphilis, vaginitis, clap, not in the groin but in the grain, an infection of her

281

inmost being, what if this was what she had to live with all her days, incurable?

Inexorcisable.

Abruptly, the flash, almost too bright to be bearable:

She had not wanted him as a friend or as a stud. But as a priest.

That's why she had shown him her manuscript—not as a piece of literary work, but as a written confession. If it had been literary, she'd have shown off her most talented work, she'd have paraded the best part of herself as a writer. But she had exposed the worst. She had laid bare the person she had violated, had exhibited the whore. She had wanted him to look at her that way and, hopefully, not find her too ugly to behold, not too soiled to touch. And having confessed, having come clean, as the saying went—(oh murder, could she ever come that way again?)—she would be forgiven.

Wash your hands, Nora, you are free of it, he would say in the confessional. You are liberated from devils. Everybody's, and your own. And the priest would murmur the words and make the cross over her. *Mea culpa,* wasn't that the expression? Go and sin no more.

It was a lie.

She had no belief in such Catholic abracadabra. It was no better than bourbon, Zen, hops and hemps, sucking or fucking.

Besides, if she needed friendship and/or absolution, there were others she could go to. Micky, for example.

I ache.

Nobody, there was nobody.

Her mother? . . . Her father? . . .

Can it all wind down to nobody?

Oh, God . . . help.

Toward sundown, Nora and her mother got into the car and hurried to the hospital. Her father was dying.

He lay in his bed, staring at his wife and daughter, hardly seeing them; it was as if he had turned his face to the wall. Yesterday he had been failing and confused but still seemed to be looking toward the light and searching for the points of the compass; today, he had found a pathway and was following it, into darkness. He was not talking at all, and barely conscious. But his eyes fluttered from time to time and frequently he licked his lips. He was frightened.

As evening settled, the doctors came again. They were still trying things. "Would you wait in the corridor?" the older one said.

The lights had not yet been turned on in the hallway. Nora and her mother walked to the windows, far away. The view through the sashes was only parking lot. Distances of cars. Everything mechanical, not a blade of grass.

Her mother started to cry. "Where will he go?" she said.

What a relentless thing to ask, Nora thought; how can pity be so cruel?

"Where will he go?" Lily repeated.

"Stop it, Mama."

"Where will I go, then?"

The second question was what the first one meant. "Wherever you can," Nora replied. "Wherever all of us can."

"What the hell kind of answer is that?"

"I don't know any answers, Mama, let me alone."

"Alone?—what's so good about that?"

"Please stop."

"I can't be alone! I was never trained to be alone. When I married him, he didn't tell me I'd be alone at fifty. What can I do at my age?"

Why didn't you think of that before, Nora was on the verge of saying. Why didn't you try to do something with your life? All those years, when I was in high school and away at college, why were you only a married woman in those years? How could you prepare for every emergency except the big one? You laid in canned goods against food shortages, a barrel of gasoline against the oil crisis, candles against blackouts. Why didn't you prepare a skill for yourself, against this goddamn inevitable, desolate uselessness?

What she actually said was, "You can run the business, Mama."

"Run the business, run the business? Me and that butterfingers Kellman? Is that what you mean? Me and that Mister Dropsy? What kind of life is that?"

"What was it for Dad?"

"I was here—he had me! Why can't I have him? Why can't I have somebody?"

If she would settle for somebody: "I may not be enough, Mama, but you have me."

"You? You'll be off and gone. Even when you're here, you're not here. I don't talk to you, you don't talk to me. You never did."

"I talked a lot, Mama."

"To psychiatrists."

". . . That's right."

Her mother started to sob uncontrollably. The lights went on in the corridor and people were going back and forth, and looking at them. Lily ran to the ladies' room.

The ache is worse, Nora said, worse than this afternoon. She yearned for dizziness and couldn't figure out why it hadn't come. In the old days, when pain was as sharp as now, she could always be sure of the vertiginous moment when the world spun away. And here, this evening, pain in equilibrium, balanced and unendurable.

"Your father would like to talk to you," the younger doctor said.

She hurried the length of the corridor. As she hastened, a firm resolution came to her:

"I'm going to tell him."

This once, she determined, this last time, before it's too late, I'm going to talk to him, I'm going to tell him as much as I can. I'm going to unburden myself and tell him about cheating at math and the razor cut and whoring in Jerusalem. Everything, all the pain.

She saw an image. The *kapora*.

Once, when she was a little girl, her grandmother had taken her to the Lower East Side. It had been the day before Yom Kippur and the shawled old lady had bought a chicken, and told Nora of her annual ritual. It was a loathsome ceremony and Nora would never forget it. The live fowl was taken to the *shochet*. He was the ritual slaughterer, the religious butcher. He had a sharp knife and a prayer book. The *shochet* grabbed the fated bird by the two feet, lifted it into the air and waved it over the head of her grandmother, and they both murmured an incantation. Thereby, all the human sins would be passed into the body of the shrieking hen, and the old woman would be shriven for another year. The *shochet* would thereupon slit the neck of the bird, and the scapegoat animal, the *kapora*, would go off into its wilderness, carrying with it the burden of its newly acquired sins.

Yes, she would tell her father about Jerusalem. He would be her *kapora*, carrying her guilt away with him. He was dying anyway; he had no use for inculpability; there was no hereafter, no retribution underground. What difference could it make to him if she told him? But oh, the difference to her! It was a small thing to ask of him. Had he asked a like favor from her, she would have given it gladly. Let him be her *kapora*.

She approached the door to his room. Almost, she ran away. Then slowly she opened it.

The nightlamp was the only illumination. It was on the small table by his bed. Half his face was bright, half in shadow; half here, half gone.

He was conscious again, and trying, with his remaining might, to smile.

"Hello, honey," he said. "I asked for you to come."

"I know, love."

"Don't stand," he said. As she started to sit down: "No, not there—I can't see you."

She moved closer, the light on her face. Tentatively, she put the tips of her fingers on the coverlet, wondering if he would touch her hand, her wrist, the scar. He didn't.

"Tell me about Jerusalem," he whispered.

Her heart stopped. He must have seen into her mind, must have been—at last—clairvoyant about her, feeling her need, her hunger, her loneliness. He was *asking* her.

"What do you want to know?" she said.

"How you were doing there."

"How I was . . . ?"

"You said you were starting a new job, and it seemed to make you happy." His voice was weakening. "Tell me, Nor."

Happy tidings, that's what he wanted. Good tidings, news of her talent and success. Nothing that had ever troubled her; only happiness, happiness. Damn him. No, she decided, I won't lie to him this time, I'll tell him everything, the whole story, working backward, whore and razor blade: I need for him to know. I need him to know and still say he loves me. I need a loving father who loves me not for the lie of my happiness, but for the truth of my wretchedness, my foolishness, my ugliness and weakness, for my scar.

"Tell me," he pleaded.

"It's a . . . wonderful job," she said. "I—it's a new magazine—the government's behind it—small, of course, but that has its advantages. For me, I mean. I get to do editorial work—and my own stories—I get to see my own stories printed. A lot of it is—what did I say it was?—confidential. It's what I've always wanted."

"And what you deserve, honey," he murmured. "I'm glad . . . I love you, Norie."

You love the wrong one, you bastard.

"I love you, Dad," she said.

285

He closed his eyes and slept a little.

When the nurse came, Nora left the room. Toward nine o'clock, the nurse came out again and said her father was dead.

The wrong one, Dad . . .

Her mother came out of the room of death, her face composed, her eyes inert. She had had her screams beforehand, Nora supposed, and might not have them ever again. Stillness, utter stillness; only her hands moved, in fidgets, as if they were thawing from frost.

"Let's go home," Lily said numbly.

"Shouldn't we be doing something?" Then, when her mother looked at her uncomprehendingly: "About the funeral?"

"He did everything himself. Arranged for the cemetery, the casket, everything."

"Shall I phone them?" She wanted something to do, anything, even to the calling of the undertaker.

Her mother wanted the same. "Leave me something," she said.

However, when they got to the phone booth in the lobby of the hospital, Lily couldn't seem to find the mortuary number and barely managed to remember the name. "You do it," she said.

The man at the other end of the line was not the stereotyped undertaker. No unctuous sympathy; nor did he pretend his occupation was an art. He was in the hauling business; hospital to mortuary to graveyard, pickup and delivery. "We'll come for the body in the morning," he promised.

As they were walking to the parking lot, Lily got out her car keys. But then, about to slide into the left seat, she was again not equal to her intention, her hands became unsteady and she gave the keys to Nora.

The ride was silent until Lily said, "Not so fast," and, a little later, warned of another car, too close. Nora was not driving fast, the other car was not too close, but it was a good sign, she thought. Nerves, yes, but a caution against mishaps; let's not compound these incidents.

"You're going too fast, Nora—what's the matter with you?"

Think of an answer.

When they got home, she said, "Can I make you something, Mama?" They had not had a meal all day, and it was nighttime.

"No, thanks."

"Some tea?"

"No, I've got to make the calls."

286

She meant to the relatives, of course. Her father's sister in Chicago, his brother somewhere in England; her mother's brother, in Florida.

"Let it wait until tomorrow, Mama, and I'll do it. The funeral's not till Thursday."

"Yes."

"Let me make you some tea." Truth was, Nora didn't want to be alone. "I'll put the kettle on."

"No, don't. I'll just take a sleeping pill and go to bed." She started out of the kitchen. As she got to the door, she remembered. "Oh damn, I took the last one a few nights ago."

"How about a drink? It'll make you just as sleepy, perhaps. Would you like a drink?"

"I don't like to drink by myself."

Her mother hadn't meant anything by it, she certainly had no intention to exclude her. It was simply that she had been accustomed to having an occasional drink with her husband, rarely with anybody else. Never with Nora. The realization was startling: she'd never had a drink with her mother, not so much as a sit-down over sherry. She tried to imagine what it might be like to get loaded with her, what they could say to one another that they had never said before, whether they could run afield somewhere, into unknown places, wondered if the newness of the event would help them discover newness in each other.

It was a desperate inspiration: let's have a drink, it said, let's sit across the kitchen table and go on a tour together, visit unexplored countries in ourselves, meet as strangers, possibly be friends.

Nora had the bourbon bottle in her hand. "Do you want it straight?" she asked. "Or how?"

"Not bourbon, honey. Scotch."

Strangers indeed. She made her mother's drink, and her own, bourbon on ice. She sat down at the kitchen table, but her mother didn't. "Don't you want to sit down, Mama?"

"Too restless, too damn restless."

"But the drink will . . ."

Not that direction. She didn't know what the drink would do for Lily. Perhaps nothing. Perhaps the restlessness would get worse, perhaps she would have hysterics. Nora took small sips of her bourbon, careful ones. I don't want to get drunk, she said. I want to see this moment deeply, I want to root into it; if I dig for treasure I may find it, something I've been looking for, hoping it was there. She took another small sip.

287

Her mother, drink in hand, walked across the kitchen to the rear door. She looked through its pane of glass, out into the night, down the steps that led to the back entrance of the store. "What are you thinking, Mama?"

"I was trying to decide whether to have Kellman open the store tomorrow, or close it for the day."

"Close it, Mama."

"I'll have to call him and tell him not to come."

"What's his number?"

"No, I'll do it."

Again offering to do the chore and, when the time came, she'd be unable to go through with it. She must not let it become a pattern, Nora determined, she must not help her mother incapacitate herself. Hands off, no more tendering of services.

She finished her drink. So did Lily. "You want another one, Mama?"

Lily came to the drainboard where the bottle and ice were. She took the drink Nora made for her, then returned to the door again, precisely where she had stood before, gazing precisely as she had before, into the night.

They were in separate rooms, Nora observed, and the silences were getting longer, drawing out to a point beyond reckoning. I must put an end to them, she thought, or we've lost it. If we, she and I, my mother and myself, if we can't on this most terrible night call a halt to our muteness with each other, we'll never find a single word again.

"Let's talk, Mama."

"I've got to call Kellman."

"Let it wait . . . let's talk."

"About what—your father?"

"Yes, if that's all we've got."

"But we don't have him."

"Mama . . ."

It was useless.

"I can't stand it, Nora."

And she started to go.

One more try. "Stay, Mama."

"I can't stand it!"

She heard her mother's bedroom door open and close. She had a fit of rage. Go in there, you selfish bitch, go in and see your husband in

288

your bed, go see the emptiness, go see his goddamn pillow with no mark of his head on it, go scream in your closet.

And I'll scream in mine.

Then she thought of her mother's helplessness. She was a woman crippled by dependency on men; on the one particular man, in fact. The loving paralysis—she had asked for it, had dreamed of it as a girl, and what she had yearned for had ultimately been realized. And now that he was dead, there was no muscle of her being she could animate, no brain, no heart, no will that hadn't been narcotized by love, and no matter what night cries of emergency she heard her daughter utter, there was no part of her that didn't cry I can't, I can't.

Is that what I'm fighting against, Nora asked, that woman-paralysis —in another way, perhaps—and can't I overcome it better than she has? If I can't, I'll wind up hating the womanhood in myself. But maybe I've already done that, maybe that's what being a whore was.

She had another drink, and another.

Christ, I'm drunk.

Whore. Tell your father you're a whore. Ask him to be your *kapora,* see where that gets you.

She made her way, somehow, to her bedroom but didn't undress. She lay down on the bed, fully clothed, and tried to cry and couldn't because, as she had once written in a high school poem, I am a woman unworthy of my tears.

She thought she was awake, she thought she was asleep.

She had no idea how many hours later it was when she heard the noise.

It was more a moan than a sob; it was so full of agony she couldn't bear it. She thought, in her besottedness, that the sound issued from her own throat. But then, because it came from below stairs, from what used to be the darkroom of the store, she imagined it her father's voice, moaning.

But as she listened, she knew: her mother. A lamentation beyond all suffering. A moan so full of anguish . . .

"Oh, Mama," she whispered.

The sobbing didn't stop.

"Oh, Mama, let me help you."

She got out of bed and hurried into the hallway, through the living room and kitchen, and down the outside steps. The night was windy, full of chill. She raced to the back door of the store and hurried in. How terrible that her mother had had to come down to her father's workroom, down to his private place to vent her agony.

She walked through the little passageway, into the darkness beyond, to the rear of the store. At the closed door to the darkroom, she paused. The moaning was more horrifying here, full of age-old ache, of torment.

"Mama," she murmured at the door.

Her mother didn't hear her.

"Mama!"

She opened the door.

They were both naked, Kellman and her mother. He lay on top of her, the flabby drone of a man; they made noises of ache and aggression.

As the door opened, they saw her.

"Oh, God."

Nora turned to run. At the door, the latch got caught and she couldn't open it.

She heard her mother behind her. "Nora!"

She couldn't get out, she had to turn. "Go away," she screamed at her naked mother, "Go away!"

"I can't be alone!" Lily cried. "I can't be alone!"

"Go away, you whore!"

The door opened, and she fled.

You whore, that's what you called her—and she isn't. Mistaken identity: you called her by your name. Go back—apologize. Tell her: not you, the whore—me. Tell her. Last chance. You lost it with your father, don't lose it again—tell her.

Tell *somebody.*

She ran to the car, found the car keys still in her pocket. Out of the driveway, onto the street, onto the highway.

Watch out, Lily's voice, don't go too fast, you're drunk, don't drive too close, too far, too fast, watch out.

Faster, riding closer to the cars, riding faster than the others, faster and closer.

Onto the city streets, what was the address now, where did the bastard live, where could she find him, what was the name of the house with the cross on the door, with the goddamn bleeding cross on the door?

She rang the bell.

Nobody answered.

She rang again.
"Father Farris!" she shouted.
No answer.
"Father, let me in!"
Don't call him Father, you idiot, your father's dead.
"Father!" she cried. "Father!"

Thirteen

A LONG TIME AGO, when the bell sounds started recurring in his dreams, they worried him. But year by year they became a friendlier sign, and he welcomed them.

Tonight, they were particularly agreeable. They were far away at first, in distance and in time; old bells, bells beyond memory, on the edge of sleep. He turned in his bed so as not to fall too deeply into slumber; he wanted the memory to stay vivid. Although they had a mournful sound, they were wonderfully benign, tolling perhaps in a garden somewhere, like Ledagrazia's, or in the seminary, bidding him awaken and come to morning prayers, and he wondered if he was scholastically prepared. He had studied his patristics but not his canon law; there was a new teacher in theology; the phrase he had written was not Aramaic, it was Greek; no flowers dancing on the head of a pin, you bonehead; angels.

Then the bells were Rome. The great one in the Courtyard of St. Damasus, knelling, acclaiming a new Pope across an old twilight.

Almost at once, a wonderful ringing everywhere, from every campanile, a quavering, throbbing resonance, pealing and rolling and roaring and echoing across the Italian hills.

Then the bell was a doorbell.

And the ringing stopped.

He lay there, hoping for the other bells to start again. But he heard another sound. Someone calling his name, calling Father.

Which art in heaven, he thought. But the outcry wasn't imaginary, it was a voice. In distress, it said.

Father!

Out of bed, he started for a bathrobe to cover his pajamas. But there wasn't time—the voice was an outcry—pajamas would have to be enough. Through the dark bedroom, a light in the living room—the voice still calling, downstairs, outdoors, Father.

Down the steps, clammy on his feet, the dark hallway, the door.

She stood on the doorstep.

"Help me," she said.

He hurried her indoors and led the way upstairs. As he had done before, he commented on the darkness. "Be careful," he said.

"Be careful." Unnecessarily, she repeated it, be careful, a number of times. Her voice made him uneasy, it sounded trancelike.

It didn't take more than the dim light in the living room to see what was wrong with her. The girl was drunk. She had her car keys in her hand. She was shaking them, jangling, an insistent agitation. He thought: Good Lord, she's been driving that way, blind.

"You could have killed yourself," he said. "Or somebody else."

She made a sound that could have been a laugh, but it had no meaning in it. "That's what I came to tell you."

"Tell me what?"

Laughter again. "Confession time. I killed somebody."

"You . . . ran into somebody?"

"No, not with my car—not by accident—I don't get off easy like that. With a gun—bang, bang."

He could take a deeper breath now—she was making it up, of course. No truth in it, but . . . trouble. Quietly, humoring a drunk: "You didn't kill anybody, Nora."

"Yes, I did!"

"With a gun, you say?"

"You're not taking me seriously." The laughter was gone; she was in a rage.

"What person—what gun?"

293

"I'm confessing to you, you bastard—and you're not taking me seriously! You've got to listen to me!"

"I'm listening—go ahead. Whom did you kill?"

"Somebody—I don't know." It was worse than drunkenness, he realized, there was something self-abominating about it, maniacal. "Somebody—a man or a woman—I couldn't tell. Or maybe it was a child." As if on a glint of remembrance. "Yes—a child! But I didn't really kill her. Do you want to know what I did to her?"

Slowly, dreading, he inclined his head.

"I brutalized her." She continued quickly, with driven fury. "She's a mean little girl—so I have to beat her. That's the only thing she understands—when I hit her as hard as I can. So I do it until she cries. She used to be a bright little girl, but she isn't anymore. She's dumb, she's stupid. She's almost forgotten how to talk—she just sits there with that spongy look on her face. They say it's my fault—I hit her too much. But it's the only time she obeys, it's the only time she pays any attention to me. And just now, she got me mad—oh, did she get me mad! She's a liar, I can't stand a liar, and it's not as if I didn't warn her. But she did it again. So I beat her and I beat her. And then that miserable thing started to plead with me—'Don't hit me, don't hit me anymore, I'll be good, I'll never tell a lie again, and I'll never cry, never, never, don't hit me, please don't hit me!' Well, if there's anything that makes me mad that's to see people sniveling like that—that's when I hate her the most. So I pushed her against the wall, I slammed her head against it, and I slammed it. I wanted to kill her—she was so ugly, I wanted to kill her. And the more she cried, the uglier she got and I thought if I don't kill her, I'll kill myself. And then there was too much blood, I didn't mean that much, and I got sick of looking at it and I—I—"

Nora twisted away in self-disgust. He thought she was going to vomit.

He couldn't make sense of what she was saying because he couldn't believe a word of it. Yet it was not drunkenness, it was more terrible than the made-up story itself, a woman lashing herself, fleeing from her own whips, agonized, running in a field of havoc.

She was quieter now, looking at him fixedly. "You don't believe me, do you?"

"No, I don't."

"You have to believe me." Her intensity was quiet now. "If I come to you to confess, you have to believe me. That's your job. And you have to give me words of comfort—that's also your job. Comfort—

forgiveness—what do you call it, absolution? You have to give me that—or do you withhold it because I'm not in the club?"

He marveled at how steady her voice had become. He tried to keep his voice as even as hers. "It hasn't anything to do with that. You can't confess with a lie—not in the club or out of it."

"You don't believe I beat a child?"

"No, I don't."

"What will you believe?" Mercurially. Bargaining. "How about theft—or cheating at an examination? How about incest—with my father or my brother?"

"Do you really have a brother?"

"No, nor a father either. Not tonight."

"What does that mean, not tonight?"

"Jam yesterday, jam tomorrow, no jam today, whatever the hell that means."

"Did something happen to your father?"

"He had a slight accident. He died."

"Tonight?"

"Tonight."

". . . I'm sorry."

"Christ, is *that* what you're sorry about? That a man gets sick and dies? Is that the kind of crap people bring into confession—as if it's their fault? I've been saying cruelty to children, I've been saying incest—and you don't give me comfort for that. Only that my father died. Mister, does that mean I only get comfort twice in my whole goddamn life?"

It was easier to deal with her now, he thought. She was bitter, she was ferocious, but she wasn't crazy anymore. He wanted to give her the comfort she asked for, but he couldn't find the key to it. With utmost caution: "No matter what you say, Nora—you do want comfort for his death."

"No! I'm not grieving—I'm enraged! *He didn't hear me!*"

This was it, then, why she had come to him. If he was cautious before, he must be doubly wary now. Don't say anything. Listen. "Was he conscious?"

"Yes, he was. Conscious enough to ask me things he wanted to hear. He made me tell him how wonderful I was, how talented, how beautiful—the Jewish maiden in the hills of Judea. He made me tell him lies." He thought she was on the verge of weeping, and hoped she would. But he could see her apply all her strength against the tears, and conquer them. "Why didn't he help me?" she said. "Why didn't he let me tell him what I needed to tell him? Why didn't he carry some of it away with him? I couldn't bear it all by myself—why didn't he carry some of it?"

"Carry what, Nora?"

"The truth."

"Which is . . . ?"

"That I'm a whore."

He had thought the craziness was over, but it wasn't. Again. Cruelty to children, incest, whoring.

As tenderly as he could: "Nora, don't do that anymore. If he didn't hear you, I will. But you have to tell me honestly. What's the truth?"

"I'm a whore. Are you going to make me lie to you too? I'm a whore."

"Nora—"

"What do I have to do to make you believe me? Something obscene? The obscenity is there—can't you see it? What do I have to do—rip my clothes off?"

"No, Nora—listen—"

"Rip my clothes off?"

She was doing it. Tearing at her clothes, rending them, ripping her blouse off, her brassiere.

"Stop it."

Awkwardly drunk, laughing, crying, stumblingly unable to disrobe gracefully, as aware of the bathetic ridiculousness of what she was doing as she was of the pain in doing it, she wrenched at herself, at her skirt, her underpants, shoes, stockings, until she was altogether naked.

"Am I obscene enough?"

He felt reduced to naked helplessness. Adequately covered as he was, he was as nude as she was, as humiliated as if someone had stripped him bare.

"Please . . . get dressed."

To add to the travesty, she picked up the car keys she had deposited on the table. Waving them in the air, she meaninglessly jangled them again. The car keys were her only habiliments—nonsensical—and they added to the contempt she was heaping on both of them.

"I won't get dressed," she said mockingly. "But I won't bother you anymore."

Naked, with the car keys alone, she started to the door.

296

"Nora—wait. You can't go out like that and you can't drive while you're drunk."

"I drove drunk before," she said. "And I'm soberer now."

She started off again.

"Stop," he said angrily. "Put your clothes on." Then, as persuasively as possible: "You can go when you sober up—I'll make you some coffee."

"Fuck off," she said.

She was out the door and in the hallway, on her way to the stairs. She'll fall, he thought, she'll hurt herself. He rushed after her, grabbed her and pushed her back into the room. His own roughness made him angry. "I said wait!"

"Get out of my way!"

"No—get your clothes on!"

She struck at him, hard. He wouldn't have thought such strength was in her, sodden as she was. Then she struck him again.

He reached for her hands. She broke away. Then her arms, to pinion them against her body. She wrested herself free, kicking at him. He grabbed her now, a full embrace, holding her, viselike, her body as close to him as lovemaking, as full of spasms, as unendurably ecstatic and as terrible, and he wanted to release her, and couldn't, wanted to set her free so that he himself would be released from her, and couldn't.

She was quieter now and, his hand free, he thought he was calming her, but he was touching her, his hand touching, not roughly any longer but gently, caressing, feeling the warmth of her skin, its nakedness.

Then he felt the paroxysm, the ache, the throe of painful ecstasy. He hadn't even known he'd been erect; perhaps, indeed, he hadn't been. Only the emission, burning in its swiftness at first, then slow and warm, like the baths of childhood.

He let her go then, and he was wet. He hoped she wouldn't see the spreading stain. He turned from her, feeling there was nothing he could do any longer, about her going or staying; his right to persuade her was over. His face averted, he didn't see her decision, didn't hear her go.

He couldn't think of her, only of himself. What sick fervor had happened to him, what raptus, what spell of insanity, to have transported him so far from himself? And how could he quickly be recalled?

Slowly, breath by breath, his equanimity began to return. He

297

would have to see to her, whether she had gone or was still behind him, watching him, knowing what had happened.

She had not gone. Unconscious, she lay crumpled on the floor in a naked heap.

Alarmed, he hurried to her. There was nothing to be apprehensive about, he realized. Her breathing was steady, strong and regular.

He looked at her, he gazed. He had never seen a naked woman before, not in the flesh. It had never occurred to him that the difference between the figment and the palpable would be so breathtaking. It was all the depths, of course, the fissures of the flesh, the clefts, the breaches, the deep cleavage of the breasts as she lay on her side, one mounded on the other; and the motion, the slow breath and stir of belly and bosom, the quiver of aliveness.

The skin: that, it seemed to him, was the most pulse-quickening difference. Unlike a photograph or even a painting, it had feeling in it; its feeling, and his; it had already been part of his experience; he had touched it, his fingers had made a pressure upon it, he had handled it.

And could again.

Slowly, quiveringly, he bent down and kneeled beside her body. For endless time, it seemed to him, he could not bring himself to extend his hand. Then slowly, inch by trembling inch, he did. Her arm was warm, the flesh was so much softer than his own. Then the shoulder, to feel the hardness of the bone, for bone was realer than the dreamlike pliant flesh. At last he touched her breast, so lightly, so delicately he hardly knew his fingertips were there. More firmly now, and a tantalizing sense that there was moisture on it, perhaps no more than his own hand had made. Again, the tangency; he had moistened her.

He looked down the body; there, the exquisite mounding, the mystery intact, he thought, the hidden thing; only the camouflage of finest hair, the triangle softly shaded from the darkness below to the nothingness above.

How beautiful she was.

Carefully, trying not to awaken her, he lifted her from the floor and carried her into his bedroom. He laid her down, still sleeping as she was, in the furrow where he had lain. Her breathing didn't change.

Again, he gazed at her.

How terrifying her beauty was. If it was exquisite, it was menacing

298

as well. He must protect himself against it, build a bulwark of denial, make his abnegation as reliable as his breviary.

Not daring to remain near her, he returned to the living room. The couch, however uncomfortable, would be good enough. Or even the floor.

He stood in the middle of the room and, for a moment, did not move. Some misery surrounded him, nameless and indeterminate, something about the room, coming nearer, closing in on him. He must not remain so still.

He moved. The trousers of his pajamas, still wet, clung to the inside of his thigh. He felt the stickiness like a mockery, a scornful rebuke.

Something stopped him, a ravage so deep and inexplicable, a hunger so insatiable that the only words he could find came from his memory of a saint: God help me to mortify my craving.

Mortify. Oh, dear God, mortify.

Against the far wall there was an old credenza. He opened it, brought out the decanter of wine. Meant for oblation, he thought, not for accidental felicities. But a need was a need. One glass, then another. He knew there was no remedy in it, even if he got as drunk as she was. But the ache was worsening, deepening, and the night wasn't offering any quicker remedies. He had another glass.

The still-damp pajama pants were a disturbance to him. He took the bottoms off and, although aware of foolishness, walked in the tops alone.

He finished what was left in the bottle, looked at it, and wondered if an oblation could come out of an empty one, and would it be called a miracle.

If he was to sleep out here, he told himself, he would need the extra pillow off the bed. Softly he walked into the bedroom.

She had not changed position, except that her right arm was outstretched, across the extra pillow. With utmost delicacy, he raised her arm and drew the pillow away.

As he straightened up, the room swam a little. He was not accustomed to that much wine. Felicities now, oblations later. No, not oblations—obligations. The binding power of promises, and debts that must be repaid . . . and dizziness. The walls, not altogether perpendicular.

She stirred a little, turned away from him onto her side.

The mound of her buttock was high, higher than he had expected

299

it might be. She was wide-hipped and he thought Song of Songs, he thought daughters of Jerusalem, tents of Kadar, he thought how noiseless the night was.

She took a deeper breath than usual and her breasts swelled. He thought the secret places of the stairs, he thought a young hart upon the mountains, the clefts of the rock.

Slowly he lay down beside her. Not beside her, he reassured himself, simply in the same bed. At a distance. He would not, he determined, not under any conditions, decrease the distance. He would turn away from her. He would not touch her, but would fall asleep, forgetting she was there.

The nightmare again. The emanation out of darkness, the amorphous creature fondling him, kissing his mouth, stroking him, sucking at his tongue, pulling at it and at the nipples of his breast, and at his penis, and all the old shame, Hail Mary, full of grace, *Deus noster refugium et virtus,* no verse appropriate to the transgression.

But this time, the hallucination persisting, not letting him go, not even after he was awake, the female creature clinging to him, sucking at him with her mouth, his eyes wide and open, in the darkness.

She did not move, but continued at him with lips and tongue, continued pulling at him.

He put his hand to her hair, he tried to stop her. "Nora, please."

Abruptly, too late, too soon, her head was away from him and she was lying on top of him.

"No," he said again.

He felt her hand reaching for him, holding tightly to him, still erect, still wanting, and he felt her fumble at herself.

"Help me," she said.

Again the entreaty for help, as she had entreated him at the door, and it was the same and different; one had no congruence with the other, yet now, one upon the other, every congruence was there.

He entered. Cries came to him and out of him, visions without words, words without visions, and all his aches were there and gone, all the mended wounds were open again, the blood and pain and pleasure, all, everything at once, none complete, nothing remedied, nothing finished that had ever been begun, no hope fulfilled, all hope fulfilled, as if now was the only chance, the last chance for joy and love, yes, even the last chance for comprehension.

And now that chance too was over, gone.

300

They lay there quietly, softly, beside each other, silent.
The pleasure stayed a while, then that too vanished.
. . . And still, none of the comprehension. . . .

They didn't stir, they lay separately, faced away from each other, wordless. How long they remained that way, he couldn't tell. He wondered what she was thinking, and couldn't even surmise. He suspected for an instant that she was asleep; her breathing was so unwavering. Then he thought she might be pretending; there was something too shallow in every breath, too soft, as if she were trying to conceal that she was there.

After a while, she quietly got out of bed. The room was darker now, the moon had shifted; he couldn't see her very well. He heard her, however, a whisper of her movement, the other side of the door, picking up her clothes, stooping for a blouse, a skirt, dressing perhaps awkwardly, without light. She must be sitting somewhere now, perhaps on the chair by the window, putting on her shoes.

He thought he heard her at the door, he wasn't sure; the door had not been closed, no need to open it, no need to make a sound. It may be, he supposed, she's pausing to collect herself, to determine what to say before departure, to finish some half-spoken sentence she had started earlier. But she said nothing.

He heard her on the creaky stairs. One footfall after another, slowly descending in the dark, and ultimately into the silence. He heard no opening of the front door, no closing, nothing else.

His head still buzzed from the wine. Not much.

He didn't move; he waited. He knew he wasn't waiting *for* anything, yet he had the unruly feeling he was in the midst of an occurrence, not the end, and that they had both been remiss in not putting a mark of finality on it. Any mark, even a word of farewell, or regret.

Yet, he didn't regret it. He couldn't understand why he didn't. No sense of shame, or sin, or guilt; no transgression he would take into the confessional. The thought astounded him. And—beyond belief— elated him.

A half-crazed stylite who lived on the top of a high pillar, worshiping the Lord ascetically, had once shrieked: beware elation in a false heaven. The hermit was right. Already, his exaltation was fading. And he knew that by tomorrow he would make a charge against himself, and not know how to defend it.

301

For he didn't even know what the act consisted of, except that he had had estrus with a woman. Estrus: what a preposterous word. The rut of animals—was that how he would hold himself to account—that he had bestialized himself? Or would he consult canon law? Reason and rationalize, write a brief, some *dubia,* the pros and cons, syllogize . . . all premises and no conclusions.

There had to be conclusions; he would find them. He caught himself making it a facile thing, legalizing. Corrupt, Cavanaugh would say; seeking excuses, extenuations, trying to make a deal with the Absolute.

He knew he couldn't avoid the prescript. Leviticus was plain: a priest shall not take a harlot.

It jarred him that he had adopted her label for herself. Already, by calling her a sordid name, he was mitigating his own offense. And he knew it was an epithet she didn't deserve. She might be a liar, yes, perhaps a woman of wild imbalances, but she was not a child brutalizer, not incestuous, not a whore. He felt puzzled at himself for being so certain of this. He had nothing to go by, no real knowledge of who she might be, no radicles of memory embedded in her past. How could he feel so deeply about her? Was this the immanent consequence of the sexual act, did the mere coupling of bodies confer the final authority: I know who she is? Was that, then, the significance of the biblical word—the quintessential knowing?

What a romantic he was. Worse, what an adolescent. He had just undergone the experience of a teenage boy and here he was, a thirty-six-year-old man, basing upon that first experience his whole comprehension of womanhood. What a fatuity, when indeed he knew—and lamented—that he knew nothing.

Not even how tonight's occurrence had differed from the substitutes. He had had wet dreams, he had masturbated numberless times in his growing years; he had not yet ceased to do so. Asleep and awake, there had been women in his visions, young girls in his school days, Hester often, the nurse in the infirmary, even one of the nuns. In his pubescent years he had been conscience-stricken not only over the act itself but over his visionary abuse of the women's bodies, almost as if he had actually raped them. It was so heinous to him, he couldn't even bring himself to confess the transgressions. Only in his midteens was he able to carry his sexual sins to the priest. All guilt, those days. But not tonight. Tonight, without any deep pangs of conscience, he had no impulse toward the confessional.

Something was radically different. In fact, nothing about this was similar to the substitute experiences. Except that they all ended in emission, there was no way to compare them. There was something awesome, even terrifying, in the act of lovemaking with a woman, as if one were overpowering a horrendous monster in one's self so as to set free one's love, one's gentleness. It was as ugly and ludicrous as violent death, and as beautiful as praying. It was an act that seemed to tell everything about one's self—the blessing and the curse. Perhaps that was the reason he felt no need for confession; the very act itself had had confession in it.

Abruptly, he knew he was lying to himself. And the frightening thing was, he didn't know what the lie was made of. Now he was making things worse, compounding falsehoods. Truth was:

He did feel guilty.

A glacial chill. He got out of bed and shut the window. He stood there looking at the empty street, the empty night.

How alone he felt. The expression came to him: lonely as sin.

He turned from the window and went to the small lamp on the night table. He lighted it and saw the tumbled bed. It held his mind a moment, longer than he wanted. Moving away, he started to look for something, not immediately sure what it was he was seeking.

His breviary. He found it in the top drawer of the bureau, precisely where he always kept it. Holding it in his hand for a while, he did not open it. At last, he set it down, unread.

Again to the window. Again the void.

He wished they had talked before she had gone. He wished they had said something, anything. He wished she had left something of herself—the bracelet perhaps, a scarf, an essence, a word or two; if only she had left something, however impalpable, in the atmosphere.

He wondered whether it always ended, after lovemaking, in emptiness. It was a high price, he thought.

Fourteen

S HE DROVE OVER THE QUEENSBORO BRIDGE,
toward Siders, and knew she wasn't going home.

There was too much left of the night; she didn't know what to do
with it. If she could sleep, she could sleep in the car; if she couldn't, it
didn't matter where she was.

Sober now, dry sober. As clear as the road ahead, bright lights into
darkness, steady at the wheel, going fast, no traffic to slow her down,
making good time, without destination.

None of the elements was unclear. She saw each of them separately, dispassionately, without animus. She blamed nobody for anything. Certainly not Farris, poor priest, taken all surprise, seduced of
innocence. Nor the oaf Kellman. Her father, for dying, a little; her
mother, not at all. She and her mother had chosen the same nostrum,
fornicating their torments into the night. It was a special-purpose
elixir in the family medicine chest, and could be labeled Lily-and-
Nora's Remedy: *Sex—Take Once Before Each Burial.* Coitus, as an

act of mourning. No crepes on doors, no ribbons of black, no sack-cloth and ashes; fucking.

Disparate. Everything clear, nothing ambiguous, but every element separate from every other one, without common denominator, as if nobody were related to anybody else, as if nobody had involved anybody else, as if even the screwing had been managed by people apart, long distance. The distance that made it possible to ascribe fault to nobody. Not even to one's self.

It was eerie to remain so remote. This is not me driving the car, she said, this is someone else. And if some wretched trespass was perpe-trated on a poor unoffending cleric, don't blame me. Blame her for everything.

But as soon as the word blame entered the picture, she knew it couldn't be someone else, it had to be Nora Eisenstadt. Was blame then the definitive badge of her identity? Was that the only way she knew she was alive? Not *dubito, ergo sum,* but *guilty, ergo sum.*

She hadn't suddenly, for the first time tonight, needed to confess; she had always needed it. It had antedated her whoring by years and years. She had been pulled out of the womb not crying mama, but *mea culpa.*

Guilty, therefore I *am.*

Guilt as the tenor of life, guilt as the climate, guilt as the ethic, guilt as the pain and pleasure, the gall and the aphrodisiac, guilt as the myth. Guilt brought down from the mountain, with the stone tablets, the extra gift of Sinai. Exalted guilt, the devil god. Satan as Father.

Tonight: a father dead and a father violated.

She didn't know where the thought was taking her. She didn't care; she would let it go, let it happen, not do an outline on the subject. Something in it refused to be categorized, wanted to stay out of context, demanded to be a free particle. Free to do what?

She drove past the turnoff that would have taken her south to Siders, and kept on driving. Nearly two hours later, she was at Montauk, as far as she could go on the Island, standing on the bluff, looking out, all directions, to the sea. The breakers were angry to-night, roaring, crashing on rocks. The wreckage was congenial to her, a kindred devastation.

It made her watch and work; it made her tired. She was facing east, clear east, and the sun, not yet risen on the horizon, was only a supposition. She turned her back to it, got into the car and drove homeward.

It was broad daylight when she walked up the back steps to the kitchen. Her mother was drinking coffee. She wore an old candy-striped wrapper and her hair, overnight, seemed never to have been touched up, there was a fall of gray in it. She looked up hardly at all.

"Would you like some coffee?" she asked.

"No, thanks," Nora said. She must sound as neutral as possible, she instructed herself; no reproach. "I just want to get into the shower."

"I won't ask you where you've been all night."

She's taking the offensive, Nora thought, shifting censure. It's not necessary, she wanted to say. I won't reprove you; don't reprove me. She said nothing.

"Where *have* you been?" Lily went on.

"It hasn't anything to do with anything."

"Suppose I said the same thing?"

"Say it, then."

"I do say it. What you saw last night hasn't anything to do with anything."

Lily was using the tactic Nora had learned in high school: impute irrelevance. Isolate the momentary concern and say that's all there is, history is not pertinent.

"Why are you blaming me?"

"I'm not, Mama."

"You ran out as if you were crazy, as if I was committing murder. I wasn't. I never was unfaithful to your father—never—not once. But he was dead. And I was . . . frightened. And I was angry too. Your father did me a terrible thing—he died. So I had my revenge."

Her hand shook, the coffee spilled, she began to cry. Nora went to her, to do something, whatever it was, the touch, the embrace. But her mother's arm struck out. "Get away—don't touch me. You're trying to make me feel guilty, that's all."

"I'm not, Mama, honestly I'm not."

"Yes, you've always tried—always. And you finally got your big chance, didn't you?"

"Mama . . ."

It was no use, not now. She walked to her bedroom and got out of her blouse. Then, into the bathroom, to run the shower; it always took a while for the hot water to come up. Back in the bedroom again, removing her clothes slowly, she tried to stretch the time, stitch by stitch, making the minutes pass.

Naked, the scent of him was still on and in her. Someone had once told her that semen had no odor until exposed to the air. It was a man who had imparted that item of trivia. Come to think of it, nothing had an odor unless exposed to the air . . . not even guilt.

Suddenly, in her bedroom, she felt a surge of revolt. She'd had enough of it. She was not going to let herself feel guilty about last night. She hadn't raped the man. She hadn't followed him into an alleyway and savaged him. She had only done to him what men have done to women, time out of history; she had seduced him. And since it was she who had done it, he might not even have to do penance for it.

Well, she would not do penance either.

Guilt had a sickly smell; she would wash the stench of it away.

She got into the shower and turned the valve until the water was scalding.

It was not quite nine in the morning of the next day when Mr. Gersten arrived. He was the mortician, in his late forties perhaps, with hair cut too close and the carefully measured speech of the graduate student.

In his profession he called himself a revisionist. He frankly admitted that he modified the religious laws to suit the secular purpose; when they were inflexible, he discarded them and devised his own; innovators must devise new tools. For example, the matter of *shivah*. It needed alteration.

Nora knew only vaguely what *shivah* was; so did her mother.

"*Shivah* are the seven days of bereavement," he said. "They come right after the funeral. You remain in your home, you sit on low benches or on the floor, you wear cloth slippers, you rip your clothes. Your friends visit you, they bring you your meals. It is public mourning."

Lily was holding on. She clung to his scholarly manner as if it were a crutch. She was studiously investigating *shivah*. Nora needed no research. "Once the funeral is over, I'll try not to mourn publicly," she said.

Gerstein said the resolution was sage, it was laudable. "Then you've decided—no *shivah?*"

But Lily was unsteady. She didn't want to reject a religious custom without feeling safe to do so. "Norie, don't you think we should do it?"

"I won't, Mama." She was as gentle as possible. "But you do what you want to do."

"It's what your father would want us to do."

"He was dead last night, and he's dead this morning."

She hadn't meant to refer to the night with Kellman; it simply came out that way. She would have given anything to retract the censuring words.

Oddly, they had a fortifying effect on her mother. "She's right. We won't have *shivah*."

"No *shivah*," he said, ticking it off a list.

Her mother had been behaving with surprising strength. Now, without warning, she went to jelly. Her eyes filled and she pleaded with Gersten. "Isn't there something like *shivah* we can do *before* the funeral?"

"Well," he said. His mind was calculating, with slide rule. "There's no law against your wearing slippers, sitting on low stools, covering the mirrors."

She nodded and he put newspapers over all the looking glasses, saying the prayer as he did so. "Vanity of vanities, all is vanity."

Then, to Lily: "Is that a good sweater you're wearing?"

She apparently knew what he meant and tried to keep her mouth from failing. "No, it's an old one—go ahead."

Reaching into his pocket, he brought out a small penknife. He cut a slash in the collar of the sweater and said, "This is a sign of grief—rending the garments. Normally it's done just before the funeral, but on this occasion . . ." He had made an exception, since he stood well with Jehovah, and wanted them to be grateful. "I will now say the prayer which means that death is our destiny, and you accept it."

"Blessed be the judge of righteousness," he began, and her mother mouthed the words, "I accept, I accept." As if it were an equitable contract that would be void if both sides did not agree.

Lily sat on the floor in the living room. Nora didn't. The guests started to appear.

The neighbors came first, the nearby storekeepers and regular customers, then friends from Manhattan. Quite early, Kellman arrived. He was unshaven and his clothes were untidy, to indicate he too was in mourning. She wanted not to watch as he greeted her mother, but couldn't help herself; she stared. He didn't kiss her, and when they shook hands it was as cautious as if their fingers were bandaged.

308

Then they went to diagonally opposite corners of the room, and he sat on a folding wooden chair. For a long time he was silent, attentive, like someone listening for a mouse, then he arose and spoke to somebody, and somebody else; at last, to Nora.

"I knew your father a long time," he said.

She nodded.

"A long time," he repeated. "Long. We both started together in the camera business. Salesmen, we were. At the old Willoughby-Peerless on Thirty-second Street." Then he added, as an observation on the epochal cycles of the race, "It wasn't Willoughby-Peerless in those days—you knew that, didn't you? It was only Willoughby's. People are inclined to forget that."

She said that she had heard that it was so, and he seemed to feel they had bridged an enormous chasm. He mentioned the change in Willoughby's again, disconsolately. He was an unlucky man to whom all change meant deterioration, death and Willoughby's.

No reference to the scene with her mother, none at all; that too was a change that could be unfortunate; he might lose his job. She had a clarified insight. His mourning of her father was not false. Kellman had been his friend and had probably never betrayed him. Nor had he, really, betrayed him last night; he had been summoned to perform a service; besides, the dead can't be betrayed. She found herself touching Kellman with pity, condoling him for his loss.

This condoling of strangers. She and her mother were both doing it. Grief was demonstrated more elaborately by visitors than by the family. Their heads hung lower, their faces were more elegiac, they spoke more touchingly of the dead. To them he was more nearly perfect, hence more lamentably to be mourned. Yes, I know, she found herself saying all too frequently, I know he was a good man, I know how excellent a mind, how gentle a heart. Sometimes she recognized him from their descriptions, more often she didn't know the man they were mourning. She wondered if they might not have known him better than she did. And it was a rueful thought that loving him more than they loved him gave her no special cognition of the man.

Her mind wandered: Farris.

Before noon, her Uncle Walter arrived from Florida. He was a portly man, robust in health, with prematurely white hair. He wore expensive clothes and a complexity of imported essences—shaving lotion, perfume, pomade, sachet for his linens—all aura of which he fouled with his huge cigar. It was Havana, contraband of course; he always knew a guy.

Embracing her mother deeply, holding her close, he didn't let her go for quite a while. He cried quickly, and quickly stopped. Then he inched his way through the crowded room, gave Nora a dutiful embrace and said, "She looks terrible. Your mother looks terrible."

Nora knew what he meant. If her mother looked more terrible to Walter than she did to Nora, it signified he was more devoted to Lily than her daughter was. "Yes . . . I suppose," she said.

"And you don't look so great yourself."

"I always look the same."

"You need some sun," he said authoritatively. "I'm taking both of you to Florida right after the funeral. You're not coming back to a bad memory. We'll go right to the airport."

"Thanks, Uncle Walt, but—"

"No buts."

"I can't. I've got a job I'm angling for."

"You are, huh?"

She knew he was relieved. They had never liked each other. "You won't mind if I take your mother . . . ?"

"No. It'll be good for her. Except . . ."

She was about to say that running away might not be all that good for Lily. The quick escape might be the slow regret. If she could use this crisis to use herself . . . start studying something, learn a craft . . . even take an interest in the store . . .

Her uncle had heard the reservation. "Kellman can run the store, can't he?"

She was about to say more but heard herself as the stern daughter of the voice of—no, not God, but prudence. What an unattractive sound it would make. Go on, Mama, run. "Yes, I suppose he can."

The place was now full of people, most of whom she had never met. She wondered how many of them were habitual visitors at wakes, *shivahs*, vigils over the dead. Except that the dead one was not here; he was in an impersonal mortuary, elsewhere. The vigil, here, was for the living.

Farris again.

If pain could only be a little less complex. Once, to a psychiatrist, she had said that the essence of her pain was that it strained the limits of her mind, tortured it to view its own limitation, threatened the brain with bursting.

Farris again.

As inconspicuously as she could, she threaded her way through the living room, down the hallway to her bedroom. She entered and locked the door.

There he was, waiting for her, Farris, the interloper.

Her self-exonerations had been useless. She had indeed attacked him, stalked him into an alleyway, committed a ferocity no less depraved than are displayed on the front pages every day. None of the hundred excuses would extenuate her responsibility; not one would ease her conscience.

Now, she made one last desperate attempt to forgive herself. She would reduce it in her mind, she said, to its insignificance, by calling it nothing more than another vulgarity in her life, a minor obscenity to take its place with more serious ones, in Jerusalem. She put a tawdry ticket on it and wrote it down as a one-night stand. A piece of bird, a piece of quail; a piece of cock, a piece of tail. Wham, bam, thank you, ma'am. Whing, ding, wipe your thing.

Disgust. And the most unforgivable part of it: somewhere, he was paying a penance for a fault that was all her own.

She'd have to lift that burden off his back.

She rooted through the middle drawer of her desk, found his number and dialed it. If it rings too long, I'll give up, she decided.

"Hello."

"This is Nora Eisenstadt."

"I know," he said.

As if he had expected her to call.

"I called to . . ." It would be harder than she had imagined, unless she went into the middle of it. "It wasn't your fault—it was mine—I called you to tell you that."

"I hadn't gotten around to whose fault it was."

He was too detached; widening distances.

"Well, when you get to it—go past it."

"Quickly?"

His voice had a barb in it; it caught and hurt. "Yes, quickly." He had made her appear maudlin to herself. She wanted to get back at him, to sound as biting as he was. "I wouldn't want you to worry yourself into a retreat over it."

"Well, if you tell me not to worry, I won't."

"Not to worry."

"Good. Thanks for the absolution."

Hurt by the taunt, she snapped at him. "I called to say it was my fault. It wasn't easy to do that. You don't have to be a shit about it."

"I'm sorry," he said. "But you needn't tell me about 'fault.' It's my business—I'm an expert."

"Well, I'm not."

She started to replace the receiver. He seemed to guess what she was about to do. "Don't hang up," he said. She waited and he went on. "When will I see you again?"

It amazed her. She couldn't talk.

"Nora?"

"See me again?"

"When, did you say?"

"I think I said never."

"Today?"

It was senseless; it was unmanageable. "No," she said.

"Tomorrow, then?"

"I'll be at the cemetery tomorrow."

She hadn't meant to mention it. Nor did she understand why he took so long to continue talking. "Then it was the truth, about your father dying?"

"Everything I told you was the truth."

"Incest, child-beating, prostitution?"

The way he lumped them all together, they sounded like a profane trinity. Clearly, he wasn't believing any of it.

She had called to exempt him of all fault, and now she wanted, deeply wanted, to see him again, ached for it, but she knew she would implicate him in more fault, and more hurtfully, without remission.

She felt as if she had locked herself into a very small, an airless space. The phone call was a foolish one, and almost vandalous. Slowly, without uttering another word, she hung up.

Fifteen

H E W A S C E R T A I N she would call him back, so certain that he stayed there by the phone, waiting for it to ring.

No wonder she had hung up. He had been niggardly, stingily holding back his gratitude for her call. And for no other peevish reason than that she had departed so summarily on their night together. She had left him with a bitter residue, not from the act itself but from the aftermath. Or the lack of it. Not that he was certain what the aftermath should have been; there was, to put it moderately, a lacuna in his experience. He knew there was substantial literature about foreplay, and had read some of it; he suspected wryly that there was less to be read about afterplay. In all this, he had the misgiving that there was somewhere a sleazy joke, and himself the butt of it.

If that were his only disquiet, he would have taken a perverse pleasure in its pettiness—it was after all merely a lovers' squabble—and he would have called her back.

But there was a deeper distress. And she had struck upon it by

313

trying, in her telephone call, to absolve him of guilt. She hadn't succeeded. He had spent all of yesterday hesitating to confess. This morning, not long after dawn, he had gone to St. Malachy's. On arriving, he had halted at the doorway of the church, and hadn't entered. He had stood there a long time, disturbed and unresolved, unable to go inside or go away. At last he had departed without confessing. All morning he had avoided, consciously avoided trying to understand why he had not confessed, for fear he might come upon an answer. . . . And in the midst of this she had called and told him: don't be penitential.

So he now stood in the hallway, with an apprehensive sense of things disassembling, uncertain how to think or if he should, wanting to call her, unable to do it, and yearning for the phone to ring.

And it did.

It was Father Warrum.

Damn the man for calling at this time, for tying up the phone.

"Yes, this is Father Farris."

"I need your help."

"What?" He was still with Nora; couldn't shunt himself so quickly onto another track.

"I'm sorry to bother you, Father, but I'm in extreme trouble. I need your help."

He heard an echo of Cavanaugh's voice. The Cardinal had predicted it so precisely, almost to the word. He'll beg for your help in time of trouble, he had said. He'll make himself an object of pity. Don't get caught.

Guardedly: "What trouble, Father Warrum?"

"I can't tell you on the telephone." His voice was shaky. "May I come and see you?"

The man sounded as if he had been crying. It was this that made Michael, almost as an act of obstinacy, stiffen still further against him. "I'm sorry, Father Warrum, but I'll be very occupied for the next few days."

"But I must see you, I must. I don't know where to turn." The suffering was deeper than tears.

"Father Warrum, I simply can't—"

"I've been arrested."

". . . Arrested?" It was real, then. "Where are you?"

"I'm not in jail, if that's what you mean. It's worse than that. I can't tell you on the phone. . . . *Please.*"

"Can you come this afternoon?"

"Yes—what time?"

"Say, four o'clock?"

"Oh, thank you—I'll be there."

As he hung up, Michael heard someone at the front door; the bell rang once, then quickly again, insistently. He moved from under the stairway where the telephone was, to see who was there. It was the postman at the wrong time of day, late morning.

Special delivery, he said, and registered; Michael signed for it. The word *Espresso* was scrawled in red across the envelope; the stamps were Italian, the handwriting was Ledagrazia's.

His hands, trembling, tore at the flap. Sometimes, when she wrote quick notes, the language was Italian. But when she particularly wanted no misunderstanding . . . This letter was in English.

> Dearly loved Mico,
>
> You called, asking for help, and I turned you away. I cannot tell you how I grieve over it. But the question you asked about Lucas and Cory goes so hurtfully to the heart of who I am that I was unable to speak. Pirandello, I think it was, said our mirror image is always someone else. So, when I look at myself I am always *un'altra,* and somehow I must compose one person out of this double self.
>
> I am a Communist.
>
> And I am a Catholic.
>
> Most foreigners do not understand how it is possible for such a great number of Italian Catholics to divide their allegiance between beliefs that are so hostile to each other. The Italian Catholic Communist would say that the beliefs are not, indeed, hostile. The Communists in Italy, he claims, are not revolutionary, they do not believe in violence, they resort to the ballot instead of the bullet— *argomenti, non armamenti*—and they do not advocate the destruction of the Church.
>
> I too believe that way. How this peaceful co-existence is possible in Italy when it is hardly conceivable in so many other places, one can only speculate. Perhaps, over the centuries, we Italians have learned to separate politics from everything else in our lives, certainly from God. Or perhaps it is just the opposite, a national schizophrenia that demands *mondo e cielo* simultaneously, love and hatred in the same bed. At any rate, there are numberless Italians

who lead this double life, some without great conflict, some in a discord that tries their souls.

I am one of the latter. Especially so, since my brother is a cardinal, and may possibly one day be our Pope.

It was my son Bruno who started me as a Communist. He is supposedly my least favorite child, but actually he is the one of whom I am proudest. He educated me. I see him more often than I pretend, and for years he has been sending me books which I read and burn.

I was an easy convert, Mico. I had a husband whom I despised, and I could never expect that the Church, as it was then constituted—and still is—would allow me a divorce. What was worse, I had six children by that hated man. I will not whisper the cruelties I suffered with him. When I wanted to put an end to child-bearing he dragged me across the piazza—where everybody knew me—and into the church, where he forced me to confess my sin. Twice I tried to abort my children. The last time I gave myself *setticemia,* and very nearly died . . . and Bruno was born.

You can imagine how fearful I have been that my double life would injure my beloved brother. I know that if I were to tell him, he would unshrinkingly defend my right to be what I am. But liberal that he is, he is still a cardinal, and in a political arena, and his defense of me would only bring misfortune to himself. So I have thought it better to hide my political beliefs.

It was when I had just become a Communist that Lucas came to recuperate in our house. Cory, who was then in his teens, spent three summer months with us. He was bright, sensitive, terribly in need of affection—and deeply troubled. He had nobody in the world except Lucas—who was both parents in one—and the boy adored him. But he felt forsaken, felt as though his brother had abandoned him to unfamiliar cities, to foreign schools, to strangers. It was useless to point out to Cory that Lucas loved him more deeply than he could ever love anyone else; the distances between them—in place and temperament—were too vast.

Lucas had indeed neglected the boy. His disregard had begun when Cory, at the age of nine, had been hurt in a street fight, and had lost his right eye. Hearing of the catastrophe, Lucas had instantly flown from Rome to be near the boy who was in a Dublin hospital. But almost immediately after the child had been discharged from the hospital, Lucas had rushed back to the Vatican, leaving Cory to the strangers in the boarding school. It was too soon. The boy groped around in a half-dark world; he was frightened and lost. . . . There were other desertions, real and imaginary, for Cory to remember.

Yet, what was Lucas to do? He had his own career to make, his own call to answer; he had the years of misery on Kilklare Island and—most terrible of all—his almost mortal illness. It would be wrong to say that Lucas was at fault. If a situation had arisen that demanded his death for his brother's life, I have no doubt Lucas would have given it.

But Cory didn't want Lucas dead, he wanted his living presence as a brother, a father, a friend. Pathetically, the boy felt that if Lucas loved him the whole world loved him. I recall one day when Cory was painting a picture and his brother was watching him. It was a lonely landscape that was being rendered in rather cheerless colors, but Lucas warmly praised the boy on how vividly the vista was materializing, and from that day onward the dismal landscape started to be filled with sunlight.

I know that Lucas looks back at those three months, when we were all together, as a joyous time for all of us. It wasn't. For Cory it was miserable. He had decided to go to the seminary in the fall, believing he wanted to be a priest. But in an unhappy, disordered way he dreaded it. He had applied to the seminary only to please his brother. And it did more than please Lucas, it made him deeply happy. I think he sincerely felt that the priesthood would do for Cory what it had finally done for himself—resolve the boy's confused longings, his turbulence, his sense of abandonment. The boy's decision to follow his brother's calling seemed to Lucas an admiring act of imitation, a tribute of the most selfless love. One evening, at dinner, Lucas said that the medicine that had been his most miraculous cure was his brother's resolution to enter the priesthood.

Nor was the boy absolutely certain that he *didn't* want to go into the priesthood. He was torn; he didn't have a

317

single thought that didn't plague him. But he hadn't the courage to be honest with his brother. He didn't want to hurt Lucas, didn't want to endanger the sick man's recovery; he had given his brother a gift of happiness that was helping to restore his health, a gift Cory couldn't retract. But at last he forced himself to discuss it.

It was late in the evening. Lucas had been improving excellently, and was even back to working a little. He was sitting at the solarium table, with his books and papers spread across it. Cory did it badly. He should have waited for a private moment, and not spoken when Paolo and I were present; and he should have prepared himself to speak reasonably, collectedly, and without the burst of emotion. In any event, Lucas heard him out. At the end of it, his response was as calm and reasoned as the boy's had been irrational. Going into the seminary, he said, was not an irrevocable act. It would be years before Cory would have to commit himself, irreversibly, in ordination. Time enough, these next few years, to go one way or another. Meanwhile, Cory would be happier in the seminary than in any other school Lucas could imagine. And he wound up by saying, without unkindness, "Do as I say, Cory. You know that I understand you better than you do yourself."

It was a strange thing to have said, considering he had seen so little of the boy over the years. And yet, in an indescribable, in an uncanny way both Paolo and I believed that it was true.

So, apparently, did Cory. He agreed to go to the seminary.

We thought that the crisis had been peaceably overcome. But that night, after Paolo and Lucas went to bed, the boy flew to pieces. I've never seen such torment and such rage. In the midst of his outburst, he started for the table where his brother's books and papers were. I knew he meant to tear everything to shreds. I got in his way, I grabbed him, struggled, pleaded with him . . . and finally I was able to soothe him.

I did what I could, for the remainder of the summer, to comfort and mother Cory. It was not hard to love him; he had sweetness and true talent. I encouraged him to paint. I

318

took him every week to an art studio in Rome. But I was not fooling myself; I couldn't pacify his rages.

On the afternoons when Cory was in the art studio, I would pretend to go shopping or to the cinema. Actually, I would go to a *luogo di riunione,* a union hall that functioned as a Communist meeting place. I would do a number of chores there—translations, typing, the writing of speeches that others would deliver—and I would generally leave them some money. Often, there would be a meeting of some sort, with speakers from everywhere.

Toward the end of one such meeting, I happened to turn and glance to the rear of the hall. Cory was standing there. The last time we had been in Rome he had caught me in a lie about a movie I had pretended to see. So this particular afternoon, he had followed me and remained for the entire meeting.

He stood there motionless, enrapt. Afterward, when I spoke to him, he was euphoric. He wanted to know all about my involvement with Communism, everything. And when I was finished, all the way home on the train, he begged me to take him to our next meeting. I kept refusing, entreating him to lower his voice for fear people would hear him, but he wouldn't stop. Nor would I agree to take him. I saw in his attraction to radicalism an unhealthy need for revenge—against his brother. And I didn't want to be part of it.

Two weeks later, however, entirely on his own, he disobeyed me and attended a second meeting. While there, he totally ignored my presence, and pretended we were strangers. And from that time until the end of the summer, he went to every meeting.

I had a fear that, as a result of his fascination with Communism, he would not enter the seminary. But he surprised me. When autumn came, he kept his promise and dutifully enrolled.

By that time I had more or less stopped going to the meeting place, for fear that others would find out what Cory had discovered about me. I never stopped being a Communist—I still give money to them—but I have become almost completely inactive.

My brother, I am sure, never got word of my involvement. But Lucas did.

It was a good many months later—I got a letter from Lucas. He was entirely well again and back at work—a monsignor now, newly appointed as Associate Chancellor of the Philadelphia archdiocese. He had news that had deeply shaken him. Cory had run away from the seminary and come to America. He had told Lucas that he was a radical . . . and how he had become one.

I can only imagine the moment when Lucas heard it, and I'm grateful to have been spared seeing it. But I wasn't spared Lucas's anger. His letter accused me of having plotted against him and his brother, and of having betrayed him. And the coldest thought he left for the very end. He said he did not ever want to be beholden to me for the ten months that we were kind to him. He would therefore not expose me as a Communist. He said, "It is repayment in full, all that you deserve."

It was a bitter repayment. But the bitterest part is that none of us are friends anymore. Cory stayed in America, went from one art school to another, from one political group to another, and became more and more radical. Occasionally, not often, I saw him when he came to Italy. About two years ago, he was back in Rome and we had dinner together. He was on fire about a woman who had made a stir in radical circles everywhere. Her name was Cristobal and she gave a speech wherever she went—it was called "The Butcher's Table"—it was inflammatory on women's rights. Cory was enthralled by her. I had heard her speech—and I could have sworn she was a terrorist. At dinner that night, I told Cory I thought Cristobal was dangerous—beware. He was drinking more than I had ever seen him do, and quarrelsome. He defended her and suddenly lost his temper. When he started to be abusive, I quickly left the restaurant. It was the last time I ever saw him.

Not long after that time, I got a letter of apology from him. I was right about Cristobal, he said; she was indeed a terrorist, and he would have nothing more to do with her. . . . But there was no friendliness in the letter, and I never answered it.

But, to go back. On the telephone, you used the word "betrayal." I never betrayed Lucas. I did not corrupt his brother. I did not convince him to be a Communist. If anyone made him a radical, it was Lucas. . . . But he has never forgiven me.

You were right to come to me for help. While I cannot report the kind of vulnerability in Lucas that may be useful to you—a crime, a disgrace, a skeleton in a closet—I can tell what his one mortal weakness is. His brother. Lucas used to think he had an affection for me and for Paolo, but his one true devotion is Cory. He is all the heart that Lucas has. There is no emotional access to the man except by way of Cory, there is absolutely none. How you can ever make that work for you I cannot tell, but I wish you everything you pray for.

One word more. You must forgive me for not having entrusted you with this confidence sooner. I was too faint-hearted. But I am glad you know this of me. You are one person from whom I do not wish to hide. I love you, Mico mio.   Ledagrazia

Composed, he put the letter back in the envelope. Why was he not astonished by it? Why did it seem so germane to what he had always known about Ledagrazia, that she would commit herself to whatever she believed in, even if it was Communism? Looking back over the years, he realized she had had a potent influence on Feradoti and on himself, pulling them leftward, sometimes successfully, sometimes not at all, yet never assailing their own integrities. She had disturbed them, angered them, inspired them—humanizing them always, calling them to heed their deepest wisdom, and their hearts. And had left them both intact.

As to Cory, Michael couldn't guess whether she had hurt or helped the boy. But Leda was neither a fool nor a villain, and he could not see how she could harm anyone. And if the boy's angers had come from having been abandoned, there was nobody in the world better suited than Leda to comfort the forsaken.

However, advice to lay siege to the Cardinal by way of his brother was no help. Michael had already tried that, to no avail. Perhaps he had not tried hard enough.

Cristobal . . . The dour warning to Cory to beware of her was, enigmatically, a warning to everyone. But how are we to beware, he asked, and of what? It was of no use to be forewarned against a generalized peril. That way, paranoia: every falling pebble becomes an avalanche. It had to be something more specific than that.

Like the face at his front door.

He saw it as he was putting Leda's letter in his pocket. A familiar face. Pressed close to the glass panel on the right. Peering into the darkness of the vestibule, both hands held to her temples, like blinders shielding out the exterior light. I'm in the darkness, Michael thought, she doesn't see me. But how clearly I see her—and know her, without remembering her name. A dark, intense face, disturbed and unsettled, weirdly sexless. At first, in a quirk of memory, he thought it was the cigar-making woman, but that couldn't be possible; another country, another time, a bridge over another river. Besides, she had had a large countenance, broad cheekboned, a Juno woman, and this visage was small and narrow, skeletally thin.

He would have to let her in.

Slowly he moved toward the front door. The first few steps and he was still in darkness. Then, just as he stepped into the light, she saw him.

That quickly, she was gone.

He hurried to the door.

She was faster than he was, seemed to drop down the steps and out of sight. By the time the door was open, she was onto the street, running, crossing it, streaking toward the end of the block.

He recognized her. That night, at the Galatians meeting, he had been able to get only the briefest glimpse of the artist, twining her sennit braid in the dimmest corner of the room. Painfully diffident, Cory had described her, what was her name, now? Cassie Macramé.

He was discomfited. Other women came to mind, in a windy street of Rome, brutalizing a priest . . .

He watched her as she ran to the end of the block. When she reached the corner, someone came to meet her from the intersecting avenue. It was too long a distance to be certain of his identity, but Michael would have sworn it was the gargoyle, Heskins.

When they turned the corner and were gone, Michael went indoors. He stood in the hallway, perplexed: what to do? He thought of calling the police, but no crime had been perpetrated, not even a misdemeanor. He saw himself as a querulous priest in a fussy cassock.

The phone rang. It startled him. He forgot that he had been hoping for a second call from Nora; the phone bell was suddenly a tocsin of alarm. He hurried to answer it.

322

The voice was momentarily unfamiliar to him, consciously disguised it seemed, muffled.

"Hello," it said. "Father Farris?"

"Yes."

"Oh, thank God."

He recognized the person, Cory Cavanaugh.

"Come at once," the young man said. "Don't waste a minute."

"Where?"

"My brother's house. Hurry, please."

He hadn't thought they resembled each other until he saw the brothers together. Then it was inescapable: a hollowness of cheek that they both had, the drawn look, ascetic. And the light in the Cardinal's study struck both their faces in much the same way, too bright on one side, burning away the features, too dark on the other, shrouding them. Particularly in Cory's face, the chiaroscuro conjured the two sides of the man, the revealed and the secret, the seeing and the blind.

He could not believe that the Cardinal was as frightened as he appeared to be; it had to be anger. "I gave you three days to leave," he said. "Your time expired yesterday. So I must tell you that last night I made the announcement to the press. On your way to the airport, you might pick up an evening newspaper and read all the details of the Synod."

Mulishly, not knowing what point he was making or what purpose it would serve: "I am not going to the airport."

The Cardinal said quietly, "Your life is in danger."

Cory, hurriedly: "Show him the letter, Lucas."

The Cardinal opened the center drawer of his desk. What he extracted was an ordinary business envelope, with the Cardinal's name and address typewritten, nothing else. He drew the single-page letter out of it. It also was typewritten, neatly, meticulously, on both sides of the sheet. He handed it to Michael. The letter had no salutation. It read:

> Send him home.
> You know who I mean. The snoop, the politician, the time-server.
> Send him home. Give him whatever reasons you choose. Tell him the lies that come naturally to you, or tell him the truth.

323

The truth is bloodshed.

It will happen to him, as it has happened to others, as it will go on happening, until the revolution has been accomplished.

Tell the false peacemaker there is no reconciliation between your people and ours. There is no peace between the reactionary and the rebel. And there is no safety for the man between them. There is only violence.

Not a violence of our making, but of yours.

When you say, as the publican said, "the half of my goods I give to the poor," then you lie. For you have taken half the world, and left the poor their poverty. This is theft, it is violence.

When you hold the world in fief, the starved of Brazil, the frightened of Chile, the diseased in the back places of Africa, the hopeless of the East; when a small Romanic enclave of cassocked men hold in fee seignory the billion wretched of the world, then it is slavery, it is violence.

When it is known that all human creatures are weak of flesh, as you yourselves are weak, and that all men commit venery of the bed, as you yourselves do, and when you do not allow men and women to shield their parts so that they may choose when to multiply, and when you invoke the damnation of God upon such so-called transgressions, then it is terrorism, and this is violence.

When you tell us that the scriptures have said that women may not be priests, that homosexuals are execrated by God, that St. Peter's rock could have been formed only of polished Italian marble and not of human clay, that the Pontiff's ring will lose its luster on the finger of a Slav or a black or a woman, then you swear falsely the passion of Jesus, and this is violence.

The violence is yours.

So we meet your violence with our own. Ours is bloody, but just. And it is swift.

We will not wait for the Second Coming. The Coming is now.

We do not believe the time-server when he says the left hand will caress the right, that the Galatians will lie down with the archbishops, that the fools and thieves and

324

murderers and pharisees will all conjoin and make Christ's heaven on earth. It will only happen when the Church has been razed, and its goods given to the poor. Thus it will not be Roman any longer, but truly catholic.

Our faith is: the world to live in, and heaven to die for. Or kill for.

Tell him to go back to Rome.

There was no closing, no signature.

He finished reading the letter, held it briefly, then handed it across the desk to the Cardinal. "Do you know who sent it?" Michael asked.

"Cory says it was Falga Cristobal."

The artist corrected him. "I don't know that it was Cristobal. But it's her rhetoric."

"What's known about her?"

"Ask Cory," the Cardinal replied. "She's one of his friends—she's a Galatian."

"She's not one of my friends—and she's not a Galatian."

"She comes to your meetings."

"To wreck them!"

"But you defend what she says in the letter," the Cardinal said.

"I don't defend the violence," his brother retorted. "But I agree with the rest. She hasn't made one charge against the Church that isn't irrefutable. She says it better and more passionately than I could have said it. And if she weren't a terrorist, we would have no difference whatever!"

It was a rarefied ethic, Michael thought. A Galatian, a man of peaceful intent, Cory was defending someone with whom he had had a rancorous quarrel. Yet, the priest had heard Feradoti express himself similarly in an effort to understand the terrorists. Were Cory's principles, then, so finely drawn—or was it, simply, that the issue gave him an opportunity to wrangle with his brother?

"Where can I find her?" Michael was looking at Cory.

The Cardinal interceded. "You will not find her anywhere, Father Farris. This letter is a threat against you—and you're departing."

"I'm going to stay and deal with her."

"Deal with her? Dear heaven, do you think you can make deals with everybody? The person who wrote that letter is rabid."

Cory: "Then so am I."

325

The prelate turned to him. "You said that last night—and I'm tired of it."

"She's not rabid and she's not demented," Cory answered. "I wish she were with us instead of against us—but she's not wrong. She says what we say, except she's willing to be crucified for what she believes in."

"Or crucify others."

Michael said it deliberately, to see if the general statement would cause the Cardinal to betray any knowledge of a man hanging on a white wall. But if the prelate had learned how Galestro had been murdered, he gave no sign of it. On the contrary, he seemed to take the term in its most hallowed sense. "Don't use the word 'crucify,' " he said quietly. "It's a passion word, not to be used for petty malcontents. She may be dangerous, but she's not glorious. She's a cheap thug."

"She's not, goddamn it!"

It was as if the profanity were a personal blow, brother against brother. In it there was such a passage of hurt as can happen only in families, Michael sensed, where the vulnerabilities are familiar and accessible. As Leda had described it, the measure of the brothers' love for one another was how deeply they could wound each other. He could see that the wounds went deep: the unguarded humanity in the older man, the suffering; and Cory's remorse—he thought the young man was going to apologize, or weep or run.

But no peace was made. The prelate was the first to repossess himself, his sensibilities hardened over, and he went back to his habit of cold contempt, and to the sensual comfort of words. "She's as cheap as a hundred little curates who nip at the sacramental wine," he said. "They want it both ways. They want to be revered for their closeness to God, and coddled for their closeness to man. Which is to say, honored for strength and beloved for weakness. They call themselves zealots and behave like helots. They want the pleasures of the belly and the bed—and now they want them sanctified. They want to be wedded to Mother Church and Susie McGonigle at the same time. And the women—like Cristobal—want to be Reverend McGonigle —fornicating at night and saying Mass in the morning. It's a bigamy they'll kill for—one mortal sin to expiate another. To hell with them."

"To hell with you, then," Cory said, with the same quiet.

Michael watched them, the two brothers, and no longer felt sorry for them. They enraged him. They could go on like this, and probably had gone on for years and years, battling bitterly, but without risk. Always they would come back to the complacent comfort of family feeling, of brotherhood, still loving one another, as obviously they did, and no real harm done to either of them or to their precious property, their family relationship. A family fight, they would call it, nothing more than that, no matter how much anger was in it; a disagreement about how toughly or tenderly the beef was to be boiled, if they were Irish; or how *al dente* the pasta, if Italian. Everywhere, the Church was having a family squabble, a very civil war. Insignificant, and who was to worry if it never got settled?

And because it didn't get settled, the Church was falling apart.

"You make me sick—both of you!" The Cardinal started to interrupt, but Michael's anger stopped him. "You think Cristobal's a villain. But so are you—so is your brother. While the two of you battle over the dogmas, she'll steal the Host. Don't you care what's happening to the Church? I don't mean the councils, I mean the Church itself. It's catastrophe! The seminaries are emptying, there aren't any nuns for the hospitals, there isn't enough money for the schools. Ask any New York curate about Mass—he'll tell you it's become a bad ticket. People have begun to think that the offertory is a small swindle, and they throw slugs in the collection box. All over the world, Catholic women are going to abortion mills or using homemade bistouries and dying of butchery. Confession has become a Saturday night joke—and soon only the crackpots will go to communion. And that's the most terrible part of it—what's happened to pure faith. It's been twisted by this argument and that, by one theological quibble and another, until it has lost its integrity and its simple holiness. Faith can't endure argument—it's not a polemical subject. But if you quarrel, that's what it becomes. Then you need arbitrators like myself—in a matter that should never be demeaned by arbitration. So don't talk to me about 'deals'—don't blame me if we wind up with a negotiated God! On your head be it—on your head!"

He steadied himself. "I don't like you, Cardinal," he continued. "And I don't like Margotto or van Tenbroek or Cristobal or Warrum —and I'm not sure how much I like Cory. But with whatever small power I have, I'm trying to reconcile you all, because I love God, and I'm not always certain how to serve Him except through the Church. And if it falls apart—!"

Frustrated, enraged by one obstruction after another, he couldn't stand the sight of them. Turning, he hurried out of the office.

327

He heard the swift footsteps behind him, then Cory's voice: "Wait, Father." The young man grabbed him by the shoulder. "That was damn well said."

"Then why the hell didn't you listen!"

It was a ridiculous outburst; the man had obviously listened. Michael took a breath and said more sensibly, "The three of us—if we could only *hear* one another—we might possibly come to terms. My God, we might even come to terms with Cristobal!"

"Cristobal?" he said bitterly. "What a fool you are."

"What about 'The Butcher's Table'?"

Michael asked the question, but Cory didn't answer it. They sat in a crowded little espresso bar, ostensibly having lunch. Actually, Michael was having the lunch, a sandwich, and Cory was having drinks, brandy. The artist had had two of them, and was on his third. Macabre, Michael thought: the brandy had dulled the good eye, but the false one seemed to glitter, vividly alive.

" 'The Butcher's Table,' " Cory said at last. "It was a lecture—a magnificent speech that Cristobal gave all over Europe. Did you ever hear it?"

"No."

"Then how do you know about it?"

". . . Ledagrazia."

Cory ordered another drink. "Did Leda tell you anything about me?"

"Yes."

"What?"

"Only about the summer you spent there with your brother . . . and the meetings you attended."

"Did she tell you about my wanting to be a priest?"

"She told me about your not wanting to be a priest."

"Lucas never forgave me for that—and he never forgave her. He thought my leaving the seminary was all her fault, but he was wrong. He thought it was Communism's fault. Wrong. How he could know all the facts and come to all the wrong conclusions—! But what can you expect of a reactionary? If he's looking for a scapegoat, he'll always find Communism."

"Didn't you leave the seminary because you became a Communist?"

328

"No."

"Then what made you leave?"

"Hunger."

"Hunger?"

"Yes . . . for women. I was in my late teens—they were all I could think about. When I tried to imagine what my life as a priest would be . . . as a celibate . . . The last four or five weeks I was there, I couldn't stand it. I'd sneak off in the middle of the night. I'd find anybody I could—a waitress in a Pavesi restaurant, a cashier in a movie theater, a cleaning woman—I'd have it over and done with and crawl back to my Hail Marys. The nighttimes were all I ever thought about. Then one morning—in the middle of a class—I thought I was suffocating. I ran out of the seminary and never went back."

"But you went back to Communism?"

"No. I ran away from everything. I followed Lucas to America —he was in Philadelphia at the time. I went to art schools and either left or got thrown out. I became an erratic rebel. With every new anger, I joined something else. The only thing I was faithful to was my painting—I was steady as a slave. I'd sell a picture, do a few commercial illustrations, take the money and get on a plane. Italy—Spain —Israel—anywhere. Useless—I couldn't find a cause I could hang on to—hundreds of them, sure—but not a single one . . . Until I met Cristobal."

"Was she your cause?"

Michael expected the artist to shade his answer, but he didn't. "Yes, she was. . . . You have no idea how she struck me when we met. I tried to paint her at that time, and I couldn't get my palette fiery enough—there weren't any scarlets!" The drink arrived and as he was lifting it to his lips, he beckoned the waiter to have another one in readiness. "The first time I saw her . . . she was going to be giving her famous speech, 'The Butcher's Table.' It was the same dingy union hall where I first became a Communist. Only it was evening— not enough light—and drearier than ever. There were folding chairs, a small platform with an ordinary oak table, the kind you'd see in a public library. The table was empty. In a little while the lights went out and there was a spotlight on the platform. Then Cristobal entered. She wore the same damn costume—dove gray, with that flaming silk throat. She started to speak very quietly about women's rights and birth control and the Church. Then, when she began to talk about abortion, she lifted things off the table. They were objects she said women had actually used to abort themselves with. Some of them were stained with blood. She showed us knives, ice picks, the quills of wild birds, acids, corrosives, the tine of a pitchfork. She would say, 'This woman died of a perforated uterus, this one had septicemia, this one hemorrhaged to death, this woman—the mother of seven children—got caught and hanged herself.' After the mention of each woman, in a terrible mockery, Cristobal would cross herself.

"She didn't raise her voice, not once; she didn't seem to be trying to inflame anybody. But it happened—the crowd was on fire. And then, when she had us all engaged on the *issue,* she did the genius thing— she engaged us to *herself*: she made us laugh. She raised the last object off the butcher's table. It was a stalk of celery. It was already limp and wilted. She held it up and let it flop about, and said, 'Even this . . .'

"Well, we needed that relief, and we howled. And from that instant, we were hers. She talked for another half hour or so—wittily —and passionately. And when she was through, we would have done anything for her—women of all ages, and *men*—we would have broken any law, we would have stolen, killed, we would have followed here anywhere. . . . And I did follow her."

"Literally?"

"Yes—all over Europe—the Mideast—wherever she went."

"You were in love with her?"

". . . Yes."

"Did she know that?"

"We lived together for sixteen months.'

"Were you happy with her?"

"I'll probably never be as happy again. For the first time in my life, one woman was enough for me. More than enough." He laughed, but it was rueful. "What a change in me! I was in love. I had had no idea that making love could be entirely beautiful—I had always reserved that for painting. I couldn't imagine looking at another woman. She was all I wanted."

"Why didn't you marry her?"

He was drunk now, and unable to hide his wretchedness. "Because I found out about her. . . . She's a spoiler."

"A spoiler? In what way?"

"She wants to wreck the Church and she's found the perfect mechanism—disorder. Wherever she goes, she gets into some group or other, and makes trouble. She sets one faction against another—and leaves everything in shambles. You saw her at the Galatians' meeting—"

"But why them? They may not be as extreme as she is, but they're also radicals. Why does she try to ruin them?"

"Because she's an anomist—she's in love with chaos!"

"Doesn't she ever fail? Don't people eventually see through her?"

"By the time they do, it's too late. She actually has her studio here in New York, but she doesn't live anywhere—she moves so fast you can't keep up with her. . . . Besides, she has another mechanism."

"Terror."

"Yes . . . Her group isn't large—perhaps a half dozen women, three or four men. But she can draw upon terrorists everywhere. Wherever we went, there was this clot of murderers. . . . At first I had no idea how violent they were. I would awaken in the morning and read that a bishop's car had been wrecked, a priest had been beaten—"

"A breviary burned."

"Yes—and I had no idea *we* were doing it. And then—as I began to suspect it—it got worse. A sacristy was vandalized, smashed to pieces. Finally, the most terrible thing—"

Michael's pulse quickened: he's going to tell about a cardinal crucified!

"—a parish house was bombed with five people in it."

Cory had stopped. How can I get him to talk about the crucifixion?

"What else happened?" Michael said.

"The last thing I heard about was the burning of a parochial school in Switzerland. Luckily, nobody was in it at the time."

"Nothing after that?"

"No. That was about the time I left her."

"When, exactly?"

"About a year ago."

Too soon, Michael realized. He had left before Galestro's murder. He would not have heard about it.

"Then what happened?" Michael asked.

"I never wanted to leave her—I couldn't bear the thought of it. For weeks before I left, I kept begging her to put an end to the violence. But it was a passion with her. I couldn't convince her—of anything. On the contrary, a terrible thing was happening—she was starting to convince *me*. I can't tell you what I was going through—like a bewitchment. But at the last moment—I was blessed—I had the guts to tear myself free. Then—when I was far away from her—what an agony it was! And she didn't make it any easier. Wherever I went, she had me followed. I was threatened—twice I was beaten—and you remember what happened in Jerusalem."

"Are you sure she was responsible for all of that?"

"Yes, I am. One of the men who attacked me in New York was Heskins. And the man who pulled a knife in the bazaar in Jerusalem was a terrorist named Ibn Lakh whom I met in Rome—with Cristobal."

"But if you knew so much about her, why didn't she have you killed?"

"I don't know. . . . I think she would say she still loved me."

"What would you say?"

"I was her possession . . . she wouldn't give up a possession." With a grimly mirthless smile: "And she was right—I *was* possessed. I couldn't get her out of my mind. Wherever I went, she was there. I became ill with thinking about her. I felt as if she were killing me, in effigy. All my hungers came back, worse than ever. I would seduce any woman, I would buy any woman, I would bully any woman into bed. Everything became an aphrodisiac: if I fingered a bit of silk, I would get an erection, if a girl laughed in an odd way, if I touched my own breast, if I saw a woman's tongue, if I looked at a certain kind of face—have you noticed that some faces are naked? I was in a state of craving all the time. When I was alone, I talked to myself in the filthiest language, I abused myself until I was in pain, I dreamed incessant dreams of self-torture, I would awaken crying at the walls.

"Then, one night, I was walking down a narrow street, about a mile from the Vatican. It was dark, it was rainy. What a child was doing out in that miserable neighborhood in pitch darkness I don't know. She couldn't have been any more than nine or ten years old. I saw her hurrying in my direction. Suddenly I couldn't move—I stopped walking. But she didn't—she kept coming closer. As she came alongside me, I grabbed her. She ran away. I went after her—I caught her—I started to smother her in my arms. She pulled her head free and began to scream. But there was nobody around to hear her, not a soul. Except me. I heard her. To this day, I hear those screams—I always will. Thank God I heard them then . . . and let her go.

"For a week afterward, I was in—what would you call it?—a walking catalepsy. Every sense was suspended—no feeling. Then, day by day, my mind began to clear, and finally I came to a decision: from that time onward, I would never touch a woman again. It's been nearly a year, and I haven't broken my vow to myself."

332

He finished his drink, seemed to absent himself for a moment. "And here's Cristobal again. Father Warrum says she's attended every meeting for the last six weeks. . . . Haunting me . . . haunting all of us."

The man looked ravaged. The drinks hadn't helped to pacify him, the devastation was too deep. Then—inexplicably—

"Goddamn Lucas!"

It wasn't a mere profanity, it was a literal curse.

"Goddamn Lucas!" he said again.

"Don't, Cory."

"Goddamn him! He used to be my confessor! Can you imagine that?"

Michael didn't believe it. "You mean you told him everything?"

"Not 'told him everything'—it was more than that—I *confessed* to him. All the time I was growing up—only to him. If I couldn't see him, I would go for months until I did. Once, I went unrepentant for nearly a year—I couldn't confess to anyone else. People didn't know, they used to think he was only a brother to me—a fatherly brother—but he was more, he was my *absolution!*"

Overwrought, he made an effort to restrain himself. "And then—a little over a week ago—when I came home from Jerusalem—I asked him to confess me. And for the first time in my life he refused to hear me."

If he had spoken agonies before, this must have seemed the worst to him. He looked utterly helpless, deserted.

"Did he say why he wouldn't confess you?"

"No, he didn't. . . . My God, can he let our political differences do that to him?—and me? I don't understand—how can he refuse to confess me?"

"You have been confessing, Cory. To me."

"No!"

"If you would like to do it more ritually—in a Church—in a confessional—"

"No! Christ, no! . . . Goddamn Lucas!" He was shaking, as if in seizure.

To get to Cardinal Cavanaugh, Leda had advised, go by way of his brother: the only access. But Cory's account of their relationship gave Michael no encouragement. There was no longer any access; the brothers were alienated.

333

Michael was depressed, he felt too dismal to be frightened; the threat against his life contained in Cristobal's letter seemed, irrationally, less important than his lack of alternative with respect to Cardinal Cavanaugh.

He walked the streets. Not sure what his next step should be, or where his next destination, he found himself at a newsstand.

An early edition of the paper, as the Cardinal had foretold, carried an item on the Synod. There was an old picture of Cavanaugh, taken on his return to Manhattan as a new cardinal, and under it the article referred to "his Conservative Synod." It was circumspectly phrased but there was no question that the journalist knew, as the whole world was learning, that the Synod was moving to unify the rightist forces of the Church behind the candidacy of Cardinal Margotto. The latter was characterized as having been in opposition not only to Pope John but even to the present Pope who could scarcely be described as radical. The date of the Synod was given: two weeks after Corpus Christi.

Michael's head thickened. There was no ache in it; on the contrary, he felt that a good, sensible, physical pain might ease his misery.

Then there was an act of God, a fortunate one. As he was about to toss the newspaper into the trash receptacle, his eye caught another item, a smaller one. The restrained headline read: JEWISH CARDINAL HONORED. The two paragraphs simply said that Natan Cardinal Halevi, the Canadian prelate known as the Jewish Cardinal, was being acclaimed today with the Humanities Laurel of the International Alliance of Christians and Jews. There were a few sentences about his liberal accomplishments and the quotation of his well-known line about one hand making the cross while the other made a fist. The award ceremony was to take place at luncheon in the Waldorf-Astoria.

With new life, Michael hailed a taxi.

It was a twist of luck. The last he'd heard, the old man was in the mountains, recuperating from an operation. And here he was, miraculously transported by providence.

As he was riding, he looked at his watch. It was not yet three o'clock. Perfect timing—the luncheon would just be concluding and he would be able to catch the Cardinal on the move.

The taxi let him off on Park Avenue and he hurried into the hotel. It was a junior ballroom that was being used for the luncheon, Michael was told, and he rushed to the elevator.

But he was not, as he had expected to be, just in time. The

334

luncheon had started at noon and had ended shortly after two-thirty. The busboys clearing the tables disagreed; one said the Cardinal was on his way back to Quebec, the other said he had gone to his room.

"Room? Where? In the hotel?" Michael asked.

In an instant, he was on the house phone.

"Who?" the old voice said.

"Michael Farris—I'm one of Cardinal Feradoti's assistants. We met in Castel Gandolfo."

The voice crackled pleasurably. "Oh, you're the firebrand who wrote that heretical book."

The teasing delighted Michael; the old man's memory was crystal.

"I'm sorry I never got back to you," the prelate was saying, "but I intended to. This is my first outing. . . . Where are you?"

"Downstairs—in the hotel."

"Come right up."

In his hotel suite, the Cardinal did not get out of his armchair. He sat at a peculiar angle, a pillow propped unevenly under him. "You must excuse me for not rising," he said with a wry smile. "If I find a position that's comfortable, I don't dare abandon it." They shook hands and when Michael was seated, the prelate leaned forward and whispered with hoarse confidentiality, "No matter how daintily the newspapers describe my operation, don't you believe it. It was hemorrhoids. They can't be described esthetically—they're a condition without heavenly grace. A cynic might say there's no divinity that shapes our ends."

He grinned and got great pleasure from watching Michael laugh. "You were a very good laugher—I remember you that way." He said it warmly, then hurried on in an eager spate of words. "Père Laqueux tells me you're still in the Secretariat—what are you up to?—no, nowadays I shouldn't ask questions, or people will answer them. How are you, anyway? Where are you staying?"

Smiling: "Mindszenty House."

"Oh, yes—I know that place. A friend of my sister's stayed there—a refugee from Hungary. He now owns a fur shop in Canada." Suddenly, impulsively: "Did you see my prize—Christians and Jews—did you see my prize?"

He picked it off the table and Michael rose and took it from him. It was indeed beautiful, a simple intertwining of gold laurel leaves. And the old man was lovably immodest about it. "I deserve it," he said, "oh, I deserve it." He giggled and flicked his head from side to side in quick, quirky movements like an ecstatic bird.

335

"I'll be seventy-five next month. Pretty good, getting a medal like that at my age, isn't it pretty good?"

"Damn good."

The old man tasted the word, then burst into a gale of laughter.

"The funniest part of the lunch was that while they were making all those flowery speeches, all I could think of was my pain in the ass. Then there was one of them—a very dusty speaker—who said I was a great libertarian, and I was always in the vanguard. And it occurred to me that in the vanguard, all men are different, but in the rearguard they are all the same."

Michael laughed again. "But you've also thought it seriously."

". . . Yes, I have." The Cardinal was suddenly sober. "You've heard about the Synod, I suppose."

"Yes."

The prelate nodded. "Tell Paolo not to worry about me—I won't go."

"I was sure of that, Your Eminence," Michael said. "But I'm here to ask more of you than that."

"You are, eh?" Circumspectly: "Much more?"

"Yes, I've done my best to prevent the Synod, but I got no closer than the asking. There's a need for a countervailing action of some sort—and I think you're the right one to start it. There's nobody in the Americas as beloved as you are—"

"Stop." Getting laurel leaves was something he could delight in—it was institutional; but this seemed like personal flattery, fulsome to a no-nonsense old man. "What are you asking me to do?"

"Announce an opposing Synod."

Meting out the words: "I do not believe in conducting a Synod without recourse to the Vatican."

"Cardinal Cavanaugh is doing it."

The old man simply left it there, not deigning to reply. Michael was chagrined at having used the argument. "You needn't call it a Synod, Your Eminence—call it a Council for Reconciliation, if you like."

A hesitance. "Does Cardinal Feradoti know you are asking me to do this?"

"No."

"He would not approve of it—not in his own behalf."

"Probably not. But this terrible humility—which will make him a most Holy Father—makes him a difficult candidate. And if we allow it to disable us, Cardinal Margotto becomes our Pope."

336

Halevi was suddenly uncomfortable, physically so. Slowly, with laborious effort, he got out of his chair and walked a little distance to a place that had no definition in the room. He seemed marooned in space.

Then Michael saw a pathetic thing, something he had not noticed before: one of the Cardinal's hands trembled, not slightly but a good deal, as if it had a palsy in it. The old man broke the silence. "I've spoken to Cardinal Margotto on only a few occasions. He always struck me as a strong man—very scrupulous. I would say he must be a deeply pious man as well. It would never occur to me to think of him as a scoundrel."

Michael warned himself: don't speak. Wait. There was a puzzle here, and it might have peril in it. Everything Halevi had said about Margotto was true. Yet Michael was convinced that if he became Pope, the repression in the Church would ruin it. And what perplexed him, this very moment, was that he felt sure Halevi's conviction was no different from his own. A libertarian like this Jewish Cardinal, who had advocated concord not only with Jews but with Protestants and Mohammedans, who had been one of the creators of *Dignitatis Humanae*, could only be opposed to Margotto. How, then, could he defend the reactionary? And how could he, Michael, deal with the old man?

As a Jew.

"Doesn't it bother you that Margotto is anti-Semitic?"

The Cardinal spoke guardedly. "I am no longer sure what that means. I have seen so-called friends of the Jews turn *against* them— either actively or by doing nothing—without a pang of conscience. And I have seen avowed enemies take up the cudgels *for* them. So I'm not sure anymore what anti-Semitism is."

Michael was shocked. It was operational double-talk. He felt harried. It was the kind of shapeless argument that was hard to oppose. And it had nothing to do with Margotto. Michael knew the truth about him; so did Halevi.

"I've heard him make specific anti-Semitic remarks on a number of occasions," Michael said flatly.

"Have you?" It was as if he had been afraid of the verdict, yet had not expected it to be so severe. His spirit seemed to weaken. "I have never heard him say an unkind word."

"Would you imagine he would do so in your presence?"

". . . No, I suppose not."

Michael was confident he had won a major point. He was therefore

337

stunned to hear the Cardinal say, "Father Farris, I cannot help you."

"In heaven's name, why not?"

"Because I am too old." He tried to bring back his good humor. "It is my worst depravity, and not absolvable."

"But you're not too old. You're as alert, as vigorous as I remember you five years ago."

"Please." He was more deeply unnerved than Michael had thought. And weighing wretched alternatives. "I mentioned a slight embarrassment—hemorrhoids—in order to hide my major humiliation: mortality. I have Parkinson's disease."

He held up both his hands, to show how they shook. And Michael realized that the quirky, birdlike movements of his head were not the vivacity of high humor but the tics of paralysis. He yearned to cross the room and take the old man in his arms, to give him some of his own muscular certainty, to hold him closely and steady him. "I'm deeply sorry, Your Eminence, and I will pray for you. But I will not weep for you—not yet." Then, quickly, to dispel any prefiguration of mourning: "We need you, Cardinal, whether you think you can manage it or not. You know as well as I do what's happening to the Church—the fragmentations, the disillusionments—and now this new thing, the terror. We need you to help pull us together. If there is an effort to be made, I'll make it for you. I'll do anything—make the announcement, handle the press, communicate with everyone who is to be invited. I'll eliminate all the nuisances. All I ask of you is that you speak, and allow your name to be used."

He replied with precise deliberation. "I'm not sure I want my name to be used."

"Cardinal—"

"Wait. I think, without meaning to, I have lied to you. It isn't my age or my ailment that prevents me. It's that . . ." He was not being evasive, far from it; he was at great pains to confront the truth, and tell it. "I'm not certain I am against Margotto. You say he is an anti-Semite. I have never seen a sign of it. Besides, I am not primarily a Jew any more than you are primarily an American—I am a Roman Catholic. I am an *old* Roman Catholic. And so is he. And we are both terrified of the new ones."

"He, yes—but not you."

"Yes, I am." He continued with an austerity that seemed unnatural to him. "They say they offer new freedoms. Well, to a libertarian like myself, that is very seductive. But then—when they tell me that I must accept their freedoms or I will be cursed . . ." He smiled

338

mirthlessly. ". . . this is only freedom to go to the devil." He paused, then went on. "A while back, when I was in Switzerland, I went to Ecône and met a number of young people who are—what do they call themselves?—revolutionary traditionalists. An egregious name, no? But the old people among them—they are not egregious—they are so sad, the heart feels like a tumor. All they want is to say the old prayers in the old way. No more. The old familiar Latin, that is all they require to take the world-fright out of them. Now I ask you, Father Farris, in a new Church where so many new liberties are allowed—to everybody else—why can't the old people be allowed to say the old prayers? We grew up with the Latin. Our parents taught it to us, our nuns at school, our priests at the altars—do we now have to reject the people we once loved, and call them sinful? Why? Why must we pray in English, why in French, why not the language we always associated with home and holiness? Or *any* language, so long as it is spoken with devotion. Why must the old tongue be forbidden? So many new liberties—but not this one, for the old? Is this the new freedom?"

A paradox. It was the accountable argument from the unaccountable source. Michael had always heard the old liturgy defended by the right, never by the left. It was as if there had been modules of persuasion, each module a kit of arguments that all belonged together, no kit divisible, reactionary ones intact, radical ones intact, not to be commingled. But this progressive old man, using conservative arguments . . . another bedlam in the Church, deeper dementia . . . or the beginning of sanity.

Encouraged: "You see? That's what I mean, Your Eminence. An argument like that—coming from you—it pushes through walls—it might bring factions together."

"You are too hopeful, my friend," he responded wearily. "We have all strayed too far from one another. We are all, I'm afraid, outside Gethsemane."

The old man walked unsteadily back to his chair, and unhappily let himself down in it. But uncomfortable as he may have been, the affliction was not at this moment physical. He had lost hope, he was viewing doomsday. "I am not of much use anymore," he said. "I cannot *recognize* things. Even if I were allowed to use the old words, they do not fit the new beliefs. And some of the old words have totally disappeared. I listen for them in the Mass and I do not hear them, they are not there. I look for the word 'breviary' in my book of

339

prayers, and the word is gone. Where did it go?—was it a false word when we learned it? We do not talk of Matins or Lauds or Vespers anymore—were they ugly words that we discarded for more beautiful ones? I hardly know, these times, when to rise to Alleluia or when to genuflect—and I am given to understand it does not matter, I can do either one, or none of them, depending on the vagaries of my mood, or the particular altar I am facing. A priest is heard to use profanity on Easter morning; Cardinal Cavanaugh tells about phalluses in Third World churches. A few years ago, I entered a hospital in Canada, and that morning there was a front-page headline which said communion will be 'revamped'—that was the word; the wafer will no longer be placed upon the tongue, but will be given into the hand. There were two interns discussing it as an item of silliness, and one of them said, 'You don't have to take it in your mouth, you can take it in your hand.' Then they both screamed with laughter, and the Eucharist had become a dirty joke." Unable to endure his own words, the old man emitted a heartbroken outcry. "Oh, dear God," he said, "what are we to do? What am *I* to do? I cannot live in this desecrated faith, and I am afraid to die in it!"

His body shook uncontrollably, and he wept. Michael went to him, touched him, smoothed his hair, steadied his hand. It would be a cruelty to call him a newly made reactionary, just as it might be a cruelty to make demands on him as a one-time progressive. He was neither. He was simply an old man, sitting on a cold hearth, chilled by the closeness of death, needing someone to warm him for a while. Michael found himself speaking Latin words to him, in prayer.

After a while, the prelate was able to come to himself a little. He tried to make a quip at his own expense. "As you can see, I'm an antiquated knight who can't mount a horse for a new crusade. Wherever the Holy Sepulcher may be, someone else will have to recapture it."

The Cardinal blessed him, Michael made a loving sign to the old man, and departed.

Walking across town, the priest had an entirely incongruous reversal. His compassion for Halevi suddenly ceased. In its place, anger, seething anger, on the edge of eruption. Whatever the old man no longer was—progressive, Jew, fighting Catholic, libertarian, humanitarian—he was still a Cardinal, a power in the Church. He still had an effective vote in a conclave that would elect a new Pope. And the lives of three quarters of a billion Catholics, on every continent, in all conditions of poverty and plenty, of erudition and ignorance, of hope and despair, of grace and disgrace, would be altered because of his vote. His, and the votes of a hundred cardinals; a hundred men, every one a celibate, and over half of them senile, some as frightened and doddering as Halevi; and they would write a name to determine the fate of the troubled Catholic world.

Walking, he was nearly a block away from Mindszenty House when he saw someone sitting on the top step of the brownstone stairway. Father Warrum.

It was just four-thirty. Michael was a half hour late; he had totally forgotten his appointment with the man. He hurried, practically ran, and came panting to the foot of the steps. He couldn't tell Warrum he had completely obliterated him from his mind—the priest's self-esteem was low enough these days, but he couldn't lie. "I'm sorry I'm late," he said. "It's been a terrible day."

"Yes, it has—for me too."

Michael unlocked the front door, led him inside, up the stairs and into the living room. Warrum refused the Coca-Cola although he looked sweaty and hot. He was wearing a winter jacket of brown wool, blue worsted pants and rundown suede shoes. With the clerical collar, the other clothes seemed ridiculous, neither secular nor religious, proclaiming to the world that he didn't know where he belonged. He looked woebegone.

"You say you've been arrested?" Michael asked.

"Yes."

"On what charges?"

"They wouldn't tell me."

"You mean the police came and they—"

"Not the police," he interrupted. "The Church."

Michael checked his irritation. "The Church does not arrest anyone."

"I don't have to be in handcuffs to know I've been arrested."

Why did Cardinal Cavanaugh have to be so damn right about this man? He was, as predicted, tricky. He had not been arrested at all, but had inveigled Michael's sympathy by saying so, had gulled him into a meeting. Before he could accuse Warrum of it, however, the latter said:

"They've arrested me exactly the same way as they once arrested you."

"I was never 'arrested' by the Church."

341

"When you wrote that book, they called you to the Vatican—to the Doctrine of the Faith."

"Have they called you to the Doctrine of the Faith?"

"Well, not yet—but they're hinting that they will." He was now genuinely harrowed. He had the manner of a man persecuted, in flight, no hiding place. "I've been summoned to the chancery this afternoon."

"What time?"

"Five."

Michael pointed to the wall clock. "You'll have to hurry."

"Please—come with me."

The crux of it.

Michael wanted to step around it, a soil on the floor. But tricky or not tricky, the man was tormented, and he didn't know how to refuse him without causing him further distress. Yet . . . "Father Warrum, I deeply sympathize with you—believe me, I do. But there's no way I can help. I am not a Galatian, I cannot even defend the Galatian point of view—I could only do you a disservice."

Warrum's trouble had overreached reason. "But you won't turn me down—I know you won't. You're a kind man, I saw that the instant we met—you're decent." His pleading stopped. Desperation made him shrewd. "Besides, you know the ropes—you used to be a radical yourself."

"I was never a radical."

"Your book—"

"—was not radical."

"It would have divided the Church just as they charge me of doing."

"Charge you? You said there weren't any charges."

"Oh, they're not actually charging me with it, but I know that's what they're going to say."

"If they do, I can see no way to defend you."

"I can't either." Then, with measured deliberation: "I *am* trying to divide the Church."

True as it might be, he hoped the man would not flaunt his heterodoxy. "Do you actually *want* to be excommunicated?"

"No!" It was a cry from the heart. "But what in God's name is so precious about Church unity? The faith needn't be a single faith—it can be many. It *must* be. Dear Christ, it's a diverse world—how can a monolithic Church be a comfort to everybody? Why shouldn't there

342

be a number of Catholic churches—High, Middle and Low, for example, as the Episcopalians have it? What's so sacred about being One?"

"If it's many, it'll be none."

Warrum didn't respond for a long time. Then:

". . . So?"

"If you say that, you *will* be excommunicated. You know that, don't you?"

Michael could see him trying to still an outburst: bitterness, heartache. "I say I don't want to be, but the truth is I am. In the Catholic Church, all priests are excommunicated. We're alone, we're the lonely—and we're kept that way. We're deliberately kept that way."

"Loneliness is not an imposed state, Father."

"It's not? What about the doctrine of No Particular Friendship?"

"It is not a doctrine."

"It functions that way—and it's treacherous! It starts with love, with compassion. 'If nobody loves you, the Church will love you'— that's Step Number One. Beautiful, isn't it?—like a beatitude. Then, Step Number Two: 'It doesn't *matter* if nobody loves you.' Step Number Three: 'It's *better* if nobody loves you.' Then the big jump, Step Number Four: 'Priests are forbidden to seek love outside the Church.' " He paused and summed it up. "The Doctrine of No Particular Friendship."

This clear-minded man, how could he be so muddled about this so-called doctrine? And how could he make such a mountain of the molehill of a minor house rule for seminaries and religious houses? It was meant to discourage separation from the religious community; even as an insensitive restraint against homosexuality it was hardly considered more than an unjust joke. "Is it so serious?" Michael said.

"Isn't it? Isn't it serious to everybody?"

"No—only to paranoiacs."

Warrum suddenly crumbled. His plea was abject. *"Am* I paranoiac, Father Farris? If I call you on the phone and beg you to be my friend, and you turn me down—am I paranoiac if I *say* you turned me down? If I come here and beg you to give me a hand, and instead you give me the finger, am I paranoiac to notice it? Am I?"

In a way he couldn't analyze, Michael was stirred. Cavanaugh could be right that the man was a trickster, but he could also be wrong; the priest's deep need was not dissimulated. Either way, how-

343

ever, there was nothing Michael could do for him. Nothing political, that is. But the man, deep down, was not really asking for political help. Or was he?

"If I were to go with you, I could not defend you in any way."

"I didn't ask you to do that. You needn't even enter the building, if you don't want to. Just come with me, and be there when I come out . . . so there's someone to talk to."

Abruptly Michael came upon the core of his suspicion. "You mean you have nobody else who would do that for you?"

"Not another priest, no."

"Surely you're not going to ascribe that to No Particular Friendship, are you—you're not going to blame the Church for it?"

He took a long time answering. Then, the disarming—the self-denuding—truth: "I'm not exactly a—safe person—to have as a friend."

Cavanaugh was wrong. The man was starkly honest. And in need.

"You'd better telephone and tell them we'll be late," Michael said.

He thought the man would weep. "Thank you," he muttered huskily. "Where's the phone?"

"It's a pay phone downstairs. Here, let me show you the way."

He led him down the steps. As they stood in the semidarkness near the telephone, the Galatian started rooting through his pockets. In a happy sort of way, he giggled, he was embarrassed.

"Do you need change?" Michael said. He knew the man did need it. All he had in his hand was a subway token, three pennies and two one-dollar bills. Poor soul, Michael thought, the Church has stopped his money and he's broke. He gave him some change for the phone and shoved a ten-dollar bill into his pocket.

The instant Warrum lifted the receiver Michael felt the dread. It was a night fright, like a bat in darkness. Perhaps it was intuition; perhaps he actually did hear the noise in the instrument.

"Put it back!"

Warrum turned. "What?"

"Put the receiver back—quick!"

"Put it—?"

Michael grabbed at the man to pull him away, but he didn't budge, stood there with that uncomprehending look on his face, the receiver still to his ear.

The detonation was not loud, hardly more than a toy pistol. Nor was the damage vast; it didn't even destroy the coin box. Only the receiver was shattered and the part of the man's head to which he had

344

held the instrument. He still remained standing, the half-headed man, a drench of crimson, then slipped to the floor, contorted a moment, and remained motionless.

The detective lieutenant's name was Carl Zeckley. He looked like a college boy, with a straw-colored mustache which, Michael surmised, was meant to make him look older, but failed in its purpose. And, trying to appear professionally distrustful, he worked hard to change a young smile into an old smirk; in this he seemed to be succeeding.

It was Michael's second interrogation. The first, immediately after the explosion, had taken place in Mindszenty House, and he alone had been questioned. This time, however, he was in the lieutenant's precinct office, it was early evening, and Cory was there. The artist too, as a fellow Galatian and friend of Warrum's, had had a preliminary questioning. Now, apparently, Zeckley wanted to see how they reacted to each other. He made a joke about it. "See if I can get you to cancel each other's lies." Then, quickly: "No offense, Father."

His smirk was even more sneering than it had been this afternoon. "You really think it was intuition that made you warn Father Warrum?"

"I did say that I may have heard a noise," Michael replied. "But I'm not sure of that—sometimes I'm surer of my hunches." He tried to smile but didn't do any better than the detective.

"You say you had no warning somebody would try to kill you?" Zeckley continued.

"I didn't say I had no warning."

"You didn't tell us about the letter." The detective turned to Cory. "Neither did you."

"The letter was sent to my brother, not to me."

"Protocol, huh?"

"Courtesy," Cory said.

To Michael: "How did you interpret Cristobal's letter?"

"The letter wasn't signed. Is it certain it came from her?"

He pointed to Cory. "He's certain."

"I didn't say I was," Cory said quickly.

"You didn't say it to me—you said it to your brother. I've already questioned him. Was he lying to me?" Having made a point, he darted quickly away from it. "How well do you know her, Mr. Cavanaugh?"

"Not very well."

345

If Cory hadn't told Michael the truth about his relationship with Cristobal, the lie might have sounded convincing, but apparently it didn't convince the detective. "Look, my friend, Sergeant Olin has questioned a number of the Galatians, and he's been told you've known her quite a few years."

"You didn't ask how long, you asked how well."

"All right—specific questions. Is she married?"

"She was, I think."

"Children?"

"Two. Or was it three? I'm not sure."

Cory was bungling; his lies were becoming more transparent.

"What does she do for a living? We got all kinds of stories from the Galatians. She's a doctor, she's a sculptor, she's a lecturer. What is she?"

"She's all of those things," Cory replied quietly.

Zeckley switched to Michael. "How well do *you* know her?"

"Not at all. I never met her."

"You were at the Galatians' meeting—she was there."

"But I didn't meet her."

"Not even in Italy?"

"No."

"One of the Galatians said she wrecked a workers' group in Sicily. Did you ever hear of that?"

"No."

"And in Rome—you live in Rome, don't you?"

"I have an apartment there, yes."

"Then . . . did you ever hear of the Liberation of the Night?"

He had indeed heard of *La Liberazione della Notte*. A number of years ago there had been a demonstration with that title. It had been a women's protest against the caveat which forbade them to walk alone in the streets of Rome at night. The unwritten restriction was enforced by brutality. A woman alone, strolling in darkness, coming home late from work, walking her dog, leaving the house of a friend, was presumed to be dissolute, looking for trouble, a prostitute. She was therefore fair game for insult, mugging, assault, gang rape. And nothing was done to protect her.

At last, the women organized a demonstration to clamor against it. Thousands of them—some said thirty thousand—assembled at the train station in Rome. They were going to march from the station to the Piazza del Popolo, and as the parade began, they all lighted

346

candles. Michael was there—it was a stirring sight—the brightly glittering procession irradiating the liberation of the night.

But it rained. The candles guttered in the wetness. Their flames failed. The downpour was not only going to dampen their ardor, it was going to extinguish the blaze of it. The demonstration would never reach the Piazza, the women would disperse. It would be a fiasco.

Then the wonderwork happened. Out of nowhere, out of everywhere, umbrellas appeared. The lights burned again, the procession resumed, the women started to sing. At the Piazza del Popolo, they assembled for one great ecstatic moment—Michael felt it as they felt it—for one single instant of triumph the Piazza flamed with a light and a hope of liberation in a darkness.

"The Liberation march was in all the papers," Zeckley prodded. "You never heard of it?"

"Yes, I did."

"She was one of the leaders."

"There were a number of leaders."

"But she hit the papers twice. The first time—the day of the march. Then—afterward—when she tried to smash up the whole group. You sure you don't remember her?"

With some asperity: "No, I don't."

Again, the sudden shift: "That weird-looking guy—Heskins—and Cassie Macramé—neither of you can tell me any more about them?" They were both silent. "Come on, Mr. Cavanaugh, they were Galatians—you saw them very often."

"They hardly ever said a word, either of them."

"But Cristobal said plenty, didn't she?"

"Yes."

"And nobody in the whole damn group knows who she is or what she is or where I can find her? You expect me to believe that?"

"*I* certainly don't know where to find her," Cory said.

The detective nodded affirmatively, but his whole manner was a cutting negative. "All right, fellas, it won't be so hard to find her. I don't imagine she'll stay shyly in the background—we'll catch up with her. Meanwhile," he added caustically, "thanks for all your help."

They left the precinct station together and five minutes later, in darkness, they stopped at a street corner.

"You lied a good deal, didn't you?" Michael said.

347

"Quite a bit," Cory replied.

"You do know where to find her."

"No, I didn't lie about that."

"Yes, you did. Where is she, Cory?—I have to talk to her."

"I told you—I don't know."

"Come on, Cory—"

"Are you out of your head? She tried to kill you!"

"What do I do, then?—hide?—run? Where is she?"

"If you think I'm going to have your death on my conscience—"

"*Where is she?*"

Sharply, Cory turned and walked away. Michael hurried after him, grabbed his arm.

"Cory—I'm going back to Zeckley. I'm going to tell him you admitted to me that you lied to him. I'm going to suggest that he arrest you—for obstructing—for being an accessory—anything he can hold you for! Now, tell me!"

"She has a studio in Soho," he said at last. "It's right off Houston. I don't know the exact address—it's called the Iron Gallery Building."

Michael did not go to Cristobal's immediately. He gave himself two cogent reasons for the delay, neither of which was the true one. First, he had to take time to concoct a plan; second, he was tired and hungry, and felt it would be unwise to challenge an adversary in his unfortified condition. While loitering in a restaurant, eating little and drinking too much wine, he had to face the real reason for his procrastination: he was frightened.

It was a harebrained notion, to go bargaining with killers. What a quixotic faith he would be placing in the conciliatory process. Not everything could be arbitrated. Surely he must know that . . . and not go.

Yet, if he did believe in the reconciling of differences, he must on occasion take a risk for it. But . . . his life?

Point was, however, if he didn't do something, sooner or later another telephone would explode, someone would step out of a dark alcove, a knife would flash. He might turn it all over to the police, and how thoroughly could they protect him, and for how long? A tenuous safety . . . Meanwhile, he had no armament; he could never, as a priest or by temperament, carry a gun.

The only weapon at his command was whatever strength he could

348

muster in arbitration. It was his only hope. So he had no real alternative. Without giving himself any merits for bravery or demerits for recklessness, he had to go and see her.

It took him until nearly nine o'clock to make the decision. He was glad it was late and nearly dark; there might be some surprise in it. And he needed to assault Falga Cristobal with every possible astonishment. Which wasn't much. His presence alone. Here I am, Dr. Cristobal, and—since you are stunned with nonexpectation—you will blurt everything, and we will come to terms. Not exactly a bombshell, but it was all the detonation he could manage.

Night in Soho, where she had her studio, would have been exhilarating to him on another occasion. The once gray and dingy industrial buildings, whose factors and merchants had long since departed, were colorful now, dizzyingly chromatic. The streets were busy with people and ventures; there was a dither. In the air, from numberless restaurants, exotic aromas of foreign foods melded with one another, not like vapors but like liquids marbelizing. The art galleries shrieked with discrepancy; somewhere, Africa beat through Beethoven; a woman sang arpeggios while a car horn stuck; there was a babel of trial and error, echo and prophecy. It excited him, if only this were the time for it.

Cristobal's studio was the upper two floors of a corner building. Like so many hundreds of its kind, it had been a loft, one of the iron edifices, sheathed in incised metal, patterned elaborately in the designs of an earlier century. Years ago, when Michael had walked in the neighborhood, this structure might have been encrusted with the commonplace grimes and soots that gave it its credible address in the commercial city, but now its magentas and scarlets and screaming yellows placed it in an unbelievable nowhere. Even its outside fire escape was a placeless thing; a cartoon of abstractions, diagonals and horizontals of frenetic color, it ascended upward into nonexistence.

The two lower floors of the building were art galleries. The big show on the street floor was a single mockup of a street collision, a Volkswagen impacted with an IBM panel truck. The lifesize, lifelike bodies of the dead and maimed were intertwined with metallic filaments and cables, and the detail of gore and ruination was so hideously real that Michael was not challenged to study it.

He hurried to the side entrance. Where the freight elevator used to be, the stairs had now been widened. He started upward, past the second gallery, closed for the night, and came to the third floor. The expansive steps had narrowed to what they used to be, cramped and

349

worn, old slate with smooth depressions made by millions of footfalls; and the hallway was lighted only enough for visibility.

The nameplate on her door was modest, cardboard, neatly lettered. She was not in hiding, it seemed to say. Falga Cristobal, Sculptor.

He put his thumb on the bell button. The ring seemed distant, in another place. He waited. About to ring again, he saw the door open slowly.

She was there.

How strange, was his thought, that she is wearing exactly what she wore before, the nonentity of color and the flame at her throat.

He felt a quiver at the sight of her.

"Come in, Mister Farris."

He heard the "Mister" as if it had been addressed to someone else. He pretended not to notice.

What he had hoped for—her surprise at his arrival—had not happened. On the contrary, it was as though she had been expecting him, wondering why he had not come sooner.

She turned, leaving him at the door, and he followed her into the studio. It was enormous. Clearly, it had been two floors at one time, but now most of the ceiling had been torn out, leaving only a gallery of small rooms halfway upward on the far wall; all the rest was space.

Space and sculptures. Stone, for the most part, huge hulking crags of rock, some hewn, some still rawly ripped from mountainsides, some in crumbles on the floor. There was wood too, laminates and timbers as fresh as forests; a few had been squared, plumbed, carved, set on plinths, totally finished . . . and ugly.

Everything was ugly. Not with the designed ugliness that artists dare when they take pride in exposing the single saving grace that hides within hideousness, but the accidental ugliness of inept craft.

He didn't know where to look or what to say. No matter what his errand, he couldn't be exposed to such immense masses of an artist's work without some responsibility to say ah. If the woman didn't require it, the things themselves demanded. But the only beautiful thing in the room was the sculptor herself.

She was the most alluring woman he had ever seen—the enigma in her eyes, the soft and lifting challenge of her breasts, the wanting of her mouth. And the sense of fervid passion, all withheld.

She watched him at a distance. Her face had a slight, a secret smile; there was a private mischief in it. Malice, pleasurable.

350

"Is there something here you yearn to own?" she said.

She knows exactly what I'm thinking, he realized, she's caught me hating her stuff, and she's enjoying my embarrassment.

"I'm unaccustomed to this . . . scale," he evaded.

Her eyes glinted with perverse pleasure. "As time goes on, you'll dislike it more."

Taunting, but where was the derision leading, he wondered.

"Here's a particularly ugly one," she said. She pointed to a stone piece, mounted high. "Prometheus, after the vultures were at him—godling sans liver. Not very attractive in concept, and hideous in execution—wouldn't you say?"

Before he could comment, she had slipped away, to another group. "There's Laocoön—you notice that I stay with the classics. If you're going to wreck, you may as well wreck the best of it."

She meant it, that her statues were ugly. She was actually getting pleasure out of disparaging them. He heard her laugh. It was low-pitched and mellow; it had a haunting background sound, like an instrument in the orchestra that doesn't carry the melody and is hardest to identify.

"Here's Hercules after one of his worst labors," she said. "Look how out of proportion his lower half is—I call him Hercules Herniatus."

Michael laughed with her; couldn't help himself. As he did, he realized how absolutely opposite this meeting was to anything he had expected. He had been foolish, he told himself, to expect she would attack him in her own studio where she could be so easily incriminated. No danger here.

Then something happened. Trivial. Upstairs, on the gallery level, a door that had been slightly ajar was being slowly closed. Then, an instant later, under the door there was a sliver of light. He had seen nobody, not even a shadow, yet he had a prescient dread that Cassie Macramé might be there, or Heskins, or both.

He pretended to have seen nothing. He hoped she hadn't noticed his eyes. Perhaps not; she was pointing to another statue.

"Here's my favorite," she said. "Niobe. Damn fool woman, wasn't she? So proud of having spawned so many children. Well, she paid for it, didn't she? Lost all of them. Every single one, murdered. And now look at her—no brain, no muscle, only tears." She had lapsed for only an instant into seriousness. Now, she returned quickly to self-mockery. "And one arm longer than the other."

351

But the return to laughter wasn't easy. "Do you really believe your work is bad?" he asked.

She was closer to him now, close enough for her scent to reach him. It wasn't perfume. It was something natural, like cinnamon or sage, or some combination of spices, exotic, oriental. She seemed to be debating whether to answer his question.

"Do I think it's bad? Yes, I think it's ugly."

"Then why are you a sculptor?"

She evaded the question. "I used to be a doctor."

He repeated: "But now—why are you a sculptor?"

"Because my husband was a sculptor."

"Did it necessarily follow?"

"No. His death did."

"What does that mean?"

"I loved him very much—and then he did an intolerable thing to me—he died. I couldn't do anything—I turned into a cipher. So one day I went into his studio—I hadn't been there since his death. I pulled up one of the blinds and the light fell on a huge stone he had been working on. I lifted a hatchet and started to hack at it. I screamed with rage and hacked and hacked." She tried to recapture her smile; almost managed it. "I've been hacking ever since."

A moment. "But surely it doesn't give you the same . . ."—about to say "revenge," he altered it—". . . satisfaction?"

"Oh, no."

"Do you sell any of it?"

Her smile was easier now; the mischief was back. "Yes, I do."

"To whom?"

"To people who don't know their own taste because they have no passion—the bourgeoisie."

"Then you get your satisfaction out of hacking at the . . ."

"Bourgeoisie, yes."

Go slowly now, he cautioned himself. Pointing to an unfinished statue: "Hacking at this is somewhat more acceptable than hacking at them."

"The murder of art—for money—is quite all right, isn't it?"

"You know very well what I'm talking about."

But she was not ready to be serious; in no hurry to discuss mayhem and murder. She would deal with those sobrieties in her own good time, she seemed to say, if at all. Mercurially, she was back to her sardonic humor again. "You mean the teenagers, don't you?—the

352

vandalism. It's really getting dreadful, isn't it? A few nights ago some boys—four or five of them—wrecked the gallery downstairs. Did you notice they have only that one ghastly object on the floor—*The Collision?* Well, those little monsters—they ruined every painting in the place. Then they broke the safety chain on the fire escape, they came up the stairs and they smashed that window. Look."

She pointed. The window had indeed been broken. A sheet of Masonite was boarded over it.

"And just in time the police came," she concluded. "You see?—it's everywhere."

"I don't mean vandalism," he said quietly. "I mean murder."

"You're late, Mr. Farris." She was totally poised. "The police have been over that ground. They left a half hour ago."

"They found you very fast."

"I found them. One of the Galatians told me they were looking for me. I had nothing to conceal, so I called them."

"Would you mind telling me what you told them?"

"Not at all. They asked to see my passport, which is entirely in order—I'm not on any wanted list anywhere. One of them commented on how much I travel, and the other asked me how I had spent the day. I referred them to three clients. One, who looked around for nearly two hours and bought nothing. The second, the wife of a respectable airline executive—I sold her a small bas-relief. The third is a well-known pianist whose hands I did in casting plaster. They took up my entire day."

There could be no further evasion:

"Why are you trying to kill me?"

She made no pretense of shock. Almost gently: "I'm not trying to kill you, Mister Farris. I'm not a murderer."

"A telephone exploded. It was meant to kill me. It killed Father Warrum."

"Do you say that I did it?"

"Do you say you know nothing about it?"

"In all my life, I've never touched an explosive. I've never set a bomb, I've never carried a weapon, I've never pulled a trigger on a gun."

"You can be a terrorist without doing any of those things with your own hands."

"Who says I'm a terrorist?"

"Cory."

"Anything that Cory and I say about each other is suspect. Since we had a very intimate relationship that now no longer exists, neither of us is to be trusted. Lovers become liars."

"He says you tried to make a terrorist of him."

"He's an inert radical. I tried to make him an active revolutionary."

"Active revolutionary—isn't that a terrorist?"

She was altogether composed. Imperturbably treating him like a child, she mildly rebuked him. "Considering that you are a diplomat by profession, you've started very tactlessly. You're to be forgiven, I expect, because you're frightened. But surely you're experienced enough to know I can't admit to being a terrorist, even if I am one. You can't really believe that I would indict myself for all those violences you're so eager to indict me for?"

"Whom do we indict?"

"Those . . . others."

"Members of your group."

"Those unidentifiable others."

"All right, those others. Why do they want to kill me? I'm not a reactionary, I'm a liberal."

"Does that make you a friend?" She was slyly laughing at him and he could feel his face redden. "There's an adage, Mister Farris, that radicals and reactionaries need each other—they keep the cauldrons of wrath boiling. But liberals—"

"—put the fire out."

"Exactly. So you're not particularly popular with either side."

"But you and I—we have many beliefs in common. The letter you wrote to Cardinal Cavanaugh—"

"The letter *they* wrote."

"—has many points with which I agree. There's hardly anything in the letter that can't be discussed reasonably. Birth control—a more equitable distribution of the Church's goods—the ordination of women—"

"Stop. This is pure parley drivel—you know that. Nothing will be achieved around a table."

"But it's being achieved. There was Pope John's Council—there will be others. You yourself—in Rome that night—women carrying candles in the rain—"

"It was nonsense—nothing came of it. Women still can't walk the streets of Rome at night. I do these little demonstrations from time to time to prove that nothing comes of such peaceable charades. There is only one thing that can work."

354

"Terror."

She corrected him. "Revolution."

"But it isn't working. You're antagonizing the very people who—"

"You're talking to the wrong people. There are millions, my friend, millions who find justification for us—*secretly*. People who do nothing about the evils of society, and feel guilty for doing nothing— they're on our side. They're happy that we do their work for them, they want us to win, they want us to assure them that they *needn't* do anything, the job will be done—we'll do it. Then there are the millions who loathe society, who have been brutalized by it—they want revenge, they want blood, and we'll spill it for them. And finally, the biggest group of all, the dreary ones, the apathetic, the millions who are dying of tedium and listlessness—the bored multitude who are crying for a fantasy—we give it to them—the new romance!"

"And you have contempt for all of them, haven't you?"

"No, but I resent doing their work for them."

"Maybe they don't really want you to do it for them. Maybe they won't thank you for it—maybe they'll hate you."

"I can stand even that."

"Can you? Suppose your revolution succeeds—and they hate you— what sort of world will you have?"

She shrugged ironically. "I'm reminded of the revolutionary who conducted Louis XVI to the guillotine. On the way, the king asked him if he would take charge of his last will and testament. And the rebel said, 'I am here only to escort you to the scaffold.' . . . That pitiless man, incidentally, was a priest."

"A lapsed priest," he amended. "Even if you succeed in decapitating society, and even if it grows a new head—can you imagine how horrible the head will be?"

"Why, necessarily?"

"If you win by terrorism, you'll have to govern by terrorism."

She didn't resist the terrorist word this time. Her reply brought his mind to a standstill.

"Why govern at all?" she asked.

Axioms he had taken for granted had to be discarded. She had no new government in mind; only a negation of all. He had to find a postulate, any postulate, they could agree upon.

"Even anarchy demands some order, doesn't it?" he asked.

"Whose?"

"You know my answer: God-and-man's."

Her bland smile didn't hide the bitterness. "You think there's order there?"

"Leave God out, then. Humanity alone."

"None there, either."

No question: her virulence was not against the Church alone, but against all government. He had thought, briefly, that she was an anarchist, but she had gone beyond that. Anarchism was based on faith in man's integrity against the corruption of government, man's gentleness against its brutality, his intellect against its stupidity, his good against its evil. But her belief was only in the corruption, brutality, stupidity and evil of government *and* man. She was all terrorist; not terror to achieve a goal, an ideal, a new order of things, but terror for its own sake. Anomist, Cory had called her, in love with chaos.

He was blocked. He could never convince her on a matter of principle; he had to attack her strategy.

"You won't win, Dr. Cristobal," he said. "Because you underestimate society. It's not as shaky as you think."

"Isn't it? Just watch," she said with cool certainty. "Any minute now, even a minor shock will topple it. And we know exactly how to make it happen. You asked me why you, a liberal, are being attacked. Let me tell you. We do not attack reactionaries and conservatives because, even if they are a real menace, killing them detonates nothing. When one of them is assassinated, nothing trembles, nothing weakens. The bourgeoisie and the poor—especially the poor—simply shake their heads a little and say tut, tut. But, in secret, they *approve.* Good, they say, another bastard killed. And they go about their business as before—even a little better pleased with the way things are. And nothing has changed.

"But . . . suppose a bourgeois gets killed—say, a moderate, a liberal like yourself. What happens? The whole middle class gets panic-stricken. They stampede, they scream outrage. 'What are they doing to us?' they cry. 'We're liberals—we've granted them everything—and look how we are repaid! We've given too much welfare to the poor, too much free education to the ignorant, too much freedom to the minorities. Let's take some of it back.' Thus, the reversal, the backlash. The liberals start to take back what they have given, they enact creepingly insidious new laws, they place a spy at every keyhole, they cheapen the schools, they shortchange the old and the sick, they cancel the milk funds. But the poor, the disadvantaged, the angry, the bitter have had a small taste of their necessities, and they've learned a trick or two. They're not going to give up what they've fought and begged for. So everybody starts to call names, to threaten, to mug, to vandalize, to break heads. The poor and the middle class bleed one another, they weaken—and they look for allies. They turn to us. Meanwhile, we have been busy. We have been pulling a stone out here and there, we have been shaking the foundations a little. The mortar cracks in a number of places. Somebody breaks a window, burns a sacred idol, plants a bomb, jackhammers a cornerstone . . . and the edifice crumbles."

It was all so frighteningly facile. The whole system of correlated phenomena was, for a woman so complex, so simply explicated. But it was the very simplistics that made it terrifying. The goal was luminously seen; the technique was easily mastered; complexity didn't dull the edge of action. It was the Italian proverb: a stiletto, because it has a single purpose, stays sharp.

"And now," she resumed, "let us get back to your first question. Why do they want to kill you?" She spoke detachedly, without any sign of hostility. "I might say that they're trying to kill you because of what you *know*. One night you gave shelter to a priest who had been beaten. What did the priest tell you? That might be a reason to burn your breviary and warn you not to meddle. Or you might be nearly strangled—again, put on notice not to interfere. Yes, I *could* say you might be murdered because of what you know."

Or what you think I know, he told himself . . . or may discover. About Galestro.

But she had not yet made her point. "But the real reason you might be killed is not what you know, but who you are. You're a dangerous man, Mister Farris—you're a facilitator. Enemies in the Church who would annihilate each other—you reconcile them, you give them the illusion that they are friends. The Vatican would have fallen apart centuries ago if it did not breed creatures like you. It would have suffocated in its lies—but you keep it breathing. You justify its pomp and its vulgarity, you excuse its greed, you hide its cruelty. What we do is pure innocence compared to the quiet terrors you defend in the Church. You do it, Mister Farris—you make the malice work—you're a facilitating murderer."

"Does it make you feel you're not a murderer if you call me one?"

"Don't confess me, Mister Farris!"

"You'd be wise to confess yourself. You're killing yourself with guilt!"

357

She laughed. "Guilt? Oh, you poor cleric!"

"The only thing that's keeping you alive is rage!"

Exultantly: "Yes—that *is* something I'll confess to—yes!"

Indicating the statuary, his arm swept the room. "And all this ugliness—you think your rage will keep your husband alive as well!"

He had no idea it would have such a convulsing effect on her. "My husband has nothing to do with this!"

He had struck home; he struck again. "You're not keeping him alive! Every time you lift that hatchet, you kill him again!"

Possibly without being aware of it, she had put her hand on the hatchet.

He pointed to it. "Go on! Why *have* me killed?—*you* do it!"

Without haste, she slid her hand away from the object.

Both remained still. When she spoke, her manner was exceptionally calm. "Do you think I could have killed you, Mister Farris?"

Her stare didn't allow an evasion. "In a moment of . . ."

"Insanity."

". . . Yes."

"I thought you might say that." She gazed at him speculatively. "Do you think I am demented?"

"That hadn't occurred to me, but since you mention it . . ."

"I'm not in any way demented, Mister Farris. One of the ways to vitiate the force of a revolutionary is to call him a lunatic. We daren't let that happen. I am not insane. Whatever craving I have for revenge is not to be put down to derangement. It's not to be denigrated—it has a very justifiable history. And before you leave here with any smug suspicion that you are all calm reason and I am raving insanity, I feel you should hear it."

"Go on."

"I was a doctor—I told you that."

"Yes."

"And a Brazilian."

He nodded.

"My father's practice was very prosperous—he was a well-known surgeon. I was a bright girl, I was sent to good schools—and I became an accomplished physician. While I was still very young, I married a fine man and we had two beautiful children. My life was very good. And what was not least important, I was performing a decent service. I was a gynecologist—my practice was in a respectable town—Belo Monte. One weekend, my husband and I took a trip. We went to a back country. I had never seen anything so primitive, such poverty,

358

nor such cruelty, especially to women. In the course of three days, I performed nine operations. One was on a young girl who was unmarried and pregnant and driven out of her home. She had tampered with herself—she was bleeding badly. I could do nothing for her, and she died. She was the age of my older daughter, eleven years old.

"When we returned to Belo Monte, I started a free clinic. I taught birth control measures, I wrote simple papers on the subject and disseminated them, I offered free abortions. Two months after the clinic opened, I was arrested. There were nineteen witnesses against me. All of them were well-known citizens, one of them was my cousin, two of them were priests. I spent five months in jail and, in my absence, my clinic was set afire and burned to the ground.

"We moved to a small village, sixty miles from Belo Monte. We bought a large house with a number of outbuildings. One of them I converted into an infirmary—very modest, as quiet as it could be. I had no shingle, no placard, not even a nameplate. And very reticently I began to do my work again, offering to help any woman who came to me in trouble. Before long, there were many of them. They came from far distances, they came sick, beaten by their husbands, abused by themselves, often in wallows of blood.

"Then the threatening letters began. The windows started to break. Vandals destroyed my equipment. A number of times I would be in the middle of an examination, and assailants would storm in upon a naked patient. Once—in broad daylight—I was on my way to the courthouse to act as a witness for a girl who had been raped—I was attacked and beaten. People stood at their windows and watched.

"The following month, I was in my infirmary, operating on a mortally ill woman. The police broke down the door. They smashed everything in the infirmary, they collapsed the operating table, and forced the woman to run bleeding into the street. And they arrested me. I spent two years in jail.

"Once, during that time, I was questioned about my allies. They knew very well I had no allies, except for a woman named Zoraia, a middle-aged nurse who acted as my assistant. But it was an excuse to starve me and give me the 'animal.' The 'animal' was an iron rod with strips of bullhide attached to it; they beat me with both ends of it.

"Six weeks before I was freed, in the middle of the night, three men arrived with Zoraia. She was weeping. All of the men I recognized; two were local businessmen; the third was a neighbor. They carried flashlights and they were armed with knives and ropes. They

359

tore off my clothes and bound me. Then they stretched me on the floor, and forced me to supervise an operation upon myself. It was a hysterectomy. Step by step, they made me tell them what to do and how to cut. Zoraia was helping them; she never stopped screaming. No anesthetic was given, no sedative of any kind to ease the pain either before, during or after the operation. When it was over, they left me on the floor, still bleeding, and went away.

"Six weeks later, I was allowed to go free. You cannot imagine how I looked forward to being greeted by my husband and daughters. But as I waited in the anteroom of the prison, I was told the news— they would not arrive. Two days previously, a bomb had been placed in our home, and all three had been killed.

"Of the people who did those things, all of them were respectable, some were police, some were in the government, some were neighbors, one was a close friend, one was a relative, two were priests, and all were Catholics."

She had told the story with remarkable self-possession, as if she had been relating events that had happened to a stranger. But the instant she concluded, her bitterness returned.

"You're quite right," she said glacially. "The only thing that keeps me alive is rage."

But it wasn't rage alone; there was the tragedy behind it, and the heartbreak. He wasn't aware that he was making a movement of sympathy toward her, but subconsciously he must have been, and she must have seen it.

"Don't touch me," she said. "I want no comfort from the Church —don't touch me!"

She didn't wait for him to go; simply turned away, walked through the confusion of statuary, and ascended the iron stairway to the gallery. In a moment, she was gone.

When the door upstairs had closed behind her, Michael stayed only an instant longer, then quickly departed. As he walked down the stairs, he thought how ugly and elegant she was, how horrifying and magnificent, how pathetic and radiant. Most of all, how suicidal. She would say it differently, of course, that she would happily risk her life for a cause, that she would sacrifice herself for a revolutionary's death, a hero's glory. But it was death itself she wanted, over everything; having no faith in humankind, there was nothing to live for, and all fury to die for. Someone so bent on death was an even more treacherous danger than he had imagined.

Facilitating murderer, she had said.

Facilitator. Yes, it was his major function, expediting, making things work, compromising differences. To Cristobal, to Cory, to Warrum, to nameless insurrectionaries behind them, he was the spoiler of noble conflict, the muddler of epic revolution, hence somebody despicable. Farris the compromiser, the man in the middle, always safe, believing in nothing, never sticking his neck out. The neutral coward . . . so they said.

Except: he called himself something else. A peacemaker. And if there were a thousand venial sins of man against God, there was one mortal sin of man against man, and it was violence.

He loathed it. It didn't, to him, represent a hero's crusade for a new society so much as a coward's revenge against the old one. And it didn't follow that the annihilation of an enemy brought about the creation of a friend. To the contrary, violence typically proliferated itself, murder begot murder. And in a faith that holds that all iniquities are somehow forgivable, he was inclined to believe that no man could ever wash his hands of bloodshed. So, if he believed in peace, even in the very process of making peace, why need he constantly be on the defensive about it, apologizing for drawing agreements instead of drawing blood?

As if peacemaking were as safe as home and slippers. It wasn't. Here, on this mission, he knew the threatening letters would continue, there would be other beatings in dark places, priests would die. But no matter. He wouldn't leave. He would stay until the task was done. Whatever dangers, even unto death.

She, however, was safe. How patly she spoke of "them" as being guilty, and of her passport in good order. Was there no way to expose her before another murder could be done? Expose what?

He thought of her studio . . . the room on the balcony . . . the door slowly closing.

He thought, too, of Warrum and Galestro.

Murderer, she had called him. If she had really made herself believe he was one, she had certainly found the perfect justification for killing him. He wondered why she had not tried it sooner, and, again, whether there would be a delay before the next attempt. The delay might be more terrifying than the act. Was that what she was after?

If only he could accomplish something.

His mission was a failure, he was the unarmed prey of killers, and

361

he felt that he hadn't—certainly not in America—one single ally.

As he unlocked the door of Mindszenty House and turned on the light, he saw the letter lying on the floor. The envelope—Waldorf-Astoria stationery—was addressed in shaky penmanship. At the bottom, the words *Deliver by Hand—Urgent.* He tore it open.

Dear Father Farris,

Pope John once said to me that we must save the Church not for ourselves but for our children. He was able to imagine that he had actually had children of his very own, such was his genius for fatherhood. The rest of us, especially those of us who have never had parishes, celibates all, find it more difficult to think of our sons and daughters.

You have made it possible for me, belatedly, to stop looking to our past and ask questions again, about our posterity.

One of the questions is: If the Church builds a new home for the young people, if it builds a skyscraper of the future, will it not cease to be recognized as a Church at all? On the other hand, if it continues to abide in a tabernacle of heretofore, will it not slowly go to dust with the disintegrating stones? I am afraid that the answer is, that if it continues to dwell where it dwells, complacent and unwilling to change, in the rich realm of its real estate, it will become heartless and hearthless, and no homing place for the young.

I have yearned, in my old age, to cast my lot with those who say that religion is a once-and-for-all canon, that it need never be changed, and must never be questioned. It would be comforting to think that is true. But alas, there is no once-and-for-all anything. If we are to conserve our cherished past, we must be willing to sacrifice nearly all of it. To live forever, we must be willing to die every day. This is easy for the young—to them death is a fantasy; harder for me—death is real. Still, in this respect, I must at least pretend to be young, mustn't I?

So, perhaps I am equal to one more crusade. I have no real choice, have I? As long as I live, I must be equal to one more and one more, until I die. Not being equal to it—that is the worst death of all. So count on me. And call on me tomorrow.

One other word, my dear Father Farris. You have done me a most charitable, a most tender service. Thanks to you, I have become myself again. I had forgotten that when a man makes a cross with one hand and a fist with the other, his hands do not shake.

In Christ's love,
Natan Halevi

Michael carefully folded the letter. It was his first token of hope, and he could have wept over it. He knelt in the gathering darkness, said a prayer for the Jewish Cardinal, and gave thanks to God.

At the most unbelievable hour—it was eleven o'clock, and dark—the telephone repairman came. The unbelievable part of it was not that he had come at night—there had been, after all, a fatality through a piece of telephone equipment—but that he finished the repair in fifteen minutes, and treated it as another instance of routine vandalism. Like the petty destruction of the cord and the receiver, the murder was insignificant.

It was insignificant to everybody. No newspaper reporters had arrived, no photographers; Warrum's body had been quickly removed and even the bloodstains had been wiped away. There had been no damage to wall, floor, ceiling, and now that the phone had been repaired, there was not a single sign that a murder had been perpetrated. If the police did not quickly apprehend the murderer, the case would probably drift into oblivion.

He himself would like to relegate it to forgetfulness, but he couldn't; he was asking when it would happen, the next attempt on his life.

Ten minutes after the departure of the repairman he had his first alarm. The phone bell rang.

He knew it couldn't have been tampered with again; there hadn't been time, and he had been here every minute. But he was unnerved and delayed answering it. He listened to it as it rang, ran down the steps and stood beside it, continued to listen, and still didn't lift the receiver off the hook.

At last he did.

"Hello."

There was no answer.

"Hello, hello."

There was no explosion, but there also was no response.

"Hello."

He hung up.

An hour later, he heard the phone again. This time he ran downstairs and answered it as quickly as he could.

"Hello." . . . No answer.

He broke into a sweat.

It was exactly as he had dreaded it: terror-by-delay.

They were not accidental, these incomplete telephone calls. This was some new way to harry him, some ingenious device to do him an undetectable injury, electronic perhaps, to his ears, to his brain, some damage unimaginable.

If the purpose was simply to put him in a panic, so be it, he was panicked. How curious that the mechanical device had succeeded where the human bludgeonings he had seen, the crucifixion, the death of Warrum, his own strangulation, had failed. He had been physically hurt, he had been horrified, but nothing had so deeply terrified him as the continued ringing of the telephone. An electrical impulse from the instrument had short-circuited his nerves.

He sought familiar remedies. Food: something easy, milk and crackers. Then prayer: he read his breviary. He went to bed.

About an hour after he turned out his light, the phone rang again. For the third time, it was nobody. That is, he corrected himself, it was the nobody that signified somebody, and he heard himself shouting into the phone, "Hello—I know you're there!"

He didn't realize, hours later, that he had actually been asleep; he couldn't have imagined he'd have been able to do so . . . when the phone rang again.

"Hello."

"Pronto."

Oh, thank heaven, he thought, hearing the Italian operator's voice. Then the stilted English of the woman, and his answer that he was indeed the Mister Father Farris.

"Michael, is that you?"

Feradoti's voice. How welcome it sounded, what a sweet echo of home.

"Are you all right?" the older man asked.

"Fine—fine. Are you?"

364

"Yes. I'm sorry to awaken you in the middle of the night. But I've been trying to reach you for many hours. I could hear your voice, but you apparently couldn't hear mine."

No silent enemies, no electronic treacheries; it had been his good friend on a bad connection. He was about to tell him how bad the connection would have been this afternoon—the explosion and Warrum's death—but he restrained himself. It would frighten the old man; he might even order Michael home, and out of danger . . . as if Rome were any safer.

"I'm so glad to hear you, Your Eminence—so happy."

"Perhaps you won't be when you've heard what I have to tell you."

He knew what it was: His Holiness was dead.

Even before he had a chance to say it, Feradoti spoke quickly. "It's not what you're thinking. The Papa is no better, but none the worse. He teeters this way, that way—he is on the edge all the time. The vigils are around the clock—and the Square is crowded at all hours."

He was making talk, delaying disclosure of whatever it was he had called about. "What's wrong?" Michael asked.

"I have to ask you to return."

His heart sank. "Cardinal Cavanaugh has been in touch with you?"

"No."

"He hasn't asked you to recall me?"

"No, he hasn't."

"Then I don't understand. Why?"

He could hear the Secretary trying to be kind. "Michael, I'm not blaming you, understand. It was a difficult task you set yourself. Perhaps an impossible one. I shouldn't have let you go—I take it as my own fault. But if you haven't succeeded with him by this time, you may as well give up. Anyway, if you go any further—it's beneath your dignity . . . and mine. Come home."

"I'm sorry, Your Eminence, but I'm not coming home—not yet."

"Michael . . ."

"I'm not going to wait for Cavanaugh. I'm going past him."

"Past him?" A note of apprehension. "How?"

Michael told of his meeting with Cardinal Halevi. He tried not to show he was proud of his accomplishment, relating only the facts, the man's illness, his qualms, his divided fidelities, his torn conscience, and, at last, his touching letter. When he was finished telling all of it, Feradoti didn't respond for so long that Michael thought the connec-

365

tion had broken. Then the dispiriting possibility occurred to him: Feradoti was angry.

He couldn't bear the silence. "*Pronto,*" Michael said.

"*Ben fatto. Mi fai troppo onore.*"

It was the highest encomium the Secretary had ever given him; not only that Michael had done well, but had done him honor.

Here I am, the priest thought, a man in my mid-thirties, and as overjoyed as if I had just won a graduation prize. And he was going to be worthy of the Secretary's pride in him, he determined, he was going to make Halevi's Council an overwhelming success.

He was impatient for dawn to come so he could get to work. At nearly three o'clock in the morning, he dressed fully and decided to go to Times Square and buy the morning paper. There would probably be a fuller account in it of Cavanaugh's Synod announcement than the early evening paper had had. Possibly it would say who had already accepted his invitation and what the cardinals' comments had been. He wanted to prime himself with all the data he could get, then devise a plan for stealing Cavanaugh's thunder. It wouldn't be too hard to do. Halevi's assemblage would be more informal—a Council for Reconciliation rather than a Synod—and could be gathered more quickly. The cardinals would come into New York not all at once, as the Synod people would probably do, but separately so that each dignitary would get his own press break. By the time Cavanaugh's Synod convened it would be stale news. And perhaps even sparse news, because it would be, he hoped, a sparsely attended meeting.

There were many things he'd have to do, he thought eagerly, and he'd need lots of help. Tomorrow he would call Cardinal Salinas in Mexico City, and if he wanted to woo Cardinal Fellinger out of his privacy, he might have to fly to Chicago. He would do it; he would do anything.

One hand makes the cross; the other, the fist. He knew it was a suspicious paradox but he was too thrilled by Halevi's indomitability to be stopped by any questionable part of it. If it was an anomaly, it was a glorious one; the old man had given him a role to play; he was a soldier of peace.

He had found an identity and he felt lifted on a cresting wave. Soldier of peace.

Peace. How differently he could think about peacemaking now that he was, oddly, a warrior in its behalf. No longer defensive; not an apology anywhere.

Peace. It was not pie in the sky to him, it was bread on earth, a

366

necessity for sustenance. It was not only his heart's hope, but his mind's certainty: it would happen. The old concept of class struggle was obsolete. Especially in America, where the proletariat was rapidly becoming the bourgeoisie, and where ethnic equality, however embattled, was becoming a reality, the divisions between the classes were breaking down. Some day the last of the ghetto pales, everywhere, would be burned to ashes. It would be a purification by fires lighted less and less angrily as time went by, and it would celebrate, beyond the equality of classes, the parity of persons.

Peace, it was his Holy Grail, his vision of beauty; it was the truth that would help disentangle the human knot; it was the reciprocal gift to Jesus for the grace of gentleness He had given him. How beautiful upon the mountains are the feet of him that bringeth good tidings and telleth: peace.

Not feet but wings, Michael thought, and on them he soared through the night streets of the city. Still uplifted, he arrived at Times Square.

Even before he bought the newspaper, he saw the calamity. It was on the front page.

CARDINAL DIES
At six o'clock in the evening, Natan Cardinal Halevi, the Canadian prelate, collapsed in his hotel room. An hour later, he died of a massive coronary occlusion. It was only this afternoon that the Cardinal was honored at a . . .

Not Parkinson's disease, not hemorrhoids . . . heart failure. Just when the old man's heart had so courageously succeeded, it failed him.

And me, and all of us.

Why hadn't the beloved prelate been spared for just one month more? One month's grace, not only for the Cardinal himself but for the young people he embraced, for the sorely embattled Church, for men who longed to make peace; only one month more.

He stood there, in the middle of Times Square, in the lights still garish at three o'clock in the morning, and thought of the three cardinals: Halevi dead, Cavanaugh cruelly intransigent and without a single vulnerability he could attack, and Feradoti, of whose pride in him he was unworthy. He thought of how bootless his task had been and how he had botched it, and how he still was not liberated of the horror of it; he must see it through until its almost inevitable failure. He thought of loss and loss and loss again.

367

He thought of Nora and saw that of all his relationships, this one, which might in another world have been loving and tender, was the most tortured of all.

And as he paused there, having no special place to go, he couldn't see anything in his life that had a spark of hope in it, or reason, or comfort. He felt utterly friendless and, in a way he knew to be sinful, betrayed by God.

Sixteen

I T WASN'T RAIN, it wasn't fog, but a vaporous mist that drifted off the bay, crossed the marshland and settled on the cemetery. It achromatized everything; all the colors, even the black of the mourners, went to gray. As if ashes to ashes meant the totality; everything had to go to ashes.

They had lowered the casket, they had thrown the handful of dirt, they had said the *El Maleh Rachamim,* asking God to give peace and life everlasting to her father's soul, and promising that his daughter's memory would keep him eternally alive. Unto the end which is no end, life unending. But somebody said, "So that's that," giving the lie to the continuum, and the funeral was over. End.

She walked slowly toward the cars, holding her mother's right arm; her uncle Walter took the left. The weeping was decorous, except for the sobs of an old, old woman whom nobody seemed to recognize.

Then, quietly, as if their motors had been muted, the cars started to vanish in the mist.

369

"Change your mind, honey," her mother said.

"No—really."

Walter said, "Come on, kid—do you good. A few weeks in the sun—you'll be somebody else."

Somebody else was what he had always wanted her to be; he'd always been searching for some way to be fond of her, and hadn't found it. "Thank you, Uncle Walt—I want to stay and get to work."

Kissing her mother, she was on the verge of wishing her a good time, but one didn't dance at funerals.

Uncle Walter opened the door of the rented car. Her mother got in and as he entered from the other side and started the engine, Lily began to cry.

"Mama," she said, but didn't touch her.

Then they were gone.

Everybody was gone, all the cars except for her mother's, which Nora had had the presence of mind to drive here, alone. And the as-yet unfilled grave. When would they fill it, she wondered, and why weren't they already doing it? Yet, what would be the hurry?

She wished she knew how to grieve. There were probably pre-scribed ways of doing it—*shivah*, was that it?—comfortable rules to follow when there was a ritual in it, when you did it with someone, with God as a last resort. There was probably even some illumination in that mode of grief. Was there no light, then, if it didn't glow from the Yahrzeit candle? . . . Gray.

She turned to go.

He was standing by the gate, near one of the two stone pillars. In the haze, his suit of priestly black was a grizzled shade; he's come, she thought, in the color of the day. He stood there recessively, as if meaning for her to know he was there, yet unwilling to force her attention. You needn't notice, he seemed to say.

Slowly she walked to him.

They stood there, saying nothing, as though waiting for the mist to clear, or hoping for the occasion to make its own discourse.

She glanced behind him, and toward the road. There was no sign of another car.

"How did you come here?" she asked.

"By train, by bus, by taxi."

"How did you know *where* to come?"

"I decided to call every Jewish cemetery on Long Island. On the fourth call . . ."

"You were very kind. To come . . . and wait."

370

"It's part of the priestly habit. Making the parish calls—the sick, the bereaved."

"You're spoiling it."

He pointed toward the driveway that ran through the cemetery. "Is that your car?"

"My mother's, yes. Would you like a lift?"

"Yes, if it's convenient. To the bus or train."

"I can take you into town, if you want me to."

"If you haven't anything better to do."

No, nothing better; nothing at all, in fact; with anybody. She felt a flush of pleasure and relief that it was somebody she wanted to be with, the only one she could currently imagine.

They drove in silence for a while, then started at the margins of conversation. She hadn't seen him at the funeral, where was he, he didn't know which was her mother until he saw Nora take her arm, how many were relatives, how many were friends, there were similarities between Catholic and Jewish burials, but there were also differences, not much difference from earth to earth.

They arrived outside Mindszenty House. She stopped the car and he didn't get out.

"You can't park here," he said, "you'll get a ticket."

"I wasn't going to park."

"Wouldn't you like to come up?"

She had a hectic moment. "I don't think so."

"I would like it, very much."

The street was narrow. A taxi honked behind them. "You'd better get out," she said, gently.

"He'll go around you." His manner suggested that anything he said she was at liberty to revise. "We never really spoke to each other. I have no vast experience in the matter, but we left things . . . incomplete."

"Incompleteness is the nature of the beast."

"Is it?" Before she could find an answer: "Please come up," he said. "I need to talk."

She was unsettled. She yearned to go with him, yet she must keep her distance. Flippancy might help. "Will you try to convert me?"

"Convert means to change something *from* something. Are you something?"

It was totally a question of religion; she was sure he wasn't derogating her total existence, and almost sure he wasn't making fun of her atheism. "No," she said. "I'm not."

371

"You don't believe in anything?"

"I don't steal money out of tin cups, I don't spit on sidewalks, I don't beat dogs—"

"—or children."

She flushed, wondering if the child-beating story would keep ricocheting. "No."

"How about God?"

"I don't beat Him either."

"Except by disavowal."

"That's right," she said. "I don't believe in Him."

"Would you like to?"

The question was as simple, as naïve as if he were an amateur at this business. She laughed. " 'Tis a consummation to be wished.' "

"You left a word out."

The omission hadn't been accidental. "If I had said 'devoutly to be wished,' it would have been a contradiction, wouldn't it?"

"Come up. I won't try to convert you," he said. "Not ever." She hesitated and he continued. "Please come up. Not for you, for me."

He opened the door, got out and went up the steps, leaving her to make up her mind. She drove around the corner, left the car in an outdoor parking lot, and walked back. He was waiting for her in the vestibule.

When they were upstairs, in the living room, it looked totally changed. Even the furniture looked rearranged, although he assured her it hadn't been. Everything was indeed the same as before, just as precise and prim, the same stiffly upright chairs, the same antimacassars on everything. But it hadn't seemed so timeworn; a house for old people who hadn't noticed the passing of the years and the thinning of velour.

Again they pretended to be satisfied with the busyness of pointless words. At last she couldn't make do with them.

"Have you ever had a woman before?" she asked.

She of course knew the answer but had a compulsion to go back to the beginning.

"No."

He flushed and she was astonished by it. "Did you say you're thirty-six?"

"Yes. Old enough not to go red in the face," he said. He made an effort—it looked strained—to pull himself out of his confusion. The words burst out of him. "I was stupid yesterday. You called—you said it wasn't my fault—it was generous—I should have thanked you. But

372

I couldn't because—" He stopped and started again. "I went to confession yesterday and a strange thing happened. I—"

This time he stopped dead still. He was routed. She wanted to tell him he needn't talk, needn't explain anything to her, but she could see it was precisely what he did need to do.

He started over again. "It occurs to me—it's never occurred before—that I'm a priest for a set of reasons I don't know I have." He laughed at himself. "That's not luminously clear, is it? I'm not really a pastor—I wasn't really the good shepherd when I was a curate. I'm really a scholar—a theologian. I wrote a book once and it gave me more trouble—and more pleasure—than anything I've done."

"What was it?"

"It was called *The Last Magic*. It had to do with divine revelation. And it just occurred to me yesterday that I shouldn't have called it Magic, but Mystery. Not form, but spirit. Not abracadabra—faith." He was struggling, having a bad time. "And it seemed such an obvious error—how could I possibly have made it? . . . And then—the strange thing—as if one thought had anything to do with the other—I didn't go inside—I didn't confess."

"Why not? Certainly you can't be lacking in faith?"

"No—not where the mystery is concerned—in Christ, in the Trinity, in the salvation of man. But in those other things . . ." He paused. His hands were unsteady and, hiding them, he put them behind his back. "What I mean—the chastity of priests—I know very clearly what the Church says about that. There's no uncertainty in my mind, none at all. Yet I find myself saying: there's no gospel on the matter, and if there is, it's contradictory. And as to canon law, it can change—any law can change. . . . And as I say those things, I know they're merely lawyer's arguments. A theologian can always find a legal license that'll justify a trespass—I'm damn good at that. . . . But I'd better face it. The truth is that I slept with a woman and took pleasure in it. And the deeper truth is, that I took pleasure and feel no guilt."

"I don't believe you feel no guilt."

"I don't—really I don't."

"Look how your hands shake."

He had unconsciously brought his hands from behind his back, and now, seeing them violate his confidence, he gripped them tightly together to keep them from trembling.

"Yes," he admitted finally. "I do feel guilty. . . . Then why wasn't I able to confess?"

373

That, she could see, was what tormented him the most. Not the act itself, but that he couldn't confess it. And he apparently didn't know why. Nor could she tell him. She felt, in every way, inadequate. He had brought his turmoil not to a fellow priest, a confessor, but to her. She wondered, erratically, if it might mean he didn't really want to take the blame for the pleasure, but wanted instead, perhaps without even knowing it, to saddle her with the whole fault of the sin.

"Michael . . . you have to talk to someone else."

"To whom? And say what?"

"Just what you've said to me."

He affected a smile. "I can't even say my breviary. This morning for the first time, I . . ."

She had never heard the word. "What is a breviary?"

"It's a book of prayer." He pointed. "There it is, on the table."

She had no particular wish to look at it, but dealing with the object itself was easier than dealing with the hurt that was in it. She lifted the book and saw the charred edges of some of the pages. If she did it lightly, she might untie things, she thought. "Do you burn the pages you don't like?"

He seemed grateful for the release. "No, I have someone come in and burn them for me."

He was only half joking. She was curious. "How did that happen?"

His indecision was only momentary. Then, apparently relieved to discuss it, he told her about the windy night in Rome, the attack upon the priest, his mission to Cavanaugh, the death of Warrum which might have been his own death, his meeting with Cristobal, and finally the heartaching loss of Cardinal Halevi. He appeared surprisingly less shaken by the fact that someone was trying to kill him than by the death of the seventy-five-year-old cardinal. The old man's demise seemed to have left him in despair.

"You say you prayed for him?" she asked.

". . . Yes."

"Then you can pray for somebody," she said quickly. "Soon, perhaps, for yourself."

She looked down at the breviary in her hands. It was beautiful, deeply used, the leather worn to intimacy. Carrying it to him, she said. "Please go back to it." Then, after a moment: "I have to go."

"No, don't."

But she was already at the door. "Nora, wait. I haven't told you the important thing."

She turned. He wasn't looking at her; he was desperate, it seemed, not to look at anything, as if dreading what he might see. "In the ritual of confession, guilt is not enough. You have to make the promise that you will go and sin no more. I couldn't make that promise."

He looked utterly lost. She turned from the door and crossed the room again. She heard a cry from him. He clung to her.

"Don't go," he said. "Please don't go."

He was kissing her, his hands were over her, the hunger and the ache were his, and hers as well, and for the moment there wasn't any death, no need of prayers or of forgiveness, no need for hereafters, perpetuities, promises of heaven. The instant was enough, the lovemaking now, for the present, for the time being, for the time *of* being.

In the middle of the night, they lay naked beside each other, and she was asleep. She was awakened by his touching her again, and she turned to him. He was whispering something and she couldn't hear it. Then she realized he was having a difficulty finding a way to say it.

"But you haven't," he murmured.

"It doesn't matter."

"It does," he said. "Show me how."

So she took his hand and helped him help her. Then, just as she was almost there, she made him come inside her. It had been so long, so nearly never that it had happened to her that she did a strange thing. She had never asked anyone to use the words to her; sometimes they had come, sometimes not, but she had never asked.

As the excitement was in her, she cried, "Tell me you love me. It doesn't matter if you don't—just tell me."

But she came without his saying it.

As they lay there, she thought: lie or no lie, it would have been better if he had said it. She scoffed at herself, the realist, wanting a fantasy.

In the morning, she had a bath while he had a shower, and it was only when they started toweling themselves that the delicious intimacy became an embarrassment, and she couldn't tell why. How distinct the functions are, she thought, how isolated by prejudice, indexed, ticketed. She doubted that they'd ever know each other well enough to have a conversation while one of them was paring toenails or sitting on the john.

375

She didn't know what he liked for breakfast. While he was shaving, she made toast and coffee; there was marmalade and a carton of orange juice.

"Exactly what I wanted," he said.

"Not hard to guess—it was all you had."

She grinned and he did too. She was very happy and wanted him to know it. She wanted him to share something that had just happened to her, and given her gooseflesh. "I always thought there could be pleasure in impermanent things . . . but no real joy."

She couldn't tell what he was thinking. Hiding a lot, saying a little. "Is permanence all of it?"

"I must have thought so." And yet, she told herself, impermanence was the nature of relationships these days—even the nature of marriages—the impermanent and the fractional. Even people who had no clerical complications were asking less and less of one another—in time, involvement, responsibility; yes, even asking less of love. Only a tyrant, a romantic or a fool could expect permanence, totality, the all-embracing, forever-enduring devotion. The fragments were getting smaller. . . . Ruefully, it occurred to her that she had been able to enjoy this impermanence because she had allowed herself to imagine that it might not be so impermanent after all.

"What are you going to do today?" he asked.

She could say it sounded connubial, husbands were always asking wives such things; or she could say it was a hint that, whatever the hell she would be doing, she'd better start doing it. Begone.

"Continue looking for a job," she said.

"What time will you be through?"

"I don't know. I'm going to keep at it."

"But not tonight?"

"No, not tonight."

"Will you come back at dinnertime?"

She wanted so badly to come back. Yet, knowing she mustn't, she had to think of some way of putting him off. Irrationally, she was angry at him for wanting something she yearned to give, and couldn't. She had a wayward fantasy: she saw herself with a lipstick in her hand, writing on his turned collar *I love you*. She hated the thought that the love might be just as true as the hostility. Answer the man, she told herself, he's asking you to return. Tell him you won't come back, you won't hurt him, won't write graffiti on his soul.

"Yes," she said. "What time?"

"Whenever you're finished. Six o'clock?"

"Six, then."

Time to leave. She wanted to kiss him. In fact, she wanted to stay, yearned to be back in bed with him again.

She catapulted herself out of there and down the stairs. Outdoors, the sun was bright, and her heart up to it. I'm still happy, goddamn it, I'm still happy, she said, and I may stay that way all day.

Even the woman who owned the employment agency didn't depress her. She was in fact a bright woman, fortyish, Sylvia Harte her name was—she called herself Sookie—and she liked Nora immediately.

"You've got good carriage," she said. "You hold your tits up."

Nora had a flash of Micky saying why don't you walk straight. Well, I'm doing it now, she thought, and because I am this woman calls me Queenie.

"Well, Queenie, it's only a part-time job," she said. "I just need somebody to take over the office for a few hours a day—so I can have a breather, and maybe go out and get laid. Do you want it?"

Nora hesitated, unwilling to mislead the woman; she liked her. "I might not want it for long."

"That's all right, Queenie," she nodded. "I know the jive. You'll sit in my chair and glom onto every job offer. You'll pick the best one for yourself, then scram. It's called the scram jive."

She talked like that, racy with old-fashioned words. She was, as she admitted, fifteen years behind herself.

Nora accepted the job, at which she was to start tomorrow. Meanwhile, today, to get acquainted, they sat in the scruffy employment office on the fifth floor of a second-rate building on Broadway and drank poisonous coffee, and Sookie told her she was divorced, no children, and how hard it was to find a man.

"Like last night," she said, "these charitable friends—they call me for a party. 'Not many,' they say, 'just a few of us. And one person in particular.' Now, it seems this one person in particular is a guy around fifty and a fine violinist with the Philharmonic. But he was recently divorced, he's living alone in this practically empty apartment—no pictures on the walls, no books on the shelves, and his new stereo's not as good as the one the wife kept. In short, he's so lonely he could fall in love with a hot water bottle. So I read up on my cadenzas, and a dozen composers I won't remember next month—and I buy myself a fussy little dress that I hate.

377

"Well, I get there and these bastard friends of mine have invited three additional unattached females. Two of them are widows, and one's a divorcee like myself. And they are—what I mean—*competition*. All my age, understand, not cute little tootsies, these are *women*. One of them's an editor—she doesn't need to practice cadenzas—she has her own music. Bright, charming and—Jesus Christ, she was just plain *nice*. Another one's the head of this committee, the one that's fighting noise pollution. If some crud is honking his horn, she steps in front of his car and won't budge until they both get arrested. She's funny, she's marvelous. But the third one, she's my favorite—she's a number-one great. She runs this vocational school for elderly citizens, and when she talks about this one special old woman, my God, she makes this crippled old lady seem like Joan of Arc. Only it's the younger woman *herself* who's Joan of Arc.

"So . . . I look at these three dames, and I think to myself, how the fuck am I going to catch up on a fast track like this?

"Okay, it's almost dinnertime and this lonely, heartbroken man arrives. And he's smart, he's got a good-looking head of hair—and the best thing about him, he's *liberated*. He's for women, this guy, he's a feminist. Of course, there are a few *little* things he's got against women's lib, but they don't amount to much. And he starts to talk about these itsy-bitsy faults that don't matter, and pretty soon we see that this guy is a front-line, first-class, vanguard son of a bitch—a hypocrite—a male chauvinist prick. . . . But as he's talking—now, get this—as he's talking, one of the three women begins to see his point a little bit. Not altogether, she says, but only an itsy-bitsy bit . . . And it's Joan of Arc.

"Minute by minute, she is switching over, she is selling us out, she is shitting in our omelet. And going into dinner she leeches onto this guy's arm and in a minute she's feeding him his food—'No, Harvey, you really *must* taste this aspic—just a toothful.'

"Then, after dinner, she wipes the crumbs off his crotch and, back in the living room, she puts him in the loveseat and herself beside him, and any minute now his zipper will be off the track. So it's only ten o'clock and they leave, and she's dangling from his arm like a charm on a bracelet.

"Now, I ask you—in three hours how can Ms. Joan of Arc turn into Lady Cunt?"

"We're caught—we all do it."

Sharply: "Not me, goddamn it!"

"You too. You bought yourself a fussy little dress you hated."

378

"What?"

"And you read up on a dozen composers you won't remember next month."

"Is it the same?"

Troubled, Sookie was really asking. As if her new employee had an answer. Nora thought of her mother, who frankly admitted her dependence on men and had no illusions of being liberated. And she wondered which of the two women was better off, the frankly enslaved one, or the enslaved one who thought she was free. She wondered too where she herself was.

But Sookie, unlike her mother, was really battling, searching. "It comes down to be-who-you-are, right?" she said. "Not who they say you are." She uttered the battered maxim so urgently that suddenly it seemed vital again.

Riding down in the elevator, Nora realized that Sookie had touched her with the banal dictum, be-who-you-are. From Socrates to the couch, know thyself.

She had a desperate need to *tell* who she was, in the hope that in the telling it would be told to her. But if she related it at all, she would have to do it honestly—to Michael Farris—not as she had written it in "Hustling in the Holy Land." Perhaps she would have to tell it in whispers, as lovers tell their secrets in the night.

Walking down Broadway, she hurried to a five-and-ten and bought a pad of paper, some pens, a large envelope. Ten minutes later she was in the reading room of the main library on Forty-second Street.

She wrote it as a letter:

Dear Michael,

After searching the soul that I do not have, I've decided not to see you again. I want you to know, however, what you have done for me; or, better, what you've helped me to start doing for myself.

Less than a month ago we met for the first time in Cory Cavanaugh's place in Jerusalem. He was a customer of mine. When I say customer I mean someone who purchases something, someone who continues a custom, who helps to perpetuate a convention, a usage . . .

She wrote the rest of the morning away, past lunch and into the late afternoon. She didn't reread what she had written, merely folded the pages, enclosed them in the envelope, sealed it, and sat there, not needing to move.

379

How wonderful she felt, how clean. She had written asking for nothing in return, not money, not praise, not sympathy, not someone else's absolution of her.

Only self-deliverance, and not even aware she had been asking for that. It had simply come. And it had never come before. Never in her writing had she securely known that it came more easily when there was no lie in it; if the truth was an agony, even if some frightened person within her cried against every aching word of it, it still came more easily when there was no lie; never had she known that the truth was the reason for writing, it was everything, the purpose, the practice, the reward. And that nothing else mattered, nothing; that the other rewards, without it, were a trick to lure the foolish; and that it, even without the others, was every prize in one.

What a gift he had helped her make for herself! What a loving gift!

She would have to do it carefully so that he wouldn't see her. If she went back at six o'clock, when he was expecting her, he might be watching for her arrival. Better to arrive earlier—five-thirty—drop the letter and run.

It was five thirty-five when she got to Mindszenty House. She held her purse close to her, clutched. The letter was inside it. Twice in the last twenty minutes she had decided not to deliver it at all, simply to appear and ring the bell and go on with the evening as if she hadn't written it. Even now, on a surge of optimism, she was still telling herself it might not be necessary to terminate whatever they had begun. But it was a vision outside the limits of common sense. Opening her bag, she extracted the envelope.

She started up the steps. She hoped he wasn't looking out a window somewhere; she hoped he was. Just as I'm about to put the envelope in the mail slot, the door will open, she told herself, and he'll pull me into the house. Or he'll see me putting the letter through the slot and just as I'm leaving, he'll call me back and insist on reading it in my presence. What has your terrible experience in Jerusalem got to do with me, he'll say, and what has the Vatican got to do with you? Then he'll tear it up and hold me, and make me stay. . . . Or, he might not.

Even if he did, what good would it be?

Quit it.

Whatever she had had with him in this brief time was more than she had had with anyone else, with nearly a year of Yoel, for example, all those months of alarum and excursion.

She was approaching the door. Arm's length from it, she had a renegade thought: Oh, God, I hope he's safe, I hope there've been no more explosions, I hope they haven't hurt him!

She stopped herself. It was a dangerous thought, meant to frighten and weaken her, catch her off guard, trick her out of her resolution never to see him again. She had no right to love him, or even to fear for his safety . . . nothing.

She left the letter at his door. Farewell, somebody's sonnet said, thou art too dear for my possessing. She lingered on it for an instant, then didn't dare to indulge in the comforting unhappiness of the verse. No poem-posturing now, she said, just run; running is legitimate on this occasion: the faster, the more quietly you run down the steps, the less likelihood of tears.

Farewell, somebody's sonnet said. . . .

Seventeen

THE SUN WAS GETTING LOW—nearly seven o'clock—
and Nora hadn't arrived. There had to be a mistake, he thought, an
accident . . . not, certainly, a change of mind, or she would have
telephoned. Still, she might have thought it would be easier, kinder
to let things drift away without event, lose their brightness . . .
disappear.

He decided to call her home. He looked for her number and found
it stuck away separately in his wallet. With the slip of paper, he
hurried down the stairs.

As he got to the vestibule, he saw her letter on the floor. He ripped
open the envelope and read only the opening sentence and felt it was
all he could stand, he couldn't read any more.

Going up the steps, he lightly tapped the letter on the railing to
make it seem less considerable than it was. But in the living room
again, it was the total presence, and he'd have to do something about

382

it. There was not enough light to read by; he turned on one of the lamps and sat in the nearest chair.

> . . . and if, as will likely happen, I never see you again, I want you to know that these moments with you have been very precious. The memory of them, however painful, will heal many other aches that may come to me from time to time. Pain healing pain is a wonder I will never try to understand, but it's good to know there are wonders left.

> Nora

He folded the letter neatly, restored it to its envelope, and sat there quietly. For a long time he didn't move.

He felt as if he had been blessed and then, bereft.

He must not, he warned himself, try to deal with the main point of the letter, that he would never see her again; too much to handle, head on, all at once. Deal, instead, with the letter's tangents—how they met, for example, at Cory's place in Jerusalem, and the artist one of her . . . customers, she had said. How curious, Cory one of her customers, when he had told Michael, quite clearly told him, that he hadn't touched a woman in over a year.

I must ask Nora about that, Michael said. Pull back, he told himself, you'll never see her again—to ask her about anything. And even if you were still together, you and Nora, you'd never refer to Cory or to any part of her past, never question her about it; you'd leave it where she wanted it left, and never feel a qualm.

No, he *wouldn't* feel a qualm. How strange, he thought, that he had no repugnance, none whatever, about her brief life as a prostitute. Even thinking of having slept with her, and her having slept with others and been paid for it, no disgust and no revulsion. Everything he had read, everything he had ever heard, the converse of the clergy, the tales he had heard in the confessional of whores diseased, and men diseased by them, all told him there was a classic, a predictable male reaction to the prostitute: detestation. The whore was a thing unclean, an abomination to God and man. There were biblical references everywhere, Old Testament and New, to the contamination of men who keep company with bawds and fancy women, and to the loathsomeness of harlots' houses.

Why could he feel no abhorrence of her, and no rancor? Why did he not rage that she had lied to him, had misled and misused him;

383

why, instead, did he feel this trembling of pity for her, why did he need to hold her in his arms, to comfort and soothe her, to murmur to her, rock her, kiss her, love her all the more?

There was no escaping it: he loved her.

He had been dreading it, holding it back from his consciousness, calling it a momentary aberration, a temporary malady of the blood, a debt to morality that he would ultimately redeem, never saying love, never allowing himself to think such an awesome word. And now that it was said, he was dismayed by it; helpless, not knowing what to do. But, one thing he did know: whatever torment it would entail, he would not repudiate it.

Love was not to be disowned. He felt as if someone had given him a precious gift, a shard of a goblet from which Jesus had drunk, and he was too humble to possess it. Yet, he could not part with it. Or a living thing—that was closer to the ecstasy and ache of it—someone had given him a living thing, a bird to care for, a lamb, a child, and if he refused it, it would languish; if he did not take it and love it and nurture it, it would sicken and die. Love love, some voice commanded him, love love and cherish it, and call it holy.

So he went to the telephone and called her, and asked her to come back. He said there had to be some way that they could see each other, that if some way hadn't been discovered by others in similar straits, they would have to find it for themselves. He heard her crying and telling him no, begging him not to ask anymore, but he couldn't stop.

"I love you, Nora. I am in love with you. And it's something so new to me—and strange—and blessed—I don't know what to do." Then: "Help me," he said.

She said that she would come.

In the beginning, they were very cautious about Nora's visits to Mindszenty House. As if she were Michael's secretary, or a typist, she came by daylight and left before dark. But after the first few times, they realized that nobody was paying any attention to her comings and goings. The neighborhood had years ago deteriorated, the block was no longer residential, many houses were abandoned, there were only a few small businesses, no neighbors to speak of, and New York was indifferent to lovers. Even Michael's concern that there might be surveillance by the chancery—or Cristobal's people—seemed groundless. Nobody was watching them. They were in a city of disinterested anonymities.

Soon they gave up being cautious and occasionally Nora would spend the night; then it happened more frequently and, by degrees, they began to live together. Although Michael had qualms about her presence in Mindszenty House, he told himself that the building was no longer a religious one—it had long since ceased to be a parish house, and had become a secular hospice for refugees. And to him, Nora was a refugee who had come crying in the night; and, possibly, one of the reasons he loved her was that she was an exile to whom he had to give a haven. This was it.

He knew that he was rationalizing to avoid the pangs of guilt. When, frequently, he did face the truth, he told himself that guilt was the price he had to pay for happiness. He paid it. And he *was* happy; they both were.

The Synod was four weeks away, three, two, and he did nothing about it. After Nora moved in with him, he no longer tried to see Cavanaugh, he tried not to think about Warrum's death or Galestro's crucifixion or Cristobal as a danger.

It was a time of illusions. He pretended none of the horrors had happened, and none of the problems existed. As to his life being in peril, he told himself that was no longer true; now that he was out of the arena, he had ceased to be in jeopardy. The notion of terror-by-delay had been a fiction he had concocted.

Only his life with Nora was real, he dreamed, and it was all happiness. He lived in an unbelievable paradise. It was as if Mindszenty House was a magical and sequestered retreat, far away from the world. And he was living in the most perfect Neverland— with the wife he could never have.

Nora ostensibly had her own room on the third floor; actually, at night, she came down to sleep with him. Daytimes, except for the few hours she spent working at the employment agency, she sat in the third floor bedroom and wrote. He had no idea what she was working on; he would hear her typewriter clacking away for hours, followed by long silences when she'd be reading, then suddenly she'd come spilling down the stairs and say, "Listen to Rilke!"

He too, at first, read a good deal. He spent hours at the library or at the religious bookshop, the Paraclete, where they unearthed things for him, old ones, out of print. He found himself being a theologian once more, a serene scholar dealing in concept; how soothing it was to forget circumstance for a while.

There had been very little further communication with Feradoti. The first had occurred weeks ago, right after the death of Cardinal Halevi. A cable from the Secretary:

GRIEVED OVER CARDINAL HALEVI. KNOW HOW PRO-
FOUNDLY SHAKEN YOU MUST BE AND DEEPLY COM-
MISERATE ON THE BLOW TO YOUR PLANS. DO NOT
TORMENT YOURSELF FURTHER. COME HOME. FERADOTI.

Almost immediately, on impulse, Michael had replied:

CANNOT RETURN QUITE YET. FEEL THAT UNTIL
SYNOD ACTUALLY CONVENES I MUST DO WHATEVER I
CAN TO THWART IT. MICHAEL.

A few days later, a letter arrived from Feradoti. Ostensibly, its purpose was to sanction Michael's extended stay in New York, but actually it was meant to bid his protégé be careful. The terrorism was worsening. He enclosed a clipping from the *Corriere della Sera*. Part news, part editorial, the article reported new atrocities the world over, Frankfurt, Madrid, Tel Aviv, São Paulo, Algiers, London. The New York paragraphs were full of errors and omissions. Father Warrum, the account said, was an excommunicant (which he was not) who had been killed by the explosion of a phone booth (it had only been a telephone instrument) in an unnamed monastery (Mindszenty House had never been a monastery). It made no allusion to any threatening letter that preceded the murder, nor was Michael's name mentioned.

Feradoti had no idea the bomb had been meant for Michael, but was sounding a general alarm: New York was becoming as dangerous as Rome; he hoped his friend would take extra precautions . . . and he wished Michael success in his "plans to thwart the Synod."

Reading the last sentence, Michael felt as if he had lied to Feradoti. His cable had, apparently, led the Secretary to believe that he was plotting further strategies against the Synod. He was not.

Nora, who knew everything about his mission—but nothing about Galestro's crucifixion—saw how depressed he had become in this planless inactivity, and tried to comfort him. "You're in knots—how can you think? If you don't worry it so much . . ."

There was the other worry as well: the threat that hung over his life. Although he had managed, by illusion, to put it out of his mind, Nora had not. He was sorry he had told her about the explosion of the telephone and the death of Warrum. She was constantly anxious.

386

"Every time you go out the door . . ." She had said it more than once.

So he went out less and less. When there was shopping to be done, for food, for anything, they tried to do it separately and quickly, with as little time away from the house as possible. It was their safety zone, their asylum.

With each other, alone, they were in a quiet concord. Because they wouldn't quarrel over momentous matters, they made a game of their minor arguments: who was to pay for what, with both of them snatching for the check, and who was to prepare the meals. Michael loved to cook and so did Nora, and they squabbled over who should do it. He liked food so spicy that it cauterized his tongue; she preferred it blander—natural food, she said. She liked it goyish, he would say.

One evening: "Next Tuesday night I'm doing the cooking," she announced. "And you stay out of the kitchen."

"What's Tuesday?"

"Your birthday, idiot."

"Hey . . . so it is."

"I promised you a party."

"Did you?"

"To myself I promised you a party. With a cake. It ought to be two cakes—you're Gemini."

"Astrology? I thought you were an atheist."

"Astrology isn't God, it's pure science." She grinned. "That's how I know about you. Geminis are tricky—you don't know who's making love to you, the celibate or the satyr."

"Purity or corruption."

"You're not corrupt, Michael. If you didn't think of yourself as a priest . . . You're the most decent man I've ever known."

She made him deeply happy and none of the worries spoiled it. Except for the one great worry . . . guilt. It was so all-eclipsing that he had to tell himself it did not exist. He knew confession wouldn't shrive him. The penitence for trespass was not enough; he must vow to sin no more; but the pledge would be a lie, making the sin a mortal one, and terrible.

He tried to stop brooding over religious matters of any kind. He started to read fewer and fewer theological books. He didn't go to church, he hardly opened his breviary, he never celebrated Mass. It was his discontinuance of Mass that brought about a troubled time with Nora.

387

It happened on a stormy evening, the Monday before his birthday. An out-of-season hurricane, the newspapers called it, and at first it was exciting—the tempest of wind, the flood of rain, the doom's-night flashes of lightning. Then, a deafening thunderbolt, a blaze of sky, and the lights in the house went black.

They were in the darkness of the kitchen, Michael preparing dinner, Nora setting the table.

"Are there any candles?" she asked.

"Yes—the living room—top drawer of the sideboard."

Before he could stop her, she was out of the kitchen, stumbling through darkness, and he could hear her opening the drawer.

It shouldn't have agitated him so deeply, he thought, but it did. He hurried across the kitchen after her.

As he entered the living room, he saw her light the match. She had a candle in her other hand and she set its wick aflame. The blaze flickered. She stood over the sideboard, looking in the open drawer, the left one instead of the right, the one he had hoped she wouldn't.

She turned to him. They were silent. The only motion in the room was the flutter of the tiny flame, in darkness.

"I meant the other drawer," he said lamely. "The candles are in the other drawer."

"There was a candle in this one, too."

"Yes . . . I see."

"It hadn't been lighted . . . it was new."

"Yes."

"There are other things in the drawer."

"Would you shut it, please?"

She pointed at something. "Is this a napkin?"

He nodded. It was an ordinary cloth napkin, table linen, no more than that, never used, never even unfolded.

"And a cup?"

Uneasily: "As you can see, yes—it's a kitchen cup."

"Not really, is it?"

"It's a kitchen cup," he repeated.

"Yes . . . but . . . would it be called a . . . chalice?"

He indicated the kitchen. "Come back, Nora."

Again she pointed inside the drawer. "Is that another breviary?"

"No, it's a missal."

"For Mass, you mean?"

He had hoped she might see the things and not suspect their significance. But he could see that she was guessing all of it—that he

388

had not said Mass in a church, had tried to improvise his own private Mass here at home, but had never used the objects, had never been able to, had not lighted the candle even once. She might also guess that he was a man suspended, nowhere, neither heaven nor earth nor hell. . . . And she was holding herself to blame for it.

He was too off balance to talk about it, but he had to do something for her sake, had to pull her away from her self-reproach. Feeling ineffectual: "Please come back, Nora."

As he started away, he heard a little sound, and thought it might be her effort not to cry. "I'm sorry I lighted the candle, Michael—I didn't know."

He returned a step or two, to comfort her. "It's all right, Nora. Really, love, it's all right."

But it wasn't all right and he couldn't make it so. He hastened away.

A little while later, she re-entered the kitchen, carrying a number of candles, two of them aflame. They lighted others, and there was a brightness in the room. Nothing more was said about the moment at the sideboard. When the electricity came back on, it was as if the instant of trouble had never happened.

Nor did they, not once during the meal, mention it. But Nora didn't look well. Her face was pale and she ate very little. She looked physically ill, but said she wasn't.

After dinner, they were both preoccupied and spoke in half-sentences. When they realized that their conversation was not meshing, they began to speak animatedly about things neither of them was really concerned about. Michael was in the middle of a hyped-up vacuity when Nora said quietly:

"Why don't you read that thing instead of fingering it?"

She was pointing to what he held in his hand. His breviary. He hadn't even been aware of it, hadn't noticed when he had picked it off the table. Quickly, with unmanageable confusion, he put it down. There was an awkward moment, and he saw that Nora was more embarrassed than he was. She excused herself, said she was tired, and went up the stairs.

She was deeply perturbed, almost ill with distress, and he didn't know what to do about it. She was aware that his religious defection was gnawing more oppressively at him all the time, and she couldn't free him of a single pang of his affliction. If only he could release her from her self-censure, and make her see that it was not her cross, but his.

He went to bed and waited for her to come down from the third floor, to join him. But she didn't appear for the longest while and he began to be disquieted. Inadvertently, as he turned in bed, he felt something under the covers in exactly the place where she would have lain. It was his breviary. Attached to it by a paper clip was the note:

> I'm getting worried about you. I'm afraid you're making yourself ill and need medicine. Please take one dose of this before Nora.

He smiled ruefully; each thought the other was getting ill. The note was crude, it was tender. Mostly, simplistic, and he had no doubt Nora knew it was. But if one has no profound remedies, one makes do with placebos.

She stood there, then, on the threshold of the bedroom, holding her wrapper tightly around herself, uncertain whether to smile or be grave. She chose an in-between. "I've been reading an article in this." She held up his copy of *Concilium,* a religious periodical. "It says that those of us who were raised on psychiatry are doing a terrible thing to the Church. We're making a neurotic of her. Even the words. We're using couch words, not Church words. We say she's having an 'identity crisis' or an 'inferiority complex'—and she's in need of 'therapy.' We've humiliated her with the dirty words of her worst enemy, psychiatry. We're giving her a nervous breakdown."

She was talking too glibly, a prepared speech, at a distance from what she needed to say. She was tightly drawn, unable to take a deep breath. He couldn't avoid it any longer.

"You're not giving me a nervous breakdown, Nora."

"I . . . think I am."

"No. Now listen to me." He saw a look of fright, a scurry of it across her face. She's going to bolt, he thought. "Now don't run, Nora—you listen to me!"

Irresolutely, she paused at the doorway, and he continued. "I'm not going to tell you I'm not in trouble. I am. But it's my trouble, not yours. And there's no way you can help me—believe me, not a single way. If we talk about this—you and I—that's a pretense that something can be done, the problem can be solved if we only put our heads together. But that's a lie. It doesn't take two minds to figure it out—it's not a hard problem to understand—it's very simple. I can solve it in ten seconds. All I have to do is stop seeing you, living with you and loving you. I simply walk out of here and into the confessional. But I can't do that—I can't imagine myself doing it—not now or ever. I know that some day I *will* walk into the confessional, but right now . . . thinking about that, it's a dying matter . . . and I can't dwell on it or I'll come apart." He felt the growing ache and couldn't allow it to increase, so he halted, forcing it to subside a little. "So . . . Nora . . . it's much worse than you think, and a great deal better. There's no solution, and there is one. That's confusing as hell, but I guess I'm compensated for the pain of the confusion with one certainty that's simple . . . I love you very much."

. . . Later, when she was under the covers, long later in the night, they talked quietly for hours. Then, after they had agreed that in future they would try to avoid raising religious questions, Nora said she couldn't help herself and had to ask one more.

"Does it upset you that you can't convert me?" she whispered in the dark.

"Have I tried?"

"No. But maybe that's your method."

"I have no method, Nora. Besides, you'd be an easy conversion."

"Why? Because I'm a Jew?"

"No . . . because you're not."

"Paradox, paradox."

"Not really," he responded. "If you believed in God—say, a Jewish God—it would be unconscionable to try to convert you. But not believing in any God, and needing Him as I think you *have* needed Him . . ."

He sensed that she was tightening. "You're wrong," she said. "I've never needed Him. I've needed courage—my own, not borrowed. . . . And I don't believe in Him."

"How can you be so certain that you don't?"

She answered the question obliquely. "My father was an agnostic. I used to call him an ag-o-nostic, because I really think he was in pain about it. He used to say, 'Don't make God and don't kill Him.' One day I realized that the implication of that is that we make God in *order* to kill Him."

"But the God we make in order to kill isn't God at all, he's another enemy."

He knew that she was smiling. "That God I can believe in."

"He's crueler than mine, you know."

"Oh, I know."

"Perhaps I was wrong about your being an easy conversion. . . . You're tough."

391

"Me—tough?" It seemed a totally new assessment of her. She had apparently thought of herself as a weakling when, in truth, she had been more and more strengthened by every onslaught of weakness. "Yes . . . maybe I am. How do you suppose I got that way?"

"Well, if you walk around in the spiritual buff all your life, you develop a tough skin. If you've got no church to run to for shelter, you harden your hide until it's impermeable. I could soak you in holy oil from now to Judgment Day and never soften you up."

Even as he said it he realized he had stung her. "I'm not hard, Michael," she said.

"I'm sorry, I didn't mean hard—not inside."

"Now that you've said I'm not, I wonder if I am." She was very still.

He knew she was worrying the thought. She would face the fault, any fault within herself—without the comfort of someone else's absolution of her—face it and not flinch. How sad and courageous she was, to be going it alone. Of all the people he knew, she needed God more than anybody, because the burden of guilt she carried was heavier than the world itself. She was all conscience, and blamed nobody for her sins, nobody but herself. Having committed so many of them, by her self-judgment, and having had no absolution for them, no peace from the agonizing memory of them, they had continued to pile upon her. No wonder she had stumbled under the weight of them, and no wonder she had at last developed the moral muscle to bear them. She was, if only she knew it, a strong woman. Strong and full of sorrow—and Someone should have come to her help. If only she believed. Yet, he knew that God was not to be persuaded—actively or passively—He Himself was not, nor others *of* Him. And to try to persuade Nora would be a violation of Him and her. So she would have to do without His comfort, and make do with Michael's. And he would have to love her for both. Even if there were world enough and time, how insufficient he felt.

He knew she was troubled and heard her, as usual, making an ironic thing of it. "Hey, if this was the first step in a conversion procedure, you flopped."

He laughed. "Go to hell . . . if I can't get you to heaven."

He heard her making a pleasant murmur; smiling. They lay there, listening to the street noises, content with their own quiet. He realized that tonight, for the first time since Nora had come to live with him, they had had a basic difficulty with one another. And he was deeply happy that they had come through so well.

Their next crisis did not end so felicitously.

It started in darkness, when they were asleep. They were awakened by the telephone. Michael struggled out of bed, looked at the clock—it was just past three. He hurried downstairs to the ringing bell.

It was Feradoti. "I keep waking you up," he said apologetically.

He was trying to maintain his habitually composed manner, but there was a shudder underneath it.

"What's the matter?" Michael said.

"I'm here with Monsignor de Gamez," he replied. "A terrible thing, Michael—terrible . . . There was a bomb—the Piazza Navona—the church of Sant'Agnese—eleven people have been killed—one of the belfries—destroyed, totally destroyed—the dome damaged—eleven people, Michael, eleven people!"

The old man lapsed into Italian, kept saying *orribile, orribile,* then he resumed: "The fragments flew everywhere—one of the figures of the Bernini fountain has been shattered—there was other damage—the Piazza has been closed."

There was a voice in the background; presumably de Gamez was saying something to the Secretary; for a moment, both voices at once, a confusion of their mutterings.

"Three of them have been arrested," Feradoti said.

"What?"

"Yes—the terrorists—three of them. Two men and a woman. The bomb must have gone off prematurely. It killed one of them and wounded the second. The wounded one ran across the Piazza—he was bleeding. There were two others in a car—a man and a woman. The police went after them, and two *carabinieri.* They didn't get very far—the *carabinieri* captured them on the Via dei Coronari."

"Who are they?"

He heard Feradoti consult with de Gamez again. "The wounded man is a clerk in a department store—his name is Alviero Bari. He's the one the police have made to talk. De Gamez says they refused to give him medication unless he told them everything. He has implicated five other people. Two of them are in La Spezia. But the most important one—a woman—a Brazilian doctor—"

"Falga Cristobal."

"Dear God, you *do* know her!"

"Yes."

"It's true, then?"

"What?"

"An attempt was made on your life!"

393

Michael didn't answer immediately. He heard the horror in the Secretary's voice. "That telephone—*amor di Dio,* that bomb was meant for you!"

"Yes." Then, hurriedly: "What else did that man say about Cristobal?"

"He didn't say any more, Michael. And in any event, I want you out of it. You're not to endanger yourself. You are ordered to come home!"

"The crucifixion—the man—what was his name?—Bari—did he say anything about that?"

"We're not able to ask him. But it's a secret we can keep no longer. De Gamez says it has been rumored for weeks. . . . When will you come home?"

"A day or so—I'll let you know."

"Today, Michael—the first plane!"

"Maybe—I don't know—as soon as I can." Then, quickly: "The other two who were arrested—what are their names?"

"I told you—you are not to deal with it any longer—you are to return."

"Please."

"I beg you, Michael—don't do anything."

"Your Eminence—listen—trust me—please trust me—what are their names?"

"What will you do with them?"

"Please!" Then, more quietly: "If you don't give them to me, I'll have to stay anyway, until I see this through. But the names may help me. . . . Please."

An instant. Another consultation with de Gamez. "The woman's name is Adela Corlina. The man is Guglielmo Luz. . . . When are you returning?"

"I'll telephone you. Please don't worry. *Arrivederla.*"

He heard the Secretary, distractedly it seemed, echo the farewell. Then he hung up.

Quickly he reached to the pencil on the table by the phone. He scribbled the three names on the pad.

And tried to calm himself.

The Piazza Navona. How ironic that that particular square had been chosen for such a savage act of destruction. The Navona, where radicals expressed themselves with speeches and demonstrations and parades, the rallying place for Italian rebellion. Havoc again, for havoc's own sake. But there, of all places—it was as if the terrorists had fouled their own nest.

Which they were now doing in an even more specific way: talking . . . betraying one another, at last . . . Cristobal.

He had three names. What could he do with them?

He thought of Zeckley, of calling him. No, he mustn't jump too soon. Anyway, he had until tomorrow, possibly even late tomorrow—the news couldn't possibly hit the morning papers, maybe not even the evening ones. Television news—earlier, perhaps. But even so, there was time to devise a plan.

He left the alcove under the stairs. As he approached the newel post, he saw her sitting on the steps.

"Nora . . ."

"I heard the phone—I was frightened," she said. "I listened. I'm sorry."

"It's all right—let's go back to bed."

She didn't get up off the stair. "What did that mean? You said . . . crucifixion."

There was no keeping it anymore, the Secretary had said. "Somebody—one of the cardinals—in April."

"Oh, no." She shivered. He sensed that she wanted to ask questions, and desisted. He knew the most pressing question, and she asked it: "You'll have to go back, won't you?"

"Yes."

"When?"

He tried to be as evasive as he had been with Feradoti. "I don't know—a day or so—a few days."

"What will determine the length of time?"

He must avoid letting her know he might be going to see Cristobal; she'd be panic-stricken, as the old man had been.

"After you've done what?" she insisted quietly.

"Never mind."

"You're going to Cristobal's, aren't you?"

"I haven't decided."

"Yes, you have—but I won't let you. Are you crazy? Do you want to get killed?"

It was exactly what Cory had said before Michael had gone to see Cristobal the last time, yet he hadn't been killed. Not that it made him feel any securer that he wouldn't be.

"I'm going upstairs," he said.

"Michael—"

But he had already started up the steps. She stayed below for a few minutes, then followed him silently.

When they were in bed again, Nora was wayward, tense, in a strange mood, as if bedeviled. No longer avoiding a discussion of the Galestro brutality, she asked a hundred questions. Morbidly, it seemed to him, she wanted to know everything that had happened from the time Michael had discovered the body until this moment, no detail spared, no anguish eliminated. It was as if she were trying to face the past dismay in all its affliction, in the hope that she'd be spared the imminent dismay: he was leaving.

But he knew she wasn't being spared, and he started to touch her comfortingly. She turned away, to hide that she was crying. Reaching over, he put his arm under her shoulder and gently drew her close to him. He kissed her forehead tentatively, not too sure of anything, then her wet eyes, her mouth. He made her stay close to him. Then they clung to each other in a blessing of safety they both knew was temporary. They said very little; the quiet, a balm. He would have liked to prolong the peace into dawn, into next week, come Pentecost, forever. But it could be only another day or so, a night or two. . . .

Falteringly, as if she had never been near him before, her hand was touching him. He kissed her breasts and caressed her body in all the places, familiar and always unfamiliar, always wondrous. He could feel her excitement growing, and his own. Then there was a cry of wanting from her, and from both of them, and the loving was joy and heartache, anger and tenderness, the first and last of it.

They still clung to one another, afterward, and it was as much serenity as an illusion of permanence would allow. In a little while, he had the blissful sense that he was falling asleep in her arms.

He had no idea how much later it was, perhaps a few hours, when he found himself awake and separated from her. He turned to touch her and no one was there.

He listened in the darkness; there was a sound somewhere, he couldn't tell in what direction. He heard her, then, in the bathroom, and the water running. She was making a low sound, a choking sound.

Startled, he got up. "Nora, are you all right?"

She didn't hear him. As he hurried toward the bathroom. "Are you okay—what's the matter?"

"Nothing, darling—I'm all right."

Her voice was casual enough. What an alarmist you are, he told himself; she's simply brushing her teeth; what in the world did you *think* it was?

Vomiting.

It wasn't the first time this evening he had suspected she was ill. At dinner, when she hadn't eaten anything, when she had looked so deathly pale, he had had the distinct feeling that . . .

He wondered if she was pregnant. Once, weeks ago, when she had first moved in, while she was in the shower and he was starting to shave, he had caught sight of the diaphragm. He had looked at the thing, trying not to identify it, glad to see it, wishing it would disappear. At first he had intended to say nothing about it, but then he realized that she had meant for him to notice it was there, not only for him to know what she was doing—he would be a fool if he didn't know—but also to know that he was a part of it. He had looked at the simple, rubber thing and had realized that for him it was probably the most complex object in the world. He turned away from it, and saw that she was out of the shower watching him. For a moment, neither of them spoke. Then:

"I know," was all he said.

Apparently, it was all she needed of him; to take the responsibility of knowing.

If she were pregnant now, she'd want him to share *that* responsibility too, and she could be confident he would. So she couldn't be pregnant, he told himself, or she'd have told him so. They had to trust each other on that.

A few minutes later, she came back to bed and very quickly fell asleep. He lay there, eyes wide in the darkness, reconstructing the evening, the night, Feradoti's call, the names of the terrorists, back and forth, everything. He thought of his enemies, Cavanaugh and Cristobal, so opposite to each other, and felt as if he were caught in the pincer of two armies.

With the first sign of daybreak, he slipped out of bed, got his clothes on, hurried to Times Square for the newspapers, scoured them—and found no mention of the Piazza Navona catastrophe. Too early.

It didn't matter. Whether the Navona bombing appeared in the papers or not, he had to assume that Cristobal knew more about it than he did. In fact, he must tell himself that her knowing—and thinking he did *not* know—was an advantage. Somewhere, buried in that thought, there could be a plan.

Again, he considered calling Lieutenant Zeckley. But what good would it do? He knew very well what the detective would say. What shall I do about the woman—arrest her? What new crime's been committed here?—not in Italy, here? . . . Or he would ask Michael what light he could shine on the last crime, Warrum's murder—did he have anything that could convincingly implicate Cristobal? Could Michael conclusively associate her with any suspects—Heskins, Cassie Macramé? Could he even cast light on where they could be found?

Yes . . . the gallery above the studio . . . the door that had closed so slowly.

Speculative and chancy, the detective would say; we can't break into a woman's property on the evidence of the slow closing of a door.

But I can, Michael realized.

The fire escape. The broken window, covered with Masonite.

And find what? Luridly: a little laboratory for the making of bombs?—what a nonsensical notion. Yet, did he have anything better than nonsense to hang on to? Yes, something *was* going on up there.

He would do it. Not now, by broad daylight . . . no good.

Tonight, then.

He would not tell Nora. She would be preparing a birthday dinner for him this evening—he wouldn't spoil that. But afterward . . . when Nora was safely asleep.

Cristobal's.

Eighteen

S H E   H A D   T A K E N a sleeping pill last night, a strong one, and when she awoke it was mid-morning. Michael had left the house; where he had gone she didn't know. He often drifted off that way, saying nothing, going to libraries, browsing in bookshops, visiting places as if he were a tourist.

She was rather glad he was out of the way today; she had other things to do, and there might be plans to make.

She had lied to him. When he had called through the bathroom door, asking if she was all right, she had said she was. These vomitings were a recent thing. The first one, after her missed period, had come at night, while Michael was asleep. None of them had happened in the daytime, so you couldn't truly call it morning sickness. Besides, she couldn't believe it happened, she had not been foolish or reckless or careless or any of the adjectives from which misfortune prescinds, she had used her device, the bad luck factor of which was said to be quite low; she couldn't be one of the exceptional Jonahs this side the probability line.

Today, the result. Two days ago, the urine specimen; this morning, the return visit to the doctor. Soon, in a few hours. It needn't, she kept repeating to herself, it needn't mean a thing.

Even if she was pregnant, it was early. It could be handled easily enough, and Michael none the wiser; she would never tell him. She could arrange to have it done right after his departure . . . in a few days, he had said.

In a few days . . . Michael, gone.

She mustn't grieve over him, she told herself; there would be so much that would remain with her after his departure, so much of Michael in the new Nora she had been able to discover, these last few weeks.

Instead of complicating her life, he had helped to make it simpler. Her work at the employment agency, from which she would not get fired, was bringing her enough money to live on, and she was writing for hours every day. How much easier it was to write now that she knew it would never be easy; she was trying to write as personally, as self-searchingly as if she were talking to Michael, telling him the truth about herself. Doing it that way, she had come to realize how fascinating this creature was, this Nora Eisenstadt, with her appetite for happiness and wretchedness. She saw her as a woman of perversity, often deeply in pain and in *need* of pain; every torment helped her understand another torment. And as she became aware that she could live in truce with her anguishes—and even possibly, some day, use them to make an art of some sort—she became available to her joys.

And she had at last found one joy she was equal to: loving him. She knew she was equal to it because it was more precious to her than being loved. What made her absolutely certain that she loved him was that she could not only count the ways, she could count the whys as well. When the sexual attraction was set aside—and God knows she didn't minimize its importance—there was a wonderful corollary to it. They had had no sexual combat. There had never been a war between them of man versus woman. She used to think that blood-letting between the sexes was a sine qua non of a love affair, its essential excitement; how sublime it was, with Michael, to realize it was only its sick hysteria.

She could count another reason. There was in him . . . the last magic. By stealth, during times when he was out of the house, she had read his book, and it had crystallized all she had surmised about him, where his beauty lay, his secret and his strength. Now she knew for certain what she had guessed, that his virility was exercised in his defense of the mystery of God. What a paradox it was that his potency of spirit gave him potency of the flesh. God was the fire of all his life, even of his lovemaking.

Yet, she knew that for all his mysticism, what he loved most about *her* was the *fact*. He knew the reality of her, knew he could trust it, it would not betray him, not abandon him or turn into something less true than it seemed to be. And his loving her—in that way—made it possible for her to be what she was, and what she would become. So that another aspect of him that she loved was . . . herself.

There were more things about him: he made her laugh. Better still, she made him laugh, and she came to see that her humor was not altogether irony, all bitterness. How heartening it was to know that there was still kindness left in laughter; it had not turned acrid.

She loved him, but she had always known that sooner or later he would leave. Yet, what a power it was to be certain that when he departed, even if he stopped loving her, nobody could deprive her of this surging energy of love; her loving was her own.

Then, why did she ache? Why this one particular hurt that could help her understand no other hurt? Why did she feel, realist that she was, that a hopeless love was time out of joint, an anachronism in an age when everything could be made to work; making things function was the credo of the era. And romance, no different from any other pursuit, had its own technology; why couldn't it be engineered to *operate?* . . . It was an eccentric question, with eccentric hope attached.

But . . . Today, just as she was about to go off to the doctor's, an accidental occurrence raised the hope higher than ever. Her heart soared on it.

Before leaving the house, she wished that Michael were at home, so she could say happy birthday to him, and hold him for a moment. Since he wasn't there, she decided to leave him a birthday note. She wrote one, sentimental, dripping jelly; the second note said happy birthday, darling, I love you. She folded it and put it on his desk. About to turn away, she saw the books.

The Clergy and Celibacy was the first hardcover one; then, *The Marriage of Priests*. Beside them, a pile of paperbacks, pamphlets, brochures. There was a badly printed throwaway with the title *Protestants Can Do It, Why Can't You?* She glanced at it; it had a racy insolence.

Then she saw the jottings. They were a pile of ill-assorted pages, lined and unlined, sheets of foolscap, bits of scrap. The top one read: *Is the marriage of priests an unalterable forbiddance?* Under it, a number of scribblings—titles and labels, for the most part, a line for each:

The gospels immutable, canon law always changing.
Living by the imitation of Christ. If in this, why not in all things?
Celibacy as discrimination.

The last note she read was on a separate slip of paper, a ragged scrap. The few words were a scrawl, dashed off in pencil, almost illegible. The jotting read:

Salvation outside the Church?

It had the shock of a flashlight in darkness. That the thought had occurred to him, in conjunction with his doubts about marriage. . . .

It was too much for her, it gave her chills and fever.

Not that she expected him to marry her, or even wanted that to happen. But if he was thinking so disturbedly about a future with a woman that he would even admit into his mind the notion that salvation—for him—was possible outside the Church . . . It quickened hope in her, and fear.

No, it wasn't possible. All that pap about technology engineering romance so it would operate—it couldn't work. And shouldn't.

He was a Roman Catholic priest. It had been his hope of salvation in a childhood too wretched and too lonely; it was the heart of his feeling as a man, it was his identity as a human being, it was the sanity of his mind. She must never tamper with it.

As between the blissful fantasy that he might change, and the aching reality that he couldn't, aching was all she could give herself.

The test was positive. She was pregnant.

"Now," said the doctor. "We'll have to do something about that nausea and vomiting."

Sylvia Harte had recommended him. Because his fingernails were beautiful, she said, and the moons were white. His hair was white, too, so was his mustache. He came out of the pages of old magazines; she wondered if he'd give her horehound drops.

He listed all the indicated specifics against the stomach sickness—

antacids, antispasmodics, antihistamines, tranquillizers. He had just begun to talk about limiting her salt intake, keeping her weight down and the routine of extra iron, when she interrupted him.

"I'm not going to have it, Doctor."

A distant smile. "I still take for granted that women will. I can't get it into my head that there's an easy alternative these days." He put the educational folders back in his file and opened another drawer. "Shall I make an appointment for you? Which hospital is nearest?"

"I haven't decided where or when."

"The sooner the better, of course," he advised. "Very little problem if you do it now."

"I'll do it in the next few days."

Leaving, she walked down West End Avenue, and tried to decide: when? The sooner the better, he had said, and she wished she could have it over and done with, right away. Tell Michael she was going to visit her mother in Florida, go to the Long Island hospital where her father had been, and recuperate a day or two at home.

But it would mean two or three precious days away from him, right now, when they had only a short time left together. If only she could keep it from him during this brief interval; how could she prevent him from knowing? Last night had been a close call; if he had awakened a few minutes earlier, if he had come into the bathroom . . .

And it would get worse, she was afraid, and harder to conceal, the odious retching and kecking; not the most romantic memory keepsake to give him as a going-away present. And the other damnable indignity: she had to urinate too often, had to stay close to a bathroom or she'd wet her pants, as she had done this morning. Couldn't the whole blasted thing be done more gracefully, more considerately, not as a female mockery? Somehow, she had to prevent him from finding out.

Meanwhile, today was his birthday and she was going to make him happy. She bought his present, a delicately tooled leather binder for looseleaf pages, one she had seen in the Mark Cross window, and had coveted herself. It was Florentine and he'd have gotten it cheaper in Italy, but she knew he'd never buy it for himself. And she was going to bake him a cake with candles on it, and his name in icing.

Shopping: a pound of chocolate—no, real chocolate, not cocoa; and the coffee she'd add to the mix would have to be espresso, cruel and bitter so that the flavor would be sweet . . . for the father of her child.

Stop it, she told herself: no child.

Still, why couldn't she play the game for a brief while? She was a mother this moment, only this moment, buying food, cooking dinner, baking cakes. Play the illusion as if it were real, make it seem so commonplace that it's credible; will it be a boy or girl? If she had ever needed evidence that she could love and be loved, the child was testimony. It had happened.

But she knew she had no need for an unwanted child to prove that it had happened. They had each other's word for it, and would have the memory always . . . and the ache.

His present, wrapped in gold paper, lay on the table to the left of his place setting. She lighted the candles and the flicker made the thinly plated silverware look like antique sterling; the Woolworth wineglasses, like Waterford. There was nothing that hadn't responded to her, nothing that hadn't turned beautiful to her hands; everything had a caress on it.

"You did it all—even this?" He was at the sideboard, pointing to the chocolate cake. As she nodded, he continued, "Packaged, though—by Auntie Flook or Grandma Glook?"

"No. From 'take two eggs.' "

He ran his fingertip over his name. He kissed her.

She pointed. "Your present."

Opening it, he gushed over the feel of the leather and the artful tooling of it.

"You're hard to please," she smiled.

He was sniffing the air. "The most wonderful part is the smell. What is it?"

"Garlic."

She had made a Jewish pot roast, bedded in onions, deeply *gedempft,* as her grandmother used to say, surrounded with richly browned potatoes and carrots gone limp in aromatic juices.

"Garlic—mm—garlic," he said.

"A man who believes in garlic—"

"Credo, credo."

"—can't be all goy."

"Let me tell you something. In the south of Italy where they're all Catholics—not a Jew among them—they use garlic as a purifying essence in the church. It used to be myrrh and spikenard, but no more. They found something better—garlic. They swing the essence of it in

404

the censers, they put cloves of it in the holy water. The priests chew it and put it in their vestments to keep the moths and the devils away. They squeeze the tincture of purity into the cincture of purity—*garlic!*"

"Liar," she said, but she wasn't entirely sure. "It's not true, is it?" He howled with laughter and she threw her napkin at him and called him liar, liar.

It was going well; her stomach felt fine. Taking her first mouthful, she warned herself not to eat too much or too fast. She had never had a nausea spell quite so early in the evening, but now, as she swallowed, she felt a slight fluttering. She couldn't stand the thought of ruining his party with her indisposition; she would have to do something. As casually as possible, on the pretext of turning lights out at the stove, she slipped into the kitchen and popped two more antacid tablets into her mouth. They took too long to chew, and the whiteness was telltale, so she washed them down with water.

He was calling. "Your dinner's getting cold."

She re-entered the room. "I'm not very hungry."

"You've hardly touched it."

"I've been eating and tasting all afternoon." She felt another premonitory sign in her stomach. I'll pay no attention to it, she determined. I'll pretend it's imaginary. If only it would go away. She felt her face getting taut, anxious. She mustn't let him notice. Ease up, she said.

"Are you all right?" He looked worried.

Damn, it's showing, she realized; there must be some other way to manage it until the antacid started working. Why did it take so long? . . . It started to work. The soothing began.

A respite now, a breather, the agitations moving downward instead of up, perhaps the trying time was over, and she'd be able to inhale deeply again. Good; he wasn't noticing. And now, with a deep breath of gratitude, it had passed.

The surge. Her body heaving.

She ran. She heard him after her. "Don't come," she muttered.

Into the toilet bowl, inside out, the sweet and sour disgust.

He was right there.

"Go away." Her voice was thick with it.

He stayed with her as if he needed her pain. He gave her a washcloth, a towel; with another towel, a damp one, he cooled her face. He touched her forehead with his hand. "Do you have a temperature?" he asked.

405

She hoped a flippancy would work. "Everybody has."

It didn't. "Nora . . . ?"

"Don't fuss, darling—I'm all right," she said. "Just too much wine, I guess."

He made no comment; she had no idea what his thoughts might be. She was better now, she said, much better. She assured him it was quite over. To avoid his eyes in the bright light of the bathroom, she left it, went back into the dining area of the living room. She knew she daren't challenge the food again. Without making an event of it, she drifted away from the table toward the most upright chair in the living room, and sat.

He stood in the archway of the living room, watching her. He seemed temporary there.

Then he said quietly, *"Was* it too much wine?"

"Yes, I think so."

"What was it last night?"

"Too little."

"Are you pregnant, Nora?"

"I told you . . . wine."

"Are you pregnant?"

"Don't I have better sense than that?"

"Tell me."

There was no escaping it. A lie, even if she could manage it, would do no good. He was not trying to catch her in a deception; he was begging to be let it.

"Yes, I am," she said.

Wordless, he moved behind her chair, put his hands on her shoulders, stooped and kissed her hair. "Why didn't you tell me?"

"Because it wasn't your affair." She hated hearing the last word come out of her mouth, and would have recalled it. Then she made it worse. "Not felicitously said, was it?"

"Why didn't you tell me?" he repeated.

She must try to speak in a firm way. Hard, if necessary. If they were kind with each other, tender, she would not be able to do this very capably. A single loving word might wreck her. She made her sentence precise; spoke it with clean-edged deliberateness. "It *isn't,* in fact, any concern of yours."

She got up, then, to move away from his touching her.

"What does that mean?" he asked.

"I can take care of it myself."

"But there's no need to take care of it yourself."

406

"There's every need. We aren't exactly in a position to handle this together, are we?"

"I'm the father." A simple statement, not a contentious one.

"Even that may be questionable."

"Don't say that!"

She felt herself choking, and wanting to choke, for having said it. What a black inspiration, what an old razor blade thought. And stupid. Because it was patently untrue.

"I'm sorry, Michael—it was an ugly thing to say. But I can't talk about it beautifully. It's not—for me—an esthetic subject."

"Not while you're sick. But in a little while it'll pass."

"Pass into what?"

They had been avoiding the center of the matter, and now she saw him confronting it. "Nora . . . whatever complexities this will present, there's one simplicity: a child will be born. You'll be its mother, and I'll be its father, and we will love it as much as we can."

She couldn't believe how ingenuous he was. There was a huge lie in it somewhere, a lie that glossed over his priesthood, that denied its every injunction against marriage, against natural fatherhood, against lusts of the flesh, against deceptions, subterfuges, failures to confess and to remain faithfully the chaste son of Mother Church.

But he wasn't a liar. If it wasn't a lie, then what was it? Could it be something of a miracle he was talking about, his understanding of such things being better than hers? Could he be talking about some special way that two people make an answer for themselves that has never been found before, a solution made possible not through any closely reasoned process, but through apocalyptic inspiration?

"How do we manage such a thing, Michael?"

"We simply manage it," he said. "People have children. If it's a question of money, I'll be able—some way or other—to handle whatever it will cost. If it's a name—if we're to get married—" He stopped mid-sentence, halted an indecisive moment, then forged ahead again. "People have children, that's all, people have children."

He repeated the phrase for the third time as if for emphasis, weakening it, and it suddenly became a mere slogan, the significance of which had been lost. She realized that he was lost as well, more lost than she was, more inexperienced in all the worldly perils and paradoxes, brave to challenge whatever he might be forced to fight, but having no notion what or who the enemy might be. All his instincts, as she had known they would be, decent; but how vulnerable he was, how sheltered he had been in Mother's bosom, and how unready he was, for anything. She hurt for him more than for herself.

"It's all right, darling," she said softly. "I'm not having this child."

She saw the start of outbreak, the tremble of his hands. At last, controlled. "I don't want you to say that, Nora—not to me, to yourself, to anybody."

"I'm sorry, Michael, I hadn't meant to say it. I hadn't meant for you to know anything about it."

Delayed, the outbreak came. "How could you do it? Why? Because you don't want the child—or because you want to get me off the hook?"

"I don't want the child—no. But even if I did—what could you possibly do about it?"

"If I have to leave the priesthood, I will! If I have to leave the Church, I will!"

"Can you imagine yourself doing that? Can you imagine me *letting* you do it? For what? For something that has no identity as yet, for a growth that can be expelled by a fall on the stairs or a bug in the bloodstream, or twenty minutes with my legs apart? My God, I've had worse torments in that position without wrecking a person I love. You think I wouldn't gladly go through it for your sake—and for mine? I'd do it tomorrow and I'd do it again!"

"You won't do it—I won't let you do it!"

"Because it's a sin?"

"Because it's a destruction of life!"

"So is not doing it! Each to his own destruction—you have yours, I'll have mine."

"It's ours!"

"No, it's not, Michael. It's mine. Whatever else is yours, this is mine. Not yours—not the Vatican's—mine. It's my pain—to do with as I please. And don't tell me you believe differently than I do. I know you, Michael. I know that in your heart you're on my side."

"No—not in this!"

"You're lying, Michael. You don't believe in that old dogma any-more—don't pretend you do. I've seen the notes on your desk—I've seen you agonizing over this. You don't believe the way you used to."

"I don't believe in what? In God? I do. In Jesus? I do. In the Church? I believe—I do believe!"

"You believe in human beings, Michael—more than you do in the Church. You believe in my right to have a child—or not to!"

"That's not true!"

Something snapped. Abruptly, she felt like an animal out of control. "How long since you've confessed?" she challenged. "How long since you've taken communion? What do you have left, Michael? I've seen you in the quiet. What do you have left—your breviary?"

She reached for the book and held it up. "What's in this for you anymore? A few prayers you've said over and over till they've lost their meaning? What's in it, Michael? What would happen if I burned a page or two?"

She was hysterical now, not knowing what she was doing. She ripped a page out and held it over a birthday candle.

"Stop that!"

He grabbed the book from her hand and, as she struggled for an instant, he slapped her.

"Oh, Christ," he cried. "Oh, dear Jesus, forgive me, forgive me!"

"Don't ask Him to forgive you—ask me! You hit me, not Him! Ask me to forgive you!"

Nineteen

WHEN HE GOT DOWN to the street, he felt cut loose from an anchorage. He was adrift on an ocean of waiting—the evening would be endless until he could prudently go to Cristobal's studio. Meanwhile his thoughts kept floating back to Nora, their quarrel still going on, the same way and differently, and in no way less hurtfully than before.

Nora, listen . . .

He must put his mind to the specific task he had set himself, the searching of a strange place. Searching for what? That too was aimless, flotsam, a tideless current.

I'm sorry, Nora—for my fault, and for yours as well. . . .

He had meant to carry tools with him, a flashlight, a screwdriver to pry open the Masonite, a hammer which he might secrete under his coat. But in his haste away from home, he had forgotten to take anything with him. Nor could he go back, risk seeing Nora so soon after their discord, in search of such strange implements.

How could the conceiving of a child have caused such an act of violence?

The fire escape outside Cristobal's studio—would he be able to get up there? Vandals might have managed it easily, but they had expertise . . . he would need leopard's feet.

He couldn't buy any of the tools he needed—the hardware stores were closed. Perhaps in another neighborhood, somewhere in the Village, say, some place might be open. Time to kill. Walking the long distance, he found a small variety store that was on the point of closing, bought a heavy pocketknife, a screwdriver, hammer, pen-size flashlight. The instant they were stowed on his person, the hammer handle held awkwardly by his trouser belt, he felt he was compounding idiocies. People would see the bulges under his coat; worse, they'd see his ineptness. His purposes were unclear to him . . . more and more space around him . . . a vastness of inconclusion.

"What do you have left—your breviary?"

No, Nora, not even that. For the moment. But all men of faith go through bad times. This is one of them. I'll come through it.

To what? The priesthood?

What did it mean, so far as Nora was concerned, for him to remain a priest? What would he give up for her?

What would the Church give up for him? Men and women all over the world—laity, priests, nuns—were asking concessions from the Vatican, negotiating, making deals, arranging sanctions, dispensations, quid pro quos, handouts. How far would the compromises go? Would women be ordained, would the sanctuaries be opened to Protestants and Jews? Would priests be allowed to marry?

Could a woman abort her child?

What did he himself believe?

How long could he go on conciliating the beliefs of others and not decide how far he would go in compromising himself? When would he set his own limits? I, Michael Farris, believe the following. Credo—what?

Less than an hour ago he had seen himself horrified by the possibility a fetus would be destroyed. Passionately he had struck a blow—literally, against a beloved face—for a principle of birth.

Was that what his credo would stand upon—would that be his limit? If he could envision a Church where priests were married,

411

where nuns wedded to Jesus were married to McGarrity as well, could he imagine a Church where diaphragms and interuterine devices and condoms were dispensed like holy water . . . and children were aborted?

Could he imagine a Holy Roman Church, the tabernacle of the resurrected Jesus, where the killing of an unborn child would not be a sin? Could this living embryo be mutilated without some mortality to Christ's life force? In a Church where all sins are forgiven, was this violence also forgivable?

If this too could be negotiated, how much of God would remain?

Maybe we were negotiating Him out of existence. Maybe the days of religion were indeed coming to an end. Maybe theology would soon have to take its place with alchemy and astromancy, a magic for dead Merlins. Maybe the mystery of God, like so many other enchantments, was becoming the prosaic predictability of the laboratory, and would soon be only a fable for the nursery.

Maybe we would keep it as an eiderdown, a solace for children of all ages—God, the night comfort. Like the shivering puppy's clock, He would go on ticking, giving the illusion to the frightened that He was a warm and tender presence, a loving zeitgeist for all lonely creatures in the darkness, when in reality he was nothing more than the ticktock of the universal technology. Maybe we would soon look upon Him as The Alluring Swindler who had seduced our faith, robbed us of reason, conned us out of our minds; had left us a mad people crying for Him at the crossroad, even when we knew He had betrayed us by not existing.

Maybe the last magic was already the lost magic.

If it was so, it would be the greatest loss of all, and more than he could endure.

The streets outside the loft building were much the same as they had been the first time he had come here, but now, it being later in the evening, the pedestrians were fewer, the noise seemed less, a night hush was falling. Even the streetlamp appeared not so bright as it had been; it flickered; sometimes it went totally dark, then came aglow again. It made him edgy.

Strange, how it didn't matter to him that this enterprise was compulsive and without clear plan, that it was illegal, that he had no notion what he expected to find indoors, that he was not objectively going in search of any specific cache or crypt or skeleton. What compelled him now was that he had no alternative but action, since no process of thought had brought him to any clarity. Reasoning, the mystical theologian in him had said, was not the best way to acquire a perception of the ultimate, and certainly not the only one.

Perception of the ultimate, what a pretentious enterprise, yet that is what he had come for. What he had come for, by way of the Vatican and Jerusalem, by way of this strange loft building, what he had come for in America, what he had come for in his love of Nora. What, in everything, he had come for.

The streets were empty now. He did not know the time; it was well past midnight, he would judge. Toward a distant corner a restaurant was closing up; at a further distance, possibly a block away, a woman's laugh went on and on, bursts and paroxysms of it, and didn't seem likely ever to stop. It was an eeriness.

He stood in a narrow passageway between buildings. Diagonally across the street, the loft. There wasn't a light on anywhere. The fire escape was all he could hold in his attention, a weird-looking thing, stair steps of wild color, every third one a psychedelic magenta so that he saw stripes of magenta light rising upward against the blackness, brightening and going dark as the streetlamp flickered. If he held the steps in fixed view he could barely make out the yellow ones as well, but they didn't want to be seen.

Neither did he. He would have liked to remain in the passageway. But there was no waiting any longer. Time, now.

He mustn't run, he mustn't hurry. With careful casualness, he started to cross the street.

The vandals had broken the chain on the fire escape, she had said. But what if it had been mended, what if the counterbalance had been locked again?

He was under it. Too high to reach. Even if he jumped, too high.

The psychedelic magenta was as bright as fluorescence. He wondered if there were purple stripes across his face, wondered if he could be seen.

How to reach the lowest magenta step? The window of the art gallery—he climbed onto its sill. Hard to balance here; he'd have to stretch for the lowest step, and do it quickly.

Too far; he couldn't reach. At the limit of his fingertips, the step was still a good five feet away.

413

He jumped for it. And didn't reach.

On the pavement now, he thought: no good, no way to get to it. If he were only one foot taller, his jump from the sill would have made it; if his arm were only one foot longer.

The hammer at his belt; it had a claw on it. He pulled it free. Quickly, excited now, he got up onto the sill again. He held unsteadily to the windowframe, to keep from falling. Raising his arm, he positioned the hammer at its furthest length and turned the claw so it might catch on the bar that held the step. Then:

Jump.

It caught and grabbed. He held with all his strength, hung there a moment by arm and hammer.

Slowly, very slowly the balance gave. The stair started floating downward. It hit the pavement with a crash. Metal clanging. The whole damn world will awaken, he said.

But no one came. And he had the stairway to himself.

Upward now, clattering a little, stopping to still the noise, upward again, clattering worse, dammit, be still, then suddenly no sound.

First landing.

Upward in utter stillness, magenta stripes, fewer and fewer of them, the yellow and scarlet steps as clear as the magenta now, upward.

Second landing.

The car came around the corner, its headlights bright.

It might not be coming here, he thought. Besides, he was high in the air, above the line of vision.

Except that the fire escape itself—the staircase resting on the ground—was not above the line of vision, it was evident, its bright colors vibrating to be seen.

The car lights got closer.

Go on, he said, ride past, don't notice.

He pressed himself against the darkness of the wall. It's the police, he thought. They've spotted that the steps are down. One of them will get out of the car, ascend the fire escape, flash a light. It's a prowler, he'll say, going to jimmy through a window; who is this criminal? Father Farris, breaking and entering.

The car crossed the intersection, picked up speed and disappeared.

Upward again, and suddenly—clatter. The third flight of metal stairs was less secure than the other two, it shook; the broken chain rattled against the metal balance. He stopped a moment, uncertainly. Then, just as he took another noisy step upward, a stroke of luck.

414

Another sound covered the noise he was making.

Plainsong.

He listened to it. Oddly, it gave him courage, told him he couldn't be wrong from now on, it was heralding his arrival.

Louder as he got to the third floor landing. Now, facing the Masonite, it was loud enough, he hoped, to obscure any noise he'd make.

He looked below. Nobody was there, the street was empty.

The magenta stripes were so shimmering, they blurred his vision. He turned away from them, toward the dark-brown oblong in the window.

Wonderful, how bright it was up here. Moon and stars and flickering streetlamp and, if you didn't let it hurt your eyes, magenta fluorescence. And the Masonite not as tight as he had feared it might be. Nailed, yes, but not too securely; only a tacking job until the glass could be replaced. He wouldn't need the hammer; he pulled it out of his belt and set it carefully on the landing. With the screwdriver he started to ease the tension of the wood. The plainsong smothered the noise.

His activity was soothing to him, giving him more confidence than he had thought he'd have. He felt a wave of excitement, a freakish exhilaration.

The wood and nail complained against each other, and something let go. Don't rush it now, he warned himself, don't let your noise get louder than the chant.

Another nail, another, a little easing at each one; no haste.

The plainsong diminished, and he stopped. The singing was almost inaudible, perhaps it wouldn't swell again, perhaps it had ceased.

Wait, he said. Don't hurry, the night is long.

He tried to loosen another nail against the silence, but it made a sound and he desisted.

The canto again, softly, like the murmur of brook water. He remembered this one, early Gregorian, there would be a crescendo at an alleluia. He would wait for it.

Slowly the voices started the crescendo passage. Still he waited.

Alleluia.

Hurrying now, one nail and another.

Alleluia.

The Masonite swung free. Not altogether down, but free enough for him to squeeze his way through. Sideways, carefully.

He was on the sill now, inside the building.

Dark in here, hardly a ray of light. Where in this blackness could the music be coming from?

He didn't stir from the sill; simply waited. He couldn't recall how far this window was from the floor. It might be a foot, a yard. Misjudging could mean a fall, would certainly mean a noise.

Patience, he said, wait until your eyes are accustomed to the darkness in the room. It wasn't as black as he had thought; moonlight, faintly through the other window.

Two feet off the floor. He stepped down warily.

Alleluia.

The plainsong came from a room above, the far one at the end of the gallery. He couldn't see the stairway to it, but remembered that there was one, remembered her leaving him and ascending it.

He descried it then, barely visible across the studio, a narrow winding thing, an iron staircase. But there was no direct passage to it; the room was cluttered. There were statues everywhere, some uncovered and some draped in muslin, pedestals, plinths, packing boxes.

In the shadows, he started slowly across the vast room. Part way, he stepped on shards of plaster, made a crunching noise and stopped. He must be more cautious now. If he tripped over anything . . .

He started to walk again. Ahead of him, obstructing the pathway, an armature threatened him: huge, lowering, a mammoth skeleton of wire and rods and cables. He edged his way around it, steadied it as it started to totter, then left it behind him; at last, past the ugliness of the mutilated Prometheus, another narrow passageway between armatures and packing boxes, and he was at the foot of the stairway.

The music, louder here.

Slowly, up the iron steps, fearful of the noisy rasp the metal made, squeaks he didn't imagine could be there.

Alleluia . . . gloria . . .

He was on the balcony that ran the length of the loft. Three doors, all closed. The sound distinctly coming from the end, the third doorway.

Slowly, along the balcony, his hand on the metal railing of the balustrade. Slowly, don't rush, slowly, he said.

The second door. The third.

And here, a few paces from the last door, he stopped as he saw the light. It was only a strip of glow, almost imperceptible, at the threshold, a gleam so faint that its luminosity was more surmised than seen; the sound from that direction was surer than the sight.

The music diminishing now, until it was as peaceful as reverie, holding its level plane, seeming to do the impossible, making melody out of monotone.

Soft as the chanting, he moved toward the sound, toward the light.

His footsteps had musical cover, but his tread was all caution. Three steps, two, and he was there.

Behind this door . . . plainsong . . . and someone listening to it. All he had to do was reach for the doorknob and turn it. Confront and be confronted.

Abruptly a thought occurred to him: there might be no one there. The room might be altogether empty except for *cantus firmus*. The thought was, in a way he could not comprehend, chilling. Music in an empty room—it was a common phenomenon—why did it seem so intimidating to him, so ominous? And why was he so prophetically certain that the room was vacant, a void to be filled only by his dread?

Slowly he turned the knob. A slight turn only, not all the way, and the sound he made was sharper than the music. If somebody were in the room, he would have been heard, a voice would have called a question, there would have been an alarm, someone hurrying to the door. But . . . nobody.

The room was, as he had imagined, empty. It was another studio, an auxiliary one, perhaps, with skylight and booklined walls, with a few smaller pedestals than down below and smaller armatures, and a table full of sculptor's implements, gouges, knives, calipers, dividers, mounds of clay, a small revolving stand. All this he saw by light that came not from the room itself, but through a separation in the curtain that hung from the archway which separated this room from the one beyond. A heavy curtain—hemp, it looked like, roughly woven, drawn almost closed; only a line of light cutting through the gap, throwing a golden knifeblade on the floor.

And as though carried on the blade, the tones of music, the *cantus firmus,* quieter now, almost inaudible, an obbligato to the spoken voices.

No, not voices. Only a single voice, as hushed as prayer. For an instant, Michael thought it was indeed a prayer of some sort, the utterance was incantatory, as if a ritual were being conducted . . . so ceremonial in its expressionlessness that Michael couldn't identify the person speaking.

He took a step across the room. Another. Halfway to the archway, he knew.

It was Cory. Muted, almost unintelligible.

A few more steps and Michael could apprehend the words.

". . . but that would make perspective only an optical device, like a stereoscope, which supposedly gives the right perspective. But there is no *right* perspective. It is all an illusion, an accommodation of one eye to another. Perhaps it would have been better to have been created with only one of them. Sometimes I think I *am* better off."

Michael moved to the curtains and tried to peer through the crack between them. Only a panel of visibility into a room not brightly lighted; scarcely anything perceptible. If he dared to part the curtains a little . . .

"The artist who has only one eye has, strictly speaking, no perspective at all. The world, for him, does not have a right side *and* a left—it has no balance. But the world is imbalanced for everybody; when were the right and left ever poised evenly with one another? When was passion ever poised with reason? And since all perspective is illusion, the vision of passion is as true as the vision of reason, and certainly more beautiful. That there are excesses of it does not . . ."

The plainsong increased in volume and Cory's words were momentarily inaudible.

As the music subsided to a whisper, Michael opened the drapery a little. Before he could see the man, he heard him speak in a changed tone.

"But this failing of sight is also a failing of the spirit . . . and in that sense, I have sinned. . . . But I can never see a woman in this. No matter how I try, she will not enter the perspective, she refuses to come into the field of vision. She stays on my blind side. She is my blackness. She's my lack as a child, she's my pain when my eye was struck. And the pain is all mine. Even when I'm inflicting it, it's mine—terror inflicted, terror felt—hurt and be hurt—guilt—and no comfort from it—"

Terror . . . inflicted . . . felt. It was confession.

As clear as their presences were clear. They were sitting across from each other, Cory and Falga Cristobal, both of them motionless. At first, because they were both in shadow, he was not certain, but in a moment he could discern that they were naked. Cory was more in darkness, and unclear, but Cristobal's nudity was plain; a woman cast in all the loveliness her statues lacked. It was a body lushly opulent, more voluptuous than he had imagined, and younger, the breasts held high and firm, large breasts with nipples in the full, her skin the color of golden topaz, and hinting at the same translucence. She glowed with beauty.

Thinking chaos, he realized there was no chaos in the room, no disorder of any kind. The unearthly thing was that it was as sensual as an act of lovemaking, yet as sacred as the confessional; at least, to Cory it might be. Yet, there was something forlorn and derelict about it, a man altogether enthralled, enslaved to sick hungers, to guilts he could never expiate, and to this woman. He had never freed himself from her bewitchment, or had freed himself only temporarily, then returned to it, and to her. It seemed tragic to Michael—not only Cory's plight but hers as well, this death-loving woman—as only bedevilment is tragic. He had an impulse to withdraw quickly, disturbed at having eavesdropped on a confession, and—ignoring his purpose in coming here—he let the curtain slip out of his hand.

They must have seen the release of it.

The voice—Cory's—called out, "Who's there?"

Michael heard the stir of the young man, moving, heard the drapery being pulled. He turned.

Cristobal was getting into a negligee, as awkward now as she had been a woman of motionless grace a moment ago. She muttered something to Cory, and the artist, aware of his nakedness, turned back into the room.

She started toward Michael. "What are you doing here?"

He had no notion what he would say, or how inapposite the words would sound. "I've come to warn you."

"Warn us of what?" It was Cory, reappearing, pulling a bathrobe tightly around himself, joining them in the outer room. "What do you mean, warn? That you'll tell you've seen two people naked, that you're a peeping Tom?"

She was chillingly more to the point than either of them:
"Kill him."

It was unimpassioned. As clinically devoid of emotion as a doctor prescribing a routine specific. But, worse, at the colder heart of it was Cory's reaction. None. It was as if it was so much a part of the moment's necessity that he had had no need to hear her direction; he himself knew what had to be done. And no need for rush or agitation.

So this was the truth of Cory, he thought, he had come upon the one great lie of the man. When all the multiplicity of plausible and

419

verifiable details had been told, they all added up to the enormous falsehood of a murderer. Specializing in what kind of murders, he speculated . . . strangulations? . . . bombings?

Crucifixions?

Yet . . . something didn't fit. Michael couldn't believe that the delicate man, the one-time seminarian, all sensibilities exquisite, could take murder as composedly for granted as he was doing now. So self-certain in the task of it that he had no haste to go into action.

Michael spoke as evenly as he could: "There was a bombing this morning—the Piazza Navona."

"We know about that," she said.

"Do you know all about it?" He waited a moment. "Three terrorists were arrested."

"That isn't true."

Still as calmly as before, but her voice had quickened. He wished he knew what the haste meant. Either that she didn't know that the terrorists had been taken—or she was lying, and didn't want Cory to know. He hoped it was the last.

He looked at Cory. No telling what he knew; he was as still as one of her statues, as stony.

"Shall I tell you who's been arrested?" Michael asked.

"Kill him."

Urgency this time. Then she did know about the arrests . . . but how much?

He must speak more quickly, he warned himself, or—murder—he wondered how they would kill him, what they would do with his body, carry it away somewhere, of course—talk quickly. He reached into his pocket for the slip of paper with the names on it. He knew them by heart, but the paper was tangible, it gave him confidence, it made the evidence something palpable they would have to cope with.

"Their names—Alviero Bari, Adela Corlina, Guglielmo Luz." He put the paper on the worktable. "Bari was the man who . . . talked."

At the last word, Cory made an involuntary movement—he looked at Cristobal. She didn't meet his glance.

"He's lying," she said. "Bari would never say a word."

"The bomb went off prematurely," Michael said. "One of your people was killed—Bari was badly wounded. The *carabinieri* picked him up with the other two. When they carried him away, he was

420

screaming with pain—but they wouldn't give him any medication until he answered their questions . . . which he did."

"I don't believe it," she said. But she wasn't sure.

Michael pointed to the telephone. "Call Rome."

The faintest flicker of uncertainty, but she recovered from it. "I have no need to. I know."

It was an edge, almost imperceptible, but Michael had won it. He turned quickly to Cory. "Bari told everything he knew—the burning of a sacristy—the bombings, the savaging of priests—murder." Now he took the chance. "He said that in some cases they reported to you—"

Cory interrupted. "He didn't say that!"

"—that you gave orders."

"That's a lie!"

"Then Bari's lying—not I. And we can both suspect why he is."

This time Cory's glance at Cristobal hinted of panic. And something else as well: distrust. I've touched something in him, Michael thought, an abscess of suspicion. It's been there; it had to be; guilty partners don't trust each other.

Caught between the two of them, Cory confronted Cristobal. "Who's lying?"

Before she could answer, Michael interposed: "What's she going to say? She's setting you up—you're the scapegoat—what's she going to tell you?"

"You bastard!" Cristobal said.

The quick glances now, between the partners, the inevitable paranoia, each fighting the specter of betrayal. Keep going, Michael said.

"Your name was mentioned a dozen times, Cory—but her name, not once! And especially on the most terrible thing—Galestro's crucifixion!"

"No! I had nothing to do with that!"

It had worked. Even the denial, because it came so quickly and revealed his recognition, meant he knew about it. Whether the artist had perpetrated the act or not, he had been involved in it. The instant Cory said the words, he realized he had uncovered himself. Something in him seemed to fracture. He said hectically to Cristobal:

"How did Bari know about it?"

"He didn't, Cory!" She pointed to Michael. "He's lying—he's trying to trap you!—kill him!"

But Cory was in a rout, fleeing from what they themselves had dealt in, terror. "How did Bari know? You promised nobody would! How did he know?"

"I didn't tell him—I swear to you I didn't! And I'm sure Bari doesn't know. If anyone told them, it was Heskins!"

It was her first mistake.

"Heskins has not been arrested," Michael said.

Cory began to shake.

Abruptly Michael realized the artist knew that the battle for his life was lost; his soul was all he had left. But Michael would have to struggle to help him save it. Knowing the man's desperation to confess, he thought he had a chance to win. He must.

"Cory, get out of this if you can—save yourself!" Michael pleaded. "She's sold you out—every single time, she's sold you out! And she'll do it again. She'll deny everything, she'll stay at a safe distance, always in the clear. If they ask her anything, she'll say 'They did it.' And you're one of *them!* So, get out of it! Let me call the police—confess it—confess everything—one way or another, absolve yourself—save yourself!"

As he was talking, Cristobal stepped between them as if to shut out the light that was passing from one man to the other. But Cory suddenly turned away from her, from both of them. The artist's trembling seemed to worsen.

Then, in a moment, he faced them again. And his face was altogether changed. Michael thought: he's seen something, had a revelation. I've won, the priest said, with a welling of relief, I've helped him save his soul. The young man seemed at peace.

He hadn't noticed them, Michael realized—the calipers in Cavanaugh's hand. They seemed not to belong there, not appropriate. Nor did the embrace seem appropriate, yet it might have been only a farewell. The artist was taking her in his arms, as if to beg forgiveness, as if to get past the quarrel in some way.

But when he stepped away from the embrace, Michael saw the other thing, the blood. He thought it didn't belong here, wrong place, wrong substance. One of the arms of the caliper was in her, below her breast, and the blood was coursing along the instrument and dripping from it, flowing quickly, gushing, starting to redden her body. The strange thing was: she remained standing for so long. When she slipped to the floor:

"Oh, Christ," he said.

He saw Cory rushing from the room. Michael hurried to her. Oh,

Christ, was all he could say, oh, Christ. As he kneeled beside her, her lips were moving, but no words. Then she did a macabre thing: she put her hand on the calipers, touched them with her fingertips and seemingly tried to smile. Again, she attempted to say something. He couldn't understand all of it, but caught the butcher-word. She was saying, he supposed, that this was another object for the table. . . .

Her body was still alive, he thought . . . but then the rigor came to her eyes. In a moment, she quivered, and was motionless.

Slowly, he arose. He didn't know what to do, where to go. Cory, where was Cory?

The police . . . he'd have to call them. He crossed the room to the telephone. It shook in his hand. He dialed the operator, had no idea what he said. Somebody was asking an address, and he didn't know it. Then, the building—he did remember its name, and gave it. Third floor, he added.

Cory . . . he must go to Cory.

The artist was in the other room, sitting in the chair he had occupied when he had been talking nakedly to the woman now dead. He had his hands together and, for an instant, Michael thought they were in the child's gesture of prayer. But they were clenched; his face was just as tight.

He had heard Michael's phone call. "They'll be here soon," he said.

"Yes."

"What shall I tell them?"

"Everything."

The artist tried to smile. "Confession . . . Will they give me absolution, do you think?"

"I can give it to you."

"No," he said quietly. Then he unclenched his hands, and loosened a little. His voice became eerily ruminative as if he were talking about an academic matter of little personal concern. "I shouldn't have gone back to her," he said.

"When did you?"

"The night after they tried to hurt you . . . the strangling . . . I had nothing to do with that."

"And Warrum?"

"Nothing . . . I was never really mixed up with the murderous things. A bombing once, but no people involved. Burnings—three of them—only property, that's all. But the violence—to people—it made me ill. You'd have been dead long ago if I hadn't begged her. He's not dangerous, I said—please let him alone. . . . I wasn't involved in any of the murders. . . . Until Galestro."

No attempted smile anymore, no further concealment of his pain. "I knew him years ago—that summer at the Feradoti's," Cory said. "We all had the same passion for plainsong. I still have it . . . it soothes me." He became aware that the music had stopped. He reached behind him to a small table on which there was a record player with old seventy-eights on it. About to turn it on, he desisted, seemed to listen to the quiet. "In those days—all the time—the music would be playing all the time. How beautiful that summer was . . . if I had only known it then. . . . I never really liked Galestro. He was a weak man, he took all sides of everything. But I was against killing him. I couldn't bear the thought that they were going to do it. But then—Falga and I—everything between us was falling apart—and I was getting desperate. She said I was a coward—she was contemptuous of me. And then I realized: she was going to send me away. There was a need, she said, for a great shock and a great occasion and a great hero. She talked in that frantic theatrical way, she mesmerized. And suddenly it happened—what I dreaded. I had the choice between losing her and being honored.

"Heskins and I did it. Up to a certain point it was easy. The gate open, the door open—the old man welcoming—the music playing. And all at once—Heskins' knife—and the man was bleeding. But it was too strange . . . the knife was protruding from exactly where his heart must have been—and he hadn't yet been stabbed in any other place—but the blood was gushing out of his mouth. I remember thinking: why was he bleeding from his mouth? 'The wrong blood,' I kept saying, 'the wrong blood.' . . . And it was all over me—my clothes, my hair.

"I heard Heskins say, 'Hold him against the wall'—but I didn't understand. Then I saw it—he had an iron bar in his hand—and nails—and I said, 'Oh, my God, don't do it!' And suddenly everything changed. It didn't seem to matter how much blood I had all over me, or where it came from. 'Hold him,' Heskins said. 'Don't let him fall.' And I heard the nails going through bone and plaster, and some places the plaster gave way, it wouldn't hold, and we had to shift him, and then the hands were nailed and I let go for a moment and the body moved a little, and Heskins said, 'Hold him, for Christ's sake!' And when he said that, I couldn't stand it and I ran—I ran from everything—from it—from her—from God. . . . And finally

I ran back to Lucas. . . . And he wouldn't confess me."

He let out a cry as agonized as Golgotha. His head upraised, he kept repeating the sound and repeating it.

Michael couldn't comfort him. He moved away, drifted onto the gallery passage where he awaited the arrival of the police. In a little while, he heard the sound of a car. As he walked along the gallery, just as he was about to go down the steps he heard the shot.

He rushed into the room, then through the curtained doorway into the inner room. Cory lay on the floor with the gun in his hand. The bullet had pierced his one good eye and the eyesocket was filling with blood. The other eye, sightless, stared in a kind of impudence.

"I don't know which of them was better-looking," Lieutenant Zeckley said. Then he added something about how sad it was that such attractive people . . .

It was, Michael considered, a routine regret. The policeman was taking grim gratification in the closing of a case.

Michael sat in a small cleared area on the lower floor of the sculptor's studio. Within arm's reach an enormous stone figure was draped in muslin; shrouds, he thought. He wondered what would happen to the beautiless colossi she had sculpted. They would probably be junked, for the most part; it wouldn't have mattered to her, she hated all of them.

Zeckley gave an order to his assistant, another plainclothesman, who passed it on to a uniformed policeman. The latter went to the phone, dialed, and spoke softly into it.

There had been others here, the coroner's man, a woman who had taken measurements with a tape, two men with lights and cameras. Only a few minutes ago, the bodies had been removed.

Surprising, Michael mused, how few questions had been asked. Zeckley was not concerned with causes or consequences, only with the facts that labeled the phenomenon, and how to put them succinctly in the report. Murder and suicide, weapons at scene of crime, witness present, case concluded. As to motive: since both corpses were nearly naked—no matter what other complexities Zeckley might suspect— he would write it down as a lovers' quarrel. How ironic for both of them; especially for the star-blighted Cristobal; how sadly bitter that she had wanted death for a cause, a hero's death—the noble fall of an earthquaking revolutionary—and she would be scribbled down as one who had died in the nasty ruction of a perverted passion.

425

"Will you need me anymore?" Michael asked.

"No, Father—and thank you," the detective answered. "You better get some rest—you look terrible."

He felt terrible; he felt ill in all the impalpable places. He rose heavily and started toward the door. Well before he reached it, he heard Zeckley say to his assistant, "Has the Cardinal been told?"

"It's five o'clock," the other detective answered. "I thought I'd wait until daylight."

"Better not. What's the nearest precinct to him—the Seventeenth, I guess. Have them send a man over."

Have them send a man over. Michael shivered. A man *had* been sent, weeks ago, from the Vatican, a man with a warning and a plea, and he hadn't been listened to, and had failed. The Cardinal had not changed. Now, another man would be sent—and still the Cardinal would not change.

Goddamn him. Cory had been right: Goddamn him.

Michael's fury was irrational, compounded of frustrations of his own, by the Cardinal's not responding to his entreaties that he compromise; it was a rage at having been beaten by the man, at having been rendered useless in a cause he had been willing to die for.

But now he had a new charge against the Cardinal, and a new wrath. It was outrage against this horror Michael had seen, this tragedy that the Cardinal might have prevented; an outrage at the man's refusal of comfort and consolation to his brother, his denial of Christ's love and forgiveness.

Goddamn him.

The lights were on in the Cardinal's house, which meant he had been told.

Michael rang the bell.

He prayed to an Old Testament God: keep my rage alive.

Mrs. Merrill, at the door, opened it narrowly. "He's not seeing anyone," she said.

"Let me in."

"Nobody—he said nobody."

He pushed at the door and she made a frightened sound. He shoved harder, jostled past her, through the dark foyer, into the prelate's waiting room, and through the double doors that led into his study.

The old man sat at his desk. He was wearing a dark robe, his face a ruin of grief. Mrs. Merrill fretted at the doorway. Vaguely Cavanaugh waved her away.

"You killed him," Michael said.

The Cardinal lamely raised his arm as if he had been struck.

"You killed him. You denied him what he needed most—you denied him what the Church must give. Whatever else it refuses—absolution—! You withheld it from him—you withheld Christ Himself!"

Tortured, the Cardinal closed his eyes. "I never wanted to confess him—even years ago—believe me, I never wanted to begin it. But he wouldn't go to anyone else—even as a child, he wouldn't. If I didn't confess him, he stopped altogether—he gave up penance. It was like an illness. And if I didn't absolve him, I'd see him growing sick with guilt, sicker all the time—he was living in a constant torment. What could I do? I had to confess him—he was all I had—I loved him!"

"Then how could you *stop* confessing him? Why did you?"

"Because I—" It was too painful; he couldn't continue.

"Why?"

"*He didn't confess to me in order to repent—he did it to punish me!*"

The old man started to tremble. Then he resumed, more quietly. "He said I had abandoned him—I was his 'cruelty,' he called me—the cruel father, the cruel mother. I had deserted him. Every woman he hurt, every time he violated love in some way, he was telling me *I* violated it! He knew it tortured me to hear what he was doing—his sick hungers—his violences. His confession was revenge." Shaking desperately, the prelate brought his forearms close to his body, tightly, like a vise containing himself.

"But I listened to him," he went on. "I always listened and gave him absolution—and every time I confessed him I took his torments into myself, and made myself sick with them. . . . But then the terrible thing happened. This time, when he came back from Jerusalem—after you saw him there—he was strangely silent, and he didn't ask to be confessed. If he visited, he wouldn't talk—he would go upstairs to his old bedroom and play the plainsong records. One night, Father Lauren called me. He had just returned from the Vatican. He's a friend of Monsignor de Gamez and he heard a hideous rumor that Cardinal Galestro had died by crucifixion. When he told me this, I had a nightmare—horrifying—my brother had done it! I knew he couldn't be guilty of such an atrocity, and I loathed myself for thinking it. That same evening, Cory came to me to be confessed. And I had that agonizing thought again—what if he *had* done it? I was terrified he might confess to me—and I couldn't stand it—so I told him no, I would no longer confess him. I kept telling myself no, he could not possibly have done it. If he had, he would have blurted it out, confession or no confession. But that wasn't the way his mind worked. He would think that sooner or later I *must* listen to his confession, and he would have the added revenge of violating not only me but the sacrament itself. So I kept saying no—I wouldn't confess him—no! And then one night he shouted at me and cursed me, and at last went away. . . . I never confessed him again—and he died unabsolved—and it's my fault. I'll never forgive myself for imagining he could have committed such an atrocity against God."

"He did commit it."

"Oh, dear Jesus—no!"

He emitted a sound that was an echo of his brother's, all suffering, a torment beyond tears.

Don't be touched by him, Michael warned himself. He wanted to keep his rage alive, but he couldn't. The old man had performed the most self-racking deed: he had defended the sacrament at the expense of his deepest feeling. And now it was not enough for the grieving prelate to know that he had done the just, the moral, the religious thing, he had not done what to him was the human thing: he had not forgiven his brother. And he could not—might never—forgive himself.

"Christ will forgive you," Michael said.

But even the consolation of Jesus gave no ease to the old man, he would not be comforted, it was a measure of his despair. He sat there, gray and sick. Michael felt Cavanaugh's affliction as if it were his own, and couldn't help him. I mustn't watch this agony, he said; he wants only the solitude of it. He started to leave.

As he reached the door, he heard the Cardinal's voice. "Please wait." Michael turned. "Could you. . . stay a few moments?"

Michael hesitated. Only a short while ago, the prelate had left instructions he wanted to see nobody; and now, one would imagine, he would have a more pressing need to be alone.

The Cardinal was at pains to steady himself; he faced Michael unflinchingly. "I want you to do me a very special service."

Even before Michael could respond, the prelate lowered his head into his cupped hands, hiding his face. The priest couldn't perceive what the movement meant, whether the old man was in prayer or simply trying to shut the world out, to absent himself in darkness. At last the Cardinal removed his hands.

"Bless me, Father, for I have sinned," he said.

An image glimmered in Michael's mind: the Pope, begging the same favor. And even more poignantly this time, Michael felt unsuited to hear the confession. He thought of his own frailties, he thought of Nora, of his own sins, unexpiated. He knew it didn't matter—he himself needn't be absolved of sin in order to give absolution. It was one of the mysteries of penance that allowed him to do so—and, ironically, it was the original version of *The Last Magic,* in which Michael had written his understanding of the mystery, that this man had so savagely condemned. Yet he felt pity for the old man, and, even if he were given the right to do so, he could not deprive him of absolution.

"Help me, oh Lord, to judge gently, as in mercy thou judgest me."

The words were barely spoken when he heard Cavanaugh's agony. Tearing the decorum of the ritual, the Cardinal cried out in a passion of heartbreak:

"Oh, Christ, forgive me! Oh, dear Jesus, forgive me for needing to be right! Forgive me that my brother is dead and unabsolved—and let me bear his sins! Forgive me that I withheld your love and mercy! Oh, Christ, oh dear Christ—!"

For a moment he could not continue. He wept.

After the confession, the prelate asked Michael to stay a bit longer. He wanted to know everything, every detail of the death of his brother, as if the knowledge were a punishment that might redress all earthly wrongs.

When Michael had finished, the Cardinal arose and walked to the window. "There was nothing the world could ever do for him—he could not be reconciled to it."

Reconciled. Michael wondered if the old man heard himself saying the word. Was he using the term as a generality? Life irreconcilable with death, with disease, with old age, heartache, loneliness? Or did he now understand the specifics of it, as applied not only to Cory, but to himself? Did his confession mean that he knew he too was one of the irreconcilable men who make a world where death comes suddenly, with violence, with terror, with devastations of the earth . . . and even without absolution?

429

The night was over. Crimson on the boundary between earth and sky, then streaks of sunlight, bright attenuated veins of gold.

There was a knock on the door and Mrs. Merrill entered. She was carrying the morning paper. Her face told them that the news was bad. How soon they've reported the murder and suicide, Michael thought, how quickly it has become part of the public malice.

She handed the paper to Cavanaugh. He held it to the light and scanned it briefly. Then, murmuring something indistinct, he crossed himself and gave the paper to Michael.

The priest had been wrong. There was no mention of Cory and Cristobal. The newspaper carried the start of an account of the Navona bombing, but it was only a secondary feature of the front page. The primary one was a huge picture of His Holiness, with the banner headline:

THE POPE IS DEAD

He too crossed himself, perused the opening paragraph, read of the Pontiff's passing quietly and peacefully in the twilight of the night before.

He put the paper down. Two deaths, a bombing and the passing of the Pope. The heaviness inside him was almost insupportable.

The prelate had possibly not noticed the story of the Navona bombing, or else was too preoccupied with the Pope's death. "Poor man. Except for his faith, he was always in doubt about everything. I hope he is no longer so." It must have been minutes later that he added. "You will be going back to the Vatican, then. And so will I."

The conclave to elect the new Pope would not be held for two weeks. The Cardinal's Synod would happen in a few days. Michael said bitterly, "The timing is perfect for you."

The Cardinal's eyes met Michael's. "No. It's too late. We are all in mourning. Who would attend a Synod now? . . . It will not be held."

The Synod canceled. It was precisely what Michael had come for, yet now that it had happened, he felt a knot of frustration. He himself had accomplished nothing. To have tried so hard, to have been rejected and insulted and physically attacked, and, no matter what his effort, to have failed; then, to have won on nothing more than a happenstance of time, the caprice of mortality—it enraged him.

If only he could feel that Cavanaugh's experience with Cory had

430

taught him that irreconcilability was at the heart of the human tragedy, if only the Cardinal could believe that Michael's mission had been to reconcile, and that it was worth accomplishing. . . .

"Would you tell me something?" Michael said. The Cardinal turned to him. "Suppose His Holiness were alive. After what has happened to you—to all of us—would you still go on with the Synod?"

The old man tried to look forthrightly at Michael, but couldn't. It was as if the priest had added another torture. At last he replied, "I have been asking myself that. Perhaps tomorrow—perhaps next year—I will be able to answer it. But right now—God help me, I don't know."

. . . Walking away from the Cardinal's house, in the early morning sunlight, Michael had a sudden insight, and the heaviness in him was lifted a little.

Only yesterday, if he had asked the prelate the same question, the man's resolve would have been adamant; he would have been cold and immovable. Today, he was shaken.

If conciliation was the answer, what hope of it with Nora?

As he approached Mindszenty House, he grew alarmed that she might no longer be there. She might have considered last night's anger the final exchange they would have with each other. Not that he would blame her for thinking so, but he desperately hoped she didn't, and that she hadn't gone.

Yet, how could they come to an understanding with one another? He who had called himself a peacemaker had set a rigid, uncompromising limit with someone he loved. But somewhere a man must draw a line, must say: beyond this point, no yielding, no arbitration of differences—for the difference in this case was life. The life of an unborn child.

Somehow he must convince Nora of this. Rationally. He mustn't be overwrought, as they both were last night. He must sensibly, and without antagonism, help her to see his point of view, that it was sane and justifiable and human. And he *could* convince her—she was not a cynic—he would find some way. Somehow, he must.

He hurried up the brownstone steps and unlocked the door. On the second floor, there was no sign of her. The dishes all washed and put away, the birthday cake in the refrigerator, candles and all, the breviary on the sideboard where it always was, and nothing of Nora anywhere, not her robe or slippers in the closet or her toothbrush in the bathroom. Not even a note.

Slowly, having already given up in his mind, he started to climb the stairs to the third floor, toward her room.

She was sitting there, at her desk, the surface of which was absolutely bare. Her books were tied together, her papers. Her portable typewriter, in its case, was on the floor to the left of her, and her suitcase was to the right. She scarcely looked at him.

Departure in everything, and he couldn't stand it. "I'm glad you didn't go without saying goodbye," he said.

She looked up and must have seen the damage that a night of sleeplessness had done to his face. "Are you all right? Did you go to Cristobal's?"

"Yes," he said. He wanted to get away from the subject and back to them. "Nora—"

"What happened?"

Telling it to her, he tried to make it sound less grisly than it was, but he knew he wasn't succeeding.

"Are you sure you're all right?" she asked. "You look awful."

He thought she did, too. Her face was pale, her eyes seemed to have lost their color. He wondered if she'd been nauseated again.

She got up from the chair and started to arrange her baggage so she could carry everything.

"I'll help you with those," he said.

"It's all right." Subdued. "I've got them organized so I can carry them myself."

"Were you sick again?"

"It doesn't matter." She didn't meet his glance. "It'll only be a few days."

"Isn't there some way—some rational way we can talk about it?"

". . . I don't think so, Michael."

"Even if we don't talk on a religious basis?"

"What other basis is there? For you?"

"Yours," he replied. "What's the simplest fact we can both agree on?"

"The simplest fact is that I'm pregnant," she said. "And from there on, we can't agree on anything. . . . Because I don't want this child."

432

"You say 'this child' as though it had nothing to do with either of us. It's *ours*, Nora. It came from loving one another."

"Please—don't. Do you think I don't love *us?*"

Suddenly they were clinging to one another, knowing there was nothing further to say, and soon they'd go their ways and never see each other again. He wanted to cry that he had cheated her, as he felt cheated too. It had been a swindle; fairer if they had never met, if he had never known this sort of love, this touching and holding and warming one's self with another's body, and the awareness of someone close in what had always been the loneliness of night. He felt defrauded and ashamed of his naïveté in having believed there was promise in it, and wanted to forget it had ever happened. Then he realized he would never forget, and never truly wanted this part of his life forgotten, and that he would always love her.

He helped her down to the street and, carrying her suitcase and her typewriter, walked with her to the corner where her car was parked. He asked her a number of times whether she was all right, as if there were something he could do about it. As she drove away she turned to look at him briefly, only for an instant; his throat caught and he couldn't swallow.

It's over, he thought, and now I must do something about confession. He took a few steps toward St. Malachy's, and stopped. It is too soon, he said. I don't know what to say to my confessor, I don't know what to say. He turned and went back to Mindszenty House, unconfessed and unabsolved.

The phone was ringing. It was Lieutenant Zeckley. They had found Heskins, he said, and picked him up. The man had had no reluctance to talk. On the contrary, he had been defiant, had boasted about the atrocities, called them heroic acts of revolution, and wanted them proclaimed. In that spirit, he had proclaimed the names of five others, including Cassie Macramé, who were implicated in the heroism. Zeckley felt sure he'd lay hands on all of them. . . . If Michael was leaving the country, would he be available for a preliminary deposition in Vatican City? Michael said, yes, he would be available.

After Zeckley's call, he remained in the dismal hallway, unmoving, irresolute about everything. After a while, he telephoned Feradoti. He told the Secretary of the deaths of Cristobal and the artist. Through all Michael's account of what had occurred, the Cardinal scarcely uttered a word. But when Michael came to the end of it, and Cory's

433

suicide, he heard an intake of breath and then Cory's name, murmured a few times, and the words *mio Dio, mio Dio.*

"I'm taking a plane tonight," Michael concluded.

He heard the same murmuring, and they both hung up.

He telephoned to make a reservation on tonight's seven o'clock flight to Rome.

He got into the shower and let the water run as hot as he could stand it, to take the ache out of his bones. As he finished, he noticed he'd been using Nora's tar soap. The shower had warmed his body, but he felt deeply cold.

Twenty

"YOU GOT TWO LETTERS from your mother," Kellman said. He opened the glass case behind him and picked the pale blue envelopes off the lens boxes. Passing them across the counter: "I got one too," he said. "She was worried because you didn't answer her first one, so she wrote to me. . . . You don't look good, Nora, where've you been these weeks?"

"I've been staying in Manhattan with a friend."

He carried her suitcase up the stairs, she carried the rest. When she had thanked him out of the kitchen, she poured herself a glass of water. Drink it slowly, she said, in tiny sips.

She opened her mother's first letter. It was a querulous plaint; she didn't like the sun, she didn't like the people, her brother's wife was a pain; she grieved for her husband. The second letter, when the conventional grieving paragraph was over, said she liked Florida better than she had expected, she'd found an excellent suntan lotion, the people were surprisingly nice, she wondered what it would be like to live here always, she'd written to Kellman suggesting that he buy half the business and he had jumped at the offer, they'd be partners, she could trust him, he'd never nick a cent. Besides, as she had said before, there were nice people here. She meant, of course, that there were men. Good for you, Mama, she thought, you'll be all right, with your vigorous tropism for sun and sex.

She vomited.

It was the first time it had ever happened by daylight. Classic now, she speculated, the classic mourning sickness.

Why had she thought mourning instead of morning? She'd better stop this maundering; vomiting was better.

She had forty-eight hours left. The day after tomorrow, at this time, she'd be in the hospital.

The retching, as the day wore on, was getting painful, hurting her stomach, scalding her throat, making her feel as if her brain were shaking loose. She had a dread, spewing as she was in daylight, that she'd have to spend the rest of the time, until the doctor took over, turning her insides out. She felt green. If only it would stop for an hour or two. She must tell herself what it would feel like when it was over, all over, and her stomach at peace again. What a relief it would be, what a deliverance.

Deliverance. Bad word. She must be careful of these connotations; they were confusing; they made her queasier.

Sick.

The hell of it was she had been on the couch too long, had read too many books for her not to realize that the war of have-the-child-or-abort-it had to be settled before her stomach would be. And to win the war, she must remind herself that this was not a child in her belly, it was a tumor, an ugly parasite; that the feeling within her was not glorious growth and enrichment, it was injury, that she was not an artist of nature, but nature's patsy. Which, by terminating the pregnancy, she would cease to be.

She vomited.

She tried another tack. It was her prerogative, she had the unassailable right not to have the child. God knows, she said, women get caught in all sorts of traps—of status and marriage and vocation—snares from which most of them never get sprung. She had been running from one after another of them all her life, and never really free. Well, from *this* trap she could really free herself. She had the *choice*.

She threw up.

At last, during a respite, something happened. She had a dark inspiration. The creature inside her, she reasoned, was torturing her because it knew she meant to kill it. Well, she would outwit the little monster—she would lull it into quietude, she would lie to it. She would tell it she had changed her mind, she was going to let it have its own way, going to allow it to be born.

So she started the perverse falsehood and kept saying it to the thing inside her and, little by little, her nausea was relieved. But sometimes, during the remainder of the day, she became confused, and wasn't sure whom the lie was convincing. Then, toward sundown, the spasms returned.

It served her right, she said: she knew clearly she had been lying, and it knew it just as well.

There was another lie, however, that wasn't so clear in her mind. She had a sense that she was perpetrating one, but couldn't identify it. It was right there, on the threshold of her consciousness, distressing her—some falsehood she was thinking or had thought, some truth omitted, some evidence withheld.

If she could only find it . . .

It occurred to her at daybreak.

It was so clear, so simple; it was thrilling and it was terrifying.

Until now, when she had thought of freedom of choice—the freedom women were fighting for—she had thought only of her right to have the abortion.

But she had another right. A right more difficult to implement, and demanding more courage than she might have if she was to exercise it to its conclusion.

The right to *have* the child.

To have it whether she was married or not, to have it whether its father was a priest or a murderer, to have it if it had no father at all, to have it whether she had money or time or even heart enough to care for it.

Thousands of unmarried women were having children today. It was not only acceptable; it even had a sort of romantic valor about it. But it was an option more easily chosen by a romantic, which she was not. The unrelenting realities loomed too clearly for her.

Until now such a choice would be made for her by others—by her Judeo-Christian upbringing, by the pragmatic traditions of her mother and her dead father, by the dictates of prudence and economy

437

and respectability; by the fact that she was a middle-class Jewish girl from New York; by her terrible responsibility to her logical and questioning mind.

But another choice *was* available to her if she had the courage to reach for it. She could have the child . . .

. . . if she really wanted it.

Did she?

She must beware of sentimental persuasions, she must stay tough.

She would not make the decision on the basis that she was pushing thirty, and alone. She would not fall into the trap of the free women, emancipated from men and the need to cling to them, and finally, in loneliness, clutching at their children. She did not want a child so that she could be its dependency. Did she want it, then, for its dependency on her? Was she hungering to be needed? Was she yearning to respond to a helpless cry, she who had known how helpless a cry can be? Seductive . . . beware.

Nor must she get seduced by tender speculations as to whether it would be a boy or a girl, whether it would look like him or herself, the first step it would take, the first word it would utter. And she mustn't get caught by the sentiment that it was now, at this very moment, a human being. It was not.

She was avoiding the obvious reason: she might have the child because she loved its father. But she knew that of all the decoys, love was the most dangerous, the romantic enticement that lures a woman to surrender self-respect, volition, common sense. She could get caught in two stages: first, she would tell herself that if she had to become pregnant, the saving grace was that she had been made so by a man she loved; second, she would wind up by yielding, by having the child because it was a loving, a divine accident. But there was no divinity in this, none. Remember that.

Michael would argue to the contrary, that this was not her child or his, but God's, and that neither of them had a right to destroy it. Wrong, it was theirs. And if she was to have this child, it was not because it was God's, but theirs—and they wanted it.

She wanted it. She had lied to Michael—she did want it. But was that enough?

No—stay tough—it wasn't. It was not sufficient simply to want a fatherless child—knowing there would be hardships within hardships which she and it would have to share—unless she could believe that this son, this daughter had some special worth.

At last she had discovered it.

438

It was the worth of the parents. Worthy . . . it was a good way to describe Michael; but, attributable to herself, it was a new idea, a beautiful dress she wasn't certain she could wear. That might be the essence of it—he had helped her to find her worth.

She didn't know exactly how it had come about; she was reluctant to say that love makes miracles. But it had done one extraordinary thing for her. It had let her look at the worst of herself, and not reach for razor blades. It had even let her expose her worst to someone else, and when he was not repelled by her, but loved her—and showed her she was lovable—suddenly she was equal to herself, and not a failure any longer. She might still, some time or other, be discharged from a job, but she would never again be discharged from life, not by anyone, certainly not by herself. Farewell to bracelets.

As to the job of having the child, she was equal to that too. No question in her mind. And probably that was the best reason for having it: the sense that she was worthy of the task—the creative task—that she could fill and illuminate a role she would never run from, and in which she could see herself, without being afraid.

Worthiness, yes . . . she could wear it becomingly, she thought.

Michael would, most certainly, ascribe this change in her to a grace of God. She knew that wasn't so; the grace was Michael's, and her own. And, for all their contrary beliefs, it was the grace of the two of them, together.

Hopeful that the same grace would be in their son, their daughter, and feeling that the mathematical probabilities were all on the infant's side, she knew she had to give birth to it.

She telephoned the hospital and canceled her appointment.

She felt inordinately calm. Even her stomach might be settling down. I'm not blissful, she thought, for bliss is perfect, and Michael isn't here, a void. . . . Well, something less than bliss would have to content her. It was more than she had ever had.

Twenty-One

THE COUNTRY WAS HUNG in black. Not only Vatican
City, but all Italy; Rome was enshrouded. He had not been a beloved Pope, not nearly so cherished as John, but death confers
affection. Not only upon the dead, but upon his fellowship, and
Michael belonged to it. In the airport, the customs man lowered his
voice to him, and the porter touched him a few times on the shoulder.
The news vendor, from whom Michael bought the papers, crossed
himself as he accepted Michael's money; an old woman took the
priest by the hand and walked in silence with him a little way.

The front pages of the newspapers belonged to the dead Pope; the
inside pages carried pictures of the Navona bombing. The Piazza
looked wartorn and desolate. While waiting for a taxi and overhear-
ing conversations, he noted that very little of the talk had to do with
the destruction—terrorism had become a Roman banality; most of it
was about the Papa and who his successor might be. He thought: the

Pope has snatched the front page from Cristobal. And he never heard the two subjects mentioned together; as if they had no bearing on one another.

From his apartment, Michael telephoned Cardinal Feradoti's office. The Secretary was not in today, an assistant told him, but had left instructions for Michael to reach him, as soon as possible, in the country.

It was mid-week. The Cardinal was never in the country except on weekends or special holidays. "Is anything wrong?" Michael asked.

"No, nothing wrong," the assistant said. Then, seemingly, a pointed silence.

The phone in the country rang a long time. Just as Michael was going to ask for another connection, he heard the familiar voice. "Michael—welcome home." Then, abruptly, without gracious inquiries as to his health or the comfort of the flight: "Can you come to a meeting quickly? This afternoon?"

"Yes, of course. Here—or in the country?"

"The country. Can you make the noon train?"

"Certainly."

Hardly another word was spoken. He had rarely heard Feradoti speak to him so curtly. It puzzled him. He was in a hurry for Michael's report, of course; yet, the Cardinal already knew the essentials of it—Michael had phoned him before leaving New York. Today, his voice had sounded tense; there might be a new trouble.

Michael unpacked in haste, and, routing jet lag as best he could, caught the noon train just as it was pulling out of the station.

When he arrived, the meeting had already started. He and Ledagrazia had time for only a quick embrace, then he hurried into the solarium.

The meeting was a surprise. He had expected a confidential gathering—Feradoti, van Tenbroek, de Gamez and himself—a small enough group so that he could give a complete report, without reservation. De Gamez wasn't there. Only cardinals were present; not a few, but eleven of them. Van Tenbroek, Feradoti, five other Italians, Fellinger from Chicago, Salinas from Mexico, Josgaru from Nigeria, and Bergfalk from Sweden. They were all, as one of the Italians later expressed it, of *la prima influenza*. Separately, each of them was a principal who might be representing others; together, they represented a wide range of political opinion, from van Tenbroek on the left to Bergfalk on the right.

441

But all of them, in meeting—and Michael invited to address it? Surely, he thought, Feradoti did not intend for him to make a report to such an influential and heterogeneous group?

But it was indeed Feradoti's intention. "I want everyone to know—openly—what your mission was, and that I knew about it. . . . And, of course, how it concluded."

Van Tenbroek added heavily, "We would also like to know the details of the Galestro . . . circumstance."

Feradoti saw Michael's discomposure. "Since the Galestro matter is no longer confidential, please feel free to tell us whatever . . ." He didn't finish the sentence but made a vague gesture to complete his meaning.

Ill at ease, Michael told it as succinctly as he could. Hearing their first questions, he realized that they had already known much of what he had to say, had already expressed their horror over the Cory-Cristobal havoc, their commiseration with Cardinal Cavanaugh, their execration of the Navona bombing. Wryly, he realized it had taken all those catastrophes to bring them finally together.

The questions ceased and the cardinals were silent. Feradoti's gravity was, Michael thought, leavened by the Secretary's pride in his protégé.

Van Tenbroek said, "Terrible as it must have been for you, you've been rewarded with success."

"If you mean the exposure of the terrorists, that was not my mission."

"The prevention of the Synod," van Tenbroek said.

Michael was on the verge of saying he might not have prevented the Synod if the Pope had died a month later, but Feradoti forestalled him. "You've done more than prevent the Synod, Michael . . . at least we think you have."

A number of cardinals exchanged glances. Bergfalk smiled to one of the Italians, Cardinal di Lillo. There was a pleasurable secret in the room.

"We feel," said Cardinal Fellinger, with pedantic precision, "that you may have had a salutary influence on Cardinal Cavanaugh."

"How do you know that?"

Cardinal Salinas blurted: "He did not attend the meeting."

They all looked at the Mexican Cardinal quickly.

"What meeting?" Michael asked.

Salinas had apparently made a gaffe. Josgaru hid his giggle behind

442

his hand. Di Lillo coughed discreetly behind a scented handkerchief. Bergfalk stroked the corner of his mouth with his ring finger.

"You may as well tell him," van Tenbroek said to Salinas.

The Mexican grimaced embarrassedly. "Apparently Cardinal Margotto arranged a meeting somewhat like this one. I was invited to attend, but I declined. I was given to understand—secretly, I must say—that many others did not attend. Among those who were absent—Cardinal Cavanaugh."

It was a good sign. Margotto's prelates were deserting him. The movement was away from the reactionaries.

Something Salinas had said—a minor phrase—had caught Michael's attention. In describing Margotto's meeting he had called it "a meeting somewhat like this one." Was this also a caucus? In Feradoti's house? But who had called it? Surely not Feradoti; it was not in the Secretary's nature to electioneer for himself. Yet, who else could have called this session—and arranged for it, away from the Vatican—here?

As if specifically to answer Michael's questions, Feradoti had risen. "I have invited you here so that there would be no false impressions—either about Father Farris's mission—or about me personally." He spoke carefully, with a clear effort to remain reflective and unemotional. It was apparently not easy for him. "Some of you may write my name in the conclave. I shall be touched by your faith in me—and not feel worthy of it. Particularly, I dread that your faith will be misplaced if you do not correctly identify me. I have been called a moderate. That is true—I am. I have been called a partisan of the blessed Pope John. That is also true—I am. But in order to be John's partisan it is not enough merely to say that one believes in everything he enacted—*one must believe in everything he might enact if he were alive today.* And that would perhaps seem to many people in the Church—and to a number of cardinals in this room—a more radical movement than John himself might have made. But I am convinced that, viewing our world as it is today, he would have led that movement. . . In any event, I certainly would. I refer to the most troubled issues of the Church—the poor, the penitential, the celibacy of priests, the democratization of the clergy, brotherhood with all mankind and not with Catholics alone, the control of birth, the causes of women."

He spoke for a number of minutes more; not long. He said nothing Michael had not heard from him many times, and in many different

443

ways, during the years he had worked in the Secretariat. But there was one difference. He was no longer trying to be politic; there was no temporizing strategy in it. He had already ceased being the diplomat, and was becoming the Pope.

And it might have lost him the papacy.

When he was finished . . . again, the silence. But this stillness was tangible, it had a depressing thickness.

They're going to desert him, Michael thought, they're going to run for cover. Bergfalk, the farthest to the political right, would be the first. He would think about it a moment, then stand up and stalk out without a word. Fellinger, the meticulous, the cautious would follow; the Italian from Torino right after him. Salinas would slip away.

Nobody departed.

In fact, it was Bergfalk who started the discussion. "None of this is exactly front page news about you, Your Eminence."

Somebody laughed, the tension eased, somebody moved his chair closer to Feradoti's. In a few minutes they were all speaking animatedly, and at once.

Not long thereafter, Michael thought it tactful to drift away from the meeting; they were all cardinals.

He wandered out onto the *terrazza* to look for Ledagrazia. Their embrace had been too brief; he longed to talk to her at length. What he wanted to talk about was Nora . . . he had a sorrow that might be soothed if only he could utter her name.

"When I heard about Cory, I didn't cry," Leda said. "But then I awakened in the middle of the night, and for the first time in all these years, I couldn't remember his face. I tried and I tried, but I couldn't bring it back. Then I remembered a snapshot I took of him, that summer he was here. He was standing right there—by the fish pond—he was painting. How beautiful he was. Well, I looked for the picture and I looked, and I couldn't find it. Then I knew it was lost, and I cried."

Her face was impassive now; no tears. Stillness for a moment, as they sat together on the white bench at the edge of the water. There were no longer any halfway carp, as Leda called them, half silver and half gold; they swam lazily, no longer needing to exert themselves to change.

He had told her about Nora. Disappointingly, she had been of little comfort; had seemed, in fact, to evade anything more than a

444

cursory discussion of the subject. It had hurt him a little. And now, unexpectedly:

"She has a right not to have it, Michael," Leda said.

"I know you feel that way." He said it with utmost gentleness, to let her know they could disagree and still be secure in their affection. "It's strange . . . I never knew you *could* feel that way until I got your letter."

"Paolo doesn't know, either." Clearly, she said it to engage him in continued secrecy, as if it were necessary to remind him of her trust in him.

"I won't tell him . . . but you will," he said.

"Me? Oh, no." With alarm.

"Yes, you will . . . when you have more confidence in him."

"Talk to Paolo about abortion? I know he's a progressive, Michael, but there's such a great distance between us."

"Perhaps you don't know how far he has traveled."

She gave him a fugitive look. Then quickly, because her subject was more disturbing, she went back to his. "Anyway—Nora—she has a right."

"Then why don't you come out—publicly—and say she has a right?"

"Come out publicly for abortion?"

"Yes . . . and as a Communist."

"Are you insane? Do you think I would do that to my brother?"

"Perhaps it might not be so shocking to him. I think he would take it with more . . . equanimity . . . than you do."

Her face had gone white. "You meant more courage, didn't you?"

". . . Yes."

It was too uncompromisingly honest, and too difficult for her to take. She suddenly was unsteady; cornered and frightened. "I don't think you and I should ever talk about this again, Michael."

He felt a pang. Another separation. Another disconnection from someone he loved. Is this what was going to happen to him from now on? Would his growing need for a purer honesty with himself and with others mean that he would alienate the people he deeply needed in his life? Would the losses come more quickly, one upon another? He couldn't let it happen.

"Leda—*cara mia*—listen to me. You're a Communist—and I don't think I could ever be. We could argue about this. In fact—we must. And be resentful—and sometimes stop talking to each other for a while. But ultimately we have to say a word or two—and listen—and

445

go back to talking. Because if we don't, we lose one another. And I can't bear to lose you, Ledagrazia."

"But what you suggest—if I come out openly and say who I am—do you realize the enormity—?"

"Then what do we all do?—stop talking?—go underground?"

"I would have to talk against you, Michael!"

"Would you be against me in everything?"

"Birth control—the ordination of women—"

"You think you could make me angry with that?"

"—abortion."

"People change, Leda."

He had not known he was going to say it. What he had so impulsively uttered shocked him and touched him with apprehension. But there was an excitement in it, as if he had thrust himself into an arena that demanded courage he hadn't thought he had.

She looked at him closely. He could see the wonderment in her face. Her eyes cleared. Abruptly she clutched him to herself, seeming to thank him for having said something expressly meant to give her strength. And he thought, with a strange happiness, how it was possible for people in conflict, but without enmity, to give courage to one another.

They clung together, recovering themselves. Then she accompanied him to the path and out to the main road where he would walk the short distance to the station.

"I will tell Paolo," she said quietly. "Not now—his passion for honesty would make *una causa* of it, as if he himself were a Communist. But after he has become the Pope."

She seemed to have no doubt that he would be. Nor did Michael.

As they were about to say goodbye, she asked, "Have you been to confession?"

"No . . . not yet."

"Will you go?"

It had never occurred to him that he wouldn't.

The priest who was to be Michael's confessor had a cold, but he said with a smile that it would not interfere with his giving absolution. He was an affable man, younger than Michael would have chosen if anyone else were available, but the important thing about him, an advantage Michael sought, was that he understood English.

"Inglese—sì—certo," the young Italian said. "I can confess you in

446

English, very surely. But why?—you speak very well the Italian."

Michael didn't try to explain; hadn't indeed explained it to himself. But now, impelled, he realized it was not that complex. Since he would be speaking about Nora, he would want to speak plainly, he would want to say it as deeply as he understood it, without casuistry, with no nuance missed because of a shade of difference in a foreign word. Especially must he not give himself the excuse that the words were alien. He didn't want to be a sophisticated cleric in the confessional, but an ordinary man who had once been innocent, and needed innocence again; he wanted to go as a child to a Father.

It was a small church, not in the Vatican, one he had never attended. But as they entered the confessional, he on his side and the young priest on the other, it was every confessional he had ever seen, the darkness was as still, the sense of confinement with one's sins as suffocatingly close, the cry of help me just as desperate.

"Bless me, Father, for I have sinned."

He heard the familiar response, he heard the snuffling of the other's cold, he heard the soft rustle of the handkerchief.

He started with the lesser transgressions. He listed the usual ones, the sins of envy and of spite, and even sins he hadn't consciously committed but which he was accustomed to confess, for conscious evil was not all of it.

He heard the responses, rote by rote, the little cough, the acceptance of his penitence, the go and sin no more, the remission from moral pain.

"I have lied to myself, and to others."

Michael heard a vague murmur of comfort.

"I have doubted God and compounded the sin by saying I was simply questioning Him on an issue of integrity. I have even once said that He betrayed me."

It was the worst sin and he should have left it for last, where he always left the worst. . . . Why did he put it before Nora? Did he really think that his sin with Nora was more mortal than his sin against God?

At last his catalogue of transgressions had exhausted itself. It was now Nora's turn. No escaping it.

"I have had congress with a woman."

There was a silence from the other side of the screen. The young priest started in English, then got lost in it. *"Che significa questa parola?"* he asked. What does this word mean?

With a twinge, he realized that he had done precisely what he had resolved not to: congress with a woman, indeed—he had hidden behind a euphemism.

"*Che cosa significa?*" the priest was saying again, and wouldn't it be better if Michael, in this instance at least, spoke the sin in Italian?

The word was ready on his tongue, waiting to be said.

Fornicazione.

But he couldn't say it.

It was a cold word, legal, clinical. It described an act, and not two people, living it. Worse, as applied to Nora, it was even a lewd word and had nothing to do with their love for each other, and what he was doing was confessing to a sin he had not perpetrated, lewdness. Only this, what he was doing now, only this was lewdness, to call his love of Nora a sin.

Love is not a sin. He wanted to cry it in the confessional, love is not a sin!

The confessor was importuning him. "Speak," he said.

And say what? Shall I say that I loved her and love her still and hope that I may love her always? Shall I say that without her I might never have discovered what a woman is, and what she may become, and might go on imagining that she is a lesser variety of man? Shall I say that if I had never met Nora—and loved her—I might forever be a man resentful of a mother who abandoned him, a nun who mortified him, a girl who betrayed him, a group of women who savaged a priest in the street? No, I say that I forgive them just as I beg them to forgive me. I say that I will not deny my love of Nora—I won't—not ever. She is no part of my repentance. I will not say she is my sin, but my blessing—without her I would die emptier, lonelier, forever a celibate cleric who had no conception that this earthly space might be nearly as beautiful as the heavenly one.

He couldn't bear the booth any longer, and ran from it.

Unconfessed and unabsolved of the thing he had come to repent, he rushed down the side street, away from the church, and onto the main thoroughfare in the blazing mid-day of Rome.

Well, it was finished, done, and he believed every word he had thought.

But the Church would not. Whether he had or had not violated canon and custom, and the explicit precepts of the Church, he had violated his priesthood and committed a sin against God. He was still an unconfessed and unrepentant man.

And a priest.

448

This was the harrowing question, then: could he continue to be one?

During the nine days of mourning for the deceased Pope, the cardinals started to arrive from distant places. They came singly, and in groups. Some were strangers to one another; some had not met in many years and were senile now, barely remembering anything except the Latin words of obsolete liturgies. Occasionally, old friends hurried across courtyards and embraced each other; sometimes they wept.

The work of the Holy See went on, and cardinals of local occupation, in their purple of bereavement, tended the affairs of the Church and prepared for the conclave.

On the last day of the *novendiale,* the visitors started to come to Feradoti's office. The first two were, coincidentally, a radical from Austria and a conservative from Germany. Michael had never met them. They looked very much alike, they both had tight faces and talked friendliness as if it were a desperation; they were vexed with each other for attending the same candidate. A cardinal arrived from India, another from Spain, then the visitors became more numerous, and the phones kept ringing. Prelates from everywhere came briefly to pay their respects to the crippled man; they covertly studied his limp, looked for signs of senility and inquired pointedly of his health. Some came and merely gazed at him. Never, at least not in Michael's presence, was the august papal position mentioned, but the significance of the sudden glare of attention was never in any doubt. He was *papabile*—not the Pope, certainly, for anything could happen in the voting—but the Worthy One.

No one had had any word from Cardinal Cavanaugh. His absence from the meeting of the Margotto faction was now public knowledge, and a universal astonishment. Rumors started. Some said that he and Margotto had had a difference; some said his horror at the death of his brother had made him ill. One story had it that the reason he had not attended the meeting was because he had not arrived at the Vatican, had never left New York, had no intention of doing so, and was not going to be present at the conclave. The story was not believed, but it persisted.

Two days before the conclave was to begin, Feradoti called Michael to his office. "By the new rules, assistants will not be allowed in the conclave except by special permission—which I'm sure the

449

Camerlengo would grant me," he said. "Would you care to be a conclavist?"

Michael had yearned to attend, and had known that the Secretary could arrange it. But when no mention was made of it, he thought it wouldn't happen. Saddened as he was that he had not been invited, he was relieved. But now, hearing the honor offered, he could not accept it. Although an assistant would not be admitted into the sanctity of the conclave itself, Michael felt he couldn't accompany Feradoti at all, couldn't enter the building with him, couldn't ascend the steps, a man unrepentant, unanointed, at a distant remove from communion —a priest who might forsake the Church. The offer smarting in him, he said to the Secretary, "You know how this touches me, but . . . I can't."

"Is something wrong?" When the priest did not answer: "If I can help you, Michael, you must tell me."

Like Leda, Michael would wait. "After the conclave."

Feradoti looked concerned, then deeply disappointed. Michael saw the regret; it was bittersweet to him.

How profoundly sad he looks, Michael thought. Never so deeply troubled as I see him now. Already he is separating himself from easy answers, from partisan solicitations, from friendships not altogether faultless, from worldly comfort; already he is burning the vigil light, he is breaking lonely bread.

"But you will walk with me, won't you?" the Secretary said. "Tomorrow, when I go there?"

Yes, he would walk with him, Michael said.

That night, weary as he was, he remained awake and thought of Nora. He kept going over their last meeting, chiding himself for not having been able to persuade her to have the child. He had had no argument cogent enough, he told himself, because he had not been able to distill what it meant to him. And now, weeks and miles away from her, he realized what he should have said: Not having the child was the violation of a mystery; perhaps, in these rational times, our final mystery: existence itself . . . Yet, he asked himself, if it *was* a mystery, weren't all the questions open?

The following morning, the day before the start of the conclave, Michael made his way through the crowds in St. Peter's Square and arrived at the office just as the postman appeared. As he crossed the desk in the outer office, he saw her letter lying on top of the heap. Stirred, he picked it up, went out into the corridor, tore open the flap and read it quickly.

He couldn't believe the news and the joy over it.

> . . . There is one other thing I have to tell you. It was
> another thing that made me happy. You will say it is my
> imagination, Michael; you will say it is too soon. But this
> morning, as I was walking to the office, I felt a movement
> —honestly I did—a small flick of life, like the touch of a
> finger, saying: you. I know, I know, I know it is too soon.
> These emanations come much later, I am told; the books
> say months from now. But still I felt it. And it occurs to
> me, that sometimes signs of new life come earlier than
> expected. Sometimes, even, they come when you expect
> they never will. Now please, Michael, don't call it a
> miracle, it's something more real than that. But whatever
> it's called, it is joyous. I love you.
>
> Nora.

It didn't matter what her reasons for having the child might be, or
whether he comprehended them; it mattered only that they were understandable to her. The child would live.

He wondered if he would ever see the child, and know it and love
it . . . and Nora . . .

He folded the letter and put it in his pocket. Suddenly her use of
the word "miracle" struck something in his mind. As if he had had a
revelation, he realized it wasn't the *child* that was the mystery. Nor
was it the Church. The mystery was the Maker.

Not the Church, not the canons, the doctrines, the gospels, not the
miters, the birettas, the papal crowns and rings, not the rites and
pageantry, the unreal and real estate, but God himself who was the
mystery.

Then why do I need the Church, he asked himself. Why do I need
my priesthood in it?

Because through it he had come closer to the mystery than he ever
could have come alone. Even that time in Jersualem when he had had
his greatest ecstasy, it was an ecstasy that the Church had told him
might be there, it was the Stations of the Cross that he had walked a
hundred times in a hundred churches.

But, on the other hand . . .

No, he must not say aye or nay to the priesthood—no, not yet.

Late that morning, almost noon, Michael appeared at the Cardinal's office and asked if he wanted to be driven to the Sistine Chapel

or walk to it by way of the high staircase.

The Cardinal smiled and pointed upward. *"La Scala Regia."*

He had known that the limping man would choose the royal stairway to the conclave; he would need every test of himself, even this one.

"Let's not go by way of the inner courtyards," Feradoti said, "but by way of the world."

So they walked the long distance, out of the Vatican, onto the city streets, the Borgo, the Via della Conciliazione, then back to St. Peter's Square through the gathering crowd. The sun was scorching and the perspiration ran down the old man's face, but he seemed not to notice. And his arm, in Michael's, held the young man more firmly than usual.

When they came at last to the beautiful Bronze Door, the place where the Church, the world and the palace all joined, both men halted. They were as still as the mid-day heat. Then Feradoti said, almost in a whisper:

"You have been a good son to me."

Michael's eyes filled and they embraced. It was hail and farewell. The old man started to mount the long stairway.

As the Cardinal reached the landing and paused for breath, the tall man appeared. He seemed to have emanated from the shadows, seemed to have been waiting there for the Secretary to arrive. Michael recognized him as he turned a little—Cardinal Cavanaugh. Both men stopped. Then slowly they went to one another. It was a long distance upward and Michael could not hear what they said. But he saw them open their arms, saw the old friends cling in a long embrace, and then, together, they continued up the stairs toward the Sistine Chapel.

A quiet joy. Those two men, brought together if only for a moment—he had helped to accomplish that. His mission had not failed. God forgive him for pride, it had gloriously succeeded. . . . Something in the Church had changed.

He stayed in the Square, lost himself in the crowd, tried to think what it would be like to be one of the laity, imagined himself without his priestly collar.

Late afternoon, he slipped away from the great piazza and went to the Courtyard of St. Damasus. As he arrived he heard the soft pealing of the bell, three times. Then the sound within, the Swiss Guards parading through the silk-hung corridors and loggias.

"Extra omnes."

That was the call. Everybody out, the cry went: all depart, except the conclavists. I could have been one, he thought. Through the windows, he saw the flaming torches, the search afoot for those who should not be there.

"Extra omnes."

Someone had once said that while the words literally meant "everybody, out," figuratively they signified the exclusion of all worldly concerns; only divine ones would now be considered. But Michael knew that even after the doors were locked, there would still be worldly concerns inside, for these creatures were not divine, but human. While he rejoiced that this was so, it saddened him to think how frail they were. Strong, some of them, men of heroic size; yet, some were feeble, even senile. Some were wise; some, foolish. Some were still available to thought, but some had done their share of thinking. Yet, no matter how similar they were or how different, they were alike in one thing: all were frail. And it saddened him to think of the heavy burden that now must be borne by men so prone to stumble. But, then, Christ too had stumbled.

And out of its frailty, the Church had learned, over the years, its one great strength: that it could change.

With a lift of exaltation, Michael realized: he need not leave the priesthood.

The Church would change.

It was no such Absolute as Cavanaugh had called it—only God was the Absolute. There were no other absolutes, not of form or formulary, all were relatives; and all, answerable to the needs of men, could change, Only He was the absolute, only He was the mystery, the last mystery, the Maker of children and other magic.

If the earth evolved, if man evolved—dear God, change was the human genius!—then the Church could do it as well, and he would be a part if it.

Meanwhile . . . what of his unconfessed soul? Could it go on in limbo? Perhaps that was where the soul was meant to dwell—always in limbo; perhaps it was not meant for a serene paradise, perhaps it was destined to struggle between heaven and hell, between love and agony.

And as evidence that he could experience both—and still believe in God—he carried a letter in his pocket.

Until the publication of EAST WIND, RAIN *in 1977, N. Richard Nash was probably best known as a playwright. Both* THE RAINMAKER *and* SEE THE JAGUAR *have been produced all over the world, and* THE RAINMAKER *has been translated into over thirty languages.*

He was one of the group of playwrights who were responsible for changing the whole current of television drama. The movement is now called the Golden Age of Television and Nash, Robert Alan Aurthur, Gore Vidal, Paddy Chayefsky, and Horton Foote were its vanguard.

Nash has also written many screenplays, including THE RAINMAKER *and* PORGY AND BESS, *and has taught philosophy and drama at Bryn Mawr, Haverford, Brandeis and the University of Pennsylvania.*

He is married to the former Katherine Copeland and has three children.